Catherine Brakefield has caught the heart and soul of the Civil War through the eyes of the South. She has diligently incorporated scripture in appropriate places to bring God's love and guidance in turbulent times. Historically accurate, the action kept me turning pages from the onset and I loved the depth of emotion she has woven into each character.

— MARCIA (MITCHELL) LEE, author of *Surviving the Prodigal Years*

*Swept into Destiny* is a wonderful historical romance that gives the reader a glimpse into the Irish immigrants in the Civil War... We experience life on the plantation, life as the poor Irish, life in a divided nation, and the war devastation that changed the culture.

— CINDY ERVIN HUFF, *award-winning* author of *Secrets and Charades*

# Swept into Destiny

*[handwritten inscription: Debra, In Christ's Love! Catherine Proverbs 3:5-6]*

## CATHERINE ULRICH BRAKEFIELD

CROSSRIVER

BREWSTER, KANSAS USA

To my grandmother who showed throughout
her life, faith and fortitude.
To my mother for her courage and confidence in me.
And to my husband who rejoices with me
each time a book is complete!

I can still hear Gran's voice vibrating
through the hillside of Camp Beauregard,
telling of God-fearing men and divided loyalties
— to the everyday patriot, this novel is dedicated to you...

# Acknowledgments

To recall all those people who encouraged me to keep this dream alive of this four book series, would be impossible for me to list. My dear family, immediate and distant, is at the top of the list as is *CrossRiver Media Group*.

*Debra L. Butterfield's* style of editing is thorough and encouraging. Her dedication to her career ensures the excellence of a finished product and brings out the best in my writing. I am very blessed to call you my editor!

Deep gratitude goes to my publisher, *Tamara Clymer,* for her encouragement and dogmatic pursuit for quality. From her layouts to this creative and fantastic book cover. You are an inspiration and truly the best!

Many thanks go to my agent, *Cyle Young* of Hartline Literary Agency, for his incomparable support, enduring confidence, and encouragement in me.

Words are often inadequate; however, God's blessings never fail. May God bless you one and all: *Jane Kirkpatrick, Cheryl Wyatt, Marcia (Mitchell) Lee*, and *Deborah Malone* for taking time from your busy schedule to review *Swept into Destiny*!

Thank you *Brennan LeQuire*, Librarian of the Bount County Public Library, for helping me acquire the research materials I desired. Your expertise helped me in my many hours of delving into the archives of the history of Maryville, about Mr. Greatheart, and the abolitionist movement. Thank you *Yosef Addis* for taking time out of your busy schedule to give me a tour of Maryville's College. To the Historical

Society of Maryville for opening their doors to me about your wonderful history, especially the Cades Cove Museum, Coal Creek Miners, and the inception of the Smokey Mountain Park.

My utmost respect and appreciation to the people of *Broadway United Methodist Church* for their warmth, shared knowledge, and hospitality.

My husband's and my trips to Springfield, Illinois, where Lincoln lived during his adult life, Washington D.C., the Pennsylvania hills of Gettysburg, the Smoky Mountains, Frankfort and Lexington, Kentucky, equipped me with the scenery of imagination you find in *Swept into Destiny*. Ireland's unique countryside of County Cork and County Limerick and meeting its beloved people helped me with the dialect. My *grandmother* and *mother* inspired my research and this unique story about the Irish immigrants and their role in the Civil War.

I thank my husband, *Edward Brakefield,* for his tireless energy in accompanying me across the byways and highways, seeking the facts about our history and our ancestors. My daughter, *Kimberly Ann,* her input and recommendations for this novel, my son, *Derek,* for his encouragement and proofreading skills, my grandchildren, *Zander, Logan,* and *Annabelle,* for giving me the inspiration to write America's history one truth at a time.

Most importantly I thank *you*, my readers. You are the wind beneath my wings, my inspiration to climb new heights along life's highway. I pray *Swept into Destiny* will entertain, encourage, and equip you knowing that with God's invisible hand orchestrating our American history, we cannot lose.

To *God* and to our loving Savior, *Jesus Christ,* goes the glory. Who through His mercy forgave a sinful nation, binding up our wounds and making this nation the greatest nation on earth. To this and future generations goes the challenge to keep America a God-fearing nation! God Bless.

# Chapter 1

*A*s the sun's golden beams peeked above the horizon, Maggie Gatlan strained to see past the early morning mist. She rested back into her saddle; no one was up. Good.

As a mother would her babe, deep forests, majestic mountains, and lush grasslands cradled the plantation's two-story brick mansion known as Spirit Wind Manor. What evil ensnared Maggie's beloved Tennesseans that she must conceal her actions from them? Only Mother understood Maggie's passion, her desire to understand her purpose in life.

The serene beauty of the Smokies that her mother's people, the Cherokee, called "Land of Blue Smoke" enveloped her. Nothing could change this surreal picture but the sad neglect of God's conscience. Not the abolitionist John Brown or Abraham Lincoln's new Republic, not even Mr. Reynolds, Spirit Wind's overseer. She shivered as she recalled his eyes trailing her form like a hungry wolfhound.

"Help!" came a voice in the distance.

Had a student gotten lost in the marshlands? Galloping down the hill, she reined up her horse before the inky black waters of the swamp. The branches of the trees rattled and swayed to the promptings of the wind, causing an eerie groan, as if the trees were aware of their fate in their soon-to-be-liquid grave. They lifted their burdened limbs cloaked with spider webs floating like ghosts on a pirate ship toward her in a morbid hello. She shivered. Where was her courage when she needed it?

"Here I be!"

She urged her mare forward, searching the shadowed darkness. Her horse's hooves sank ankle deep into the mire. She spotted a man covered with mud and slime, clutching a moss-covered log. Only his head and shoulders were visible; swamp water covered the rest of his body like a black coffin. The nauseous odor of rotten eggs saturated the air. She swatted at the mosquitoes swarming her head. "I'll send someone—"

"Miss, I be in a bad way."

A stranger of no consequence to her. She glanced up the hill. The Glenn was a half a mile away. One conscionable act had led to this consequence.

"Miss, please?"

She dismounted. The slurping noise of her boots chilled her ears, and she sank deeper into the muck until she could no longer see the tops. As she neared the man, she held out the end of her riding crop toward him. "Take a hold, sir."

"Saints be praised." He stretched out his arm, his blackened fingers just five inches from the stick. "I, I can't reach it… my body… won't move. Help!" Like a drowning man, he reached for her. She made a desperate lunge. His head sank and disappeared into the murky water. Seconds later, he came up gasping, clawing at the log.

Jesus help us. The inky waters swirled about her knees. Then her left riding boot wouldn't budge. Grabbing onto a web-covered limb, she inched her foot out. The ill-fated boot was instantly lost and her skirt was sucked down like a bucket in a deep well. "Ow!"

"What?" Strong hands grabbed her waist. A large man swept her into his embrace with ease, his eyes gleaming into hers with amusement. "What is a dandified lady like you doing in the swamp?"

A dirty red bandana wrapped his forehead, and curly black hair covered his head. This was not the time to be chivalrous and he was hardly the man to offer it. His close-clipped black mustache curled about dimpled cheeks and there was a glint of amused contempt in his black eyes.

"I live here. Now unhand me. This poor man needs your attention."

Dark of face, swarthy as a pirate, his hot glare swept her face like fire. "I think you're hardly wearin' the right clothes to be livin' here."

Before she could reply, five men swarmed her like a passel of angry bees. "Where'd she come from?"

"She lives here," retorted the man whose arms she occupied.

"I don't mean that literally, you foolish man!"

The six ill-tempered men glared back at her. "What'd you do to him?" Without waiting for a reply, they hoisted the man out of the muck, up on their shoulders, and carried him toward drier land.

"How dare you. I heard his cry for help and rode as fast as I could. I thought of leaving… but stayed. I deserve your praise. Not condemnation."

"You? Help the likes of us?" His bold eyes stared at her. She coughed, covered her nose, then pushed with all her strength with her other hand against his chest. The smell of him was enough to gag her.

She felt his hand supporting her back drop away. She clutched his neck, her wet riding gloves scrambling for a better hold. She glanced down at the rancid waters, then up at him. His sweat-stained shirt clung to his sinewy chest in moist folds. She shuddered.

"Here is a difficult decision for you, to be sure. To accept my help or to remain in your swamp? What will it be?"

He was dirty and ragged, but, despite his dishabille, his eyes were as bold and black as a swashbuckler's.

"Matthew's snake bit," a man yelled. "Get out of there, Benjamin."

Her rescuer's powerful legs made a slurping noise in the quagmire. "Wait, my boot."

He ignored her plea.

Maggie beat against his chest. What was he made of, granite? "I need my boot. Unhand me you nasty vagrant! And let me grab my—"

"Vagrant? We're Irish, fresh off the *Dunbrody*."

"That decrepit ship? Then you are pirates, here to pilfer Spirit Wind. Admit it."

"We like to keep our business to ourselves."

"Enough of that." A man on the bank swiped the air with his mud-caked arm. "Quit sparking her and get out of there before you both get bit!"

"Sparking?" With one stroke of his massive arms, the Irishman swept Maggie over his shoulder as neatly as a bag of oats.

"I've heard about you ruffians. How dare you touch me with your filthy hands. You think I want your ghastly smell on my clothing?" Kicking her feet, her booted foot hit him hard in his leg.

"Ouch! The lass's toes are as rock hard as her head." The man's large hand spanked her.

"How dare you!"

"Don't you drop her, Benjamin. No namesake of mine will ever harm a—"

"Drop me?" Maggie peered around Ben's back. Seeing the Irishmen upside down, it was hard to focus, but she got enough of an eyeful to notice Ben's father's broken white teeth smiling back at her.

Ben's dad laughed. "She's a bit high and mighty, maybe you ought to throw her back. Seeing how she lives here and all."

"Why you bag of rags you call men, I'll have you know I am the daughter of the owner of the property you have so rudely littered with your presence."

"I believe she's been damaged by this place." Ben swatted her rump again. "She's got spunk, though she be ugly as sin what with her face red and swollen with mosquito bites."

Coming to consciousness, the snakebitten man groaned.

"Three snake bites. And a passel of leeches sucking what life be left from him," Ben's father muttered.

The back of Maggie's head hit the ground first. Ben ran toward the prostrate Matthew. She rubbed her head. The man had the manners of a hoodlum. Blowing a tendril of hair from her eyes, she set her chin, determined to retrieve her boot. "Ouch." She pulled out an inch-long pine needle from her toe, then glanced up at the lone pine tree. "This is your fault." Hopping on one foot, she proceeded toward the swamp.

"Ben, check the lass for leeches."

Is he referring to me? She glanced back. "Oh, no…" She slapped his extended hand and aimed a calculated palm to his cheek. He ducked, then laughed as he hauled her up into his grasp and carried her up the hill tucked beneath his arm.

Off went her boot and stockings; up went her skirts and pantalets. "How dare you!"

He ran his dirty hands up her ankles. "Got him."

She gasped in horror. Lodged just beneath the fleshy part of her knee, a large black bloodsucker had latched onto her leg. She shuddered.

The groans of the snakebitten Matthew floated like the mist toward her. She bit back her scream. Just how many of these bloodthirsty leeches did he have on him?

Ben's father knelt next to her, a pocketknife in one hand and the stub of a dirty cigar between his lips. The smoke encircled his head like a wreath; all she could see clearly were his deep green-blue eyes.

"Be of good courage." His gentle words consoled her.

Jesus, let him be as merciful as You.

Maggie had heard stories how the New York Irish would rob you in your bed, then cut your throat and drink your blood. For the first time, she realized the true gravity of her situation. She was outnumbered and totally at the mercy of these pirates.

The man lowered the blade of his knife, the cold steel touching her flesh. She bit down on her bottom lip.

"Get this stogie from my mouth and touch it to that bloodsucker, Ben."

Resting on her elbows, she dug her nails into the soft dirt and scowled at him.

Ben grimaced. "What if I burn her?"

"Do your best just to burn the leech, and don't leave his tentacles in her flesh, could be it might start a bad infection."

Streaks of sweat broke through Ben's hairline. Maggie closed her eyes. She opened them only to see another leech, smaller than the first, but getting larger by the second… on her blood.

They began the procedure again. She felt faint.

The man with the snakebites groaned. No telling if he'd live or die, with snakebites and these blood suckers. What a fuss she was making over a couple of leeches.

The second one dislodged, Maggie covered her calves and flopped back onto the ground. Only the ordeal wasn't over.

Ben leaned over her, a whiff of his foul breath whisking past her nostrils before his lips reached her ear. "I've got to check you again. I don't like this any more than you do."

She shoved him aside and rose to a sitting position. "Really? Do I have your word on that, you filthy Irishman?"

"This is a difficult task to be sure." Ben's eyes gleamed into hers. His voice was soft, but there was a vibrant note in it. "I'm... attempting hard to be objective, but I find myself... wishing it weren't the nasty job of dislodging these ugly suckers. I'm thinking you should find another place to take up residence."

She gritted her teeth, ignoring the callused fingers of this stranger running up and down her calves. Her arms were shaking from the exertion of keeping her upper body in a semi-sitting position.

After his inspection, there was only concern for her written in the deep crevices of his downturned lips and the droop of his shoulders. "There's two more on the back of both her legs just below her knees."

"Well, you know what we gotta do, son."

Maggie rolled over on her stomach. The cold blade against her hot, moist calf sent a shiver through her body. The smell of smoke, burning worms, sweat, and swamp water penetrated the sultry air that promised a hot June day. "Ahhhh. Mary, Joseph, and the Saints... Jesus help me!" the snakebitten Matthew cried.

She had never heard such pain uttered from a man's lips before.

Ben's dad rested back on his knees, and wiped his forehead. "I think we've got them all. Let's see how Matthew's comin'."

"I'll leave you to... um, you know." Ben turned her over. His mouth contorted, suppressing a grin.

She gasped. Her riding skirt was tangled around her knees; her knickers had been pushed up, too, and her stockings lay in a heap on the grass, exposing her bare toes and white skin against the green of the grass.

"I have never saw the likes before." His finger touched the dimple in her knee. "Dove-white and they even feel as soft as a dove's underbelly—"

Her open palm whacking his cheek echoed across the hillside. She covered her legs and, beneath the folds of her yards of skirt, pulled on her stockings and lastly her boot. An uncontrollable shiver coursed through her veins, the dark, muddy swampland taunting her. Going back into that swamp to retrieve her lost boot was not something she relished. But she must. How would she explain her missing boot to Mr. Reynolds?

Ben followed her glance and offered her his hand. "Take it if you like. I'll only offer it once."

There was something vital and exciting about his grip. His riot of curly black hair fell about his soiled red bandana in mischievous abandonment, only there was nothing frolicsome in his gaze when he strolled past her. Pausing before entering the gaping hole of the foul-smelling swampland to remove his boots, Ben glanced over his shoulder at her, and was gone.

Goose bumps popped up across her arms, recalling the leeches. "I don't want that old boot, please come out from there—"

"Got it!"

"Oh, you did?" Maggie hopped down the hill, grabbed the dirty boot between thumb and forefinger and examined it for leeches.

"But I'll throw it back in, after all you don't need it."

"No, please, I'll clean it up. You spared me a great amount of explaining."

"And money purchasing such fine boots, I wager." His eyes appraised her. "'Twas not easy. I had to do some feeling about before I recovered it."

Maggie looked at his mud-caked arms, aghast. "Oh, but you... you must have three times more leeches than I."

"Your kind worried about my kind?" He stepped closer.

My, he was tall and strangely chivalrous in his barbarous sort of way.

The snakebitten man's groan split the air between them like a lightning bolt. Maggie followed Ben up the hill and knelt down. The man's face was pasty white in a sea of black whiskers, his arms just skin covering bones. She glanced at the other Irishmen. Their cheek bones shone beneath mud-blackened, gaunt faces, and homespun shirts darned so many times there was more thread than cloth, plastered their shallow chests.

Sudden fear clawed her throat. Their needs were far too many for her to comprehend, and she had her school to protect. "I, I must return home." Grass and dirt particles clung to her wet and putrid garments as she rose. She shook her skirts, trying to rid them of the decay, and backed away from the living corpse sprawled on the grass.

Her mare nickered softly as she stuffed her muddy riding boot in her saddlebag, then reached for her horse's reins, trying to block out the memory of death and deprivation not more than ten yards away.

Ben arms reached past hers, looping her mare's reins through his arm, he bent his shoulders forward, cupping his mud-blackened hands. Her stocking foot curled around his palm as he lifted her easily into the saddle.

A spark in the depth of his liquid eyes—bold, yet gentle—the lift of his chin, the thrust of his shoulders, displayed his pride and unbeaten spirit. Poor wretched people the Irish, there was little hope for them of elevating their position in society. It's a good thing they carry their pride with them.

"I'm sorry. I wish there was something I could do. I'll bring some bandages and soap and clean drinking water back with me."

"Sorry, are ya?" Ben said, his hands drawn into fists by his sides. "We know about you landlords from our native Ireland." His chin poked forward like a boxer's. "The potato famine we left and then coming to America and no one givin' us work and our children and women hungry and sick. Lost amidst this sea of conscience and consequence, we are." In suave finality, he saluted her as eloquently as any southern gentleman, only in tattered rags. "We can take care of our own. Been doing it for more than 300 years and don't need the likes of you tellin' the likes of us how to survive."

The audacity of this man throwing her goodwill back into her face without even a 'thank you kindly' added to the end of it. "This is America, not Ireland, and we do things differently here." She took off at a gallop, jumped a hedge, and headed for the safety of Spirit Wind.

Ben's eyes had said more than his hateful words. He didn't believe she'd return. Well, she'd show him.

# Chapter 2

*M*aggie, those Irishmen are a filthy, rowdy bunch, don't get too close to them." Mr. Reynolds' goatee, which reminded her of their billy goat, bounced up and down with every word. "They'd love to get their filthy hands on you." His gaze circled her figure like the coil of a snake.

"Yes, Mr. Reynolds," she said, knowing full well they were not the only ones who wanted to get their hands on her. She held the pitcher of water firmly to her apron, trying to quiet the turmoil in her stomach as he slithered closer.

His morning's coffee, leather, and bad breath whiffed past her nose as his thin body bent over her like a poplar in a windstorm. She dared not look up.

"Your father should be back from Virginia tomorrow. Remember what I told you, or else I'll keep you to the confines of Spirit Wind another day."

"I understand, Mr. Reynolds."

He treated her like one of his concubines. Or perhaps wished she was.

There was no doubt Father suspected her mother and her of questionable activities. Maggie had voiced her views to Father that every person, including slaves, needed to be able to read and write. Because of her age of fourteen years and her mother's affiliation to the Society of Friends, Father had given the overseer, Mr. Reynolds, full power over her and Spirit Wind.

Reynolds snapped his whip across his polished black riding boots, the repetitious noise rippling like waves against rock. "The work in that infested snake pit will whittle their numbers down." He chuckled. "I'll be doing my countrymen a favor, what with the herd of Irishmen that come to our shores every year. No need to worry about running out of their practically free labor."

Maggie bit back her response. She had to find a way to show her father the truth about the arrogant Reynolds. He was always careful to display kindness and consideration when Father was around. Reynolds was neither. He'd threatened a whipping and ordered her to her room, demanding she tell him what she had been doing riding so early in the morning. How could she deny her whereabouts when her mosquito-bitten face told Reynolds so plainly? So far her little school in the Glenn remained hidden from Father's and Mr. Reynolds' eyes, but for how much longer?

Reynolds stepped closer. He licked his thin lips as his big palm stretched out to grab a curl that had strayed loose of her chignon. She backed away. "I must be leaving now." Her personal servant, Hattie, followed with a basketful of bandages and liniment hidden beneath cinnamon rolls and scones. They loaded the water, tablecloth, silverware, and baskets into the bed of their buggy and off they went.

What would Ben think of her now? She'd promised to return immediately. That had been three days ago. Was the snakebit man named Matthew still alive?

The closer Maggie and Hattie rode the stronger the scent of swamp and the rancid smell of death grew. The sun shone down without a cloud to shade her from its burning rays. The sweltering afternoon would likely be just as humid in the evening moonlight. Her father allowed Mr. Reynolds to hire these Irishman to dredge out the swampland, too snake-ridden and disease-infested for their slaves to accomplish. Was Ben aware he and his Irishmen were of less consequence than their slaves?

As they drew near, one Irishman from the sea of twelve stood from his crouching position on the grass. His long legs soon ate up the distance between them. He removed his tattered hat and bowed. Black eyes, bold as brass, stared into hers, with a hint of humor that masqueraded behind a square chin and insolent lips, drawing her gaze to his.

"Lordy, Miss Maggie." Hattie's large eyes opened wider. "These poor men need more than just water and scones to cover their jagged bones. I don't see how their elbows don't poke a hole through their flesh."

The sudden set of Ben's square jaw confirmed Maggie's suspicion that he had heard Hattie's remark. It was evident the only thing Ben hated worse than poverty was pity.

Maggie ignored Ben's outstretched arm and descended from the buggy. Spotting a large flat rock, she walked over and set down the checkered tablecloth. Some of the men were huddled over a fire, stirring a pot of tangled wild grass and a few late dandelions.

Hattie nodded her head slowly. "What I says, I knows."

She always saw more in one glance than Maggie saw in a half-dozen. "Hattie, return to the kitchen. Tell Cook to give you that fried chicken, biscuits, and greens she made for our dinner and bring back a pitcher of milk."

Ben took up a corner of the linen to help her arrange it on the rock. His presence was unnerving.

"Miss Maggie, you're going to get me in a passel of trouble." Hattie looked around at the men who were rubbing their muddy fingers on the grass, their eyes fixed on them and the food. She bit down on her nails like a beaver chomping on wood. A habit she had whenever she grew nervous.

"Have I ever gotten you in trouble? You need not fret. Mother will uphold my actions."

"Really?" Hattie removed her fingers from her mouth and wiped them on her apron. "Just where was she three days ago? You locked in your bedroom like a canary in a cage."

The men mumbled among themselves, chuckled, and then spoke in Gaelic.

Maggie could feel the heat of the men's stares as she waved good-bye to Hattie. Ben's eyes turned darker, more menacing. Now all that was left for her to gaze at were the puffs of dust trailing the buggy.

"What do you think you're doing here? My kind don't care for your kind."

Don't care for me? Her blue tarlatan, flounced with cream-colored

Chantilly lace, sat high and hugged her neck. Why did her collar suddenly feel like a noose? She pulled at her collar, avoiding the Irishman's angry eyes.

"So, you were locked in your room," he whispered. He stared at her, deep in thought. Had he noticed her discomfort? He bent closer and thrust a dirty index finger in her face. "Don't be getting yourself in trouble on our account."

Her lace pantalets beneath her skirt hoops were sticking to her skin like a rain-drenched doily. Her discomfort was most likely due to what had transpired three days earlier, and Ben's eyes weren't helping the matter any. She grabbed her large basket and the small basket of silverware off the ground. "I tried to find some way to help that poor snakebitten man." She bit her tongue; she'd almost told him how the work at the Glenn had stopped. The children were desperate to learn and risked a beating to be educated. She slapped down the silverware on the rock. As if he cared.

"We can't afford to lose this job." Grabbing the pitcher, Ben followed her. She ignored him, lamenting over the teaching days she had lost imprisoned in her room.

Reynolds had watched her and her mother like a hawk on a rabbit. Only the trusted Eli, their head house slave, was able to get away and warn the other slaves from the adjoining plantations not to come to the Glenn. She laid out the warm rolls and the smell of cinnamon floated in the air.

Ben set down his pitcher. "Some of the men have wives and children to feed. This is the only paying job we've had since leaving Ellis Island. We don't need your kind of help."

His words were pure foolishness. "What good is a job if you lose your life doing it?" Maggie whirled around so fast the heel of her shoe got caught in some tall grass, throwing her totally off balance and falling toward the pitcher of water.

Ben snatched her into his swarthy arms, swinging her against his chest, then carried her to a stump and plopped her down with a finality that left her dizzily reeling in a total state of confusion. "My... shoe," was all she could think to blurt out.

He fished through the tangled web of grass and debris. Grabbing it up, he bowed down and placed the shoe on her foot as chivalrously as Prince Charming. Only the irate eyes that stared into hers declared she was not his Cinderella.

"A regular Sir Galahad, my Ben is." Ben's dad's eyes twinkled back at her as if daring her to contradict him.

She turned away to hide her embarrassment. It was as if Ben thought himself better than she. Though poor, ragged, and half-starved, he was not, by any means, broken in spirit. Disillusioned? Yes. He knew there was no hope of their two worlds ever uniting. "You need not fear losing your jobs. Father has waited for over a year to find—"

"Someone stupid enough to risk his life in this snake-infested swamp?" Ben layered a hand on each hip and laughed mockingly.

"Exactly." She stuttered, straightening her skirts in an attempt to regain her composure. Walking back to the makeshift table, she said, "May I be so bold as to inquire of your full name?"

"Benjamin McConnell at your service. Most of my friends call me Ben, as you already know."

"You are different from the other—"

"Irishmen you have encountered? You mean I've not yet learned my station in America?" Ben mocked. "Or that we didn't slit your throat, nor drink your blood?" A deep belly laugh followed. "No, lass, 'tis but a fable that likes to follow us."

The other men muttered in Gaelic, nodding their heads.

Maggie let out a sigh of relief. "That is good to know."

Ben clicked his tongue on the roof of his mouth. His eyes didn't miss her confusion. "I believe this land of opportunity will soon see that our Irish spirit will overcome the poverty—and the fables—that have followed us." He raised his blistered hands and swept the landscape like an artist would his canvas. "Someday I will have a grand place like this."

The men laughed.

"You capture a leprechaun, did ya, Benny, my boy?" one of them said. "You think he be leadin' ya to that pot of gold?" The men slapped each other on their backs at the joke. Maggie looked at Ben and bit back her laughter, wondering. Her parents had little money when Father came to Tennessee and carved his fortune out of the wilderness. If anyone could—

"You can laugh if you want," Ben replied to the men in a bellow that a bull would be proud of. "But I'll be gettin' my land."

Ben McConnell had grit. Maggie's heart beat wildly, recalling Jesus' words *…if you have faith as a grain of mustard seed, nothing will be impossible for you.* Her spirit felt drawn to this man with the rugged cleft chin who dared any to question his dreams. "My father is English. His family didn't have a cent to call their own when they landed on Plymouth Rock. If he could do it, I see no reason why—"

"What strange bed fellows wash up on the banks of these American shores." Ben's glance swept her form like a hot summer breeze. "In Ireland, the Brits were our enemies; 'twas them the reason we left our homeland. Nearly starved us out, they did, and only the hardy ones found passage to America. Now we meet again."

Maggie looked away from Ben's penetrating gaze, recalling Mr. Reynolds' whip cracking its warning through the air and snapping against bare flesh. The thought sent a chill coursing through her bones like a stark February wind. Many a time she had doctored the backs of those who had met with Mr. Reynolds' whip. She wished never to smell the putrid scent of infected flesh again.

She dared not look up. She feared Ben would see her tortured memories and her sympathy for them and their pitiful fate. "Where is that poor man Matthew, with the snake bites?" Time was of the utmost to her. "Mr. Reynolds, my father's overseer, warned me not to take long or he'd ride out to see what has delayed me. It was all I could do to keep him from following me. I shall leave after I have seen to Matthew's wounds. Hattie shall be here shortly. Now, if Mr. Reynolds does come," Maggie warned him hoping to be taken seriously, "please, do nothing to rile him. He is a wrathful man and quite unforgiving." Maggie looked around. "Where is Mr. Matthew?"

# Chapter 3

*B*en ignored the ache in his shoulders and the twitch in his leg muscles as he lifted the heavy stumps in the swamp. His mind was on more pleasant things like Maggie's bright eyes and the sweet melody of her voice.

"Son?" Ben's father's salt-and-pepper head poked through the branches of the tree he was hauling. "That Mr. Reynolds is up on the hill yonder and wants to talk to us."

So this is Mr. Reynolds. Ben kept his eyes shielded by the branches of the large oak tree. He spread his legs apart, crossed his arms, and listened.

"I'll take the taskmaster's whip to your backs if I hear a hint of someone going to the authorities on this." Mr. Reynolds glanced down at the dead man, then gazed at Ben.

Ben stepped out of the shadows. This Englishman better watch out. He was a free man here and would like to see Reynolds try and whip him. More likely Reynolds would use the copperheads to do his nasty work.

"I expect this swamp to be drained out by the end of the third week. I need cotton fields, not snake-infested… well never mind that. What with Maggie and Mrs. Gatlan feeding you from the king's table, I expect you not to give me any trouble, you hear?"

Mr. Reynolds jabbed the toe of his boot into the corpse. When Ben told Maggie that Matthew had died last night, the lass's eyes pooled with tears, sayin' she blamed herself for not being there to help nurse him. This Maggie girl was strange to be sure.

"Well, what are you standing around for?" Mr. Reynolds checked his gold-plated pocket watch and looked up at the sky. "You've got another hour of daylight. Get to work."

Ben walked forward. Grabbing his hat from his head, he placed it firmly in his hands, curling the brim. "Sir, may I have a moment of your time?"

"Out with it."

"If we had a team of mules at our disposal and a couple of drags, we could get the job done faster than with our brute force and shovels."

Mr. Reynolds fingered his goatee absentmindedly. "I suppose. Well, it'll have to be a team I don't mind losing. What's your name, boy?"

Ben stepped closer, turning his eyes downward at the pasty-white man with the receding hairline and thin build. "Benjamin McConnell, sir."

"Who's the head man of you Irish? You?"

"No, sir."

"Well, you are now. I will personally hold you responsible for any..." He glanced at the dead man, his lips curling with disgust. "Mishaps to my mules. Now get back to work." Reynolds mounted his horse. "I demand an honest day's work from each one of you, and I'll expect a truthful report each day." He turned and galloped away, his gray brocade coat flapping in the breeze.

"There are some things more painful than truth, but I can't think what it is." A man who stood a head taller than Ben, slapped him on the back. "Lighten up, lad. You frettin' won't get our job done."

Ben plunked his hat back on his thick wooly hair. "I say we show this peacock Englishman how Irishmen can do a job." He handed his hatchet to a spindly looking man who had a hard time holding up his own weight, let alone pushing over an obstinate stump.

"You take this and if you see any snake slithering along the water, you yell out and fling this. Hopefully you'll be lucky and hit him before he bites me." Walking toward a large half-rooted tree that he had been working on most of the afternoon, he threw a chain around it and tossed a shovel to the big man who had jostled him. "Here, put that big bulk of yours to service and see what you can do to uproot this... uh..."

"Jim, Jim McWilliams."

With Ben pulling and Jim pushing, the slurping noise of the roots giving way had all the men pushing and heaving the heavy dead tree out of the way of their irrigation ditch.

"Okay, men, let's get moving and clear a ditch from this point to twenty yards." Ben turned. "Come on, Big Jim, let's clear out another stump."

"You talking to me?"

Eyeing the man, though as thin as he, Ben could tell there were muscles behind the leanness of his bulk. "Who else?"

Ben lay down on his coat beneath the star-drenched sky. Hands behind his back, he smiled. The day had ended well. The men were pleased with their work. He could tell by the proud lift to their heads. Then there was Maggie. A good Irish name, to be sure. Was her mother Irish?

"Mr. McConnell."

From out of the dark mist that surrounded the low swampland, two forms emerged. "Mother of my merciful Savior… are you a figment of my dreams or flesh and blood?"

Two women approached, cloaked in hoods and long, flowing capes that shrouded their forms like the mystery that surrounded their presence. To Ben, it was an answer to his prayer when Maggie's lavish brown eyes looked questioningly into his.

"The saints be praised, so it is you." Ben didn't miss Maggie's soft smile that swept her full lips, her pleasure to see him obvious. "What are you doing out so late? It must be close to midnight, near as I can tell." This was no place for such fine ladies.

A woman of stately form, a head taller than Maggie, stepped forward, graceful in movement. The embers of the campfire cast shadows and shades about her high cheekbones and glistening black hair. Maggie looked from him to the lady beside her.

"Mr. Reynolds has retired for the night, so Mother and I decided to see to your needs. Mr. Benjamin McConnell, I would like to introduce my mother, Marie Mahal Gatlan."

"It is an honor to be meeting ya." Ben bowed.

The stately Mrs. Gatlan smiled. "I know about you Irish. My father was of Irish descent. My mother, who was from this country, taught me many ways to prevent infections."

Ben rocked back on his heels. "Could this be? A high and mighty Englishman married to an Irish woman?"

Mrs. Gatlan laughed softly. "Yes, and my Indian mother and my Irish father were married by Dr. Isaac Anderson who, at the time, was a circuit rider. He later began Maryville College, which my mother and I attended. White, Indian, and free Negroes, they were all welcome."

"Saints preserve us. He sounds like a great man indeed!"

"He was." Mrs. Gatlan sighed. "Dear Mr. Greatheart, it is hard to believe he died just six months ago, upon the entry of 1857. Maggie had just graduated from his college."

Maggie bit down on her bottom lip thinking about the conversation she had overheard between Mr. Reynolds and her father. "Now maybe Anderson's abolitionist ways will cease in Maryville!" She hadn't heard what her father replied for she'd run up the stairway for fear of disclosing her horror. When had acting like a compassionate human being become wrong? "I can't believe how—"

"And the world we knew seemed to disappear with him." Her mother sent her a beware look.

Maggie hadn't noticed that Big Jim and Ben's father, as well as the other Irishmen, had moved closer to Ben and were listening intently to their conversation.

A noise in the brush and Hattie's curly head came into view. She was winded from running and bent over to gasp in a few breaths of air. "Mrs. Gatlan… the Mr. is back from up north and asking for you?"

"Maggie, stay and hand out the food, but do not tarry long. I am sure your father will have much to tell us regarding his trip to Illinois. He went to hear Mr. Lincoln's reply to the Supreme Court's decision regarding the Dred Scott case."

"Oh?… Mr. Reynolds thought Father was in Virginia visiting family."

Mrs. Gatlan put a finger to her lip. "As your father had hoped." Her mother and Hattie hurried back along the small foot path that wandered around the hillside through the grass and brush to the back quarters of Spirit Wind Manor.

"Your father is an Englishman from Virginia? And your mother is from Tennessee?" Ben asked.

"Father's ancestors were some of the first Englishmen that came from England to the New World. Most people find it difficult to believe, knowing my father's nature, but he adores Mother, and they make quite a combination. Mother encouraged my father to employ you. So, you see, you must do a very good job and show Father that my mother was right about Irishmen."

Maggie did not wait for him to reply. But instead, went to work and unloaded her basketful of bread, cookies, cornbread, milk, bacon, ham, and eggs.

It was clear she respected and admired her mother. Ben looked around at the men. What a ragged bunch they were for such high-minded women to spend their time helping.

"We will do our best to finish the job set before us." He eyed the food. The aroma of fresh-from-the oven bread still warm to the touch tantalized him, and the bacon, crisp and warm, was just the way he liked it. Ham swimming in gravy and buckwheat cakes dripping in syrup, when had he seen such a feast spread so fine?

Big Jim's tongue licked his lips as he devoured the food with his eyes. Ben's stomach growled before Maggie had even laid out the last morsel.

"Maybe we should sample a few of those buckwheat cakes and ham." Big Jim reached forward swiping his finger on some syrup that had spilled onto the tablecloth.

Maggie laughed, a gay musical sound that echoed in the moonlit treetops. "Please, gentlemen, help yourselves. I shall return with fresh goods tomorrow evening." She paused, looking out into the dark swampland that seemingly dropped off into nothingness from the crest of the hill. "Our good Lord willing," she said, gazing at Spirit Wind.

What was troubling Maggie? What sorrowful memories haunt the floors of such a beautiful place? Ben crushed his hat brim beneath his thick fingers. His conscience pricked him for the way he treated her earlier. His stomach growled from hunger. But something more important than food needed his attention. "If my dad had returned from a trip up north," he whispered. "I would not be tarryin' with the likes of us, but rushin' to his side to learn about the odd sights and sounds he'd seen."

Her face was pinched with emotion and there was a strange fretfulness in her eyes. "You are right. I need to head home." She covered her head and turned to leave.

"Allow me to accompany ya back."

"There is no need. I can find my way home, perhaps better than you."

"Indeed, you will probably have to point the way back to me." It was with misgivings that he grabbed hold of her arm, wondering her reaction.

Her womanly scent engulfed his senses. Lavender, roses, and flour… she wasn't a stranger in the kitchen. Ah, a woman after his own heart.

"So you like to bake?" He peeked beneath the hood of her cloak, searching for the sparkling-eyed lass with the kissable lips. The melody of her laughter complemented the night wind.

"I do and I like to make desserts the best of all. In fact, I wouldn't mind starting off every meal with dessert."

"That would explain it."

"Explain what?" Maggie lifted her hood and Ben was quick to drink in her beauty.

"Explain… why I find you so sweetly delectable."

"Oh, you are a rogue. Mother said to beware of your fancy Gaelic flattery, or else I'd surely learn to regret…"

"Regret?" Ben stopped. Did this lass with the pert dimples on each side of her beautiful pink lips have the capability of bewitching an ignorant lad? All manner of answers swirled through his thoughts and not one of them a pleasing retort.

"Regret I ever met you," Maggie whispered.

The soft sound of the wind running its fingers through the grass and its whispering notes as it played with the fringe on her cape, wrapped his hungry body with the sonnets of warmth and hospitality, melodies of love and mercy more beautifully recited than any Christmas choir could have sung.

The trainings of his departed Scottish-Irish mother who loved reading poetry and who taught her son the gentlemanly arts of chivalry stood Ben in good stead now. He took Maggie's hand gently in his and kissed it. Her slight tremor pleasing, he looked up into her liquid eyes, not missing the slight sigh that followed.

"I shall never regret meeting you. You embody what I felt on my first look of America, that spirit of liberty I felt blowing like the wind, so free and true. I was like the apostle Thomas of the Bible, I was. Until I saw it with my very own eyes I didn't believe America would be any better than Ireland. And I remembered 2 Corinthians 3:17, 'Now the Lord is that Spirit: and where the Spirit of the Lord is, there is liberty.' Now I know I have found my destiny. I will have my land."

"Oh my." Maggie sighed softly and removed her hand, her vibrant eyes searching his. "I will pray God protects you from the trials that lie ahead for you. It is not easy starting over and… and some southerners are talking about seceding from the Union, and then there is Father. He can be a vengeful taskmaster."

# Chapter 4

*M*aggie's eyelids fluttered open, blinking in the morning sunlight pouring through her window. Something had awakened her. There it was again, that thump, thump, thumping noise. Only that wasn't what had awakened her. Then what? She folded back her downy coverlet and lowered her bare feet. The morning light streamed an oblong path on the shiny wood floor. No one awakened this early but the servants. Her bare feet pitter patted along with the thump, thump, thumping.

Where had she placed her wrapper? Her boots rested beneath her discarded dress of last night's escapade, which now lay draped across her St. Anne upholstered chair. She grimaced. Nothing saintly about what she'd done, recalling Ben's touch and the goose bumps that traveled up her arm when his firm fingers wrapped around her hand. Fiddle-faddle. She hadn't time for men.

Would life ever get back to some normality so she could resume her work at the Glenn? Mother was always supportive of Maggie's ambitions. With her desire to educate the slaves, was she putting Mother's reputation at risk among the high-society of the South's elite? She tiptoed to the french doors and stepped onto her balcony, hugging the shadows of the stately brick walls.

The warm breezes played with the folds of her long lace nightgown this the twenty-ninth day of June. Below, on the clothes line, hung three large parlor rugs and one of their servants was thumping an India rug with a wire-handled paddle. Father sat on the veranda, just below her window.

"Well, Chief Justice Taney's ruling on that Dred Scott Decision has me baffled. Abraham Lincoln gave a fine speech on the topic, and I wished not to find myself siding with that Republican abolitionist; however, I must… as I realize the aftermath of the Supreme Court ruling."

Maggie could see her mother was as baffled as she with what her father had said.

"I wish you had not gone to hear Mr. Lincoln speak. Politics always upsets you and the doctor has warned you about apoplexy."

"Nonsense, Marie." Father slapped his napkin on the table and rose. "I'm glad I took the journey to Illinois. That Lincoln fellow in Springfield brought up a good point regarding the Court's decision. If 'all men are created equal' and have 'certain inalienable rights, among which are life, liberty, and the pursuit of happiness,' are these rights just for white people of Great Britain and America and not colored people? Why should the Supreme Court stop there? What Lincoln said was the Supreme Court could then decide to exclude other undesirables, for instance, French or Germans or your precious Irish from suing the US Court for their freedom. The Court could rule against the people with an iron fist."

"Oh dear." Mother rose, her arms outstretched toward Father. "Please be careful, dear husband, do not upset yourself so."

Her father, deep in thought, continued to pace back and forth. "I remember what my father said about Thomas Jefferson's fears, something about if the judiciary has the sole power of constitutional interpretation then the Constitution is a mere thing of wax in the hands of the judiciary, which they may twist and shape into any form they please."

Her mother grabbed his arm, and Father cupped her face in his large palm, gently kissing her on the cheek.

"You see, my love, our forefathers prayed and carefully wrote the Constitution to protect United States citizens from would-be tyrants who would attempt to dictate to a nation what they will think and what they will do."

"What can we do? We didn't elect the Supreme Court judges, so now what?"

"Listening to Lincoln, I couldn't help think what my father would say of that young man's speech." Father reached for her mother's hand. "My family came to America because of the kings and lords of Great Britain who liked to dictate laws and impose their beliefs on their subjects with an iron fist. As long as those Supreme Court judges do not rewrite the Constitution, I believe these United States can survive even our judicial judges."

"Now sit and finish reading your paper." Her mother pulled her father toward his chair. "Our forefathers knew civilization is prone to breed tyrants. Just look at what the whites did to my mother's people, the Cherokee. But surely not even the Supreme Court would ever think of rewriting the Constitution."

"Never! Americans wouldn't stand for that. After all, it would mean that the Supreme Court would be tampering with constitutional rights."

"I fear a lot of our southern neighbors in Tennessee might have spoken out against Dred Scott being freed and again about secession, if not for this ruling."

Father sat back down, taking a sip of his coffee as he contemplated his next words. "Pray, Marie. Pray that God intervenes for these United States. I am certain our southern neighbors are happy with the Supreme Court decision, but is it right? Is it just?

"We must uphold the God we trust, the God that heard the cries of the American patriots and freed them from the grasp of a tyrant." Father pointed heavenwards. "It is to Him, our King, we answer to Him alone in the life hereafter." He patted her mother's hand. "I believe my father would have liked this Lincoln fellow. I do not agree with the Republican Party or the abolitionists, but I cannot help admire Lincoln."

"I am glad to hear you speak this way. But I don't know how you will manage to keep order in Maryville with these secessionists traveling through eastern Tennessee. Our neighboring slave owners are certain to vote to secede from the Union. Being mayor during this trying time will be difficult. The Quakers of Friendsville and the Society of Friends of Maryville sway toward supporting the abolitionist activity."

"Mr. Reynolds has provided me a measure of reassurance. That it is all just idle gossip. The Society is not affiliated with any abolitionist activity. Still, I want you to keep clear of that ladies group."

Picking up his paper, he slapped the folds open with exuberance. "Oh, and speaking of idle gossip, I almost forgot to show you this. Our neighbor found this and asked me about it." He rested his paper on the table and withdrew something from his inside coat pocket. "He is hoping to gather more information as to how his slave acquired it. Do you know anything about this?"

Maggie's thinly clad body immediately felt the chill of the banister. Ignoring the discomfort, her eyes stared at the object. Father had withdrawn a writing tablet from his coat and handed it to her mother, then picked up the paper and began reading.

Maggie bit down on her lower lip. Father was watching her mother discretely over the top of his newspaper, but her mother was completely unaware of it. The item looked like Susie's tablet, with her blue paint mark on the wood.

Her mother kept her eyes shielded with her long sooty lashes. She took it, inspected it, and then laid it down on the table, tracing its edges. Her fingers shook ever so slightly. "It's a writing tablet."

Father threw down the paper and with hands behind his back began to pace again. "If any of our respectable neighbors, or our zealous overseer, thought there was someone teaching their slaves to read and write… why… they wouldn't hesitate to hang us from the nearest tree, or at the least, tar and feather the whole family and… and make an example of us to fellow slave owners!" Her father's face grew redder with every syllable.

The woman beating the rugs stopped in mid swing, looked at her father, then resumed.

"Do you understand me, Mrs. Gatlan?" His eyes pinched closed, as if he was feeling hot tar wash over his body. "Always remember your station in life. Do not converse with the help. You have women of the other plantations to spend your time with."

"I will choose my own company and, as my husband has provided such an admirable example, not to bend a knee to anyone but my Lord and Savior."

The thumping noise stopped.

Father stomped over to the dining room entryway, then glanced toward the servant cleaning the rugs. "What are you staring at? Resume your work."

The thumping resumed. The heels of Father's boots clicked on the stone patio, he halted before her mother and stared down at her. "I take the risks for this family, Maria. I trust you will remember this."

Then before Maggie's startled eyes, he knelt and laid his head in her mother's lap. "You would look terrible in tar black… please, let me deal with this." He arose as quickly as he had knelt, offering her his hand. "My love, are you coming?"

"Always." Her mother accepted the proffered arm and gave it a pat. "So, where is the book I asked you to buy on your trip up north?"

Father drew a package out of his coat pocket. "You are my better half. I will never be mad with you for long, my love, nor deny you anything."

Her mother tore at the brown paper with a relish equal to a mother bear defending her offspring. "Mr. Gatlan, we should not remain ignorant as to the outcry regarding this book."

Maggie looked down, *Uncle…?*

Her mother patted the cover. "*Uncle Tom's Cabin.*" She gave Father one of her sweeping smiles. "Good, now I shall see for myself why this book has upset so many northerner households." Raising herself on tiptoes, she kissed his lips. "Don't worry, husband, Maggie and I will not let you down. You have nothing to fear whatsoever. After all, God is on our side. Now, come and see my roses before we go in for breakfast."

Maggie let out a sigh of relief. "I wish I could find a man who loved me that much." She hurried and dressed in her newest riding outfit. The soft velvet folds, the color of a crystal blue sky, fell gently over her petite waist and swished to the floor. Mother said it brought out her eyes and complexion beautifully. This would be a good day to spend with her friend Irene as well. Her little boy, Will Jr., was growing up so fast. And she could always ride by the swampland and see how Ben was doing, too. Her riding boots tapped a merry rhythm on the spiral stairway, and she slid into her seat at the table without Father noticing her tardiness moments after he and Mother entered from the rose garden.

She had much to tell Irene about Ben. Maggie stared at her hands as she toyed with her silverware. After all, she should be concerned about the Irishmen's and… Ben's well-being. Recalling their walk in the moonlight, there was something about him she could not ignore. Another idealist like that Lincoln fellow, not very practical, especially for these times. Still, there was something exciting about him, she had never met someone so—

"So, where might your mind be this morning?" Her father tapped her shoulder. "Reliving your night's excursion?"

"What?" Maggie glanced at her mother.

Her mother rolled her large expressive brown eyes toward Father. "We saw Mr. Reynolds in the rose garden and—"

"Maria, please. This matter must be settled promptly." Her father sat down in his customary seat at the head of the table. "I've asked you a question."

Maggie felt as if a peach seed had found residence in her throat. She coughed. "Would you please repeat the—"

"Just where are you planning to go this morning? And where were you last evening?"

"To Irene's. I thought I would bring over some of Cook's biscuits and scones. Irene and Will Jr. love Cook's biscuits."

"Oh?" Her father's blue eyes focused on her like a hawk on a chicken. "Is that your only reason for leaving my watchful eye? You are not planning to divert your ride toward the swamp by chance?"

"I… why do you ask?"

"Because I've been told by Mr. Reynolds that you were walking with a young Irishman in the moonlight last evening."

Maggie looked down at her plate. Had Reynolds been following her? She felt like a prisoner and Reynolds her warden. She glanced at her mother and sucked in her breath. If Mr. Reynolds had watched her beneath the cover of night, what was to prevent him from watching her go to the Glenn?

Father threw his napkin on the table and stood, his chair falling back in his haste to rise. "I will not have this! You understand? He is beneath us, and I will not have you being seen with an Irishman."

"I wouldn't worry," Mr. Reynolds said.

Maggie gasped. She hadn't noticed when he came in. He strutted like a peacock to the dining table, pulled out a chair next to her, and then motioned for her father to sit back down. Reynolds reached over her, looked right into her face, smiled, and grabbed a scone. His enormous mouth bit into it slowly, consuming it in one bite… not taking his eyes off her.

I hope he chokes.

"Those ragged men have got to go into the swamp waters. There is no way around it. And I'm certain a few of them will meet their Maker when a cottonwood snake gets a hold of them."

*Chapter 5*

*B*en removed his shoes and socks; they were his only pair and he wouldn't want to waste them in that water again. It took him a full day to dry them out when he'd fetch Maggie out of the bog. He wiped his forehead and the back of his neck with his worn-out bandana.

Now came the part he and the others dreaded. Since Matthew's death, no one had ventured into the swamp. They had accomplished all they could on dry land. Their irrigation ditch lay before the mouth of the swamp like a gaping grave awaiting its victim. Only the victim would be the marshes and snakes of the swampland.

Ben took a deep breath. He would have to wade in waist deep and see what he could do with wedging out the vegetation that prevented the flow of the water from escaping into their ditch.

"Ben my boy, let your dad do this. What with that spot of rain we had last night, the snakes will be crawling to be sure."

"Not to worry, Dad, I've got this." Ben removed his tattered shirt, draped a rope over his shoulder, and waded into the water. The slimy mud oozed between his toes.

"You'll need more help doing this; you can't do it alone, my boy."

Ben watched a snake slither across the swamp and avoided him. Carefully he moved his legs toward the big tree, its limbs now tentacles of mossy green vegetation, slippery and slimy like the back of a reptile. He shuddered. Still, he'd not let another man do what he was afraid to do.

Removing the rope from his shoulder, he fastened it to the trunk of the tree, then ran it across the bog and heaved it toward land. He hoped the rope was long enough to reach the men on the shore and hitch to the two mules.

His eyes looked toward the one patch of sunlight that filtered through the darkness of the swampy brown-black waters. He waded farther inwards, now up to his waist. He was almost there, just a few more feet. At the end of his rope, he glanced back over his shoulder. The tree had stop moving. What was hindering it?

A snake, its little beady eyes staring into his, perched on the tree as if daring Ben to move it any farther. "Oh, I see, this be your house. Sorry, fellow, but your house must be moved. Now, you don't give me any trouble and I won't bother ya."

A strange noise, like the sound of a dozen insects, erupted. Was it coming from the snake? Or was it the blasted mosquitoes?

"That be a pygmy rattlesnake, son. Don't you be fighting him! Get out of there and wait to do any more until he slithers away."

Why, that snake's barely twenty inches long. Has Dad gotten senile? "Listen, small fry, let's carry on this conversation another day. I've got to get this here tree out of our way, you see? You just sit there and enjoy the ride."

Ben turned and pulled with all his strength. Come on just a few more feet and he'd be done. Big Jim extended his arm for the rope. Sweat poured down Ben's face. He wiped his eyes with his arm and mosquitoes flew about his head and shoulders. He blinked, the salt of his sweat burning his eyes. He'd sure be a pretty sight if Maggie happened along today, and yesterday she hinted she planned on doing that very thing.

He heard that insect noise again. Big Jim yelled, rushing toward him. Like a bullet, the snake's bite shot through Ben's back. The snake bit again.

"There's a cottonmouth swimming toward ya!" his dad yelled.

"Ahhh…" The cottonmouth bit him in the leg. His left side felt like it had gone to sleep. He lost his balance, his head swimming. He gasped for air but only the muddy swamp filled his lungs. Someone grabbed his arms. Someone else wrapped something around his middle.

"Dad, I can't feel my legs."

"Lay him down here. Good. That's good."

"Ah…" The sharp steel blade of his dad's knife gleamed in the beams of sunlight. "I'd like a bit of warnin' before you be cuttin' into my back."

Someone stuck a sliver of wood between his teeth, but he could not hear what he was telling him. His ears were pounding along with the bell ringing in his head. He bit down, stifling his cry when the blade cut through his flesh. Once done, he spit the wood from his mouth.

"Don't have to take all my…"

A woman's voice?

"Maggie? Sorry I can't get up. Something's wrong with my legs." Ben was dizzy again, he was falling. How could that be, he was lying on the soft grass—velvet it was to his exhausted body, velvety as Maggie's riding habit. "Maggie… Give me your hand." Fingers as soft as a dove's underbelly they were. He looked up at her. Her face turned dark. Dark as pitch. The ebony waters pulled him down, down… he couldn't breathe. Coming up for air, he gasped… "Hold on to me, Maggie. I'll not get out without your help."

# Chapter 6

**M**aggie bit back her sobs, setting her face like the granite tombstones gracing the family plot. Ben turned to her, his face muddy, his eyes unblinking. Was he seeing her, or the black waters? She looked away. Ben's only hope for survival was if she could hide her feeling for him.

"Get him out of here." Mr. Reynolds swept the air with his arm. "I don't care where he goes, he's useless to me now."

Ben's dad's hat looked like a corkscrew in his hands. Maggie doubted it would ever regain its shape. Iron wheels scraped the dirt and pebbles of the worn farm lane, and their buckboard came into view. Maggie let out a pent-up breath of air as a bright blue jay flew past her to her mother.

Eli yanked on the reins of their team of white horses, crossing his arms like a large black Roman centurion ready to do battle for his queen.

"Just what is going on here?" Reynolds asked her mother, his confusion at her presence obvious.

"We are here for Ben McConnell." Her mother motioned for Eli to carry Ben's body to the buckboard. Maggie wished she could jump up and down with glee as she had done as a child when Mother appeared like an avenging angel to her rescue. Eli jumped out of the wagon and bent over Ben's prostrate form.

"We can take care of our own, Mr. Eli, if you please." Big Jim knelt, scooping Ben into his hands gently. But Ben's lifeless legs were too much for one man to handle.

Eli grabbed the bottom half of Ben and together they lifted him onto the wagon where Maggie's mother sat near a mattress and quilts. Carefully she laid a pillow beneath his head. Ben's teeth chattered like a woodpecker and she watched him hug his arms across his chest. Chills. The day was humid enough to wring water out of her muslin dress.

"But, but," Reynolds stammered. His goatee bobbed up and down with every quiver of his pointed chin. "I want this Irishman taken to the poor man's ward in that hospital in Knoxville, Eli. Do you hear me? I order you to take this, this cripple there."

Eli stood in front of the kneeling Mrs. Gatlan. His solid, six-foot height resembled a brick wall, whereas, Reynolds, a thin willow. As unmovable as cement, all Eli was missing was his Roman sword. He looked down at Reynolds off the tip of his nose. "I only obey Mrs. Gatlan."

Maggie stood in awe, recalling the bleeding back of Eli when he was beneath Reynolds' iron hand. Evidently, Reynolds remembered, too. His body vibrated with sustained wrath. "How dare you disobey my orders."

"Mr. Reynolds, might I ask your services?" Mrs. Gatlan pulled out her slender leg and stretched her foot forward. He hurried to her aid, eyeing Eli who ignored him.

Her mother walked about the hillside, her lavender barred muslin skirt spread twelve yards of fabric on her swaying hoops. Her small, white-gloved hands clutched one another in exaggerated exuberance. What is Mother up to?

"Mr. Reynolds, you are so intelligent. Your idea to hire the Irish was a splendid one. And with your… careful supervision, they have done a marvelous job. I can hardly believe they have accomplished what for years Mr. Gatlan and I thought an impossible task. And to think, not even these mules have been damaged. Now, just how much longer until this is completed and when will you begin the cotton crop?"

Reynolds placed his thumbs in the corners of his vest and cleared his voice like the pompous blue jay that just flew by. One would think he was the one that directed the efforts to drain the swamp, making it into a farmable piece of real estate, not Ben's brains and the Irishmen's hard labor. Maggie's mother continued.

"Mr. Reynolds, I am in need of their aid." She placed a hand on Mr. Reynolds' arm and smiled sweetly into the overseer's startled expression. "Dear Mr. Reynolds, Mr. Gatlan will explain my desires to you upon his return from Washington."

Mr. Reynolds' face became vivid red in the glow of stark sunlight. "I think you have fabricated this—"

"Don't you go callin' Mrs. Gatlan a liar."

"Why you upstart blackie. I'll put you back in chains, give you the whipping you deserve, and send you to the fields." Reynolds slapped his whip against his riding boots. "I am in control here when Mr. Gatlan's away."

Her mother, head erect, stepped forward. "No longer." Her voice echoed above Reynolds' whip thumping his leather boots. Her eyes gleamed into Reynolds' steel glance, daring him to question her authority.

Maggie scurried into the wagon bed like a mouse caught in the cupboard, shaking from head to toe. This was definitely not part of her plans. She was well aware of how much influence Reynolds had on her father. Maggie prayed silently for God to intervene.

"No one interferes with my authority." Reynolds pointed the whip in her mother's face. "You will pay dearly for this offense, Mrs. Gatlan." He grabbed his horse's reins, and in one fluid motion, mounted and was off in a fury of hooves and flapping gray coat.

Relieved to see him go, Maggie hurried to her mother's side.

"I have roused the demons in him." Her mother watched him leave.

"Mother, he meant what he said about getting even with you." Maggie leaned against her mother, drawing strength from her. Mother circled her with her arm.

"The only way to fight evil is to 'Put on the whole armor of God, that ye may be able to stand against the wiles of the devil… the shield of faith wherewith ye shall be able to quench all the fiery darts of the wicked. And take the helmet of salvation, and the sword of the spirit, which is the word of God.'"

Mother thought God and the Bible could rectify any conflict. "We have not heard the end of this, Mother. We may have gained a foothold, but I fear we might lose a stride or two before this feud with Reynolds has ended."

"Feud? He is bent on destroying everything I love, and that is an act of war." Her mother patted her hand. "Eli, help me into the wagon, please. We need to be off. Are the cabins ready for occupancy?"

"Yes, ma'am. My wife had them cleaned and fresh linen placed on the beds."

Maggie's mother looked down at the Irishmen, her kind eyes not missing a one. "Clean water and plenty of soap for baths?"

"Yes, ma'am."

"Gentlemen, please follow our wagon to your new accommodations. Cabins, water to bathe with, and food awaits you. You will begin on the northern swampland tomorrow."

Was Mother right? Would Father side with them… or Reynolds?

Eli helped Maggie onto her horse. She wished she could ride straddle and wear pants. Then she could jump into the saddle as easily as Mr. Reynolds had.

Her father had changed so. Mother rode straddle like Father when Father first saw her. She was half Cherokee Indian—her mother's father chief of the Cherokee of Tennessee. Maggie stared into the mists toward the Glenn. Mother had told her about those days so long ago when she and Father had carved Spirit Wind out of the wilderness and trusted God for their daily provisions.

Ben's father ran toward the wagon and thrust a tiny leather pouch into his son's palm. "Take this wee mustard seed I brought from Ireland. Me own dear father gave me these seeds to remind me that with God, nothing is impossible. Faith as small as a grain of mustard seed! See for yourself, we are here in this blessed land." Ben's father smiled through his tears. "'Tis better than kissing the blarney stone, it 'tis. God can restore you back to a full man. If He has a mind to, and if you believe He can!"

Her eyes met Ben's momentarily, then turned to gaze at the lowlands. God please, please heal Ben. He had saved her, but could she save him? Would Ben ever walk again?

# Chapter 7

*B*en hated being a cripple. Each morning, he would rub his legs, praying for life to return to his numb limbs. Nothing. Eli was his constant companion. He bathed him, carried him to the buckboard, and then carried him to his wee cart so he could oversee the swamp clearing.

Big Jim was his legs and ensured Ben's orders were carried out to the fullest. But he worried about his dad; he was trying to work as hard as two men and him up in age. His dad's color was better. The ruddiness of his cheeks also displayed his faith renewed. Now, more than ever, Ben was determined to get that piece of land. His dad and he burned with the desire to prove that the signs saying "Irish need not apply" were only hurting the Americans. Irishmen were tireless workers, smart, and not afraid to get their hands dirty.

It was hard for Ben to accept the aid of Eli, knowing that people like Eli were keeping the Irish from attaining jobs and food. And what about the Glenn? What was going on there?

Each morning before the sun rose, batches of slaves would disappear into the night, only to reappear an hour or two later, before the rooster crowed his first alarm. They'd hide the contents of their pockets and not breathe where they had been. An uprising of some sort was coming about, to be sure. Should he alert Maggie?

He heard a gentle knock on his door and then the soft voice of his nurse. "Are you up, Ben?"

"To be sure, I be, and as decent as I am able with half a body at my disposal." Ben swept back his hair from his forehead, then nodded at Eli who kept an eagle-eyed vigil on Maggie while in Ben's room.

The first sight of Maggie always astounded him. This morning the rays of the sun shone on her back, and she looked like an angel with a halo of sunlight floating about her hair and shoulders. Her eyes held a strange magic that mesmerized him every time he glanced within them.

Deep pools of color, those brown eyes took on a gleam of their own whenever she wore vibrant scarlet or sky blues. To be sure, she was a vision, that Maggie Gatlan. It was getting much too hard to fight the tide that welled within his heart each time she touched him, be it as she lifted his sheets to massage his legs, like she was doing now.

"I take it you're getting even with me for that first day we met," he said.

"I never thought about it that way." Maggie chuckled, then continued to rub on the liniment she had brought. "Let me know if this burns."

The smell resembled what he used on his mule whenever the animal became lame. "Could it be horse liniment you be using?"

"Do you feel anything, Ben?" Red from the liniment, Maggie dipped her hands in a pail of cool water. "I hope the liniment didn't burn your skin." She touched his legs. "Do your legs feel hot?"

And him wishing he could feel that gentleness… he bit his lower lip. "No, but I be smelling like a horse, to be sure."

Maggie turned her face away from him, glanced at Eli, shook her head, then reached for a cloth. Was she trying to hide her disappointment? She dipped the cloth into the water, then covered his now reddened legs, her mouth quivering ever so slightly.

Eli cleared his throat. "I'll fetch some fresh drinking water."

Ben scrunched his eyes shut and lifted his arm across his face. *Merciful Jesus, what have I done to deserve this?*

Maggie gently shook his shoulders. She smelled of apples, flour, and horses… with a bit of the sunshine thrown in for good measure.

"Ben, there's a preacher coming to town for a tent revival. He, he's wonderful." She bent closer, her soft green sprigged muslin with the puffy sleeves brushing his chest. She'd tied a white lace shawl in the front about her bodice. The song, "The Wearin' o' the Green" came to mind and he started to hum it.

"Ben, listen." Her eyes were serious enough to be dressing him for his wake.

"Lighten up, lass. You're much too young for me to be laying extra years upon your pretty face. I can take care of myself."

"He has a reputation in the north of being a healer. I've seen it. Mother and I want to take you. Will you go with us, please?"

Ben rose to a sitting position. Maggie plumped the pillow behind his back. It felt good. He started to hum "The Wearin' o' the Green" again, watching her as she rushed to get him a cool drink of spring water from the bucket Eli had just fetched. Her long hoop skirt swayed with every motion of her hips, dress and petticoats swishing across the just-washed floor so clean he could eat on it. Her waist looked small enough for Ben to wrap his hand around. Dainty and innocent she be. Not at all knowing about the disappointments of life, atrocities of war, death, and starvation, Oh, to be innocent.

"Do you know the song, 'The Wearin' o' the Green?'"

Maggie shook her head as she carried toward him a tray laden with a steaming bowl of soup, a glass of milk, and a piece of bread.

"I'll be tellin' it to you, then."

"Okay, but take a sip of this first."

Ben did as she directed. He didn't realize he was hungry. He finished the bowl of soup, then smiled up at her. "Now, where was I? Yes, 'The Wearin' o' the Green' is an Irish folksong, dating back to the Irish Rebellion of 1798 when we rose against the British."

His fingers traced the deep green borders of her dress. "Back then wearing green clothing or the shamrocks was considered a rebellious act, punishable by death." Ben laid his head back on his pillow. He watched Maggie's expression as she touched the gold cross she always wore about her neck.

"Yes," he whispered. "Just a simple trinket and a color and the English would hang men, women, and children alike if their orders were not obeyed." Clearly, she was having a tough time digesting this.

"Well, I'll be tellin' ya the last two verses. Though I doubt I'll be doin' it proper.

> *She's the most distressful country that ever yet was seen*
> *For they're hanging men and women there for Wearing of the Green.*
> *But if at last our color should be torn from Ireland's heart*
> *Her sons, with shame and sorrow, from the dear old Isle will part*
> *I've heard a whisper of a land that lies beyond the sea*
> *Where rich and poor stand equal in the light of Freedom's day.*
> *Ah, Erin, must we leave you, driven by a tyrant's hand*
> *Must we seek a mother's blessing from a strange and distant land*
> *Where the cruel cross of England shall never more be seen*
> *And where, please God, we'll live and die, still Wearing of the Green.*"

Ben grimaced, directing his gaze to Eli. "Free indeed. What has freedom gotten the Irish in America, but want, hard work, and more want?" He looked around the cabin quarters, a bed with clean linens, a table, chairs, a cupboard laden with plates and cups and full of bread, butter, cheese, and meat. More than he and his dad ever had in Ireland, to be sure. Then on the pegs, more clothes and another set of shoes. "Who needs freedom if one is provided with the wants?"

"Ben, look at me." She pulled his chin around. Her eyes looked deeply into his. She was a strange one.

"Ben, what you wish for will come. Don't lose hope in America." Then she jumped, like he'd pinched her. He wouldn't say the thought didn't enter his mind a half dozen times a day, but he was truly innocent of the action.

"Rich and poor stand equal in God's eyes, Ben. Hear this preacher. What have you got to lose? It's the American way." Maggie shrugged her slender shoulders and laughed. "Well it's the Christian American way." She wagged her finger in front of his face. "Never, never, give up your faith or hope in Jesus."

"When is this preacher man coming to town?"

"Sunday."

"But it be Tuesday. And my dad and Big Jim's leaving on Friday. All us Irishmen have been ordered out by Mr. Reynolds. Our job is done here." He jingled his pocket. They had made forty gold pieces, and if not for the generosity of Mrs. Gatlan, they would have made much less. But would that buy the splendors of this cabin? Hardly. Winter was approaching. What would they do with no roof over their heads or warm coats on their backs?

"If you could see to it that we Irish could stay on longer—"

"I wish that was possible." Maggie grabbed the sandwich she had made and the tall glass of milk and handed it to him, then sat down on her chair, glancing toward Eli. "Father said we could either sell a few of our slaves and hire you Irish, or else let you go."

Ben nearly choked on his bite of sandwich, nodding in Eli's direction. "And of course, all you being related, it would mean splitting up families."

"Exactly." Maggie glanced back at Eli, then looked down at her hands. "Mother refuses to do that. But she is very fond of every one of you—"

"And what about you?" He wanted to say Maggie dearest, but choked back the words.

"I'm praying, Ben. I told my father we could build a few more cabins and let you stay at Spirit Wind while you look for work. Once word gets around how you dredged the swamp, there will be plenty more work for you." Maggie laid her hand down on the coverlet, then just as quickly got up and began to pace the cabin.

"Can you come, Ben, to the revival? Maybe your dad and Big Jim would come. Don't you see, this is what our country needs right now. Southerners are talking about seceding from the Union. Oh, I can't bear to think about that." Maggie rushed to his bed and knelt, her eyes pleading, searching his. "Come, and keep an open mind."

"But I'm not sure our religion permits this. Does this preacher believe that Jesus is the Son of God?" He leaned forward, their faces nearly touching. It was all Ben could do not to kiss her pleading lips.

"Yes, Ben, truly he does and he believes Jesus can heal just as He did when He was on earth, only through God's Holy Spirit."

Ben searched her face. "If you can get your father to allow us to stay until the following Monday, I will see if I can get my men to come to your tent revival. I know my Jesus and if He's there… well, we'll just see."

Maggie caught her breath. "It would be a miracle from God if Father grants you Irish more time."

# Chapter 8

The smells of horses, harness, and Mother's lemon verbena sachet drifted past Maggie's nose. She couldn't believe all the carriages traveling the street heading toward the oval tent erected on a large hill just outside town. From here, the tent resembled a gigantic mushroom.

Dust clouds from the horses' hooves rose to greet the walkers. Some smiled and nodded to her; others who were strangers coming into town for the revival, looked curiously up at them.

She and mother glanced at each other and laughed. The clanging of harness, conversation, and singing filled her ears. Indeed, their little assemblage must make quite a site. Adorned in their silk dresses, a combination of pink and plum, with lace parasols raised high against the bright Tennessee sunlight, she and Mother sat perched like nobility next to Eli in an old buckboard with Ben sprawled out in back. Behind their wagon were the Irishmen all decked out in their Sunday best, gray broadcloth with wide black cravat, ruffled shirts, and black derbies, compliments of Spirit Wind.

There couldn't be a prouder bunch of Irishmen. Three abreast, shoulder to shoulder, a dozen of them marched in perfect step to the tune of "The Girl I Left Behind Me" as they sang. "I'm lonesome since I crossed the hill, And over the moorland sedgy, Such heavy thoughts my heart do fill, Since parting from my Sally. I seek no more the fine and gay, For each just does remind me How sweet the hours I passed away, With the girl I left behind me." Ben's bass voice, strong with feeling and emotion, had her wondering if he left behind a girl in Ireland? A stab of jealousy slapped her chest unexpectedly and for a moment she was indignant. He's most likely got a half-dozen pretty girls pining for him in Ireland!

"O ne'er shall I forget that night, The stars were bright above me, And gently lent their silvery light When first she vowed to love me." Ben glanced her way and smiled. "But now I'm bound to America's shores - Kind heaven then pray guide me, And send me safely back again, To the girl I left behind me."

Eli hummed along.

"I wish I could have encouraged your father to come," Mother whispered. She twirled her parasol, blocking any view Maggie may have glimpsed of her mother's disappointment. "Your father used to love to go to revivals and church socials before we got so high and mighty in society. Now he just goes Sunday mornings, and I think it's more an obligation than a chance to talk to his Lord and Savior. I just don't know where I've gone wrong."

Mother was the anchor of Maggie's faith. It was due to her father's loyalty to her mother that he allowed the Irish to stay on. For Mother to doubt was unusual and too human for Maggie to digest. Mother was above any Christian she knew and on equal terms with the late Reverend Anderson. Maggie patted her mother's lace-gloved hand. "You always say that our good Lord gives each of us our own wills to choose or not to choose. I am confident Father will change his mind, especially when Jesus heals Ben."

The tent smelled like moldy bed sheets. Ben adjusted his eyes from bright sunlight to dark shadows. Eli had plenty of arms ready to carry Ben to his spot on one log seat. Clouds of dust rose from the dirt floor, stirred up with the boots and goings on of the crowd finding their seats, making it harder to see.

"I don't want to be here, take me home," one little girl wailed.

Carried in on a stretcher, her attendants hurried through the crowded aisle bumping into people in their urgency, taking the first seat in front of the preacher's platform. A stout man with a stogie hanging out the corner of his mouth bumped Ben's arm. "Sorry. Say, what are you here for, healing or salvation?"

"It'll not hurt me to grab a little bit of both." Ben smiled into the soft, pudgy face of his stogie-eating friend. "What be your reason for coming to this foul-smelling place?"

"Curiosity." The man puffed harder on his cigar. "When I heard tell that this preacher was having a revival down here, thought I'd check him out. It will be interesting to see how he'll do with this crowd. Heard tell he did real well with the abolitionists up New York and Boston way."

"Oh, Mother, can anything good come from the North?" Maggie whispered.

"We shall soon find out. Look, just two rows from the front, isn't that Matron Burns from the Society of Friends?"

"Why, yes, and there is Miss Peabody."

A man walked onto the makeshift stage made of a few planks of wood hammered together. He was a thin man, and his black suit threadbare at the cuffs. In his hands he cradled a Bible as worn as his clothing.

"He doesn't look like he was so well received in New York," Ben heard Maggie whisper, "unless, that's the way people dress up there."

Ben chuckled. Most likely Maggie had never been up north, and he and his friends were mostly the only northern folks she'd seen. He glanced to his left at his dad, now clean shaven, with his pants creased at the knees and pressed razor sharp, and his Sunday go to meeting shirt on. Big Jim had fared as well as the other Irishmen, thanks to Mrs. Gatlan.

Ben sat up a little taller. With all the bad he and his friends had encountered in New York City, there was still good to be had, if you were willing to work for it.

The preacher opened his Bible. "My message today will be on disciplining your doubts." The preacher flipped the pages of his Bible. "But before we begin with my sermon, God has weighed something heavily upon my shoulders for me to read. Please turn to 2 Corinthians 3:17.

… 'Now the Lord is that Spirit: and where the Spirit of the Lord is, there is liberty.' Is this liberty for a few or for all? We need to ask ourselves this."

The crowd booed him. Maggie's face turned pale white.

The preacher laughed, then lifted his hand. "Well, now that I have your attention—my dear friends, the Bible is the Bible and we need to remember *that* first and foremost. We must fear God and obey His Word and never, never take it out of context.

"Now understand what the Bible here is talking about. God is talking about the Lord's glory, and we being transformed into His likeness, which can only come from accepting our Lord, our Savior, and the Holy Spirit."

The preacher walked down the steps and took hold of the little girl's hand. "Only Jesus can set us free. Not man's laws." He looked out at the crowd. His voice rose higher. "We are all slaves to Satan until we allow Jesus Christ in our hearts as our personal Savior." He turned to the little girl. "Do you believe that?"

The little girl nodded.

"Do you believe that Jesus is the Son of God who died on the cross for your sins and that His Holy Spirit has the power to heal our infirmities today as Jesus did when He walked the shores of Galilee?"

"Yes, I do believe," the little girl said.

Silence pulsed in Ben's ears. He held his breath. The preacher grabbed both her hands into his. "Then in the name of Jesus Christ, I cast out this evil and demon spirit of illness. Satan, I bind you and the forces of evil in this little girl's body, and in Jesus' name I command you to leave her and her family alone! In the name of my Lord Jesus Christ, little girl, rise and walk."

The little girl rose to a sitting position, swung her legs over the edge of her pallet and stood up. The crowd gasped. The little girl took a hesitant step, then another, and another. Tears flowed down her face. She hobbled on wobbly legs toward the preacher. "I can walk, I can walk, oh thank you!"

"No, little one, thank Jesus!" The preacher looked up over the mass of people. "Would you like to be free from your sins, free from what ails you, free from the shackles Satan has placed over your hearts and minds? Then bow your heads, please, and repeat after me. Lord Jesus, I am a sinner and not worthy of your grace. …Lord, forgive me of my sins, …I repent of my evil doings and ask for Your Holy Spirit to come into my heart. I accept by faith Your salvation message, being born again into Christ's family. 'For that which is born of flesh is flesh; and that which is born of Spirit is spirit… For God so loved the world that he gave his only begotten Son, that whosoever believeth in him should not perish, but have everlasting life.' Deliver us from the evil one, Jesus, now and forever more, amen."

Ben repeated the words as the murmur of voices swelled around him. Maggie's sweet voice blended with his, and he wished he had the nerve to reach for her hand. Before he could utter the last syllable, Big Jim had scooped him up into his strong arms and marched him down toward the preacher.

Ben wanted his legs back more than the air in his lungs. But somehow, that paled in comparison to feeling the freedom he experienced repeating those simple words of the preacher. Whatever happened, being a life-long cripple, a lowly beggar, or fighting in a war he didn't believe in, he had that narrow road to follow that led to Jesus and a celestial home to go to just beyond the hilltops. Maggie's cheeks glistened with tears. What plan had his Savior crafted for them? Or would his decrepit flesh waylay him from his intended mission?

# Chapter 9

"Come in," Maggie answered in response to the gentle knock on her bedroom door.

Hattie opened the door, then slammed it shut. "There's no stopping that devil now." Laying her back against the door, she gnawed on what was left of her nails. She reached for her rabbit's foot, rubbing it intensely.

"What's this?"

"Cook's, she lent it to me."

"You know I don't believe in Cook's superstitious mumbo jumbo."

"Yous got your cross; we gots our rabbit foots."

The feeling of Maggie's smooth gold cross beneath her fingertips gave her pause. *Lord, tell me how to convey Your message to the unsaved.* "This isn't a charm; this is to remind me that I'm a sinner and need my Savior, Jesus, to guide me, to keep me on the narrow road to His—"

"Your Mother will soon be at those very pearly gates if'n you don't get downstairs… oh, come quick. Mr. Reynolds is… and your father is …"

Reynolds' angry voice drifted up from the study as Maggie followed Hattie down the winding staircase, clutching the cherry wood banister like a life preserver.

"He's nothing but a liar. He was never a cripple." Reynolds leaned over her mother's chair, yelling in her face. Maggie hurried toward them, pushing Reynolds aside.

"How dare you speak to my mother like that!" She turned to her father who sat at his desk, his eyes cast downward, his face a block of ice. "Father?"

"I want Ben McConnell and his Irish cronies off this place today." Reynolds was an inch away from Maggie's face. She kept her focus on his beady eyes, much like a snake's, that is if she ever had the misfortune to see one this close. That thought made her laugh.

Reynolds backed away. Totally baffled, he looked from her to her father. Her hands shook with rage. She buried them in her billowing skirt.

Like an archangel, Mother stepped in front of her. "It is not for you to decide who may or may not reside at Spirit Wind."

"Are you going to allow your half-breed wife to talk to me like this?"

Father's chair scraped across the wooden floor. His heavy footsteps walked slowly toward them, as if he dreaded his journey's end. What was wrong with Father? How could he allow Reynold's to speak that way about her mother?

"Maggie, are you certain Ben was crippled? Could he have been faking to acquire help for himself and the Irishmen? This sort of deception has been used before." Her father studied her mother's face to see her reaction to his words.

Maggie rose to her full height. "I am certain, Father. Ben was not pretending. He could not feel anything from the waist down. I nearly burned him with that horse liniment. See," she said, holding out her hands, "there is still a bit of a burn on my thumb here."

Father inspected her hands, turning them. "And he acquired miraculous healing from this, this... faith healer?"

"That is preposterous!" Mr. Reynolds slammed his fist on her father's desk. "Mr. Gatlan, how can you be taken in by a faith healer and the wiles of your wife and daughter?" His steel-gray eyes stared at him.

Father glanced at her mother. Like ice cracking with the first gleam of the sun, father's hard face melted into a smile. He hugged her mother close to his broad chest. "I could never live without my better half."

"Well." Reynolds huffed. His eyes narrowed into slits of hatred; his thin lips menacing, he snarled. "I can no longer be a part of this... woman's deceit. She has cast a spell on you both."

Reynolds stormed toward the study door, then turned, his hand on the brass knob. "But I warn you, you'll wish I hadn't left, what with that abolitionist John Brown and his armed insurrection to free the slaves. You'll be killed in your beds by the black hands of your slaves, of whom you are so diligent to protect."

Maggie looked from her father to the door wobbling on its hinges like a rudder of a lost ship from Reynolds' departure. "Well, I say good riddance."

"You might not think that way if you read the headlines of the paper this morning. There's trouble brewing, Maggie. This John Brown fellow isn't going to quit until he's burned us out of our homes."

"Well, we have Ben and his Irishmen to protect us." Maggie smiled. She envisioned Ben's strong arms wrapped around her waist, only this time all for the right reasons. Oh, just think how thankful he must be toward her for taking him to the revival. Ben had run up the aisle, grabbed her and swung her around, kissing her smartly on her upturned cheek. She placed a forefinger to her lips; she could just imagine.

"Daughter, Ben and the Irishmen are leaving. Seems that word has come about a job opportunity in Kentucky."

Maggie was already halfway to the door, her head in a whirl, half-anticipating Ben's touch again. And those eyes, laughing, jesting, all wrapped into a delightful package of mirth. "When Ben knows how much we need him, he'll stay, you'll see."

"Then we must sell some of our slaves if we keep the Irish on," her father retorted, walking toward his desk and sitting down. "There's not enough in the money box for the Irish and feeding and clothing our slaves. Besides, I've run out of work for them to do until spring. Maybe in April I'll be able to train and sell some of my Thoroughbreds for the races and harvest some cotton and tobacco."

"It will be a tight Christmas as it is," Mother said. "Your father just paid Mr. Reynolds a sizable amount of money... how did that come about, dear?"

Her father shrugged. "I thought I had paid him his wages for the year and only owed him this month's pay." He pointed to the books. "But see here, it says I owe him, and... wait a minute. I did pay him. Someone scratched off Reynolds' initials. I paid him the total amount of $3000 in cash last month."

"It is his word against yours, dear husband."

Maggie couldn't believe her ears. "What now, Father? And who will run Spirit Wind?"

"Eli can through the winter months." Her father opened a drawer and withdrew his pistol. "Or else I could resign as mayor. I wouldn't mind it. I prefer working outdoors."

"No," her mother replied. "This is a critical time in Bount County and Maryville needs you."

"I suppose you are right, dear. Then we will need to hire another overseer come spring." Her father pocketed the pistol and headed toward the door. "Reynolds isn't getting away with this."

Her mother took him by the arm. "Reynolds will only deny it." She patted his pocket. "Let it be, it's only money."

"Marie!"

"I am glad we are rid of this dishonest man. Finally, I have my husband back."

"But, Marie."

"With that type of man, you would have to kill him or forever watch your back. You know I am right. Now, husband, can you deny this?"

"That is my intention. He's the worst kind of polecat. I can't believe I was so deceived by him. And I need to put him in his place before he tries to do any additional harm to my family."

Mother looked up at him pleadingly. "Please, husband, let it be. The Good Book tells us to not to repay evil for evil."

"Marie, this is life. You can't always turn the other cheek; that could get you killed."

Her eyes beseeched his. Finally, Father relented. Mother grabbed Maggie's arm. "Come along, Maggie, go and say your goodbyes to Ben. But I wouldn't let him know about our troubles, might be he'd feel obligated to stay on and help us."

Ben threw his few possessions into the middle of his blanket along with the food Maggie had given him, tied up the corners, then placed a stick through the knot and tossed it over his shoulder. He fell in line with the other Irishman traveling down the road they'd been traveling for three days.

Big Jim began the middle lines of "Garryowen," picking up where they'd left off last night while drinking their coffee. "Our hearts so stout have got us fame, For soon 'tis known from whence we came Where'er we go they dread the name, Of Garryowen in glory."

Maggie's brown eyes bubbled up from his heart to his thoughts. She was a rare one. She'd said goodbye without an afterthought as to the success of their venture. Confident in their ability, she was.

"Ah, the jiggle of money in my pockets feels good," Big Jim said, pacing himself next to Ben.

"Indeed." Ben chuckled. Big Jim's large grin nearly swallowed his cheeks. "What are you going to do with yours?"

"I'm planning to buy me a little farm." Big Jim spryly walked around a puddle leftover from the previous night's snowflakes that had melted with the first sunlight. "What be yours?"

"A little land to call my own sounds pleasant to be sure." Ben pointed to the large building. "Is this Stearns' coal mining camp?"

A short, burly man with sideburns that swept to his wiry black mustache walked out of the coal mining headquarters. They had arrived at the noon hour, evidently, for he swiped his mouth with a checkered napkin. "Ok, your bunk is in Building B, find you a cot and settle in. I'll be there shortly to sign you in."

Walking down the lane made by the heavy wagonloads of supplies and coal, Ben's boots crunched in the dirt heavily layered with coarse coal dust. Men with faces powdered with coal dust sat on stumps or on a little piece of grass as if to feel and touch a piece of greenery amidst the bleak and blackness. They looked up at them, not bothering to move their heads in a nod, just the whites of their eyes moved, then they continued eating their lunch.

"The sun has just reached the top of the sky and these men look ready to drop," Ben whispered to Big Jim. One guy, surely no older than thirteen, looked up at them and grinned, then blinked, squinted, and looked down at his plate. "You're newcomers."

"How'd you be knowing that?" Ben stopped and caught a whiff of what the boy was eating. If the food didn't taste any better than it smelled, he doubted he cared to be trying it at all.

"'Cause your face is clean and your clothes don't smell of smoke or coal."

"What's wrong with your eyes?"

"Sunlight bother's them."

Before opening the door to their new sleeping quarters, Ben squared his shoulders and glanced back at the youth, recalling his earlier days in Ireland. Bedding down in a grass hut, breathing in the mud of the moors on his sodden face. *Jesus, get me out of this place like you did in Ireland. You have not predestined a life for me here in the coal mines, I am sure.*

Ben picked a cot by the window. He felt the mattress and noticed it wasn't too clean, but it was softer than sleeping on the ground. He reached into his pockets for the bits of paper Maggie had given him.

Six months of recuperating from his wounds had not only helped his body, it had given Maggie time to teach him how to write his name and read. He wasn't real good with the writing part, never did have the opportunity of putting his thoughts on paper or of writing letters and such, but he knew he'd be doing a lot of that now.

"Okay, men, form a line and we'll get you signed up proper for your weekly checks," the foreman said as he entered the building. He pulled up a straight back chair and sat down at the only table gracing the wee room littered with cots so close Ben had to side step to reach his pillow to lie down on.

Ben was first in line. Proudly he wrote his name in big bold letters. "How long are you fixing we'll be working here?"

The man with the sweeping whiskers looked him up and down like he was a piece of meat on an auction block. "Depends how you work and if you can keep up working twelve hours a day, six days a week. You get lunch given to you, but you have to pay for your breakfast and dinner and, of course, the lodging."

"So we don't need to live on the premises?"

The man shrugged. "It's a free country, but kind of hard to work the hours living off the coal field."

Ben moved over so that the next man could sign his name "What if a body only cares to work until they get up enough money to buy them a little farm?"

"That's fine. Like I said, it's a free country unless you owe a debt to the company store." Sideburns looked up, staring a hole in Ben's face, then his face softened. "Look, if I was you, I'd stay clear of the company store and the bar at Whitley. That little old farm could probably be yours say in a year or two." Sideburns wagged his pen before Ben's face. "But if you kick up your heels, you'll most likely turn out to be a lifer, like most of these gents." He pointed to the open door and the men having their lunch. "Of course, you can always rent one of the houses out yonder if you have a notion to settle down."

Ben crossed his arms. "Then for sure I'd owe my soul to this coal mining camp."

Sideburns chuckled. "You learn fast, kid."

# Chapter 10

hildren find your seats, please." Maggie chuckled watching how quickly everyone obeyed her. Seeing Susie she smiled. Susie's neat brown red-checkered calico flattered her gentle curves. Her starched white turban accentuated her oval face, high cheek bones, and beautiful large, expressive eyes. My, she's blossoming into a beautiful young lady. Where have the years gone?

Realization dawned that two years had already past since Ben left.

Maggie hugged her Bible, walking down the rows of long tables, checking each one's work. She tapped Susie on her shoulder. "Where have you been for three days? We've missed your sweet face here at the Glenn."

Susie looked up from her tablet, her large liquid brown eyes, surrounded by sooty black lashes gazed into hers. The moon peeking through the windows lit her face with an iridescent glow, then suddenly her lower lip quivered. She bent her head onto her desk, her shoulders heaving with her sobs.

"What has happened?" Maggie whispered as she knelt down.

"I'm pregnant, Miss Maggie. And I've had morning sickness something awful."

Maggie covered her mouth. How could this be? Each boy met her gaze, their mouths a round *O* as each shook their heads in denial.

"Twern't one of them, Miss Maggie." Susie looked up with tears making rivulets down her oval face and splattering onto her desk. "Mr. Reynolds been having his way with me and my little sister."

Maggie plopped down into the nearest chair. She was aware these things went on, but not to anyone she knew. Well, she would alert Mother as to the charge. Mother had been attending Maryville's Society of Friends meetings. Maggie placed her hand in her pocket and grasped Ben's letter. He'd be here the day after tomorrow. Should she tell him?

The school had flourished after Mr. Reynolds left Spirit Wind. Now she knew why. Maggie thought Reynolds was busy taking care of his own plantation he bought adjoining Spirit Wind. Now, Reynolds' extra-curricular activities had come into play again. She bid the children good-byes and hurried to her horse.

"They hung him, Marie. Right there in plain daylight for everyone to see." Her father's disheveled state said it all. He must have ridden all night to get back from Virginia this early in the morning.

"There, there, it can't be as bad as all that." Her mother guided him to a chair. "And you must remember your age; a fifty-year-old man should not be riding in the dark and going for days without sleep."

"John Brown had it coming, Marie. What with raiding the federal armory at Harpers Ferry. Why, it's clear what he was trying to do, arm the Africans in a revolt against us. General Lee was stupendous. Brown's five sons dead, and Brown hung for treason. Do you know, until his dying breath he did not repent of his deeds? Even with that rope hanging about his throat, he had the nerve to act like he was a religious martyr dying for a sacred cause, and him looking down at the crowd like he was some dignitary. Then he handed the guard a note and the guard read, 'I, John Brown, am now quite certain that the crimes of this guilty land can never be purged away but with blood.'"

"Oh, my!" Her mother covered her mouth with her hand and paused, then resumed her task at hand and set down a steaming cup before him. "Here, drink this tea. It will calm your nerves."

"The northerners were crying and saying that the court hung a hero. And some of the southerners yelled back at them that Brown was the devil and that hanging was too good for the likes of him." Sweat seeped from her father's forehead and he wiped his face with his handkerchief.

Her mother picked up her cup of tea and gulped it down, dabbed at her mouth and then her brow.

What would happen now? Maggie shuddered, recalling Reynolds words. A slave uprising? With their northern neighbors considering Brown a martyr, the South could little expect aid if the slaves did revolt.

"There will be more talk about—"

"I don't want the South seceding from the Union, Marie, and I don't want this slave issue on my conscience either. Why, most of our neighbors never even owned a slave! Well, maybe, one or two, that doesn't count. And I found out that there are slaves in the north, too. After Virginia, I went up to Washington to see for myself what was brewing.

"Why, you can't believe the factories I saw in Pennsylvania. Children as young as ten years old working in deplorable conditions, and those Irish, my, my." He clicked his tongue on his teeth. "The women, so tired, dressed in rags… I don't even know if this Lincoln fellow understands what's he's up against. How will our slaves take care of themselves… they don't even know how to—"

"That's being taking care of."

"And no one knows?" Maggie's father got up from his chair and gathered her mother into his arms giving her a shake. "You are certain that Reynolds knows nothing about what we are doing at the Glenn. I cringe to think how he would not hesitate to rally our neighbors against us. He seems bent on ruining me."

"We have more to worry about than that." Maggie stepped forward. "Mr. Reynolds has been having his way with—"

Mother's look silenced her words.

"What is it, Maggie?" Her father lifted his tired head. He looked like an old man. Father had always been a pillar of strength, a colossus of wisdom in the most perilous of times.

"A friend is coming to visit from Kentucky," her mother said.

Was mother afraid to tell Father it was Ben?

"He should be here sometime tomorrow. Now, husband, why don't you go and lie down, you look exhausted. I have something I need to attend to in town, but I promise, I will return before you are up from your nap."

Father looked from Maggie to her mother questioningly. "Who's coming?" The candle's glow displayed the deep haggard crevices of her father's face.

"An acquaintance of your sister's." Mother smiled into Father's worried face.

"Oh." He kissed her on the cheek. "Well, I am a bit tired. I believe I shall retire with a good book."

Her father climbed the steps to his bedroom, one foot dragging behind the other, his broad shoulders bent.

"He, he looks like the weight of the South is upon his shoulders."

"It is, Maggie. Our gracious lifestyle is changing with the times and there is nothing we can do about it. Come now, we must hurry before the meeting begins without us."

Ben packed his saddlebags carefully: a clean white shirt, a pair of dress pants, and his new derby hat, along with food and his canteen. He'd been counting the days when he could see Maggie again. He was hoping for an invitation to spend Christmas with them, but didn't want to accept Maggie's invitation until he was certain of his future. He could hardly believe his good fortune as 1859 drew to a close.

He'd not told Maggie about his farm or his fine horse. He patted his dapple-gray stallion Caedmon on his ample neck. "'Tis not a finer Thoroughbred anywhere, and I gave you a fine Irish name meaning 'wise warrior,' so be livin' up to your name, if you please." He'd be riding to his Maggie in style, mounted on his white horse.

"Son, hurry. The auction will begin before we get there."

"You and Big Jim can go without me. I haven't got the heart for it." Ben jumped into the saddle, not bothering with the stirrups, and urged his horse forward. "You know my feelings."

His father swished his hand in front of his face like he was shooing a fly. "We're landlords now and need a proper look to our plantation."

"Well, we don't have to follow in the steps of these people we always loathed. Dad, having slaves when we've just gotten out beneath the yoke ourselves, makes no sense, no sense at all!"

"Who needs to make sense of it? We're in America and yours and my citizenship will soon be returning to us final like. Now, my boy, let us be off."

It was a day's hard ride to Whitley, but it was on Ben's way and he enjoyed the company. The quiet town had become a bustling metropolis overnight. Buckboards filled with rifles, and wagons carrying men, women, and children littered the dusty main road. It made it hard for a body to be getting to the large tent staked at the end of the road. People scurried about; ladies in fine silk dresses and lacy parasols blended with the men's suits and vests adorned with fancy gold chains and watches.

Big Jim leaned forward and whispered, "After that John Brown hanging, I'm not sure that some of these aren't his abolitionist friends roaming these hills ready to take a pot shot at us."

"You'd think with all the yapping about slavery Dad would get it in this thick skull that it isn't fashionable anymore. What with Kentucky statesmen yapping about going the Union way, most likely we'll have to let our slaves go free if war is declared."

Big Jim poked his finger at a wagon. The bed was filled with men, women, and children. "'Tis not a nice memory, but I'm recalling a similar wagon, only littered with the bodies of my dead mother and father. Starved to death they were because of the potato blight. In Ireland we had our freedom, but were life-long bondsmen to our landlords."

"True, there are more shackles that can tie a man's feet from freedom than slavery. Being in debt is one of them."

"Those poor folks in the coal mines for another, spending their hard-earned money in the saloon and the company store. You did the right thing, Ben, holding our money. Like a bank you were."

A tall, muscular man with a crown of curly hair and a chin that poked out enough to hang a coat on ran past them. His feet were bare; his trousers barely covered the knees of his long legs. A volley of gunshots followed.

"You on the white horse, get him!" The sheriff motioned with his gun.

Ben bent low, putting his heels into his horse's sides; he shoved the running man to the ground. Then leaped from his horse and held him down in the dusty road with his knee. "What has he done, sheriff?"

"I've got to get back to my family," the black man said.

"That's your crime?" Ben said, wishing he hadn't tackled him. A man shouldn't be separated from his wife and children.

The sheriff locked the man's wrists into handcuffs. "Now stand up!" The sheriff nodded his head in thanks to Ben. "Got to get this buck to the auction block."

"Okay, let's start the bidding."

Ben was tussled back and forth as the men around him barked out their price. The bid rose to $75, then stopped. What good luck, most of the slaves had gone for over a thousand, too far from Ben's limited pocket book. Just before the gavel hit for the last time, he yelled out $100. There was a murmur in the crowd. Someone said, "Well he did ground him, let the Irishman have the runaway."

"The black man named Jacob goes to—"

"Mr. Ben McConnell, if you please."

Jacob's previous owner, a short, burly man, eyed Ben up and down. One eye was larger than the other, like he'd been squinting into the sunlight too long. "Well, keep your horse saddled. I spent more time hunting him down than him working my plantation, and I paid $1000 for this buck."

"Did you ever think of purchasing his family?"

"I would gladly. Only, his family got passage up north by the Underground Railroad. Jacob was with them, only he got caught and sent back to me. Good hunting!" The man patted Ben's shoulder and walked away laughing.

# Chapter 11

The courthouse curtains were drawn and the windows closed. A musty smell engulfed the room. Maggie couldn't breathe in enough air. Her pulse slammed her ear drums and she inhaled deeply, preparing for the next onslaught of verbal attacks.

The woman in the bright sapphire blue bonnet glared at her. "Mr. Reynolds is a fine gentleman. His slaves are his property to do with as he chooses. We should not take a slave girl's word over a gentleman like Mr. Reynolds, that he, he had his way with her. How preposterous!" She laughed.

Maggie trembled with anger. Fine gentleman? A polecat was more of a gentleman than Reynolds. She gripped the side of the table, determined to remain calm. The wood felt smooth and cool, solid as the Holy Bible. "The girl had no reason to lie. We are Christians first and our duty as such is to uphold God's laws. Fornication is a sin and we cannot allow any woman to be raped, especially an innocent young girl." She leveled her eyes on the group, daring anyone to argue this point.

"And, of course, you have never sinned, Miss Gatlan?" replied the woman in the sapphire blue bonnet. The murmur of the thirty women of the women's society buzzed about the room like nervous wasps. The president pounded her gavel on the table, void of everything but a poinsettia plant brought in to give the courtroom a little color. Maggie grimaced. More than color was needed here. The president nodded for Maggie to proceed.

"Have your consciences been seared? What is wrong with you,

ladies? Can't you see that we cannot turn a deaf ear or blind eye from these… atrocities? When the Jewish council told Christ's disciples not to teach in His name, Christ's disciples said, 'We ought to obey God rather than men.'"

Maggie's eyes scanned the group. Only two women, donned in black bonnets and black dresses, met her gaze. "John 14:23 states: 'If a man loves Me, he will keep My words: and my Father will love him.' And what does James 1:22 say? 'But be ye doers of the word, and not hearers only, deceiving your own selves.'"

The two women in black rose and left the room. A gleam of the setting sun filtered through the door and into the meeting of Maryville's Society of Friends. Dust particles rose like little fairies from the feet of two departing ladies.

"Well," a lady drawled, "I do see Miss Gatlan's point. No telling what a husband would do if not for his good wife's direction in reading the Good Book." The lady fidgeted with her collar and cleared her throat. "But I can't rightly see how we can judge Mr. Reynolds until one of us asks him."

"He'll deny it, Mable," another woman said. "Most likely say it was… someone else that got this girl pregnant."

The president smiled at Maggie. "You may sit down now."

Maggie took one last look at the women. She'd failed. Why God? Why hadn't the Bible verses she quoted done any good?

"Is there any other business?" The president looked around. "Then I call this meeting adjourned until next month."

Matron Burns motioned for Maggie. She was an elderly widow whose husband had died some ten years ago. She had a set of eagle eyes she used to acquire knowledge about everyone in Maryville as well as everyone in Bount County. She was a large woman, with ample hips, a high sloping forehead, and gentle hands, ready and willing to offer a dish or give aid to a down-and-out neighbor.

It wasn't too late. With one word Matron Burns could change the tide of indifference. People flocked to her for kindly and wise advice, and she usually ascertained everyone's problems with a single word. She gave Maggie a gentle pat on the arm.

"My, you have grown into a caring young lady. You must be proud of her, Marie." Her hoops swayed to her large torso and hit the sides of the chairs as she bustled toward the door. Maggie felt like a dog that had tried to please its master, but had fallen short. Just a tidbit of praise for a job as inconsequential as the air one breathed.

With the room empty, her mother busied herself with straightening the chairs. The noise of her footsteps echoed in the stillness. Placing her dainty hand to Maggie's cheek, she smiled. "You spoke the truth when everyone else ignored it. Remember that, my darling."

After everyone else's rejection, her mother's praise gave solace to Maggie's wounded spirit and made the night's defeats a victory.

"That's all any of us can do. You didn't desert Jesus." Her mother's face glowed in the half-light filtering through the windowpanes. "Remember, Maggie, you are never alone when you stand up for truth. 'But the hour cometh, and now is, when the true worshippers shall worship the Father in spirit and in truth.'"

Streaks of burnt orange and blues swept the horizon. Darkness would engulf them soon. But she had shared this moment with Mother, and she knew she would never forget it.

As they walked in silence toward their carriage, she felt someone touch her shoulder. She turned to find one of the women clothed in black.

"Could thee follow our carriage?"

Marie stepped forward. "Ada. I thought I recognized you."

Ada ushered Maggie and her mother into the Quaker's house. A fire burned in the stone hearth and a kettle of something bubbled just above the yellow-orange flames. Lively red curtains at the windows offered some cheer to the brown walls. Blue and red checkered goose-feather pillows adorned two wood-spindle rocking chairs. A handcrafted baby rocker sat between the chairs. The young woman Ada addressed as Elizabeth smiled back at her as she rocked the cradle.

Two bearded men sat at a wooden table. The older one, wearing reading glasses, looked up from his Bible, then laid his glasses aside. The younger of the two stood up and smiled at Elizabeth.

"This is my husband, Amos. Husband," Ada said, "this is Mrs. Gatlan and her daughter, Maggie. They are in need of our services for two girls who have been abused by their master."

Ada summed up in one sentence what had taken Maggie ten minutes in front of the woman's society to explain.

Amos, dressed in black trousers and a white shirt, reached for a log and laid it beneath the bubbling kettle. "Where are these girls residing?"

"At Mr. Reynolds' estate, which is next to Spirit Wind, their manor."

"Ah… yes. I have heard of the good thing thee are doing. Please, sit thee down." As he rose, his chair scraped across the shiny wooden floor. His wool socks made no noise on the floor as he walked closer to get a better look at them.

Was this man referring to the Glenn? How did he know about that? Maggie looked at him curiously. "Sir, to what are you referring?" She could be arrested for teaching slaves to read and write. The school must be kept secret.

"Ya, so thee are Miss Maggie?"

It was obvious the Quaker had seen the alarm generated by his words. He motioned with a hand to Elizabeth. "Go fetch the boy."

Maggie moistened her lips, eyeing the drink of the younger Quaker man, evidently the husband of Elizabeth whom she heard addressed as Isaac. Her throat felt as cracked and dry as her lips.

"Would thee like some tea?" Ada offered them two seats near the fire.

Maggie nodded and took a seat. She cupped her cold hands around the warm mug and sipped the brew. Blackberry, her favorite. Jonny, one of her students, entered from a back room. What was he doing here?

Jonny was an energetic ten-year-old who could do with an extra ten pounds, only it was hard to get him to sit still long enough to eat a complete meal. His bright brown eyes spotted her across the room. He skipped toward her, his bare feet tapping a tune to his happy words. "Miss Maggie, I'm going to Ohio, goin' to join my mother there." The boy held out the slate and chalk she had given him. "See, I was just studying. So I can help my mom to learn how to read and write like the white folk."

The baby awoke and let out a scream, as if to join Jonny's elation. "That's wonderful, Jonny." This home must be one of the stations of the Underground Railroad. So now these Quakers knew about… "But if you learned about my school, what if—"

"Thy secret is safe with us," Ada replied.

"Please excuse me while I feed the baby," Elizabeth said.

Maggie's mother patted Jonny on the head. "You're Mr. Reynolds' house boy, correct?"

"Yes, ma'am. He mighty bad to just about everyone, especially the girls, but some of the boys, like me, he likes to have his way with, too."

"Mr. Reynolds is giving southern gentlemen a bad name." Her mother returned Amos' stark, disapproving gaze. His long black beard and dark hair resembled the pictures in the paper of John Brown. Maggie shuddered. Her mother, however, appeared unafraid, probably because of her outrage.

Marie tapped her finger on the table at Amos as if chafing an obstinate pupil. "We care for our people, every last one of them. I am sure you have read *Uncle Tom's Cabin.* I have, too. I doubt very seriously that Harriet Beecher Stowe ever visited the South, or else she would have known how southerners care for their people, and why Mr. Reynolds is no longer in our employ."

The glow of the fireplace etched her high cheekbones and distinguished profile. "Yes, we are slave owners and proud to be called southerners, aware that we, too, are slaves by choice to our evil natures where sin abides! As Galatians 5:1 states, 'Stand fast therefore in the liberty wherewith Christ hath made us free, and be not entangled again with the yoke of bondage.' Only Jesus can set us free from the bondage of Satan's yoke."

The fearful looking Amos stood and bowed, a merry twinkle in his once hard-as-steel gray eyes. "I am a southerner and proud, as thee, Mrs. Gatlan, to bear the title. Though Mr. Reynolds is geographically considered a southerner, we know he is not a gentleman of the South.

A wolf in the chicken coop doesn't make him a chicken, now does it?"

"Why…" Her mother stepped back, her hand on her heart. "Sir, you have captured this deplorable situation admirably."

"Truly, Mr. Reynolds is not a southern gentleman, whereas, thee and thy husband's good deeds clearly prove otherwise." Amos walked to the mantel, turned, and smiled. "The South's most valued reputation can be visibly seen in its charming people. I pray we shall never lose our charm and chivalry."

Mother's face lit up with her sweeping smile. "You have lifted a heavy burden from my shoulders with your kind words."

Ada placed a bowl of steaming stew, cheese, and a piece of bread before her mother and her. "I believe we can safely say, unless Reynolds repents of his deeds, we shall not meet him again once we've entered those pearly gates."

"Praise the Lord." Maggie huffed before picking up her spoon and smiling at Ada. She knew she shouldn't wish any soul to Hell, but Mr. Reynolds had chosen to play the saint while doing the devil's work, and if anyone deserved residence, it was he.

The odor of hickory and pine filled the small cabin and crackled amidst the slurping and spoons tapping the soup bowls. Amos finished first, his eyes staring back into Maggie's. She gulped the last of her soup.

"I don't care to use women, but we are short of helpers. Two of our… brothers have just been shot and killed by bounty hunters. We will need one of thee to volunteer thy services, and a strong man, someone who is a loyal abolitionist.

"Thee are a diversion, and shall travel only to the first Underground Railroad Station. Thee will then return to thy home and family. The man must plan to continue and prepare to lay his life down for the mission. He must be trustworthy, brave, intelligent, and most importantly, a follower of Jesus. 'No man having put his hand to the plough, and looking back, is fit for the kingdom of God' Luke 9:62. Hopefully, he will be able to leave his charges at the railroad stop in Lexington; however, he must be ready to travel all the way to Ohio and on to Canada, if need be."

In spite of the warm fire just five steps away, in spite of Maggie's shawl covering her back, she felt a cold chill climb up and down her spine. Ben McConnell, he was the only one she could trust. But she hadn't seen him for two years. What were his political views? What were they getting themselves into?

Her mother patted her hand. "Maggie is busy with the school. My sister-in-law lives close to Lexington, so I will be the woman. I am not afraid to disguise myself in whatever clothes are appropriate for the success of getting these children safely to Canada."

# Chapter 12

*B*en glanced out across the Appalachian Mountains. A dusting of snow laced the pines, maples, and dogwoods. He inhaled deeply, stroking his dapple-gray stallion. "Caedmon, I'll never tire at lookin' at the bright greens, browns, and reds of the foliage." He shivered when a gale blew through the mountains and burrowed deep into his homespun coat.

The night had been a chilly one and though the sun was up and felt warm, an occasional chill crawled up his spine. He'd gotten soft sleeping indoors on the feather bed he and his dad had made from their flock of geese and chickens. He couldn't begin to count the times he'd dreamt of Maggie sharing the covers with him once she became his bride.

Deep valleys of fog floated like misplaced ghosts out for a lark, and bare granite boulders pushed up from the red dirt. His horse's stride and his daydreams of a better tomorrow ate up the lonely miles. Only the layer of leaves beneath his horse's hooves disturbed the stillness. It wouldn't be long now and he wouldn't feel ashamed proposing to her. Soon he would have the finest racing horses in Kentucky. He patted Caedmon's neck. He'd proven a worthy sire of a few horses. Ben needed a few more, too, to plow his fields that would yield him a good crop of hay, oats, and maybe a little tobacco. He'd heard tobacco grew well in his part of the country.

Spirit Wind's stately brick fortress, tall of columns, wide of verandas, now loomed on the horizon. He stopped Caedmon, spat into his hands, and removing his hat, rubbed his unruly hair flat. That ought to do it.

Glancing up, the sun now gleamed on the topmost peak. What is that? Something had caught the sun's rays. He'd have to remember to ask Maggie about it. He nudged Caedmon into a canter, his eyes peering between the trees as the lane wove about the hillside. He visualized Maggie's sweet lips and big doe eyes with lashes thick enough to be lost in and a waist small enough for a man's hand. As he reached the manor, he tied Caedmon to the hitching post, straightened his coat, and took the steps two at a time. Reaching for the knocker, he gave it three hardy hits.

"Top o' the morning to ya. Is Miss Maggie about?" he asked when Eli answered the door.

"One moment, sir, while I fetch her." Eli led Ben into the parlor.

Ben glanced back at Eli. Hmm… he acted like he didn't know me. Ben looked at the intricately scrolled ceiling, the floral wallpaper adorning the soft blue walls. Cherry wood Chippendale furnishings graced the large rectangular room with bright blue, turquoise, and brown upholstery fit for an English lord. He absorbed it all, memorizing it for his and Maggie's future home.

He checked to make sure no one was around, then spit into his hand and flattened his hair again. That was a step in the right direction. Only he'd need to clean his hands before shaking Mr. Gatlan's. He looked around again, then wiped his palms on his coat. He pulled down his vest and polished the tops of his boots with his trousers by placing one then the other against the back of his legs. Surely, he had nothing to be fretting over. His fine clothes told clearly of his accomplishments, and they'd impress Maggie and her father.

The doorway gaped open like the hole to the coal miner's tunnel. Where's Maggie? She should have been expecting him. Maybe she didn't receive his last letter. Or more to the here and now, he hadn't received her rejection.

"Ben?" The man who had left some two years ago was but a scarecrow. Maggie hesitated. This man dressed in fine brocade sharply sweeping his well-muscled shoulders, ruffled shirt, and smart-fitting trousers, was a stranger to her. Only the face was familiar, the broad forehead, dark eyes, and thick wooly hair. Even without his beard, he still looked like a pirate to her. She covered her mouth; she couldn't help chuckling over his attempt to tame his unruly locks as thick as a sheep's.

He ran his thick, work worn hands through his black hair. "Guess my attempts to tame my mane didn't work too well."

His strong, rugged chin jagged out a fraction of an inch. His sparkling eyes an invitation for any woman. Maggie glanced downward in her embarrassment. If Ben could read her mind, then he would know just how good he did look. Did the man she'd grown to care about while he was paralyzed, the man she'd nursed and learned to love, still exist?

"What is it, Maggie?"

Could he be trusted? She needed him to be the measure of the man she and mother needed for their mission. She felt she would burst at the seams. There was scant little time to learn about this new man who stood before her.

Three lives were at stake, not counting the ten lives that would be in peril of the hangman's noose if they should fail. Dear Lord, if not Ben, then who? Trust in the Lord with all your heart. …Ben's concerned eyes melted into hers. Lord, oh how I want him to be the right one! She grabbed both his hands and laughed from the pure joy of his touch. "My, what a proper gentlemen you've become. Have you eaten? You can join us." She tucked her fingers around his elbow.

Ben's lips creased into a lopsided grin. "I'm a land owner, Maggie. I bought my first slave before departing from Kentucky."

Maggie's heart leaped to her throat. What will he think about her abolitionist friends the Quakers and Mother and her helping the children?

"'Twas my father's idea. He thinks in order to become a proper gentlemen we need a couple slaves. But I don't be seein' the need. I like workin' my own land, and don't care to be givin' the experience to another."

Yes, that was the Ben she'd grown to love. Nothing could change her Ben, not land, wealth, or becoming a proper southern gentleman. She let out a sigh. "It is good you came, especially at this particular moment."

"What's the matter, Maggie? A secret of sorts?" Ben searched her face.

"Yes." She hugged his arm. "I will disclose it later. Now you will meet father as an equal. I shall not mention that you used to work here. Father will never know. Mother and I have only said that you are a friend of Aunt Louise."

They entered the dining room and she began her introduction. "Father, may I introduce Mr. McConnell from Kentucky. He shall be staying with us."

Her father rose and extended his hand. "Nice to meet you, Mr. McConnell. What part of Kentucky are you from?"

"Near Emerald, sir. My dad and I have a hundred acres of the best rolling hillside I've ever seen. We plan to purchase an additional 200 acres next year, the good Lord willing."

Father was impressed, as Maggie knew he would be. "Well, have a seat here so we can talk."

Her father sat back down. "I look forward to getting more acquainted with you. Where did you study? I have never heard an accent like yours before." Father twisted his mouth toward Mother. "Where have I heard that accent before, Marie?"

"From myself, to be sure." She sent him a smile from across the table that Maggie could see warmed Ben through and through.

"Indeed, I'm Irish and proud of it."

"And I quite agree, Mr. McConnell." Her mother lifted the platter of meat. "Would you like some ham, and how about a cup of coffee to wash down that scone?"

"Why this is going famously well, having someone here that my wife approves of is a good start to my day." Father then directed his conversation to Maggie. "How about it, daughter, you want this strapping young man to attend our Christmas Ball? I'm sure the ladies will enjoy meeting him."

Maggie hesitated, not wishing to share him, then, seeing her Father's look, immediately complied. "I'm certain they shall."

# Chapter 13

*B*en waited at the bottom of the winding stairway for his first glimpse of Maggie. Mr. Gatlan, dressed in a black tuxedo like his own, joined him. "I don't believe the welcoming I received, Mr. Gatlan, and you decking me out in the king's finest for this ball."

Mr. Gatlan patted him on the back and laughed. "I've enjoyed our time together, and I like doing for a young man like you sporting promise. My grandparents came to this country to get away from the prim and pomp of the lords and parliament. Not that we don't have our own in America." Mr. Gatlan looked up. "Ah, now here come two visions of loveliness to erase every thought of politics from our minds tonight."

Two women of equal beauty and grace stood in regal fashion with a crown of curls adorning their heads. Dresses of glittering satin and lace billowed about their tiny waists to sweep the floor beneath their dainty slippered feet.

"I've never seen the like," Ben whispered. In awe, he watched Maggie float down the stairway as if on angel's wings. He was further awed as to how he would get beyond the hoops of her skirt to waltz with her. Reaching for her arm, his heart thumped against his chest like an Irish drum during the battle of Erin, or so the folklore went. He sighed.

He could accomplish anything when those soft velvet eyes looked into his. He needed to put in words her poetic loveliness. He led her to a secluded spot in the hallway and bending low whispered, "Behold thou art fair... thou hast doves' eyes within thy locks; thy hair is as a flock of goats—ah, thou art fair…"

Maggie chuckled, unfolding her lace and satin ribbon fan in front of her face so all he could see was her beautiful eyes. Her bare shoulders told him the truth. They were rolling with humor like the waves off Dublin Bay.

He pulled at his shirtwaist, his mood slightly dampened. His comment had not the effect he'd hoped. Solomon's words had worked their spell upon his love—where had Ben gone amiss? Still, he had the girl of his dreams on his arm, and he wasn't going to allow a minor setback to disrupt the evening.

Eli led everyone in the back hallway toward the ballroom located on the third floor of the mansion. The room's domed ceiling allowed the stars entrance. It gave the effect of dancing amidst a star-drenched sky with only the full moon to peek in every so often past an obstinate cloud.

"Ben, come, we must greet the guests." Maggie led him to one of the curved walls where the french doors opened to a balcony.

"I have never seen the like."

"This circular room enables the dancers to move easily around and see." Maggie smiled and pointed to the french doors and balconies. "The dancers shall always have fresh breezes to cool their faces."

"You can see for miles around up here. I cannot but notice that it would make a strategic lookout point." He glanced over at Mr. Gatlan. A square chin, length of leg, and a balance of shoulder, there was nothing cowardly about that profile. It would be just like Maggie's father to plan a lovely ballroom, while providing a safe lookout point for any enemies that might dare embark upon his manor.

"It is, as my father puts it, a British move." A wistful sigh escaped her sweet lips. "I often come here when I need solace and a place to pray. Here objects that looked huge before now appear small." She sighed. "I often wish I could make life's problems as minute as they appear here."

Ben took her hand, drew it to his lips and gently kissed it. "Sharin' a heavy load makes the burden lighter."

She lifted her eyes. Ben grabbed his breath. Such sadness.

"I wish we could stay here all evening, but we must go in. The dancing shall begin soon."

"'Tis well it should. You needing a little joy tonight and Ben McConnell is just the man that can give it." He raised her fingers to his lips and not taking his eyes from hers, kissed them.

Ben cut a striking figure with his broad shoulders, thick hair, and sweeping smile. He was quick on his feet, agile enough to withstand even the nudging of the clumsy couple in front of them and told the man "Not to worry."

How she wished Ben had directed his comment to her not to worry. Why would he? She had not had the nerve to tell him her dilemma. Her father waltzed by. He didn't know and it was best he did not.

Reynolds' slaves were hiding beneath the floor of the Glenn. Susie had confided that Mr. Reynolds had left for Knoxville and would return in a fortnight. That would be tonight. He would know when he returned home that Susie and her sister had fled, giving him the perfect reason to come and demand an answer from Maggie as to their whereabouts.

The soft mellow notes of a violin began, then the orchestra joined in and the beautiful notes of "When Irish Eyes are Smiling" wrapped her emotions in a cocoon of detachment from the other dancers. Ben's deep baritone lent a Gaelic charm to the lyrics as mystic as moonlight on water.

"For your smile is a part Of the love in your heart, And it makes even sunshine more bright." His lips close to her ear, he sang the sonnet as if he'd written the words just for her. "Like the linnet's sweet song, Crooning all the day long, Comes your laughter and light."

The gentle notes of Ben's voice encircled her with its charm. Her body bent and obeyed his promptings. Her billowing skirts swirled about their pivoting steps. Waltzing with Ben was divinely thrilling. The promptings of his arm circling her waist, his gentle commands moving her about the room, swaying, dipping, twirling in one motion, one body. Her breathing ceased its normal rhythm. Her heart throbbed.

"For the springtime of life Is the sweetest of all There is ne'er a real care or regret; And while springtime is ours …" He lowered his head, gently kissing her forehead. Maggie closed her eyes, wishing that the song would never end. "I pray it shall always be springtime for us, Maggie my—"

"Oh, Ben."

Magic filled the room and the hours passed by blissfully. Christmas waltzes and steaming cinnamon and cider punches—alarmed she glanced down at her full plate suddenly ashamed. Ashamed and sharply aware that Susie and the others lay hidden beneath the floors of the Glenn, thirsty and hungry while she took her pleasures.

The strong night wind rustled Maggie's hoop skirts and lifted her long silky curls. She and Ben had left the dance, quietly departing the house through the kitchen door. The parcel of food Cook had prepared Maggie cleverly hid beneath the folds of her velvet cape that she laid across her arm.

The wind played with the dry leaves and wild grass spiraled about their feet. Looping her chilled fingers in Ben's, he suddenly brought her closer. "It's like the wind upon the moors." Removing his top hat, he bowed his swarthy head, his eyes gleaming into hers. Her heart beat against her rib cage like a canary. This is the moment she dreamt of. How could she kiss him, knowing she'd brought him here to entice him? Her dear mother was risking her life for Maggie's students. Oh, why had she started the school? She would never have known about Reynolds raping Susie, otherwise.

She could have been pleasantly oblivious and Mother would have been safe. Now Ben would soon be caught in her web of deceit… But she wouldn't have known Ben.

Her thoughts lapsed between present and past, recalling that day long ago riding her horse and hearing the Irishman's cry for help in the swamp. That Bible verse her class had memorized reverberated in her head: *We have obtained an inheritance, being predestinated according to the purpose of Him who worketh all things after the counsel of His own will.* The words she had muttered *then* came as clear as a bell to her now. "One conscionable act led to this consequence."

She ran her hand along Ben's face, feeling his strong chin and smiling lips. The distasteful flavor of deceit filled her mouth.

Ben swept her into his embrace. Maybe he thought she was being coquettish… his emotions were as wild and reckless as the winds.

She pulled away and walked farther up the hill, her lips burning with the lost love of his kiss. But there was more at stake tonight than her selfish desires.

"What is wrong?" His hands cupped her shoulders; he turned her, lifting her chin, searching her face.

The moon cast an iridescent glow on the hillside, making trees appear taller, like giants. Could Ben see in her eyes the mammoth responsibility that lay before her? She could not allow Mother to dress like a man and drive the wagon to the Underground Railroad station clear to Ohio. Father wouldn't allow it. Father would get caught up in this mission of death. If the bounty hunter caught them, he had the law on his side and could kill her parents on the spot. Ben was her only hope. Should she play the role of a fainting damsel in distress? Or blindside him with the ghastly truth? She'd rather lose Ben instead of her parents.

"Is this about that slave problem?" His piercing black eyes burnt hers like fire.

"I, I fear I am putting you in jeopardy." She pulled away from him and began walking, her arms hugging her chest.

Ben followed. "I gathered a little of the turmoil you feel from the heated discussion at dinner yesterday. So Reynolds is bent on complete victory over Spirit Wind? It would not surprise me in the least if he would not take vindication on his slaves, knowing how much you care for yours."

Maggie turned and gazed up at him. How could she not admire him? How could she not believe that, like the Irish chieftain of yore, he would avenge this foul deed and come to her rescue? "So, I see you are not only a southern gentleman outwardly, you are also the Christian patriot within. A pleasing combination, one which is akin to my mother's." She hesitated. "And Father's."

"So what does your father know of your deeds of hiding my true identity?" Ben took her hands into his and she felt the warmth of them travel through her chilled body. "I am not certain, but Mother knows the truth. And whenever Mother decides upon a path, Father is quick to defend her and travel the same rocky road. He always says that she is his conscience, without which, he would be a shell of his former self."

"You are your mother's daughter and I can well see the resemblance. If my mother be still alive, she would approve of ya."

"What happened to your mother?"

Ben plucked a blade of grass and began sucking on it. "She died in Ireland, during the potato famine. Upon her dying breath, she told us to be off and leave for this land called America. God would bless us if we did not lose sight of His Son, Jesus. Truly my mother's words came true more than ever when Jesus gave me back my legs." He glanced at her. The moon cast its glow on his face, part shadow and part glare. "I see worry in those deep brown eyes of yours, Maggie. Worry that I feel God himself would want me to wipe away... so tell me, what is wrong?"

A gust of wind blew her skirts and curls in wild abandon about her form. Ben was so strong, so confident. Then Amos' words came clearly to her thoughts, *most importantly, a follower of Jesus.*

"'No man having put his hand to the plough, and looking back, is fit for the kingdom of God.' Ben what does that Scripture mean to you?"

"Jesus is everything or else He is nothing to ya." Ben eyes stared into hers. "He that is not willing to sacrifice *everything* for the cause of Jesus, is not willin' to sacrifice a'tall, and not fit for God's kingdom."

"Come, I will show you the Glenn, where everything first began." She pulled him forward until they reached the Glenn.

Her footsteps echoed in the chilly cabin; she closed the door against winter's gale and the shutters rattled. Then she heard the children beneath her feet. She fumbled for a candle and lit it.

Ben put a finger to his lips.

"What? It's just the tapping of the bare branches on the window panes." Maggie turned toward her desk.

"I'm sure there is someone beneath the cabin. Is there a crawl space?"

She reached inside her cape and laid down the package and wondered how soon Ben would guess the truth. It would make telling him easier for her and perhaps he'd enjoy a good joke. "I am certain it is just a squirrel or worse, a skunk, getting out of the cold."

Ben eyed the package. "Smells like you are planning to feed the squirrels with the chicken from our dinner." He knelt down and began knocking on the floorboards. He found what he was looking for. "A trap door?"

"Ben, look at me. You are right; there is someone here, three children. I'm helping the, I mean I am a part of the Underground Railroad and I did not wish to endanger you."

Ben looked up at her from his knees. A curious position and she chuckled in spite of the seriousness of her predicament. "The children are waiting for Mother to take them to the Underground Railroad site in Ohio."

He rested back on his heels and wiped his forehead. "Saints preserve us, what have you gotten yourself into?"

"More than I care to admit." She reached for his arm and he rose. "Kind of like a reverse proposal?" she chuckled.

"Indeed, but it is plain as the nose on my face that I have much I need to learn about you. So when did you start working on this railroad?"

"I wish I was working on a real railroad. This type of railroad is a game of life and death, two *conductors* have lost their lives." She opened the hatch on the floor used for storing kindling, now used as a hide out for runaway slaves. Susie, with cobwebs in her tight curls, stepped out, then Little Sis and Jonny.

Susie blinked, looking at Ben curiously. "Who's he, Miss Maggie?"

"A friend. Here, children. Sit at your desks and eat." She rushed toward the window, peeked out and did the same on the other side of the cabin. "Did you hear anyone outside?"

"No, ma'am, just you."

She let out a sigh of relief.

Susie took large bites of her fried chicken. "Master Reynolds warned me before he left for Knoxville that I'd better do everything I was told until he returned or else he'd give me a double whipping." Susie looked down at her plate. "I know I should have been brave and waited for the Quaker like you told me, but I couldn't."

Maggie patted her head. "It's alright, sweetheart, soon you will be safe."

Ben muttered. "'One conscionable act led us to this consequence.' I understand now."

"No, you don't. I've beguiled you, Ben." Her hot tears obscured his face. Guilt and her selfish desires burned in her bosom. "I led you here hoping you'd take these children. So you'd risk your life and my mother and father's lives would be spared."

His arms encircled her trembling shoulders. She buried her head into his chest and cried. From out of the pits of despair, he comforted her.

"And I am lost, Maggie my lass, lost upon this sea of conscience and consequence, like my Irish comrades. I could no more turn aside and allow you or your parents to do this life-threatening task than I could walk by a lovely lass stuck in the swamp." Ben kissed her forehead. "Only God knows where He's takin' us."

"I've changed my mind. I'll find someone else, it's—"

Ben quickly silenced her words with his hand. "First rule you must learn is never say 'too dangerous' to an Irishman."

His eyes twinkled into hers. Does he think it's some kind of lark? Oh, I'll never understand him!

Ben chuckled, embracing the children with his lighthearted merriment. "Well then lad and lassies, you'll be spending Christmas with me on this railroad leading to your freedom."

# Chapter 14

The cold wind chased slate gray clouds across the face of the full moon. In New York, it would have been snowing. But in Tennessee, it was a blinding rainstorm.

Ben burrowed deeper into his homespun coat. One hand held the reins of Caedmon, the other held the rope he'd tied to the wagon. He glanced back at Mrs. Gatlan and the children huddled like little chicks beneath the wings of her cape on the wagon seat next to her. Ben and Maggie had attempted to discourage Mrs. Gatlan from coming.

Then when Mr. Reynolds appeared on their doorstep moments after the last guest departed, demanding his slaves. Mrs. Gatlan said it was the only way for the countryside not to know the truth. Maggie needed to stay and teach. Mrs. Gatlan would go and pretend she was on a visit to her sister-in-law.

He reached down and wrapped the rope around his saddle horn. The mud-caked wagon wheels no longer rolling, now slid up the hill like tiny wooden runners. He would clean the wheels once they reached the top of the hill. Caedmon neighed softly, shoving his shoulders into pulling the wagon forward, encouraging the little mule that pulled the wagon up the hillside. Ben was trusting on the rain to obliterate their tracks leading into Kentucky, and if Reynolds sent out the bloodhounds, the dogs would not be able to pick up their scent.

Susie and her younger sister were quiet and obedient children. However, the boy Jonny was a tad too noisy to suit Ben. Still, he thanked God for small miracles. Gatlan's mule was a willing beast and with the help of Caedmon, pulled the little cart through the woods without complaint. He glanced back. He'd wrapped Mrs. Gatlan and the children in a quilt and they looked quite comfortable. Only the tops of their heads were wet. He wished he could rectify that.

He shifted the brim of his hat and a stream of icy water washed down the front of his coat. He shivered. If he was following the right trail, the cabin should be just over this hill apiece.

The Quaker said to look for a burned-out tree; there would be a note inside. The pouring rain made it hard to see. The only light he had came from the lightning that ripped across the dark sky like daylight… brief but helpful. Now wouldn't be a bad time to pray. He especially liked Psalm 91 during a rainstorm. How did that go? He remembered his dear departed mother and how she would say it, "abide under the shadow of the Almighty… He is my refuge and my fortress: my God; in him will I trust."

A flash of lightning illuminated the tree he needed. He jumped off Caedmon, reached his hand inside the tree, and grasped the note. It had been sealed in a glass jar. He opened the jar and removed the note, but couldn't read it. He walked back to the wagon and handed it to Mrs. Gatlan.

She held it up. Just then a flash illuminated the sky. "Even the lightning doesn't provide enough light for me to read this, and the paper is turning into mush in the rain." Mrs. Gatlan placed the note back into the jar. "I believe the Quaker said the cabin is after the mountains, in the valley. I think I have been there before." Lightning bolted and its thunder rumbled. Mrs. Gatlan pointed to the small lane the brief light had revealed. "There is the lane. I remember now. Mr. Gatlan and I came here once hiding from the Indians."

Something in the thicket just to the left of him rustled. A bear? Perhaps it was a lone wolf out for some pre-morning breakfast. Or the bounty hunter. He raised his gun. A shot could arouse the countryside. He holstered his gun and drew out his knife.

A man crouched not more than three yards from Mrs. Gatlan and the children. It looked like the man was asleep. Ben approached slowly, calculating his every step. He'd have to knife the man between his lungs, or else hit the jugular vein.

The man's black hat had fallen from his head. At least he thought it was black, hard to tell it being so dark and wet. The man struggled in Ben's grasp. Why, he's just a kid.

"Thee need not harm me. I have come to guide thee to the next station." Sweat and rain streamed into his eyes.

Could it be the man was telling the truth? He was dressed in strange looking black breeches, a black vest, and coat. "Where is the note left for me?" Ben challenged.

"In that hollow tree."

Ben pushed him toward the wagon, his knife poised and ready in the small of the man's back. "You cry out, and you're a dead man. Mrs. Gatlan, do you recognize him?"

"Yes, you were at the Quaker's cabin. Your sister had a—"

"Not my sister, my wife, and we had our first child just a month ago. He's colicky and not sleeping well."

Ben wiped the rain from his brow. "Alright, lead the way." Couldn't slight the man for taking a catnap, what with a baby waking him up every two hours. He chuckled. Must have been powerful sleepy to nap in a chilly rainstorm. "Go ahead and get in the buckboard."

They traveled up the mountainside for a half a mile. Black smoke spiraled upwards over the treetops. From the ravine that concealed them from the cabin's inhabitants, Ben could just make out the cabin and the stone chimney. The Quaker stopped. "Something is amiss. Wait here."

The Quaker picked up some kindling wood and opened the back door. A young girl dressed in black met him. She then walked up to Ben. "Thee must go. Two bounty hunters are in the cabin. They say they have come for smoked ham and bacon. Empty the contents." The girl's hands shook as she handed them two covered baskets full of food and a jar each of milk and water. "The men did not see me. Mama said I must leave the baskets here for her to retrieve."

Mrs. Gatlan took one look at the girl's frightened face and gathered up her skirts. "I'm staying. Child, I shall not have your family face those bounty hunters without me."

Ben saw a flash of petticoats and hurried to help Mrs. Gatlan down, placing a restraining arm to stop her. "They might figure you're part of this."

Mrs. Gatlan handed him a note. "Head for Lexington. Look for a carriage shop. Walk up to a man dressed in a straw hat, smoking a pipe, and playing checkers. Ask him if he's been waiting long. If he is the right man, he'll call you Cousin. You should be relieved and able to return home. If ..."

Ben knew the rest. "Do not be frettin' your pretty head, I'll get them to Cincinnati and beyond, if need be."

The cabin door opened. Two large men, with the young Quaker man between them, shoved the Quaker down the steps. "You're lying. I'll whip the truth from those lying lips of yours."

Susie whimpered, and quickly covered her mouth. Caedmon started to neigh. Ben covered his stallion's mouth.

"Reynolds!" Mrs. Gatlan whispered. "Go on. I'll stall them."

"I can't leave you here."

Mrs. Gatlan patted his hand. "Do not fear," she nodded her head toward the noise of an approaching wagon. "My husband will be here shortly."

Ben looked at her puzzled. "How—"

"Because after thirty years of marriage I know my husband. Now go."

The girl led the mule and wagon down the ravine to a cave. There she and Ben covered Caedmon's hooves and the mule's with burlap so the animals wouldn't leave hoof prints. Then they wrapped the wagon wheels in burlap.

"I will take you down the hill to the trail you must follow."

Ben helped her up, placed the children in the bed of the wagon and wrapped them with quilts and blankets. The rain had let up. Now only an occasional drizzle fell. He tied Caedmon to the wagon and jumped onto the wagon seat. The girl kept her eyes straight ahead and told him when to turn.

The wagon wheels slid in the wet road full of deep puddles that oozed of blood-red mud. How had Mrs. Gatlan faired? Her plan must have worked because the bounty hunters had not followed. Ben stopped the wagon.

"I'll be backtracking to make sure Mrs. Gatlan came to no harm. Remain here until I return." Ben ran back to the cabin, inching his way toward the dimly lit cabin. Angry voices came through a partially opened window. Ben crammed his body into the shadows of the cabin and looked in the window.

Like the ticking of a clock, Reynolds snapped his whip on his riding boots. "I get back what's mine. You high-and-mighty do-gooders don't fool me." His angry red face stood two feet from Mr. Gatlan's. "You're stealing from me in the name of your sanctimonious honor!"

"You have no evidence that my wife or these Quakers have done any stealing. Have I made myself clear?" Mr. Gatlan pointed to an empty chair. "Come, sit down, let us talk this over like civilized human beings and enjoy the hospitality of these friendly people. Why, look at this ham. Come enjoy your coffee. It is too cold and damp to be about on a night like this."

Ben let out a sigh of relief, then turned and ran toward the woods and to the wagon. At least the Gatlans had bought them a little more time. "I must leave you." The Quaker girl climbed out of the wagon. "A Quaker home is just up the hill. Mama wants me to warn them not to come to their cabin in the morning."

Ben looked up and down the trail. Reynolds was out for blood and revenge. "What will happen to you if you're caught?"

The girl shrugged. "We will pray for thy safe journey."

Ben glanced at the sleeping children. "They worth all this?"

"They are God's children." The girl was gone, swallowed up by the night with her dark coverings.

Susie had been the first to rise. It was a lonely stretch of road, and the sun had just begun to peek over the horizon. Ben didn't see any call for her not to ride beside him on the wagon seat. She was a cute little lass, full of questions about the Irish and mostly about what he thought about Miss Maggie.

"Have you a girlfriend?" Susie asked. "Bet Miss Maggie is not your first, you bein' handsome and all."

He'd taken the girl to be eleven, maybe twelve. Yet her thoughts were all grown up. "This is a difficult question, to be sure."

"Your face has gone and turned red as a turnip ready for pluckin." Susie giggled. "You do like Miss Maggie, I can tell …"

"Yes, I do," He fingered the two-day-old stubble on his chin and recalled the moment following the dance. Maggie's glowing face, her thick deep lashes setting off the light brown specks in her eyes. But it was clear she did not feel the same for him. She had only needed a favor from him. "We're from two different worlds." And fine clothes could not be making the difference.

"So? Mr. Reynolds and me are from two different worlds and that didn't stop him from having his way with me." Susie looked down at her hands. "Who's going to want to marry me, Mr. Ben?"

"You think you've been damaged, do ya? Well, 'tis not your fault. Like my departed mother would be tellin' me, don't be wasting your sufferings. Lean on the good arm of Jesus and let Him be leadin' you through the tough times."

A tear dropped onto her brown arm.

Ben was at a loss for words. Jesus, I need Your guidance here. He cleared his throat. "'Before I formed thee in the belly I knew thee.' That's from Jeremiah 1:5 and God may just have a purpose for your babe."

"My baby."

Ben patted Susie's arm. "You're not the only woman that has gotten that way. And you won't be the last. The Lord was born a pauper in a stable fit only for the animals, and a bastard to the entire outside world, them not knowing His regal Father." On the distant horizon, the golden beams of sunlight crested the winding dirt road to greet the new day like a bride awaiting her groom. "Not a more beautiful sunrise have I ever seen."

"Mama says it's a good sign when the sun rises bright and clear after a rain. That new life was about." Susie wrapped her arms around her stomach.

Two riders appeared on the road, galloping toward their wagon. There was no way to avoid them. "Get in the back and cover yourself.

Pretend you're sleeping."

Susie scrambled over the wagon seat, and fell into the wagon bed with a hard thump. "Ow!" Jonny cried.

"Hush, riders coming."

Ben planned to ride by them. One of the men blocked his mule. "Pull up, you sorry Irishman!"

He'd recognized that voice over a tumbling waterfall. "Big Jim, what are you doing here?"

"More like, what's you doing with these children, son?"

"Dad?" Ben blinked. Holding his hand over his eyes, sure enough, his dad's bearded face and bright green-blue eyes came into view, and by the look of his scowling mouth, not too happy to see him. Or was it his cargo? "I, I got me a delivery to make."

His dad came alongside. "We know. We met a bounty hunter in the tavern last night, hired by Mr. Reynolds, he was. Bragging how Mr. Reynolds plans on getting those slaves that had the adus..."

"Audacity, Mr. McConnell," Big Jim replied.

Ben's father scratched his head. "Don't know why these Americans have to use so many fancy dandy words to be tellin' the plain truth." He bent low, as if afraid his voice might carry to another ear not to his liking. "He's planning revenge to those slaves who escaped from his farm and he's in the killin' mood to those who are trying to help them." Ben's dad rested back on his saddle. "It made the hairs on my head stand on end, it did."

Big Jim rode his horse around the wagon bed. "One, two, three children, what's your plan?"

"Got to get them to the next station before—"

"There ain't no next station. Least not in Lexington or even Paducah. That blood thirsty bounty hunter said they've taken out every Underground Railroad stop from the Smokies clear through Kentucky. Only, we met your conductor and he told us he has your provisions ready and waiting for ya at Hobbs Corner. There's a big sign just before you enter Lexington. Go down the hill to your left. The horse and carriage are there. New clothes and food, too."

He slapped the reins across the mule's rump. The old wagon moved off with a creak and a groan that sent the wheels splattering into the puddles across the muddy road.

"What can we do to help you, son?"

Ben couldn't believe his ears. He put a finger to one and gave it a tug. "Am I hearing right? I thought you didn't believe in the Underground?"

"I don't. But I don't believe in scalawags telling free Americans what they will do and what they will think, either."

"Americans?" Ben questioned.

"Yep. I'm a property owner now and I demand my rights according to the law of the land. And this bounty hunter has set my blood to boiling."

"If what that bounty hunter said was true, Reynold's plans on getting even with the Gatlans, Maggie and her mother." Big Jim removed his hat and took a swipe at his forehead with his arm.

Big Jim's frown told Ben he was powerfully worried. Well, he couldn't be in two places at once. "You hear that bounty man right?"

"Yep, he was slobbery drunk, but he was tellin' the truth to be sure. Funny thing is, I got the feeling he don't like Mr. Reynolds any more than Maggie does."

Merciful Savior, please keep Maggie and her mother safe. Ben rolled his tongue around in his dry mouth. What would Reynolds' next move be? "Take Caedmon back with ya. Travelers might wonder why a fine horse like Caedmon is hitched to such a rickety wagon."

"But it might be a horse is what you be needin' to get home on."

Ben glanced back at the children. No telling when he'd return home. There was no guarantee the conductor in Ohio would be at his station.

# Chapter 15

Thick snow flakes floated down like fairy dust. The children were having fun playing with them. The transition from wagon to carriage at Hobbs Corner went well as did the change from their plain clothes to their Sunday finest attire. "Mr. McConnell, look at this one." Little Jonny's palm held an exceptionally large flake. "Could I make a snowball with this one? How did you say to make them?"

Ben laughed, ruffling the boy's hair. "No, get in. We're entering the town now." Ben closed the tarpaulin shades of the carriage, and climbed up into his seat. Clicking to the horses, he peered down the road into town, remembering his orders. "Look for the candle in the upper window. Knock on the door and say it's your cousins from Kentucky, come for a visit."

The town was lit up with candles. Even the road had candles sitting in the snow lining the streets.

"Where are we now?" Susie said, peeking out.

"Put your head back in." Ben adjusted the starch collar about his neck. He'd come to the end of the road.

A church bell rang, then another church picked up where the first bell left off. Suddenly there were more bells clanging and people coming out of their houses. What was going on?

"Merry Christmas," someone cried. Carolers walked past the houses singing "Hark the herald angels sing …" Two men leaped from the shadows and ran toward their carriage. Ben leaned a shoulder toward his shotgun; just his luck to arrive on Christmas Eve. How was he going to use his gun with all these people milling about? Merciful Savior, help me to be knowin' what to do.

"Hold up there." The men grabbed his horse by the bit.

Some people on the curb stopped their singing. Ben's sharp eyes darted from the man holding his horse to the man standing below him. Suddenly he remembered that this was Ohio, a free state. "Kindly remove your hands from my horse. This gentlemen and lady are looking forward to seeing their cousin whom they haven't seen for quite some time."

A large man finely arrayed hurried out of a stately mansion, clanging the black wrought iron gate shut behind him. "Dear cousins, what has kept you? I expected you two days ago." The man adorned with a silk lapelled dinner jacket and a wide black cravat centered in his frilled shirt pushed his way forward.

"Dr. Keenly?" Ben asked.

"Yes!"

The two men stepped away. "Well, I guess we were mistaken." The tallest of the men moved in front of the carriage, blocking Dr. Keenly. "Look here; we're looking for some runaway slaves. We've been trailing them now for over a week. I've been told they'll be coming here. If you hear anything, you're to let me know. We'll be over at the tavern."

"My good man." Dr. Keenly laid his hand on the bounty hunter. "It is Christmas Eve. This is hardly the time to fret over slaves."

"Just remember, I can have you put in jail for harboring slaves, and for knowing who is hiding them. I've got the law on my side. Remember that."

"My cousins have come for a visit and my advice to you is to return to your families and enjoy the peace that Christmas brings us once a year."

The juicy roast beef swimming in gravy, mashed potatoes, green beans, and corn added to the aroma of the cinnamon spices of the apple pie fresh from the oven. The holly and popcorn decorated evergreen tree adorned with candles and bright tinsel glowed in the center of the room.

Ben stretched his feet toward the mammoth fireplace, sipping his wine and feeling his eyelids close in peaceful bliss. Dr. Keenly, a surgeon, was one of the most affluent persons of the Underground Railroad.

Ben smiled, watching Susie's face light up each time Dr. Keenly spoke about the bright future that awaited her.

"It is only a matter of time before you will become free to do as you wish." Jonny and Little Sis had retired after dinner. But it was clear Susie was thirsty for more. The carolers outside the floor length windows raised their sweet voices to the tunes of "Joy to the World," and "It Came Upon a Midnight Clear."

The worst was behind Susie and her sister and the best was yet to be.

"Ben, you have performed your task famously. It is a shame circumstances forced you to take the children from Tennessee to Ohio on your own. But your heroism will not go unnoticed."

"I didn't do it to be praised. I did what was needed." Taking a sidelong glance at Susie, he added, "'Twas not a burden. They are good children, and I hope you keep them together."

"I will try. The children will be free to return to America once this slave issue is rectified. For now, I shall send them to Canada the day after Christmas. Mr. Reynolds has placed quite a sizable amount upon their heads."

"But I thought I could stay here." Susie looked from Ben to Dr. Keenly, then down at her hands. "I need to be going back after my baby is born. I'd like to return to Spirit Wind. Go back to school. Miss Maggie needs me and I need her."

Dr. Keenly squirmed in his chair. "You need to think about employment first. Now, what can you do? Now that you are free, so to speak, you must think about keeping a roof over your head and food on the table for your child and your sister. You'll need clothes and a proper education."

"How much will I need?" Susie's eyes widened with concern. "I get all those things free at Spirit Wind."

Ben looked away. What Susie needed was Maggie to take her into her arms and console the frightened girl. It's a hard road to go alone and freedom comes with a price.

"But you don't want to go back to Spirit Wind. Why, I read Harriet Stowe's *Uncle Tom's Cabin*. My wife and I couldn't believe the atrocities the southerners commit against their slaves."

"I don't know anything about autre-ities… that word, all I know is that Miss Maggie and her mama are kind, sweet, and understanding, always has been toward me. Most white folks in the south are. There never was an unkind word, nor act of violence between the Gatlans and our kind. No, sir. Miss Maggie would give us her last morsel of food before we'd go hungry." Susie sat up taller in the big high-backed chair and crossed her arms, her jaw set. It reminded Ben of Cook when her temper got riled over someone talking against the Gatlans. Susie pushed out her bottom lip, ready to do battle at the false accusations of her beloved teacher.

"Miss Maggie told us we are all slaves one way or the other. Slave to our passions, slave to our ambitions, and the only one who can set us free is Jesus. All we got to do is ask Him into our hearts. But that Mr. Reynolds is a bad apple. I don't think it's the color of your skin, it's the color of your heart—"

A knock on the door split into Susie's next words like an axe to a tree. Dr. Keenly's butler walked toward the front door.

The loud, demanding voice on the other end caused the back of Ben's hair to bristle.

"Speak about the devil and he be knocking on your door," Susie whispered. She rose and rushed into Ben's outstretched arms.

"I need to see Dr. Keenly this instant. I don't care if it is Christmas Eve."

Ben quickly got Susie into the back room where Dr. Keenly hid the slaves. He carried Little Sis and Jonny down the back steps and into the hidden room. *Why is it Reynolds is always one step ahead of us? Does he have an inside channel with the devil himself? So much for being a free state.* Ben deposited the children and then tiptoed back, hugging the wall. *The kind doctor might need his services.*

"I'm Mr. Reynolds of Tennessee and you are harboring my property. Are you aware that I could shoot you where you stand?" His voice yelled above the carolers. "But I'd rather send you to prison and have you rot there for your crime!"

Dr. Keenly turned to his butler. "Go for the sheriff." Then Ben heard the doctor's reply, clear as a bell. "You have just threatened a pillar of the community. We'll see what the sheriff thinks."

There was a shuffle of feet. "Doorman. Remove this unwanted guest. How dare you accuse me of wrong doing? You have no evidence against me. You are not welcome here, Mr. Reynolds. Get off my property. You can wait at the gate for the sheriff."

"I'll do better than that. I'll get a search warrant. Then I'll be on my way with my slaves and have Mrs. Gatlan flogged for stealing my property!"

Dr. Keenly, his hands in his coat pockets, walked back into the room. His kindly face a jigsaw puzzle of lines. "I can't move the children farther north until after Christmas. What do you suggest, Ben?"

"You've got a good hide-a-way here in your mansion." Ben placed his hand onto his chin. "I need to be leavin' and have Reynolds think I have the children. Now, I'm in need of a decoy." He looked over at the young servant boy who looked to be Irish. Ben walked over and whispered to the doctor. "Your servant boy is of slight build. With the proper clothing, he could pose as Susie, if he is agreeable."

Dr. Keenly talked with the boy. The servant boy nodded his head, all smiles, evidently imagining a daring adventure.

"I'll need three fresh horses," Ben said, eyeing the boy. Did he have the right to sacrifice one child for another? "Boy, this is dangerous work. You willing to chance your life this night? I can't promise you won't get killed—"

"I am." The boy nodded. "Yes, sir. I'm willing to go with you."

"But you're exhausted." Dr. Keenly squeezed Ben's arm. "Your muscles are as tight as a rubber band, ready to break."

Ben straightened his shoulders and smiled into the kindly doctor's face, then back at the youth. "I've been tired before. Besides, Maggie and her mother might need my services."

With Dr. Keenly's aid, they wrapped all four feet of his prize stallion, a big black Thoroughbred named Samson. Ben sure hoped the horse lived up to his namesake. He could use a strong hand tonight.

A horse neighed in the distance. Samson's ears poked forward in the horse's direction. Dr. Keenly held the stallion's upper lip tight. "No, you can't neigh back tonight, my boy. Leave those introductions for another day." He patted the horse's thick muscular neck. "I know, Samson, yes, those bounty hunters and that no good boss of theirs are out there."

Ben led a mare out, her saddle packed with supplies for the trip home. He glanced at the servant boy named Matthew, riding a chocolate mare.

The full moon shone bright in the clear sky and Ben couldn't help but wonder about that first Christmas Eve. Jesus sure loved us to leave His throne to live here with the likes of us and all the meanness of men.

Leaving the city, Ben glanced over his shoulder. The trail of hoof imprints in the snow, though obscured somewhat with the burlap, made it evident to Reynolds which way they had gone.

Matthew pulled the top of his hood over his face, his dress and cloak nearly covering him as he straddled his horse. Matthew had drawn the line at playing a girl by refusing to ride sidesaddle.

Back out in the open, Ben looked both ways and kicked Samson into a canter. The more miles he could put between Reynolds and his bounty hunters the better. Ben's pistol slapped his thigh, reminding him of what he just might have to do to rid the countryside of one bad apple.

After crossing the state line into Kentucky, the night passed slowly into dawn, and sometime in those dark hours, Ben noticed that his region of Kentucky had gotten a dusting of snow as well. Nothing to worry about; the roads weren't icy, but the burlap wouldn't do him too much good.

Samson didn't know when to quit, dripping wet with sweat, he pulled on his reins to go faster. Ben was afraid he'd wind the stallion. As it was the little mare had had enough. He glanced over his shoulder at Matthew.

The boy was slumped over his saddle. Asleep? He halted Samson and grabbed hold of the mare's reins. "Matthew, wake up."

Matthew shook his head. "Sorry."

Only the clump, clump, clumping of the horses hooves on the snowy wet and muddy road pulsed in Ben's ears. His land lay just to the left of him. It was clear the boy had had enough. Besides, he didn't want Matthew in danger. Reynolds wouldn't stop now. He'd want to take his revenge out on those who had instigated this plot to get his slaves to Canada. Maggie's beautiful face popped uninvited into his head. He needed to get back to Spirit Wind. His dad and Big Jim could protect Matthew and take him back to the doctor's in a couple of days.

"You did well. I couldn't be prouder of you if you were my own son!"

"But I want to go with you." The boy's smooth face and bright eyes looked up at him eagerly. "Please, sir, I can help ya."

Ben patted him on his thin shoulder. "Yes, in a couple of years, indeed, you'll make a fine young man I'd be proud to ride alongside of." Leaving Matthew with his father, he lit out across country. The hours melted away beneath Samson's feet. A sudden noise behind him made him dart into the woods. He reined up in a nearby thicket covered with tall burly wild grass and brown trees, and waited.

Three men on horseback galloped past him, then stopped. "I think… I don't know, boss, those tracks were hard enough before to follow… now they're nowhere to be seen." The tall man astride a milk-white gelding pulled hard, grabbing his left and then his right rein, seesawing on the bit, venting his anger on his horse.

Ben knew it was Reynolds before he saw his face, just by the vicious way he treated his gelding.

"You fools. I told you not to go so fast. Now we'll have to flush them out." Reynolds' face was a red as Hade's fire.

"Boss man, this doesn't make any sense. Why are they coming back? They were in Ohio. Why—"

"Because Susie adores Maggie and she knows I won't stop until I get my revenge. That Ben McConnell… well, he's nothing but a love-sick pup." Reynolds held up his fist and shook it. "But I'll show them both. I'll get my revenge. On Maggie and that half-breed mother of hers." He stretched out his whip. "I plan on using this on Susie and that Gatlan woman." He chuckled. "Maggie and her dad can watch."

That man is sick with hate. Ben lifted his revolver from its holster, then holstered it again. He'd be no good to Maggie if he landed in prison. He waited, hoping the three men would separate enough for him to whittle down the numbers.

One of the bounty hunters swung around to his area. Quietly Ben lowered his bulk from the saddle and grabbed the rope out of his saddlebags. Tying Samson to a tree, he pulled out his knife and moved two yards away, crouching down. As the man came near, Ben jumped up and wrestled him to the ground, then knocked him out with a hard punch in the face. He gagged the man with a strip of cloth from his shirt, then cut some rope and tied him.

Samson looked up, his ears pointed toward his left. Then Ben saw him. The man was on foot. Ben crouched behind a tree, waiting for him to find his friend. Well, he'd bind this second bounty hunter like the first and dress him like a turkey on Christmas morning.

Just when the man was about to yell out to Reynolds, Ben tackled him to the ground headfirst. The man coughed, spewing mud and snow. Ben boxed his ears and then tied his mouth, then his hands and feet. Leaving him there lying face first in the mud, Ben stood up, his mind alert, straining his ears, his eyes trying to penetrate the woods. Where did Reynolds go?

The wind howled in his ears as flakes of snow fell about his head and shoulders. Crouching low, he made his way toward Samson and the mare. The hairs of his neck pricked. Did Reynolds have him in his sight? Well, he wasn't going to wait around to get shot. He jumped into the saddle, leaning low, and galloped through the woods toward the road.

He heard it before he felt; the bullet hit his shoulder. "Ahhh …" He dangled on Samson's neck, trying to reach the reins with his good arm. The frightened horse took off at a run. Another rifle shot echoed through the hillside, splitting the snow-filled air like a clap of thunder. The bullet hit him in the leg, tumbling his mind into a half conscious, half stupor, where pain became a dream. A third bullet whizzed by his head and Samson groaned.

"No!" Ben clung to the horse's massive neck and felt the horse's blood oozing through his fingers. Samson's forelegs wobbled beneath his weight; he neighed. "Jesus, help us." The horse stumbled forward. Ben squeezed his eyes shut against the dying horse's agony. Head down, Samson's forelegs faltered toward a ravine, and he and Ben somersaulted down, down…

# *Chapter 16*

*E*li shook his head and left the room. Maggie hoped her mother had not seen the exchange between them, but mother never missed anything.

"No news about Susie, Little Sis, or Jonny. I'm sure everything will work out right. After all, God's word clearly states, 'And we know that all things work together for good to them that love God, to them who are called according to his purpose.'"

"Now, stop your worrying." Mother led her toward the table brightly arrayed with cranberries, sweet potatoes swimming in butter, fried okra, carrots in cream sauce, steamy squash, corn bread, and honey rolls. "Come and eat. The turkey is tender and oh so juicy, just the way you like it."

The dogs barked, then they heard a knock on the door. Eli hurried to answer it.

"Is Mrs. Gatlan in?"

"Now who could this be?" Her mother hurried out of the room.

"Mrs. Gatlan, I hate to bother you on Christmas day," the man's high pitched voice could be heard throughout the house. "My daughter's time has come and gone. She has herself a beautiful baby girl, only now she's taken ill. Mr. Reynolds left strict orders I was not to bother the doctor. Now what am I to do? Not that any doctor would come on Christmas Day, us being up in the Smokies and all."

The man's emotions were out of control with grief. What other reason could it be for him to be shaking like a leaf in a storm? Mother never turned her back on someone in need. Maggie might as well get ready to accompany her, but first she needed to give Cook her present. Grabbing it up, she hurried into the kitchen.

"Merry Christmas, Miss Maggie," Cook cried out, her face shiny from the steam of her bubbling pots.

Maggie produced a neatly wrapped present from the folds of her dress. "Merry Christmas, Cook."

"Lordy, Miss Maggie, you shouldn't of." Cook opened the package, then rushed toward the mirror. She placed her new hat on her head and surveyed it, turning this way and that. "Humpf! Don't know how you managed to make this ugly puss of my mine look like a proper lady, but you did!"

"I'm so glad you like it." Maggie clapped her hands together. It looks as good as I imagined it would!"

"Well now, Miss Maggie, that's enough of that huggin'. You'll get your clothes mussed. Now go sit down and finish your supper."

"There has been a change in plans. Could you pack up the picnic baskets with our Christmas dinner?"

"Surely Mrs. Gatlan is not figuring on going to do her doctoring on—"

"To quote Mother, 'Christmas Day is just like any other day when someone is in need.' You know Mother." Maggie left the kitchen, the rustle of her long skirts swishing across the hallway announcing her entrance. Her face must have displayed her shock at seeing her life-long friend's father standing on their threshold.

"Maggie, sad to say it's Irene." His brow was a patchwork of wrinkles.

Maggie patted his arm. "Now don't worry I'm sure Irene will be fine. Mother has doctored many a woman during and after childbirth."

Father's quick footsteps pounded the floor boards as he left his study. Puffs of smoke from his pipe floated before his face, making it hard to see his expression; however, his tone of voice was unmistakably leery.

He pointed his pipe at Mr. Sturgis and said, "Just how does Mr. Reynolds figure into this?"

Mr. Sturgis fidgeted with his hat, his thick fingers folding the brim in rolls. "He gave us a loan on some equipment so now we're beholding to him." Staring down at his boots, he added, "Well, I'm much obliged." He slapped his hat on his balding head, and patted it down. "I'll be on my way. I'll tell the Missus to expect you." He backed down the steps not taking his eyes off her father. He climbed up on his wagon and slapped the reins on his horse's rump. The rickety buckboard creaked and wobbled every time the wheels hit a pot hole. "Giddy up!" His voice rose above the clamor. He sped down the road leaving puffs of snow and dust behind him.

"You get the feeling that there's something more to Mr. Sturgis' beholding nature toward Reynolds?" Her father turned, his eyes softening. "Maggie, I'm glad you're going with your mother. She oftentimes takes on more than her body can handle. And I believe this is one of those instances. I'll give you two days, then I will ride out to check on you both."

"But husband—"

"Either you allow me this, or I will disallow you to leave." Father pointed the stem of his smoking pipe at her, his eyes blazing. "I should have killed Reynolds when I was in the killing mood. That man brings sorrow wherever he travels."

Maggie breathed deeply of the crisp air. She gazed at the white frame house, resting graciously on the hillside.

"Hey!"

She'd know that voice anywhere.

Will's strong legs made the distance from the barn to the buckboard in seconds. He grabbed Maggie in one of his bear grips and swung her high as easily as he would a sack of feed corn. His deep blue eyes sparkled up at her and complemented the sapphire blue sky.

"Put me down, you big ape," she commanded.

"I'm relieved to see you both." Will shoved his ash-blond hair off his furrowed brow. "Come and see my beautiful little daughter. We've named her Little Irene."

Maggie nodded toward the buckboard.

"Mrs. Gatlan, allow me to help you down." He glanced into the bed. "What have you got here? Looks like you plan to feed an army."

"You can get those things later, just hand me my black bag in the corner, there." Her mother clutched the bag to her chest, then opened it carefully. "I was afraid something might have broken on the way up here."

Will peered over her shoulder and glanced into the bag.

"What are you looking for?" Mother tilted her head questioningly.

His sparkling blue eyes met hers. "You by chance have a pint of breast milk in there?"

Her mother slapped him on the arm. "Always the kidder." Will chuckled good humoredly. "Honestly you haven't changed, William. I can still remember your dear mother chafing you for playing pranks on your teachers during grade school."

Taking the elbow of her mother and her, Will walked them toward the large frame house with the sloping veranda. "Wish this was a prank I was spouting and not the gospel truth. Little Irene's been on goat's milk ever since my wife got the fever."

"Has a doctor been out?"

"Yes, but he weren't no good so I sent for the best. Right, Maggie?"

"Mother can heal anyone or anything." Maggie smiled into her mother's frowning face.

"Not my doctoring. I just do a lot of praying that the Great Physician will guide my hands. Now what did this doctor say?"

Will leaped up the three steps that led to the porch, his face now solemn. "Said we should have sent for him sooner 'cause it was too late, infection's already set in, too bad to treat. But he wasn't any good." He glanced toward the closed door. "Before we go in, I got to tell you, Mr. Sturgis went and got remarried. Yeah, that was our Christmas present you can say. Mrs. Sturgis died with pneumonia in the spring. Mr. Sturgis married Miss Ellis six months later.

"That woodsy woman? The one the gypsies go to for their concoctions?"

Will nodded and shoved open the door.

A sickly sweet smell met Maggie's nose before she'd even crossed the threshold into the darkened room. "Some light and a little air might help?"

Will shrugged. "I'm certain Miss Ellis won't mind."

Walking toward a window Maggie pulled back the curtain. Dust particles like winged parasites looking for their next prey floated in the sunlight that streamed through the greased over windowpane.

"The late Mrs. Sturgis would have a fit if she knew the state her house was in," Mother whispered.

"Hey!" A hoarse voice cackled, shuffling boots followed.

"Oh, I'm sorry, I thought no one was...."

"Maggie, Maggie," a child's voice cried, shaking off the long claw-like fingers that hastened to snatch him back. The small boy's other hand clutched the folds of a dirty quilt as his little legs ran in boots too big for his feet. "Me wants to go to your house." His small eyes looked into hers as his little arms reached for her skirts.

Maggie patted his back. His face was dirty and tear stained, and his thick brown hair full of tangles. "Why, you sure can, that is if your father says it's okay."

Burying his head deep within the folds of Maggie's skirt he pleaded. "Please, Father, me wants to go to Maggie's." His small shoulders heaved with every sob.

"Well, I never saw the likes," said a nasally voice from the corner of the room. "That's the gratitude I get for everything I've done."

"My son meant no disrespect, Miss Ellis, I mean... Ma." Will crossed the room with his long strides. Grabbing his son, he turned him from the folds of Maggie's protecting skirt. "You get over there and tell your grandma you're sorry." The five-year-old boy struggled under the hard hands of his father. His eyes were as wide and frightened as a young fawn's.

"Don't bother," retorted Miss Ellis. "I don't care about such nonsense." Making a face at Will's little boy, she pointed a long finger at Maggie and said, "You've gone and spoiled him, ain't no hope for him now."

"How's Irene this morning?" Will picked up his son and wrapped his arms around him.

"Humpf. I'm sure now that Doctor Gatlan is here, she'll be fine. All I've heard for days on end was Mrs. Gatlan this and Mrs. Gatlan that.

Maggie this and Maggie that. A body gets sick of hearing it. No, Miss High and Mighty can't try none of my conjurations…it's got to be Mrs. Gatlan's or nothin'. Just as stubborn as her ma, Irene is. Well, I'm tellin' ya' signs wuz put fer man to read and there's an unnatural sign on that one if'n I've ever seen one." She plopped herself into the closest chair, her voice faltering against the steady pounding of her bow-back rocker hitting the ivory colored wallpaper with a thud, thud, thud.

Maggie's mother smiled at Will Jr. "Why don't you and your pa go into the yard and play? Might be you can find a few clusters of snow left over from yesterday. You could make some snowballs."

"Want to, son? Want to have a snowball fight with your pa?"

The boy nodded. Will extended his large hand engulfing his son's.

She and Mother watched the pair go out the front door. "Where's Irene?"

Miss Ellis motioned toward the guest room. Maggie knocked gently and opened the door. Her mother gasped, holding her hands to her nose.

"Inflammation, I knew it as soon as I walked in the house."

A metal-framed bed emerged in the semi-darkness. Irene lifted her delicate hand. "I prayed you'd come—"

"Oh, you're so hot. Mother come feel her."

Irene's lips quivered as tears filled her large eyes. "My father married Ma Ellis and she's a compulsive gambler. Mr. Reynolds has bought up the note on the farm. He's confiscated my father's slaves and left us for ruin with no way to pay back the note."

Irene pressed a hand to her brow. "Will and I tried to help Pa out and now we stand to lose our place. Oh, Maggie, I have such a terrible headache…. Will has some of Reynolds money; he was due here yesterday, but never showed. What are we going to do? Oh, why did Father have to marry that woman? She's not even a Christian; she believes in spiritualism."

"Now, stop worrying, you're going to make yourself sick for sure." Maggie kissed her gently on the forehead.

Her mother leaned forward. "Some men need a woman in bed with them. They don't care who that woman may be." She winked at Irene.

That seemed to make Irene feel better because her sobs subsided.

"I'm going to heat some fresh water and give you a proper bath. Would you like that?" Her mother patted Irene's arm.

"I'll get the water." Maggie reached for the basin and pitcher. Outside the bedroom, she paused near the hand carved bassinet. Little Irene lay in a soft pink-netted gown that her mother's skillful fingers had made. Her arms ached to take the child to her bosom. "Be patient, Little Irene, your mother needs me more."

She and her mother worked on throughout the afternoon, bathing Irene and cleaning the bed sheets. Then Mother sent Will into town for the doctor. Irene needed stronger medicine than the herbs and teas they'd brought. Will came back with a bottle of a foul-smelling liquid and regrets from Doctor Ankins. He'd done what he could for Irene and had a pressing engagement on the other side of town. She turned away so Will would not see her disappointment. Most likely, a party with his friends was the doctor's pressing engagement.

In the days that followed, Maggie watched helplessly as the fever raged and did its foul work on her best friend's body. Spasms and hallucinations plagued Irene, drawing her back into the realm when she'd delivered her baby. Her cries for water became pitiful sobs. Maggie pressed the cool water to the cracked lips, but Irene was beyond knowing, locked in the agonizing abyss between life and death.

Will pushed opened the door, his large shoulders filling the doorway. In his arms, nestled Irene's baby.

"The fever's playing tricks on her. She's been mostly out of her mind, don't expect much," Maggie said.

"Thought maybe seeing her daughter might help." He beamed down at Little Irene. "Isn't she beautiful?" His eyes soft and tearful, he walked to his wife's side, knelt beside her bedside, and whispered, "My darling, here's your daughter. She's going to be as beautiful as her mother."

Maggie's heart wept for them. She blinked away her tears as she looked at her friend and the small bundle wrapped in Will's arms. His eyes met hers, his bottom lip quivered. "Is she?"

Irene's eyes fluttered open. Eyes that a short moment before had been glassy bright with fever looked up at him, now clear as a spring brook in April. Her lips formed his name.

"My darling, look who I brought." He held the baby close to her cheek. "Here's Little Irene."

She caressed her daughter's head. "My beautiful baby... Take care... my baby." Her eye lids fluttered closed then opened with a start. "Don't... blame... God," she muttered. Her breath came in short gasps. Retching in pain, she placed a hand to her stomach.

"I hear music," she whispered. A peaceful smile crept across her parched lips. Her eyes wide, she followed the beam of the setting sun coming through the open window. "That garden's beautiful. There's Mama." Irene half raised up out of bed. Will put out a supporting arm. Her body fell back—limp.

"Irene, Irene."

Maggie took the small babe from within the crook of her father's arm. Will buried his head in his wife's soft hair and wept.

Mr. Sturgis stood in the doorway. Unabashed tears covered his face and his lips quivered. Maggie went to console him, but he pushed her hand away. Waving her and the baby away, he turned on his heels and stormed out of the room.

Maggie blinked as sunlight streamed through the open doorway. She searched the landscape. Her thoughts were still hazy over the night before. Her father had come for them. Angry voices had wakened her shortly after midnight. Miss Ellis' nasal sounds had been the loudest. Now at breakfast, Mr. Sturgis had not appeared.

Maggie and her mother asked where he might be. Only then had come a hint of the explosion that erupted when Mr. Sturgis told Miss Ellis about Irene's death.

Miss Ellis stared at Maggie, then her parents, one side of her mouth parting across her teeth like a dog's snarl. "Ain't none of your business where my husband is. You just get before supper time and take that babe with you. Foolishness," she muttered. "I just might commit the old fool."

"What? Where's Sturgis?" Maggie's father demanded.

"He's in one of the slave quarters, drunk as usual."

Maggie looked around. "Where's Will?"

"Up at the grave plot, I expect."

Mother's eyes, steeped in worry, looked into hers. "Jesus is caring for Irene. It is our duty to care for the living. Go to him, Maggie. He might not want Irene to be buried here. Irene, like her children, is welcome at Spirit Wind."

Maggie nodded. In the distance she could see Will slumped beside a granite headstone. She prayed for the right words as she walked to his side.

"What am I to do, Maggie, with a sick newborn and my five-year-old boy?"

"Mother—"

"I don't want your charity. I want to know why God had to take my wife." He nodded his head toward the slave quarters. "That's what can happen to a man who marries out of grief."

"God has given us the Good Book to read and seek guidance from, not to whittle out half-truths and pick out of His words what we choose to accept and obey. Your father-in-law has made the Bible into his personal wish book. You can't go against God's laws and expect His blessings. He knew Miss Ellis wasn't a Christian when he married her."

Will shrugged. "He thought he could change her. Only, she ended up changing him."

Maggie rested her hand on the crook of Will's elbow. "God tells us in 2 Corinthians 6:14, 'Be ye not unequally yoked together with unbelievers: for what fellowship hath righteousness with unrighteousness? and what communion hath light with darkness?'"

Will turned, his bloodshot eyes staring into hers, his wet cheeks reddened by the north wind. He moved his lips as if to say something, then turned away, looking at the slave quarters. "The truth always comes to the surface eventually. Well, I'd best get the hole dug."

"Mother wanted me to tell you that Irene is welcome at the Spirit Wind plot, that is, if you feel she would be happier there. Mother is looking forward to caring for Little Irene and Will Jr. Your children will fill the vacuum losing my brother to whooping cough and my sister to typhoid left. Father, well, he could use your help at Spirit Wind as head overseer. Reynolds has left our estate in an awful mess."

"He has?" Will straightened his shoulders. His large hands puckered into fists at his sides. "Well, then, I guess you've got yourself a new overseer." He tossed the shovel down and grabbed her arm. "I never saw my wife happier than the day you and your mother showed up, and Will Jr. already loves you. Come on, let's tell my father-in-law."

Sturgis sobbed and laid his cheek on the soft dust of the floor. "I'm the one that needs the help. Why are you leaving me and taking my daughter?"

"If you're in need of help, how can you possibly help your wife?" Maggie asked.

His sobs subsided. His eyes narrowed into slits. "You're no Christian. If you were, you'd show me some compassion. You're nothing but a hypocrite and worse than my wife could ever be, passing judgment on a poor sinner. Who are you to judge? Get out."

Will had their horses hitched to the buckboard before Maggie finished packing Will Jr's belongings. Maggie's mother put Will's boy on one side of her, then Miss Ellis pushed Little Irene into her arms and thrust a bottle of the precious goat's milk from her claw-like fingers into Mother's hands.

"There," she said, her scowling face contorting her features. "Now be gone with ya!"

"Not until I've tied up this stubborn goat." Her father and Will pushed the goat along, then tied him to the back of the wagon. "How much you want for the goat?"

Miss Ellis rubbed her bony fingers together. "A hundred will do."

"That... a hundred? Why that scrawny goat's not worth more than ten dol—"

"Pay her, Mr. Gatlan." Mother smiled back into Father's irate eyes. Without another word, he reached in his pocket and slapped $100 worth of bills into the woman's open palm and climbed in next to his wife. Maggie mounted her father's horse.

Will tipped the brim of his hat to his mother-in-law. "I'll be over tomorrow for my wife's body and the rest of my things."

As they made the last turn in the road toward Spirit Wind, a lone rider appeared on the horizon. "Who could that be?"

They didn't have long to find out.

"Mr. Reynolds, what brings you this way?" Her father's tone was cordial, but Maggie could feel his suppressed anger in the vibrating baritone of his words.

Will moved his horse closer to hers, scowling back at Reynolds.

"I've been at Spirit Wind, was coming to see your daughter." A smirk spread across half of Reynold's face, like a rabid animal. "What a pleasant surprise that I should find you here." His gleeful chuckle sent an ominous warning to her heart. "I wanted to tell you before you found out from someone else. Ben McConnell's dead. Shot the scum myself."

Maggie gasped. Ben's face flashed before her mind. She felt the coldness seeping like an icy wind through her body. Ben's dead? No! She gulped, then met Reynolds' gaze. She would not give him the satisfaction of becoming hysterical.

Reynolds' eyes darted from Maggie's face to her mother's. "Caught him delivering my slaves to the north."

"Were you able to get your slaves back?" Maggie's father displayed only concern.

"No. Unfortunately, I was too late. McConnell led us a merry chase. Making me believe he still had them." He shrugged. "So I killed the wolf that raided my chicken coop." Reynolds raised his hat in a manner that only could be interpreted as a victorious salute. "At least he won't be raiding any more chicken coops. We don't want another John Brown on our hands. Most likely if I had followed your instructions, Mr. Gatlan, that night I found Mrs. Gatlan at that Quaker cabin, I just might have outran him."

Her father cleared his throat. "Only stands to reason to keep on the main road. Shortest way to the north."

Reynolds rested his arm on the saddle and leaned forward, like a mountain cat ready to pounce. "Only it must have been an inside job, some abolitionist sympathizer. Well, I'll find them, male or female." His eyes rested on Maggie's mother. Two cat eyes gleaming in the sunlight. "And prosecute them to the full extent of the law." Reynolds pointed a finger in front of her mother's face. "You just see if I don't."

Her father jumped to his feet. "Are you suggesting—"

"Please resume your seat, Mr. Gatlan. I have a baby to nurse back to health." Her mother's sweet smile wasn't lost on anyone. "Good day to you, Mr. Reynolds."

They left him sitting on his horse watching their dust. Her mother kissed the sleeping babe on the forehead. Will Jr. grabbed her arm and hugged it.

How dare Reynolds threaten Mother. She was the very heart and spirit of them. The epitome of God's infinite love.

Ben's face flashed before her mind again. Her heart would forever lie with Ben.

# Chapter 17

The fire crackled in the old wrought iron stove and the teakettle whistled. Maggie chuckled, her eyes merry as she surveyed her room full of students. "Children, the teakettle whistles its best song when neck deep in hot water. Remember that when faced with adversity." She smiled warmly at her newest student, Polly Toole. "Now, Ida, please stand and read John 3:16 to the class."

Thirteen-year-old Ida was exceptionally well dressed today. Her red and green plaid dress became the Christmas spirit. Her hair was done up with matching fabric, and stood out on either side of her head in stiff curly braids. "Now, don't be shy, you have a beautiful voice and we all want to be able to hear you."

Ida stood up, turned, and peeked over her Bible, her eyes sparkling at Cain. That explains the reason for her picture-perfect appearance. "All right now, Ida?" Maggie glanced out the window at the frosty landscape. She couldn't believe it; five more days would usher in 1860.

Suddenly, the cabin door flew open and Eli stumbled inside, bent over, and gulped deep breaths of air. Maggie threw her body against the door, shutting out the wintery gale that swept away the warmth of the little room. She shuddered. Had the dreaded time arrived?

"Mrs. Gatlan says to get to your owners right quick. Take to the woods and don't look back. Those children belonging to Spirit Wind can stay put. Sheriff Pundy is on his way." Eli sat down at one of the benches, his bulk too large for the small table. The children, prepared after many preliminary drills, ran and gathered their coats and hurried out the door. Maggie grabbed the remaining books and pencils as Eli told her the sordid details.

"Mr. Reynolds bolted into the house earlier, knowing full well the master was gone. He pushed me aside and found Mrs. Gatlan reading *Uncle Tom's Cabin* while rocking Little Irene to sleep. Told Mrs. Gatlan he was gettin' the sheriff, that she's—"

"They're in here!" Reynolds hateful voice penetrated the log cabin. A shiver ran up Maggie's spine. She rested her hands in the folds of her skirts and waited.

The wooden door of the cabin ricochet against the tongue-and-groove walls, then slapped Reynolds in the face. He thrust the door aside, pulling Ida along by her pigtails.

He shoved the child onto the floor and laid his dirty boot on her stomach. "Now you tell me why you are here? I don't want to hear one of your lies, tell me the truth or I'll whip you within an ounce of your life. I swear!"

Maggie cupped her hands into fists. Ida was so proud of her appearance. Maggie shook with rage and in her authoritative voice said, "You are on private property. Get out, now!"

Reynolds removed his boot and stomped toward her. His face as red as the devil's horns, he hurtled a fist in her face, stopping short an inch from her nose. "I'm going to own Spirit Wind someday, you just see if I don't. I'm going to put your Indian mother down on the reservation where she belongs and you—"

"Me? I'd like to see you try and do something to me." She locked her fists by her side for fear she'd use them on his worthless face. Nothing in life mattered now that Ben was gone, and this man killed him! "How dare you threaten my mother and me. There is no law against me doing what I like with my slaves, if I want to educate them so what?"

"It's illegal to educate slaves and besides that, you're educating others too. Don't deny it. Look at her."

"Ida came to visit us. Can you prove otherwise?"

"I'll beat the truth out of her!"

"The countryside already knows of your bullying tactics. I will merely state the obvious. That you had beaten this poor girl to submit to your whims."

Reynolds banged his fist on one of the desks. Ida cried, rolling over and covering her face. Maggie bit her lip. If she appeared weak before Reynolds, all would be lost. She had to make him think he couldn't achieve anything by beating Ida.

Sounds of horses snorting and hooves flying through the woods now swarmed the Glenn. She looked at Eli. Both knew her secret was over.

"What's all this about?" Sheriff Pundy said.

"I found Mrs. Gatlan reading this." Reynolds withdrew the book like it was a saber.

The sheriff looked down at the title and read, "*Uncle Tom's Cabin,* say I heard about this book, heard it was a passel of lies."

Maggie stepped forward. "Wouldn't you like to read it for yourself and find out about the lies?"

Sheriff Pundy looked up. "May I?"

Reynolds pounded the desk. "No! This is banned in the South, didn't you know that?"

"Reynolds, calm down. What else have you got on the Gatlans besides a book? I don't see how this proves they're doing abolitionist activities."

Reynolds, his face a combination of red from the cold north wind and his hot temper, banged his big fist down on the desk again. "Look around, sheriff, this school has enough desks in it to teach all the slaves in Bount County. Here's one for proof." He bent over and pulled Ida to her feet by her pig tails.

Ida whimpered, but didn't cry out. Reynolds pointed a finger at Maggie. "Besides this, she and her mother are part of the Underground Railroad. They helped three of my slaves to escape. Actually, it was three and one half; Susie was pregnant! I demand you arrest them."

The sheriff examined the book closely. "I don't see how a book can hurt you by reading it."

"That's how the abolitionist movement got started." Reynolds walked closer, towering over the five-foot-eight man. Reynolds' stature was intimidating and he knew it.

The sheriff tossed the book on a desk, then walked up and down the aisles. His boots thumped like a war drum. Pundy was known throughout the county for his fair play—that is to say, unless he felt bullied.

"*Uncle Tom's Cabin*, the school, and now your runaway slaves, when you put it all together, guess I have no choice." Pundy turned, his eyes softening. "Maggie, your father's not going to like this. I'll let you gather up some of your things before I take you and your mother to jail."

A large shadow loomed over her. Eli now stood in front of her. She couldn't see beyond his back, but by the tone of his deep voice it was clear his face was set in stone. "No one is takin' Mrs. Gatlan or Miss Maggie to jail. Not until the master comes home, Sheriff Pundy, sir."

Sheriff Pundy knew of her father's temper and authority throughout the county. He cleared his throat. "Well, I see no reason not to wait until Mr. Gatlan returns home."

In the days that followed, Mother bought Eli a ticket on the railroad so he could race to Illinois and overtake Father with the news. Then Mother bought Ida from Reynolds for an exorbitant price to take care of Little Irene and Will Jr., but mostly to keep Ida away from the ill-tempered Reynolds.

Will McGuire rode across the countryside to gather supporters in a petition to not jail the Gatlan women. Generally, the neighbors didn't want to get involved. So Maggie, fearing a jail term, set to work to make sure anyone who wanted to continue with their education, could homeschool themselves. They had been taught the basic reading, writing, and arithmetic. Now it was up to them to continue to practice it. Just before her father was due home, Maggie took one last ride to the Glenn.

The cabin looked as forlorn as she felt. An empty cavity filled her heart, where once her mission and her love for Ben had resided. She could only imagine what anguish he had gone through.

He would never work his land and she would never teach again. Never again. She knelt and rubbed her hands across the trap door, the way Ben had. What would it have been like to belong to that tall, merry-eyed Irishman who was as fierce looking as a pirate, but had a heart as big as that pot of gold at the end of the rainbow Ben's dad always talked about?

"Daughter?"

Maggie whirled around and ran to her father's outstretched arms. She buried her head in his shoulder and wept. "Oh, Father, I'm so sorry for getting you and Mother in this trouble. Can you ever forgive me?"

"There, there." Patting and stroking her hair, he pulled her an arm's length away. "So we got ourselves another slave girl?"

"Yes, and I know you said that we must be careful with our finances. And now we'll need to employ a lawyer."

"But we shall. I've already hired Honest Abe. He waits for us at Spirit Wind. He almost didn't accept the job. What with his tight schedule and all. He's making plans to run for the presidency in the next election. But this fight is so dear and close to his heart, well, he couldn't resist. Your court date is scheduled for Monday morning."

Tall and gangling, Abe loomed over every man with easy grace. Maggie felt the hidden strength behind his piercing, steadfast eyes. His square chin jutted out like a prize fighter, as if daring anyone to argue with him. Maggie offered him her hand as they entered the courtroom, her petite hand gobbled up in his mammoth one. "Are all northerners as large as you?"

A rolling rumble sputtered from within Abe's mouth, like an artesian well of mirth. His eyes were as merry as his smile. "Are all southern ladies as pretty as you?"

"No wonder Father has joined your allegiance, Mr. Lincoln." She drew closer and on tiptoes whispered, "But I fear for your safety."

Just moments ago, angry southerners lining the road had yelled obscenities at Mr. Lincoln as he approached the courthouse in his buggy. He had to run into the building before a volley of tomatoes and other rotten fruit damaged his distinguished looking hat and suit.

"I must apologize for my fellow countrymen. They are listening to propaganda. You are a brave, compassionate man, Mr. Lincoln. Have you always been this willing to sacrifice your life for your convictions?"

A clamor of tomatoes hit the courtroom windows making Maggie jump. She'd meant her question to be a jest.

He patted her hand, his eyes serious as they looked into hers. "Die when I may. I want it said of me, by those who knew me best, that I always plucked a thistle and planted a flower when I thought a flower would grow."

"I pray some of your wisdom might rub off on me." She laughed, then fear grabbed her heart, despite her determination to make light of the moment. "I shall pray you do not leave this earth until you have finished the work our good Lord has intended for you. The Almighty has a plan for these United States and I believe you are predestined to accomplish this."

"If we do right, God will be with us, and if God is with us, we cannot fail. Remember that, Maggie. Whatever happens here, remember that."

Hours went by, but Mr. Lincoln's strong claims of insufficient evidence were ignored, the jurors' stony faces and akimbo arms conveying their resistance to the defense. The words of Matthew 13:15 swaddled like solace her wounded heart. "For this people's heart is waxed gross, and their ears are dull of hearing, and their eyes they have closed; lest at any time they should see with their eyes and hear with their ears." Maggie listened intently as Lincoln addressed the jury with his final remarks.

"It has been said of the world's history hitherto that might makes right. It is for us and for our time to reverse the maxim and to say that right makes might. There has not been anything entered into this court to prove that Maggie and her mother, Marie Gatlan, have willfully stolen Mr. Reynolds' slaves. Mr. Reynolds has used his powerful might to sway this jury. With no evidence, there should have been no trial and hence no verdict."

Lincoln waved his arm in the air. "Remember this before deciding the fate of your neighbors: Character is like a tree and reputation like its shadow. The shadow is what we think of it; the tree is the real thing. Vote the right, not the might."

The jury retired to reach a verdict. Ten minutes later they reentered the courtroom. The judge rapped his gavel. "Order in the court. Jury have you reached a verdict?"

"We find Mrs. Gatlan and Maggie Gatlan not guilty of harboring slaves. However, in order to assure that Mrs. Gatlan will disperse the school and burn all abolitionist material—"

"Flog her, flog her!" someone yelled.

A gasp went up in the courtroom. The judge pounded his gavel to no avail. Two burly men, masked and armed, grabbed Maggie's mother and hauled her out into the courtyard. Two other men immediately barred the exit of the courtroom.

"No! No!" her father yelled as he bolted up from his seat in the courtroom. Two more masked men held him there. Chaos reigned, women screaming as the crowd pushed their way to the exit. Two men grabbed Mr. Lincoln and Maggie and rushed them into an inner room. They blindfolded her and tied her hands, ignoring Mr. Lincoln's protests.

At the first sound of the whip slapping across her mother's back, the crowd in the courtroom grew silent. Once, twice, three times. Maggie hung her head, wishing she could block out the noise. She heard her mother groan. Then nothing.

An hour later, the bailiff untied her and removed her blindfold. Her hand flew to her neck and grasped Great-grandmother Gatlan's heirloom necklace that now hung there. Just before entering the courtroom, Mother had clasped the necklace around Maggie's neck and whispered, "Daughter, you will need this when I am gone. Always remember God will never take you where His grace cannot protect you." … Mr. Lincoln! Maggie looked frantically around the room, but he was gone. She prayed he had escaped safely to Illinois. Perhaps the north was the only safe place to be. It was certainly not here.

The bailiff's arrogant face scowled into hers and fear wrapped her body like cold iron. Would she be whipped next? They were all slaves now, slaves to this new wave of hate that had grabbed her beloved South. What was it Mr. Lincoln had told her earlier? I have said nothing but what I am willing to live by and, if it be the pleasure of Almighty God, die by.

"What did your father expect would happen hiring that Lincoln fellow?"

"A fair trial. Now may I leave?" The blood would flow soon. She had no doubt if Lincoln was elected to be the Republican choice for president that the South would rise and secede from the Union. Too bad, she liked Mr. Lincoln. He and Ben would have gotten along beautifully.

Ben. Would she ever stop thinking about him? Oh Jesus, help me to forget Ben and help this nation remain whole and beneath Your sheltering arms.

"Just make sure you don't go educating those slaves again."

She heard the key in the lock and hurried toward the door. "Mother?"

# *Chapter 18*

*B*en groaned and looked up. All he could see was rock and more rocks. A couple of hungry looking vultures attempting to gorge on Samson that he had chased away with his stick now observed him for a possible dinner. Or was it closer to the supper hour? What's the difference, he wasn't eating… those vultures were.

His left arm, still oozing, was a bloody mess. He must have been lying there for days. Dear Lord, what I could use right about now is that handy angel to fetch me another cup full of water. Had he dreamt it? It seemed real enough at the time.

He looked over at the stream running down the mountain not more than an arm's length away. More likely he'd gotten water from there. He missed something… Christmas, he was looking forward to eating turkey with Maggie. Night, day, night, day, four he counted in all. He'd yelled for help until his throat was hoarse.

He laid back. What was the use? Lord take me to heaven with ya. I'm too far gone to be of any help to anyone. Maggie, what about her? He'd had a dream…

"Anyone be down there?"

"Dad? Is that you?" Ben tried to yell, but his throat was so dry, he only managed a hoarse whisper. He rolled over with difficulty; his bullet wounds and being near starvation had taken their toll. Sitting, he stretched his good hand out for a rock; eyeing one nasty long-beaked vulture, he swung his arm. The vulture rose higher and higher in the air. "Go a little farther, my winged meat eater."

"Look, there he is… quick, Big Jim, hoist me over."

That's Dad.

"Then I'd have another man ailing and not being able to do his share of the work." Big Jim's baritone echoed through the mountains. "Here, grab hold of the rope and tie it around that tree. Be quick."

Ben looked up, raising his arm toward Big Jim. He rolled his tongue around his mouth and rested his head back on the hard ground. Dirt and pebbles fell across his face. Big Jim grabbed Samson's stiff foreleg and pulled at the dead horse.

Ben choked back his dry tears. Samson's stiff limbs, the glassy eyes… reaching out his hand, he felt Samson's silky coat for the last time. The horse had kept him warm in the cold nights. "He was shot trying to protect me." Ben licked his lips. "Water?"

Big Jim lowered his canteen. "Careful, this might hurt, your lips are cracked and bleedin.'"

"Can't believe I'd have that much blood left."

"That Reynolds fella and his bounty hunters been bragging up and down the Tennessee and Kentucky border about killing you, but your Dad wouldn't give up. Said he would believe that when he saw your dead body for himself. We've been looking for you ever since Christmas. And here you are. Can you grab hold of my neck?"

"I'm so happy to see ya I might strangle it a little too tight." Ben felt a surge of energy run through his veins as he clutched Big Jim and they made their way out of the ravine.

"The saints preserve us." Ben's dad kissed his cheeks, wetting them with his tears and then did a little jig. Now, loaded on the back of the wagon, Ben rose on one elbow and gazed out toward the ravine. Samson, I'm sorry. He laid his head back on the pillow and sobbed. Samson kept him company. His warm body solace for a while. That is until Ben had to use his revolver on him. He couldn't stand to see the big fella suffer any longer.

Tears rolled off his cheeks. "Did you hear if the children got to Canada safely?" he whispered.

"Yeah, they did. Only don't sound like Maggie or her mother faired too well. Hear there was a trial. Didn't hear the outcome."

Ben puckered up his lips, coughed, and whispered, "A trial? They wouldn't dare hurt those sweet southern ladies."

Big Jim followed behind, straddling his big bay gelding. "Things are different. Tempers are flarin', not so sure who they'll burn next. You can sniff it in the air. Like a keg of dynamite ready to explode."

Maggie gently bathed her mother's lacerated back. Downstairs her father's angry voice rose like a roaring tide exploding its banks.

"What do you mean you can't find the men responsible for whipping my wife?"

"Gatlan… be sensible. The men were wearing hoods."

Maggie peered over the upstairs banister. Sheriff Pundy, usually a mild-mannered man, was getting equally angry. Maggie could tell by the way his voice quivered and his face turned redder by the second.

"How can I arrest who I don't know?"

Her father slammed his fist down on the table. "What I can't figure is how you and your deputies could let them get away."

The sheriff slammed something against the table. She couldn't see what it was. "Two of my deputies are in the hospital with multiple gunshot wounds. Get it in your head that these are times we've never been in before. I can't trust anyone. Part of this is your fault. Why did you hire Abe Lincoln, of all people, to be your wife's lawyer?"

Her mother groaned. "Maggie, help me up."

She turned the corner of the doorway, and ran to help her mother. "Mother, don't try and get up, you need to sleep and let these wounds air. Doctor Jordon said that's the only way to speed the healing."

"Your dear father will make himself hoarse with all this yelling. Now help me."

When her mother got something in her mind to do, it took a crowbar to pry it loose. Maggie knew it was no use arguing. She tenderly rubbed her mother's wounds with salve, wrapped gauze around her mother's back and chest, then put on the lightest garment she could find, a cotton shirtwaist and skirt.

"Hand me my shawl. There, that should do." Her mother looked at herself in the mirror, pinched her pasty-white cheeks and chuckled. "Too bad I can't add some of the red on my back to my cheeks."

As soon as they stepped into the hallway, her mother grabbed the spiral handrail and Maggie held her other arm. With every downward step, her mother groaned.

The half glow of the setting sun illuminated the tall windows graced with lace shears and red-velvet curtains, as red as the faces of her father and Sheriff Pundy. What could Mother do? There seemed no way to halt the volley of heated words that grew more volatile with every mouthful.

The polished wooden floor met their steps beneath the winding stairway. Her mother paused. Taking a deep breath, she anchored her shoulders back and plastered a smile on her face. The men hadn't noticed them standing in the hallway.

"Mother, you're so brave," Maggie whispered. "I don't think I could have come through this as well as you. But, oh, I wish so that it had been me and not you."

Mother kissed her on the cheek. "The past is behind us, Maggie. Now let us face this present storm and calm it before a typhoon erupts."

Father had his back turned toward the doorway, his body rigid as a post, his hand upraised as if to hurtle it into the sheriff's face. "I want these men to come to justice, do you understand? I don't care if you arrest all of Maryville. You can start with that bailiff. How dare they do this to my wife?"

Sheriff Pundy wasn't looking at him, but at Matron Burns and Miss Peabody crying in the corner of the room. Maggie could only see Matron Burns, who dabbed at her nose with her lace handkerchief as she gazed out at the rose garden.

"I can't remain silent any longer or else I'll bust my corset stays. I just can't believe this happened." Matron Burns raised her handkerchief to her moist eyes, then blew her nose. "What is our country coming to, flogging women?"

"You forget, Matron Burns, Mrs. Gatlan is half Cherokee."

Matron Burns turned, waving her linen handkerchief as if to infuriate him the more. "Pishposh. She's more of a lady than I and it's as plain as that revolver sitting on your hip!"

Miss Peabody's thin face twisted in wrath. "No woman deserves such treatment. Sheriff, you must put a halt to this barbarism."

Sheriff Pundy twisted his coffee cup around in his hand. "I know I'm throwing a log on an already blazing fire, but talk in town is Reynolds is planning something. But I can't arrest a man from gossip."

Leaning heavily on Maggie, her mother entered the room and shuffled her feet to her husband.

"Marie, what are you doing up?"

Pulling him down to her height, she kissed him gently on the cheek. "My dear husband, do not worry. All is well," she whispered.

The sheriff turned away, his face revealing his embarrassment with the deep red flush that burned its way from his neck to his pudgy cheeks. "Mrs. Gatlan, I… am sorry."

"I am proud of my Indian heritage, and proud to be a southern lady." Mother's eyes flashed about the room, taking in at a glance each face. "Jesus was whipped for no crime and I shall bear my stripes remembering my Savior's sacrifice. I pray this discourse and hatred that presently rips through our beautiful southern heritage, Christ's love will dissolve."

Tears welled in her father's blue eyes. His scowling face relaxed and the upsweep of his lips crested into a smile. "You are better, my love?"

"I have improved much beneath the gentle hands of our daughter." Her mother looked around. "How are Little Irene and Will Jr. doing?"

Her father patted her slender fingers. "Very well, you need not worry. Ida is always by their sides."

How handsome her father looked, wearing his white shirt and cravat. His black pants hugged his solid hips, quite the contrast to the sheriff who had allowed his wife's good southern cooking to go to his belly.

Her mother, always the hostess first, said, "Matron Burns, Miss

Peabody, how nice of you to drop by. Did either of you have supper? Maggie go and tell Cook to start the fires. Tell her there will be three more for supper this evening."

"Yes, Mother."

The sheriff sucked in his stomach, then laughed and patted the bulge that refused to disappear with any prompting from him. "Well, as you can see, I never refuse a meal."

Supper went well. The candelabras flickered their light against the thickening darkness, casting shadows on the papered walls. Then a commotion on the front lawn, the hound dogs barking and growling, drew the happy dinner party toward the full-length windows. Gun shots rang out.

"Oh my!" Matron Burns jumped away from the window. Five hooded men on horseback rode up. "We want your wife," one man yelled.

Father opened a drawer and pulled out his revolver.

Sheriff Pundy shoved him back. "I don't want bloodshed." He opened the door. "Now, you men get out of here if you know what's good for you." He patted his chest where his badge shone in the moonlight.

"We want Mrs. Gatlan," one man yelled.

"You have done enough to her." Her father shoved the sheriff aside and thumped his thumb to his chest. "You speak to me, you cowards, hiding your faces underneath a pillowcase. Might as well hide under your bed because you know your deeds are foul."

Will ran around the corner armed with a rifle. Eli and a dozen slaves stood behind him. "Get off this land before I shoot you down like the cowardly dogs you are."

One of the hooded men fired at Will. Will dropped him with one shot.

The sheriff had drawn his revolver. "Get out of here before you're all lying dead like your comrade."

"We're not done with you abolitionists yet." The lead man turned, leaning on his saddle. The voice was strangely familiar to Maggie.

"Sheriff, you sure you want to be standing next to them? You could get accidently shot on your way home. Or worse still, in your bed." He chuckled. "You can't be everywhere and if you don't stop this investigation into Mrs. Gatlan's whipping, my men and I will keep on vandalizing the countryside until you plead for mercy."

"How dare you threaten me and mine!" Maggie's father shook with rage. Swerving his right hip, he laid back his broadcloth coat.

His pistol was on that hip. Her mother, seeing the movement jumped in front of her husband.

"Marie, get back," her father said. She refused. "Woman, do as your told."

She ignored him. "Mr. Reynolds, why are you so full of hate for us? You delighted in flogging me, and I had hoped you had vented your temper enough as to lose some of your hatred for me. Or am I just a channel you have chosen to bully others weaker than yourself?"

Reynolds growled deep down in his throat. Maggie shuddered. "Mrs. Gatlan, you're the lifeblood to your husband. I want him to suffer because I hate him more than life itself." His hand disclosed a pistol. The boom of flint and powder temporarily deafened Maggie's ears.

"Ahhh …" Her mother fell backward.

The smell of gunsmoke filled the air.

"No!" Her father caught her before she could fall to the ground. Will shot back, winging Reynolds in the arm. The men turned and galloped off.

"Eli, ride and get Doctor Jordon."

Sheriff Pundy grabbed his horse and galloped after the men.

"Get Reynolds!" Her father looked down at his wife's motionless body and cried, big sobs racking his shoulders.

Will and Eli jumped onto their horses and galloped after the sheriff.

Her father scooped up her mother's limp body, carried her into the house, and laid her down on the sofa. Maggie placed a pillow behind her head.

"Lordy, lordy, what next. The devil is prowling this house. Lookin' to devour us all." Cook's large torso quaked like jelly, her turbaned head wobbling back and forth.

"Cook, calm down." Her father's tone was authoritative.

"Get a basin of water and some rags. Quick," Matron Burns said.

"Marie, Marie, can you hear me, darling?" Her father took her mother's lifeless hand in his, kissing her fingers. Laying his head on her breast, he sobbed. "Marie, please don't leave me. Please, I need you so. Without you I'll be half a man."

Her mother's eyes fluttered opened. "My love." A sweet smile lit the drooping corners of her angelic face. "Don't hate... forgive..." Her hand reached up to stroke a blade of sandy-brown hair from her husband's forehead, then stroked his cheek. "Jesus told me to say... 'love your enemies'... don't hate, darling. Not even Reynolds, nor our daughter. Remember... 'do good to them that hate you.' We will be together always, my love... in the sweet by and by. Our daughter... don't blame... remember 'if ye forgive men their trespasses, your heavenly Father will also forgive you... if ye forgive not... neither will your Father forgive yours...'" Her eyes went suddenly glassy. "True love... Jesus' love... endures—"

"I will never love again if you should die!"

"Redemptive... love." Her jaw dropped forward; her eyes stared blankly at them.

Big tears rolled down her father's cheeks and chin and splashed down on her mother's hand.

"This can't be," Maggie cried. "First Ben, now Mother—dead?" Father crumbled to the floor, reaching for her mother's hand. "Marie... Marie... I don't want to live without you beside me."

Maggie pressed her hands to her father, weeping openly on his shoulder. He pushed her away. He gently placed her mother's hand on her chest and kissed it, then burying his head on her chest, he sobbed for what seemed to Maggie an eternity.

When he arose, his eyes accusingly gazed into hers. "This is your fault. You, you had to start that blasted school. You had to include your sweet mother in your scheme. If you hadn't, your mother would still be alive. I warned her. I told her that." He kissed her mother's forehead, then her lips.

Maggie cringed on the scarlet-rose velvet carpet. Father's eyes, cold as ice, glared at her.

"I'll go and get the undertaker," Father said.

"I'll have Cook keep your dessert warm," Maggie replied.

Her father eyed her and frowned. "I won't be home tonight. I've got things to do in town."

Maggie hurried after her father. "But… Mother said—"

"She was delirious."

"Father, no, I believe she came back from heaven to tell us this, to tell you this."

Her father looked down at her from the bridge of his nose. She clutched his arm.

"Quit pawing me." He pulled her arm away, a shiver coursing through his body as if detesting her touch. He backed away from her. "Go about your business and I will go about mine. From now on, we are strangers. Do you understand me?" His eyes took on a strange gleam. She shuddered. "We are strangers that share the same name and the same house." He slammed the door behind him.

Like concrete statues, Matron Burns and Miss Peabody held their handkerchiefs to their gaping mouths, unable to give either comfort or support. Maggie hung her head in shame.

"Lordy, lordy, Miss Maggie," Cook said, patting her on the back and weeping openly. She grabbed the corner of her apron and wiped her eyes. "Mr. Gatlan's gone crazy with grief."

Not a cloud in the sky. Wasn't it supposed to rain? She wished for a torrential thunderstorm so as to inhibit the viewers. There seemed no end to the people crowding the pews, bumping into to one another to give her and Father their condolences.

The Reverend Brown's eyes softened and his mouth worked its way into a grin. "I shall never forget the first time I met your mother, she just a child of eight when I baptized her up on Mt. Gilead. Back then people sat on tree stumps or beneath the brush arbor in our makeshift church. She was determined to follow Jesus and she never swayed from her faith."

"Thank you, Reverend. I remember my mother telling me about that baptism." Maggie smiled.

"Did she tell you about meeting the late Reverend Anderson? How we had to wait for him because he was a circuit rider then?"

Maggie nodded.

"Mr. Greatheart," muttered Matron Burns coming up beside her. "He established Maryville College, and in walked Marie. She became Reverend Anderson's star pupil."

"And because of me, mother lost her life." Maggie bowed her head.

The Reverend patted her heaving shoulders. "Dry your tears, child. You did what you had to do, and your mother did what she had to do." He paused watching the crowd of people coming through the doors.

"Maggie, I am so sorry about what happened to your dear mother," said Elizabeth Toole, leaning heavily on the arm of the slender girl standing beside her. "Polly was determined to come. We don't understand why people have to be so mean to one another."

Polly nodded. Her tight curls bobbed about her head.

Maggie wished more time could have been spent teaching her. Evidently, it was enough to strike up a friendship. She sent the girl a warm smile.

Two women dressed in black from head to toe walked past them. Her Quaker friends found a seat in the back of the church. Then four men walked in. They were strangers.

"Who are they?" Matron Burns was quick to comment. "I don't care for the guns they're toting, either."

The Reverend patted her arm. "Well, I think everyone is here. I might as well start the eulogy." He moved to the pulpit and the crowd quieted.

"Often a person's life and character command our special interest because it is so clearly evident that God has taken a great interest in him or her. For instance, I believe God took an interest in Sam Houston. His parents moved here from Virginia in 1807. Sam went on to become the governor of Texas. Then there is Chief Timpson of the Cherokee Indian tribe. I remember Reverend Anderson telling me like it was yesterday when he married Marie's parents, a Cherokee princess to an aristocratic Irishman." The crowd chuckled. "Yes, what a combination. Marie's mother was dressed in white doeskin, her father dressed in a black tuxedo. The union brought the Indian tribe and the white settlement harmoniously together."

Reverend's gaze rested on Maggie. "Now Marie had the Holy Spirit in her. Everyone that met her felt it." Her father slid forward in his seat, as if ready for a speedy departure. She could feel the crowd of people overflowing the pews, waiting for the reverend's next words. This was not an ordinary eulogy. The reverend had a point to make.

"Spirited, determined, and faithful to Jesus. That was Mrs. Marie Gatlan, never afraid to look a person in the eye and tell them they were wrong and then do the right thing, no matter what the consequences." Reverend clutched his Bible like it was his anchor. "One conscionable act begets a consequence. I am reminded of Ephesians 1:11 and 12 'In whom also we have obtained an inheritance, being predestinated according to the purpose of him who worketh all things after the counsel of his own will: That we should be to the praise of his glory, who first trusted in Christ.'

"Marie was not afraid to die for what she believed in, and she believed mind, body, and soul in the saving grace of Jesus Christ." He slammed his fist on the podium. "It would be well for us to remember this when faced with the decision whether to turn our backs on a person, be it Indian, Negro, or white that needs our protection. What lies ahead for the South, only God knows. And only God knows what every individual man or woman will do when their life is on the line."

Her father hurried down the aisle, his hands in his pockets, his broad shoulders bowed as if fighting a turbulent storm. The big oak door slammed shut behind him.

# Chapter 19

*B*en felt stronger each day. And on this eighth day in May, with the robins and bluebirds chirping and the sun warming his back as the plow made spirals in the rich, virgin dirt, he paused to pray. Humbled, knowing only the good Lord could have planned for him to have the money for his land. Now an invitation arrived from one of the most high-society houses in the county, it was, indeed, a happy morning. A horse neighed and his mule, Nellie, neighed back. Stopping the plow, he looked up to see Big Jim galloping toward him.

"He's in a bit of a hurry, Nellie." Ben wiped his forehead and neck with his bandana. "What's got you up so early?"

"What's got you so happy pulling a plow at daybreak? Why don't you have Jacob do this back-breaking work?"

"'Tis my own land I plow and proud of it. Mine and my dad's. Why just look at this good dirt." Ben scooped up a handful. "I can grow anything in this. Ah, a top of the morning for me to be sure. Besides, Jacob is painting the house, nothin' fine about painting like it is in digging in your own dirt."

"Spoken like a true Irishman." Big Jim rested his arm on the horn of his saddle and lifted his hat off his forehead. "You been invited to that big ball in Lexington next week?"

"Indeed, I'll have the prettiest lass on my arm as well."

"Who might that be?"

"Maggie Gatlan. Just wrote her another letter. She should get it soon."

Big Jim dismounted, running the reins over his horse's head. Clearly, he was in a thoughtful mood.

"It's too lovely a day to be broodin.'"

"How many letters have you written Maggie?"

"About a dozen." Ben laughed. "She being the only girl that has made me feel like I have only half a heart without her—"

"It's not easy, this thing your dad has laid upon my heart to say."

"Dad has had too many problems clogging his thoughts." Ben recalled the conversation at the dinner table the night before, about seeing Maggie.

"When your dad thought you were dead, it took ten years off his life." Big Jim frowned. "He wants me to follow you wherever you go. He is fearful those bounty hunters will find you and haul you off to jail."

"You'd think you're in Ireland the way Dad talks. Here in America, you are innocent until proven guilty, and Dr. Keenly from Ohio assures me I have not a thing to be frettin' over."

"Dr. Keenly has been good for you. And all this outdoor work has put the color back in your cheeks and the spring in your step. Still, that doesn't take away the fact that Maggie hasn't answered your letters. What are you going to do at this fancy ball without a girl on your arm to twirl? Prop up the wall with ya good looks?"

"She'll be there."

Big Jim crossed his arms. He'd gained a ton of weight, all muscle from the work on his farm. Together, they attracted the ladies proper when they rode into town every Saturday for their cup of ale. One mug was all they'd allow themselves. They learned well watching the miners dwindle their livelihood away at the coal mining company store and tavern.

"You're hiding something. I can see it in your eyes." Big Jim was sure to pry it out of him. He was as stubborn as a mule and as ornery as a donkey when he got his mind set on something.

"Dr. Keenly introduced me to Mrs. Louise, hostess of the manor we will have our ball at. And Mrs. Louise knows the Gatlans. They're kin to her and assure me Maggie will be there."

"That so?" Big Jim did a jig. "My, my, we surely have acquired the

Irish luck and a wee bit of a leprechaun's knack in acquiring wealth. We came here with barely a shilling between us and now look at us—land owners. You taking the arms of the landlords as equals like the ones we once served in Ireland. This is indeed a good land, this America."

"'Tis not the luck of the Irish, nor a leprechaun's shenanigans, but the blessings of our Savior, to be sure, I am praising. I read the other day that Lincoln might be nominated to be the Republican candidate for president. Did you complete your citizen papers that Dr. Keenly gave us from his lawyer?"

"Mine's still in the drawer. You might need to help me. Are you a legal citizen?"

"Proper I am and I'll be voting in my first presidential election. And I'll be voting for this man Abraham Lincoln."

"Five states have threatened to secede from the Union if he gets elected." Big Jim moved closer and whispered. "Did you tell your dad?"

"No and I do not wish you be telling him." Ben swiped his hat off his woolly hair. "Well, I must be getting back to my work. I want to get this field plowed and seeded before the ball."

"Have you got a suit?"

"Dr. Keenly has set me up to be a proper gentlemen, to be sure. He even taught me the social graces so I'd not embarrass myself with Maggie and has provided me with a fine seamstress to fulfill my desires for a special gift for my beloved."

Maggie awakened refreshed from her day's travel to Aunt Louise's. She rose from the featherbed and tiptoed toward the wide veranda that overlooked the spacious lawns and elegant buildings of her aunt and uncle's thousand-acre estate west of Lexington, Kentucky.

Nothing seemed the same at Spirit Wind without Mother. Father was but a ghost of his former self. If not for the loyal Will, there would be no one to rely on, no one to talk to. She was fearful of coming to Kentucky, fearful something would happen to her father, what with his moods turning so violent of late. Then there was Reynolds. The sheriff had combed the woods for him, but he had vanished.

There was a soft knock on the door. "Yes?"

The door opened slightly and a maid poked her head in. "Miss Maggie, will you be joining the family for breakfast?"

Maggie considered declining. The household had been asleep when she, Eli, and Hattie arrived. Hattie pushed past the maid, carrying a box into the room. Her new print dress fluttered behind her flying feet. "Yes, she is coming, soon as she's properly dressed. What time is breakfast?"

"Well …" the maid drawled. "Master likes to have his eggs benedict by nine. But Mistress Louise says he shall have his breakfast when Miss Maggie comes down and that put a stop to Master's comment right off."

"Miss Maggie will get dressed right quick."

The maid pulled at the door, then hesitated, shoving her curly black head through the crack. A large grin displayed even white teeth and eyes as big as saucers. "I declare, I don't think there's much preparation you need to do. What I see is Miss Maggie's already beautiful. You're just improvin' on perfection."

Hattie turned in a huff and rushed forward. "You mind your folks and I'll mind mine. I declare, I got a whole lot more to show you about Miss Maggie's attributes. Waits and see when I get done with her." Hattie pushed the maid out, closed the door with a soft thud, and leaned on it.

"That child has a lot to learn about etiquette." Hattie's sharp eyes assessed Maggie. "You look a whole lot better than last night. I swear, the bags beneath your eyes could have carried your pendant."

Maggie looked down, fumbling with the lace cuffs of her wrapper. Her father and Will said they would come; still the maid had not mentioned their arrival. How would she explain Father's absence? "I miss Mother. She'd know how to handle my father."

"You can't hide from life just 'cause your mammy gone. Now look here," Hattie's tone gentled. "I've got just the thing to perk you up proper."

She undid the lid and held up a rose-pink satin gown edged with garlands of deep scarlet rose buds, black velvet ribbons, and foamy with cascading lace.

"It's beautiful, but where did you get it?" Maggie touched the satin that glimmered in the morning light like dew on a rose petal.

"A gentleman sent it to you."

Maggie stretched the folds apart. "Why, there has to be at least fourteen yards of fabric here."

"Go try it on."

Maggie bit her lip. Should she? "I don't know who sent it."

"It won't hurt none to see if it fits." Hattie held out the dress, inviting her.

It was so lovely and Hattie had a point. What would it hurt? "Okay, but keep your eyes on the clock. I do not wish to be late for breakfast."

"I'll get your corset. Hope the length is right. I'd hate to try and hem this before the ball tomorrow."

"Oh, it just has to be."

Maggie hated corsets and wore them only when the occasion called for it, and she always found a reason why it didn't. But this occasion was different. Roses were her favorite flower and she loved the lace. It wasn't gaudy, but finely woven and tinged with onyx.

Someone had gone to extra special care to make this gown. "Oh, Hattie, what if it doesn't fit?"

The last stay tied, Maggie stepped into her hoops and then the petticoats. She raised her arms. Hattie let the dress down slowly. It circled her arms in wistful folds. The puffy sleeves hugged her shoulders; the neck dipped just before her bodice. She touched the soft rose buds that circled the yoke and traveled up toward her shoulders.

"These buttons are made of pearls. I never saw the like." Hattie stepped from behind her, fluffing up the skirt. "Now let me get those slippers. I knows I saw them. Where they go?" Hattie fumbled in the box. "There they is." Running toward her mistress, she carefully placed them on Maggie's feet.

Another knock on the door.

"Oh, Hattie, are we late?"

"I told that troublesome maid we'd be there whcn we gets there." Hattie rushed toward the door, her finger out, her mouth ajar like a can of jam. "Look... Mrs. Louise... please come in, Miss Maggie was just trying on a gown from one of her admirers."

Maggie rolled her eyes. Admirers? She hadn't one. She turned, ready to greet her aunt whom she hadn't see for years.

Louise's hoop skirt hardly made it through the doorway. She paused, her slender hands going to either side of her powdered cheeks. "My, I can hardly believe my eyes. My little Maggie is all grown up. Oh, and so lovely. Your waist looks as tiny as a child's; my how lovely you will look tomorrow night."

"She has a perfect twenty-inch waist." Hattie smiled knowingly. "Bet it be the smallest in this state as it is in Tennessee."

"Why, I suspect it is." Louise chuckled. "And I suspect that Maggie will be the loveliest lady at the ball. My goodness, I am feeling so very old."

Maggie rushed to her side, the satin floating about her like a misplaced cloud, and gave her a kiss on her cheek. "I am still the girl that always adored my lovely aunt. And you are as beautiful as you always have been."

Louise held her close. "I am afraid to relinquish you for fear you might vanish. I tried to stay up, but Blake insisted I get to bed, what with a houseful of overnight guests arriving. And I must admit I was tired and so glad to feel my pillow beneath my tired head." Louise kissed her smartly on her cheek. "Has my wayward brother come with you?"

"He said he had some pressing business…" Maggie lied. Her father had left for Virginia without a word. She had shown him the invitation. He had looked at it and left the invitation on the table.

Maggie stroked the rosebuds and satin, trailing her fingers down the black velvet ribbon. "Should I wear this tomorrow evening? I don't know who it is from. Is it proper, Aunt Louise?"

"Well, let me see. Turn around. Good. Now curtsy. Now let's see you waltz around the room." Louise hummed a tune.

Every movement of Maggie's quick feet, every bow, sent the yards of satin floating about her as if it had a life of its own. Slightly winded, she stood before her aunt and waited. The robins and blue jays arguing over the food in the birdhouse outside her window broke the silence.

Louise looked up at her with tears in her gentle brown eyes. "You remind me of your mother. She was slender of form and so graceful." Louise rose from her seat in a flutter of rustling taffeta and grasped Maggie's palms in hers. "She had a beauty from within that people noticed most… " Louise drew her close and kissed her on the cheek. "You have that same gift, Maggie. Don't ever lose it."

Maggie bowed her head. She felt undeserving of such praise. Oh, Lord, help me to be ever watchful of Thy love like my mother was. She rested a hand on the glimmering fabric of the gown. "But, how can I possibly wear this without knowing who sent it?"

"Let me see the card." Louise read the note. "Of course I cannot be certain, but I believe your secret admirer is your father. Yes, it would be just like my brother to do something like this."

"Really?" Maggie rushed forward and examined the writing. "Or… it could be Will McGuire?" It was obvious to everyone at Spirit Wind that Will was determined to make her his bride before the year was over.

"What's the matter, child?" Louise asked.

Should she confide the awful truth to Aunt Louise? Maggie wished it was her father's. This gift would mean he had forgiven her. Then maybe he would surprise her and be here tomorrow.

For the first time since her mother's death, Maggie felt bathed in God's love. "He brought me to the banqueting house, and his banner over me was love." Recalling Song of Solomon 2:4, she glanced at her aunt; God was comforting her through Aunt Louise.

"Yes, yes, come in, so good to see you." Louise McCullen smoothed a strand of her chestnut hair smiling at every one who stepped from the tiled coach entrance. Her tall slender profile etched a gracious shadow beneath the pavilion. Her husband, Blake, loomed like a protective elm tree next to his wife's right side and Maggie was on Aunt Louise's left.

The butler, Tom, helped each guest to the well-worn steps that had served many fair young damsels dressed in flowing yards of billowing evening gowns. Tom smiled politely at every guest, his black tux with long pointed tails admirably displaying the wealth of the McCullens. The mansion had been in the McCullen family since 1813. The twenty-bedroom estate allowed their out-of-town guests to stay overnight in preparation for the gala ball.

Maggie surveyed the brightly lit entranceway of the grand hallway. The long, impressive stairway swerved gently upward to display the second level and above it, a dome of stained glass windows that Aunt Louise's husband, and architect, designed.

A moment's pause between coaches and Aunt Louise glanced over Maggie's figure. "How lovely you look tonight."

Maggie curtsied, praying her aunt would not notice her tear-stained cheeks. If she had, she graciously chose not to comment.

"Maggie, this bright blue becomes your sparkling eyes. Royal blue always brought out the highlights of your mother's hair, too, though yours is not jet black." Louise tilted her head to one side as if examining a painting.

Maggie looked away, tapping her pocket. She'd received a letter from Will that he would be here tomorrow for the dinner and dance. He had ended it by writing "Your Adoring William, P.S. Mr. Gatlan will not be accompanying me. He has business in Springfield."

"Blake, will you greet our guests and direct them to their rooms, please? I want to show Maggie the garden before it's too dark."

Blake's twinkling hazel eyes met Maggie's. He bowed. "Maggie, the bloom of youth is in your countenance. And I can see by the heightened color of your cheeks that you are in need of more compliments this evening to affirm this." He reached for her hand and kissed it. "You are a breath of fresh air to my Louise. She feels twenty years younger just being with you."

Aunt Louise led Maggie down the steps. "You are shorter in height than Marie, but you resemble your mother so closely that I feel I am talking to her when I speak to you. Marie was a beautiful, stately lady who will always remain alive in my memory."

Louise cupped Maggie's arm in hers, their hooped dresses folding into one another companionably. The sweet-smelling lilacs and honeysuckle graced her senses, mingling with the freshly mowed grass and the apple and plum blossoms.

"Your mother tamed your father, you know." Louise laughed, soft and sweet; it had its own melody and complemented the birds singing in the trees. A hummingbird flew by them and landed on a rose bud just a few feet ahead. Maggie felt as if they had become a part of nature, strolling with God's creation.

"People thought it was the other way around, that your father taught Marie and tamed her of her Indian ways. Not so. Marie was already a lady when your father met her. As you know, her father was Irish, a lovely man, gentle of spirit and a man of great wealth in Ireland. When your father met Marie, it was love at first sight. But Marie's father didn't approve of Gatlan, said he was too head strong."

"Really?" Maggie glanced at her aunt's face, as if to confirm what she said was true. "All Father ever told me was that he was from one of the best families in Virginia and naturally, I thought he was—"

"He was, but my brother would not conform. He listened to a different drumbeat that most Virginians found offensive. At least our father thought so. That is why my brother struck out on his own to claim his fortune in the wilderness of Tennessee. Why, I don't even think he ever used his first name after he left home. Wilber. He never liked it, so he didn't use it. Always went by his surname. That's your father, and my younger brother, the black sheep of the family."

"And only my Mother could tame that restless spirit within him, especially when he got into one of his foul moods." What chance had she? Father refused to speak more than a sentence or two to her. At Spirit Wind, he wouldn't even look at her.

Louise bent down to stroke a tiny rose bud. "Sometimes I much prefer the rose bud. You can imagine how beautiful it will be. Then when it blossoms, it only remains in its splendor for, oh my, much too short a time. So I like the rose bud, it lasts longer and you can imagine the best longer."

Louise searched her face. "Wilber was sixteen when the War of 1812 began and he ran off to enlist, against my father's wishes. The only good thing that came out of my brother's reckless temper was that he brought my future husband and love of my life, Blake, home with him." Aunt Louise hugged her arm and chuckled. "I believe my older sisters and brothers might have spoiled Wilber. What else could have made him the way he was? Always demanding his way, always dead set on having his way."

Maggie couldn't believe her ears. "Then Mother truly changed Father." She couldn't remember a day that her father wasn't smiling and happy as long as Mother was close. How he always rushed in looking for her when he had returned from Virginia or Illinois. "Oh, Aunt Louise, Father has lost his better half. He said so when he was kneeling in a pool of Mother's blood. Cook thinks that the devil has gotten hold of his spirit. What am I to do?"

"Pray. Your father is a good man. As Jesus would say, your father has strayed from the flock. But being a black sheep lost in this field of goats of the Southern secession, it is not a good thing."

Maggie bit her lip. Should she tell Aunt Louise the rest of her nightmare? That her father blamed her for her mother's death? That her father would only speak to her in front of their slaves?

Her aunt grew quiet. Maggie's face must resemble a quagmire of emotion. Why else had Aunt Louise chosen to take her aside when she had a house full of people to welcome? Guilt and shame washed over her like the tide. "We should go in. I am keeping you from your guests."

"Your father found his reason for living when he met your mother. She was just fourteen and he sixteen. Now that she is gone, Blake and I were afraid he would react this way. But Blake has confidence in your father. Your father saved Blake's life during the war; you should ask him about that someday. Blake says your mother's influence helped Wilbur find that narrow foot path to Jesus' grace. There was a favorite verse Marie always recited when he got into one of his moods. Do you happen to know it?"

Maggie searched her memory. "Mother had many verses she recited." Then she recalled what her mother had said the day she died. "Something about forgiving? She told my father not to hate. That it would destroy his chances to love… true love endures." Maggie buried her face in her hands. "Father retorted that he never wanted to love again. Not without her…"

Horse harnesses and carriage wheels grating across gravel filled the wordless silence. Aunt Louise rested her gentle hand on Maggie's trembling shoulder. "We have just a few more moments together."

She took hold of Maggie's hands, her kind eyes smiling into hers. "Don't be sad, Maggie. Your dear mother would want you to remain hopeful. Hope in the Lord. Remember, hope is faith reaching out in the darkness—grabbing His nail-pierced hand. Jesus will reach back, inspiring us through the storms of life, through the rejections of our loved ones—in spite of our heartaches, believe in God. Jesus will shed His redemptive love upon us. Remember, my darling, the night is always blackest just before the sunrise."

Maggie blinked back her tears. Oh, how she wanted to believe. Jesus help me to hope. But she had let so many people down. "You don't understand, Aunt Louise, I feel somehow cursed. Everyone I love dies."

"Child, what are you saying?"

Aunt Louise's face blurred before her tear-filled eyes. "Before my mother's death, I was instrumental in another's death. An Irishman who sacrificed his life to take three slaves to freedom, Ben McConnell. I shall—"

"Wait, what is his name?"

"Ben McConnell."

"Unless there is someone using his name, he is far from dead. He shall be at the ball tomorrow."

# Chapter 20

*B*en paused before climbing the steps, gulping down a deep breath, then skipped up the cement incline and grabbed onto Blake McCullen's extended hand.

"I'm Mr. Ben McConnell. How do you do, sir."

Blake grabbed hold of his arm and gave it a shake. "You feel too solid to be a ghost."

"Me, a ghost?" Ben gave him a belly laugh, thinking him in a joking mood. "You'll know for sure I am flesh and blood when you see me at your table gobblin' vittles, sir."

Blake drew him inside. "There's a girl in here you need to persuade."

"What?"

Blake guided him into a room where bookcases lined the walls. A large circular table with sketches layering its shiny wood finish stood in the center of the oval room. His sharp eyes searched Ben's face. "My niece, Maggie Gatlan. She thinks you're dead. Know anything about that?"

"You mean she did not receive my letters?" Ben hit his forehead with the palm of his hand. "Saints preserve us. Where is she?"

"She hasn't come down yet. Fix your eyes on the stairway. And watch your words, or you might be missing a few teeth." Blake looked him up and down as if to measure what kind of man he was.

"Did she get my present? A gown I especially had made for her?"

"*You* sent it?"

Ben cupped his arms behind his back, pacing back and forth. "I do not understand. I told her to be expecting it. She did not get my letters?"

Blake crossed his arms. "Wilbur."

Ben cocked his head. "What did ya say?"

"Wilbur Gatlan. I am afraid he might have confiscated them. How much do you know about the tragedy that has befallen the Gatlans."

"Tragedy? Is Maggie all right?" Ben eyed the spiral staircase that wove like a celestial harp up to the second floor and then to the third. He had half a mind to climb up there and knock on every bedroom door until he found Maggie. He took a step forward.

"Hold up." Blake motioned for his wife. "Louise, we need your expertise in handling a delicate situation involving your niece. I'll hold down the fort and greet our guests." Blake glanced at him and then to his wife. "Louise, Ben McConnell has arrived."

Louise looked at Ben slightly bewildered. "Maggie is of the understanding that you are dead."

After an agonizing pause, she said, "A divine intervention to my niece's heartache. But we must handle this with care." Louise grabbed hold of his arm. "Right this way, Mr. McConnell. I'll fill you in on Maggie's nightmare."

Mrs. McCullen ushered Ben into the study. A roaring fire snapped and crackled in the hearth, illuminating the walnut scrolled walls that gleamed with candlelight sconces every five feet.

"Someday I'll have me a desk like this." He walked over to the large mahogany desk scrolled with bear and claw legs, rubbing his hands along the smooth rich grain, and then walked behind it. Moving the tails of his coat to either side, he sat down in the big wing-tipped leather chair. "Fine indeed." It fit his height exactly. "This is just the way I want my chair, when I build my house."

"Your house?"

Ben looked up, startled. "Maggie, my darling." He rose and hurried toward her.

She crossed her arms, as if to block his entrance into her life.

"What is wrong? Have you not been getting my letters?"

She stood there draped in the rose creation he had designed for her, draped in his dream and looking better than his dream could even make her. So beautiful, so… cold—as ice she was. This was not the way he had envisioned their meeting.

"I see you like the dress. It is a vision of loveliness on you. I could never have imagined how lovely…. But you want no part of me? I've been praying for this moment ever since I woke from my stupor. Maggie, forgive me for whatever sin I may have committed to ye."

"You, you don't know how I longed…" She turned away from him.

"I should have come to ya; I should have. But my dad, he was needing me. He was the one that found me at the bottom of the cliff, half dead.

Her beautiful Irish-brown eyes with a hint of a tear beseeched him. The Christmas ball, the dance, the Glenn. One conscionable act had led to this consequence. With a tear in her eye and a prayer on her lips, she bid him safe passage. Had she forgotten that night? That memory had kept him alive. Would this be the end of it now?

"Reynolds shot me and left me for dead." With every word, he stepped closer. With every look she cast his way, hope coursed through his veins like water dropping into his parched heart. There was still a wee bit there for him. A bit of a flame, and that was all he needed.

"Maggie, my bonny lass… In that dress, you look like the princess I see in my dreams. I thank you kindly for wearin' it."

"You sent this?" Her pearl-white arms traveled the length of satin. "However could you have afforded this?" Her eyes shone glassy bright in the firelight.

His heart beat irrationally in his chest, like it wanted to escape into hers. "Oh, I've missed you." He took her into his arms. She melted into his strength. Someday the words he longed to hear on her lips would come.

Gently, he kissed her soft draping curls pouring like a waterfall, they were, on her bare kissable shoulders. She turned her face away. Her profile etched in the glow of firelight, he would not forget, not in a million years—no matter if destiny should separate them this night.

Maggie's tears glistened like dew drops on pink cheeks and wet her red lips. Ben gently wiped each tear away with his thumb. Her pain-filled eyes questioned his. "What happened that night?"

Ben put a finger to her lips. "What matters is that we are together. I would have come for you, if I had known about your dear mother. I want always to be there for you."

"There is nothing you could have done. Reynolds is still on the loose, and I fear that Father might be trying to find him."

Ben led her to a settee near the fire, sitting her down; he sat next to her, taking her gloved hands, feeling the warmth of them. "'Tis a man's right to mourn for his wife and to seek out her killer."

"Father blames me for Mother's death."

Her soul cried to his and he prayed for the right words to say. "He only puts the blame on your shoulders because he cannot face the fact that it is his. He hired Reynolds, and then was blinded by that man's deceit. Your father will come to this truth. You'll see. He's too much of a man not to be seein' the truth and admittin' it. Just give him a wee bit more time." Ben turned her, cupping her face. "'Tis not our job to question the almighty hand of God. He determines when we shall leave this earth for the life that awaits us beyond the sunrise."

"Father must have kept your letters from me." She rested her head on his chest.

"'Tis a father's privilege; I hold no malice toward him, but forgive him." He reveled in their closeness, her soft head near his. "Who am I to be courtin' a princess? A ragged Irishman without a shilling to his name is all I am. 'Tis the good Lord who saw fit to give me more." He kissed her hair, drinking in the silkiness and inhaling the scent of roses.

"I know the likes of your father, proud and fiercely protective. He will come around with our prayers. You'll see."

A soft knock on the door and Aunt Louise entered. She stood in the light of the hallway, her slender profile and hooped skirts filling the archway like the fairy queen in the books his mother read to him when he was a child.

"Maggie, I am praising God for his mercy that your Ben is alive. Now come, eat and enjoy the festivities."

Ben offered Maggie his arm. This moment felt more like a fairy tale than reality. He needed some encouragement to believe he wasn't dreaming. "Indeed, I have a wager with Mr. McCullen that I can eat him under the table."

Maggie lifted her face toward the chandeliers twinkling with candlelight above them. The polished wood floors and tall banisters gleamed with the deep richness of fine mahogany. Chippendale chairs with Queen Anne cabriole legs adorned the room's tall arched walls. At one end of the room a large stone hearth blazed a cheery fire. A settee with ball-and-claw feet nestled within a nearby alcove, spreading an invitation of a semi-private interlude to the couples. At the opposite side of the room, the members of the band busily tuned their instruments.

As if mesmerized, Ben and she walked toward the tall french windows, the curtains blowing in the promising summer breezes. Dogwood blossoms lay glistening and white before the setting sun. Crab trees burst with riotous pink blooms and the grass rolled like a carpet of aqua blue on the fervent hills.

"As far as the eye can see," muttered Ben, giving her hand a squeeze and nodding toward the double french doors that displayed a tantalizing peek of the wide covered veranda just a few steps away. "Let's go outside while the musicians are tuning their instruments."

"But I promised Will the first dance."

Will had ridden hard to get here and had arrived shortly after supper. He'd been so kind, so hardworking, she had agreed out of duty. She felt she should be with him now.

"'Tis a little more time I am asking."

Surely she could spare few moments more alone with Ben. They had so much to catch up on. "All right, but I must hurry back to the ballroom." They slipped onto the veranda that overlooked the spacious lawns.

"The last rays of the setting sunlight are as bright as my mother's eyes." Ben chuckled, clearly pleased with the day's accomplishments.

If not for his mountain of curly hair, she would not have recognized him. He'd filled out well. He'd allow his sideburns to grow down the side of his face, drawing attention to his solid broad chin. He appeared taller than she remembered, definitely more muscular than six months previous, most likely due to working his land. His broad muscular shoulders, bulky in his tuxedo that tapered down to a small waist, made him look as if he'd been born into nobility, not the peasantry of his heritage. His profile displayed a broad forehead, high cheekbones and square jaw, an uncompromising face. Many young women at the ball tonight turned his way when he walked by.

Golden beams of sunlight glowed across the darkening horizon illuminating the trees in a dozen pastels. The smoke from the hickory logs of the barbecue pits that had brought them their tantalizing meals earlier of roasted pork and mutton, floated on the breeze. The noise behind them of clapping hands and her uncle's strong voice rising like an eagle's cry reminded them that they were not alone.

Uncle Blake stepped up on the small stage where the band sat. "Any time you're ready, Jake."

Jake smiled, set down his glass of punch, and walked to the center of the stage where a table waited with his violin. He picked it up, cradling it like a father would his child, his gifted fingers guiding the bow skillfully. The musicians hurried to his side. Jake's voice rose just loud enough above the magical notes of his violin. "Gather your ladies fair. The ball is about to begin."

Fifty pairs of men and women swayed and dipped to the eloquent tempo of the music.

"Oh, there's Will," Maggie said.

Will had seen her in the same instant. The room had gotten so crowded it took him a few minutes to make it to her side. She moistened her lips, recalling the strained conversation after dinner, Ben on one side of her and Will on the other. It was a blessing to have at least the meal without the two battling their brawn about like two stallions. She turned, flipping open her fan, cooling her flustered face.

"Ben, I promised Will I'd dance the first dance with him. I, I just don't know what we'd do at Spirit Wind without him."

"I see." Ben chuckled. "What does a ghost expect, coming back so suddenly? I'll busy myself with one of the other ladies, if you don't mind."

Will eyed Ben for a moment, then popped out his chest like a champion Thoroughbred, sweeping his glance to Maggie.

Ben watched Will maneuver gracefully around the dance floor with Maggie, her quick agile feet keeping in perfect step to Will's. That's a good thing for her. She'll need quick foot work to not get trampled on with my big feet. So, he had been replaced by this Will. Did he suppose that a beautiful woman like Maggie wouldn't attract another stud?

"Ladies and gentlemen, get yourselves ready for a good old-fashioned reel."

A reel? That just might be more like what he was used to back in Ireland. A few of the ladies eyed him with interest. He rubbed his hands together and stepped forward.

Before long beads of perspiration broke out on the most carefully powdered foreheads. Soon all doors leading to the gardens were flung open, and still the dancers begged for more. Ben found his rhythm and twirled a lass around who had a waist as tiny as a water glass and skirts that billowed around his legs like a sail on a clipper ship. The lass proved to be a cheerful counterpart to his governing feet, and they laughed at each other as they flew about the room.

Then Will danced by with Maggie pivoting gracefully, her pink gown swaying to Will's careful guidance and her eyes adoringly staring into his. Ben felt a twang of jealousy. Aw, 'twas fickleness at its best and me spending a month's wages on that dress only to have another man twirling her about the room. Well, 'tis high time he gave her a twirl, but how with that ape of a Will claiming her every dance?

The musicians took a break. He looked to see where Maggie was. Will was leading her to the punch table. Crooking his elbow, he gave his dance partner a wink. "Would you care for some refreshments?"

The lass opened her fan, covering her face, her long lashes batting like a butterfly caught in a storm. "Something in your eye, lass?"

"Oh." She tapped the cuff of his coat. "I just adore your accent. You are simply too charming." She hooked her arm in his and he led her to the punch bowl. Cozying up to him she halted him, reaching up on tiptoes. "My name is Amy." She tore up her dance card. "There. I want to dance with you all evening."

Just then he caught Maggie's eyes viewing the act. He laughed. "Amy is it? A beautiful name, to be sure."

Maggie pretended she hadn't noticed Amy's arm wrapped around Ben's. Amy noticed. She gave Ben's arm an extra hug, looked at Maggie, and smirked. She cringed at the tinkle of Amy's voice. Blonde hair, cornflower blue eyes that darted from one man to another like a honeybee looking for nectar, that was Amy Jackson. However, tonight Amy's eyes were fixed on Ben's. Her pale blue watered-silk ball dress with festoons and lace complemented her eyes and complexion. Where did she get that dress? From Paris?

Ben noticed her staring at Amy and him. She bit down on her bottom lip and looked away. Had her jeering thoughts shown up on her face? It was hard to tell what Ben was thinking. Oh, how embarrassing. When Ben's lips weren't creased upwards and his eyes not smiling, he was a different person. He loathed snobbery. She recalled that first day in the swamp. Swarthy, with his tossed curls and his eyes as bold and black as a—

"Ladies and gentlemen," Blake said, standing tall and lean. Aunt Louise stood next to him, adorned in a black satin with puffed sleeves and a princess lace collar, looking like a queen arrayed for her king. "Grab the ladies of your heart and prepare for a challenge of skill and endurance on the dance floor."

Ben took Maggie into his arms. Someone mouthed her name, she didn't know who. Ben's eyes mesmerized her. Grabbing her around the waist, he guided her into the array of dancers.

Hips and hoops layered with silks and dripping with laced petticoats, swayed to the music. Her heart pulsated to his strong moves. Dipping and swaying, they made their circle around the room to the tempo of the waltz. Step, turn, step, turn, like the rhythm of the waves, he drew her to his side.

The soft enchanting notes of the waltz mellowed away and the lovely "Sweet Evelina" began. "Way down in the meadow where the lily first blows, … She's as fair as a rose, like a lamb she is meek, …" She took a deep breath. When the minstral bands came through their town, she listened with a quickened heartbeat, singing along with the lyrics. "Dear Evelina, sweet Evelina, My love for thee shall never, never, die." The song reminded her of Father and Mother and the love they had shared. "My love for thee shall, never, never, die…" Father sang that to Mother. Her parents had been so happy together. Could she hope for such a love?

"Maggie," Ben whispered. "Are you enjoyin' yourself?"

"I… are you?"

His white teeth gleamed and he broke into a loud merry laugh, his bold eyes raking over her. He turned her into another pirouette, his eyes fixed on her face, a glint of amusement within their black depths as if he knew of her attraction for him. "If you would be preferrin' Will's company, it matters not to me."

"It doesn't?" She willed her arm not to tighten uncontrollably around his. She wanted to shake some sense into him. Didn't he know how her heart burned for him? She needed him more than a flower needed the sun to grow or the rain to quench its thirst. But he'd never know, not unless he whispered the words she longed to hear. No, I'll not be the first to declare my love. She raised her chin just as Jake's strings began the lovely "Lorena."

"The years creep slowly by, Lorena," Jake sang mournfully as they danced about the ballroom. "The snow is on the grass again, The sun's low down the sky, Lorena, The frost gleams where the flow'rs have been."

"I believe it matters to you," Ben muttered between clenched teeth. "I know it matters to me."

Couples left the dance floor. Men took out their handkerchiefs, ladies their fans, cooling their heated faces.

"Are you sure you are able to continue dancing?"

She wouldn't give him the satisfaction of quitting. Amy looked longingly at him. Maggie turned her head. Nor would she give Amy a chance with her Irishman again. "Lead on you... you, you, black pirate you."

His long legs ate up the dance floor, her face fanned by the breezes made in his wake. Her silk dress flew about their forms in a sunset of rose, white lace, and deep velvet-black ribbons. Only a few dancers were left, Lorena's enticing sonnet weaving about their forms. "A hundred months, 'twas flow'ry May, When up the hilly slope we climbed, To watch the dying of the day..." Was she destined for Lorena's fate?

Her billowing silk, ribbons, and lace dipped and swayed in perfect rhythm to the soft, sweet words. "We loved each other then, Lorena, More than we ever dared to tell..." She closed her eyes, bearing the truth of poor Lorena's fate. "And what we might have been..."

Ben bent her backwards, lowering his face to hers. She waited for his lips, hot and moist and exciting, to mingle with hers. He pulled her up, his dark eyes snapping with elation like a pirate who'd just run off with the prize. He broke into a loud, merry laugh. "I think you be preferrin' me over any other buck here. Why don't you admit it?"

"Oh!" She slapped his cheek and the noise echoed in the lapse between instruments and laughter. She lifted her skirts and ran through the open doors into the gardens.

The night winds felt cool on her perspiring face. The words of "Lorena" followed her fleeing skirts. "But then, 'tis past—the years are gone..." How embarrassing! Everyone had seen her display of affection for that worthless Irishman. She blended her voice with Jake's, singing, "I'll say to them, 'lost years, sleep on!'"

She strolled beneath the shadows of the maples. Glancing over her shoulder fearing Will, or worse, Ben, would come after her. She needed to be alone.

How could I have ever thought I cared for him? He deceived me into loving him. I never want to see him again.

A soft footstep, then another. It came from a nearby tree. "Who's there?"

Reynolds' pale face, his goatee looking silver by the moon's glow, appeared in front of her.

She turned to run. Something hit her from behind. She opened her mouth to scream. His dirty hand grabbed her like a vise, pinching her mouth closed, then he forced her to the ground. His knee pressed against the small of her back. He wrapped a cloth around her mouth, then pulled her to him and snarled. "At last." His words spit vile in her face. She turned. He forced her to look at him and pushed her toward his horse tied to nearby tree. "Get up there."

He got up behind her. Her hoop skirts rose like a misplaced bell on the neck of his large Thoroughbred. He reached over her and gathered the reins, nuzzling her curls at the same time. "I saw your father two days ago in Springfield. He was there clapping and cheering when Lincoln got the nomination for the Republican presidential candidate. He's on his way here. But I beat him to you." He sniffed her neck, groaned, and ran his hand underneath her petticoats. "You're so fetching tonight—"

She elbowed him hard in his stomach, pulled the rag from her mouth, and screamed.

"Why I ought to—"

"Whip me like you did my mother and then shoot me? I'll die before I allow you to lay your filthy hands on me." Maggie elbowed him again in the gut.

"Why, you—"

The horse neighed, prancing about and shaking his head against the tightened reins. She struggled to loosen herself from his grip. Someone jumped on Reynolds' back. The horse reared, and Maggie slipped down into a pile of dead leaves in a heap of silk and petticoats.

"Are you alright, Maggie?" Will said. "Anything broke?"

Maggie swiped her rump. "Just my pride."

"What should I do with him?" Ben hauled Reynolds up by the nape of his collar.

"I'll take him." Her father rode up on his big Thoroughbred.

"Father!"

He jumped off his horse and swept her into his embrace, kissing her on both cheeks. "I can't believe I lost track of that polecat."

"Father, he knew you were in Springfield. Said Lincoln—"

"Right, I was afraid Reynolds was planning on assassinating Lincoln. Well, Abe got the votes this time that could take him to the White House." Father pulled her away. "Let me get a look at you." He seemed to like what he was seeing because the rare smile Father reserved only for Mother spread across his face.

"Maggie, you're beautiful, and all grown up. You got your mother's looks... and her spunk." He crushed her to his large chest. "Daughter, I'm sorry for the way I acted toward you."

She melted into his shoulder and wept. Father had come back, just like Aunt Louise said he would. "Father, what's going to happen to us in the south if Lincoln gets elected?"

Father buried his head into her curls, whispering, "The inevitable, Maggie. War."

# Chapter 21

*M*aggie set her Paris original gently down on her hair and stared back at the image in the mirror. "What do you think, Hattie?"

Hattie, laying the last of Maggie's toiletries in the trunk, walked over. "I think you need to tip it off your forehead so people can see your eyes."

"Daughter, are you ready?" Her father, tall and stately in his black coat, cravat, and tan breeches, was pulling on his gloves. "The carriage is here and we need to get on our way or else we might miss our train ride to Illinois."

She glanced at her wool shawl, then over at her lamb coat. "Should I take the lamb instead of the shawl? What is February like in Washington D.C.?"

"Cold. Take them both; Illinois is a tad colder than Tennessee. February and March are bone-chilly and cold in Washington, D.C. That hat is becoming, but you'll need your wool hat and mittens, too."

"I've packed them, Master Gatlan," Hattie said.

At the bottom of the stairway, Lawyer Peabody, Matron Burns, Will, and Doctor Jordon waited.

In a rush of words, Matron Burns said what Maggie was thinking. "Don't you worry. I'm sure speaking to President Lincoln will help the Southern cause."

Doctor Jordon shoved his spectacles up the bridge of his long nose, and nodded. "Just because South Carolina, Mississippi, Florida, and Alabama have seceded from the Union, doesn't mean that Tennessee has to."

"I wish that was all of them," said Lawyer Peabody, his mouth puckered in a frown. "Georgia, Louisiana, and Texas have seceded, too."

Voices outside greeted their ears, then a rock was hurled at the window. It fell short. A bunch of southern crackers, some on mules, yelled, "You Lincoln lovers, get out!"

"What's got their feathers in a ruffle?" Matron Burns stared out the window. "Why, that's John's boy. I bet between the five of them they may own one or two slaves a piece."

Will drew out his gun and fired in the air. "Get out! Before someone gets hurt."

"You men, disperse," Sheriff Pundy hollered as rode up with his posse. "We're not at war and there's no need to start one here. Mr. Gatlan is trying to prevent a war and—"

"That's just it. We don't want him to prevent one; we want war! Those Yankees aren't going to tell us whether to have slaves or not. Us Tennesseans want to go with our kind, the Southern cause!" The men whistled "Dixie." Others began to chant, "We want secession. We want secession."

Father stepped forward. "Gentlemen, please."

Josh, the lead cracker, lowered his pistol, his face red with shame. "We don't have anything against you, Mr. Gatlan. You have always bought our goods and treated us fair. But we're southerners through and through and can't let our kin down."

"Humpf!" Matron Burns placed her plump hands onto her ample hips. "If the South marched into the sea, would you follow them?"

"You don't think I know that?" Father walked forward and laid a hand on Josh's horse, giving it a pat. "I'll fight with you, if need be. But I know you, like me, don't want to secede from these United States we fought for in 1812. We know the bloody mess war is. You sure you want that, Josh?"

Josh looked down, unable to meet Father's eyes. His mouth worked the chewing tobacco around his teeth; he turned and spat. "I know what you're sayin' is true enough. But a man's got to do what he's got to do for his kin."

The men started their chant again. "Secession, secession—"

"Stop!" Sheriff Pundy rode his horse into the middle of them.

"Disperse this minute, before I have to lock up the group of you." The men turned and took off galloping toward the mountains.

The servants loaded Maggie's and her father's trunks into the carriage. Maggie hugged Little Irene, kissing her on her pudgy cheek, then shook Will Jr.'s outstretched hand, pulled him toward her, and kissed him on his cheek. His little eyes looked up at her, so innocent … like Irene's. Oh, Irene, I'm glad you're not here to see this. Cracker against slave owner, neighbor against neighbor, and the war hasn't even begun yet.

"Will, are you sure you can handle everything while we're gone?" her father asked.

"Don't worry about a thing."

That was like telling the wind not to blow. Maggie looked up at her father, noticing the deep creases around his eyes and the dark circles beneath them. Lawyer Peabody stepped forward.

"I'll get a postponement on Reynolds' trial. Just concentrate on getting an appointment with President-Elect Lincoln. Or better yet, use those twenty days before Lincoln's inauguration to become his friend."

Will stepped closer to Maggie and whispered, "Tell your father to be watchful; there may be an attempt on Lincoln's life." He reached for Little Irene, his eyes searching Maggie's. She looked away. Will had asked Father for her hand in marriage. He'd consented. Only, she couldn't give Will the answer he desired. He bent close, sweeping his lips across her cheek. His voice deep with emotion, he whispered, "You be careful."

She shivered, feeling the cold wind blowing across the mountains. What would it be like in Illinois and Washington? What would be the welcome from the Yankees or would they be facing hateful stares and venomous gossip? There was no way to hide her southern roots, nor would she want to.

"Here, allow me to help you, Mr. Lincoln." Maggie folded the clothes Mr. Lincoln had decided in the last minute to take to Washington. It was clear his thoughts were not on clothes or household items needing to be shipped from his Illinois home to Washington, D.C. His wife, Mary, had gone on a shopping trip to St. Louis. She would join them in Indiana.

"Thank you, Maggie," Lincoln said. "Gatlan, you have a very caring daughter." He rested his big frame down on one of the chairs hand crafted for his tallness. Rain pattered on the windowpane. Maggie walked over and looked down at the growing crowd waiting to see Mr. Lincoln off.

"Mr. Lincoln, you will need an extra sweater and your scarf and coat. It is a cold, damp day outside and you need not acquire a chill. Father says trains are always cold. We are planning to follow and meet you in Washington."

One of the soldiers General Winfield Scott had ordered to accompany Lincoln hurried into the room. "Are the president's trunks ready?"

Lincoln's valet checked the contents and closed the lid.

Lincoln rose and went to the soldier in charge. "I would like Gatlan and his daughter to accompany me in my private train car. Please collect their trunks and belongings."

Maggie followed Lincoln downstairs and out the front door where a crowd had gathered. The rain pounded on the porch roof and echoed in Maggie's ears along with President Lincoln's words.

Lincoln's deep chest rose and fell rapidly. Was it because of the rain? Or was it because of his deep emotions for his neighbors and staunch supporters? His long arms spread out wide as if to circle them all with a farewell embrace.

"Here I have lived a quarter of a century, and have passed from a young man to an old man. Here my children have been born, and one is buried. I now leave, not knowing when, or whether ever, I may return, with a task before me greater than that which rested upon Washington. Without the assistance of that Divine Being… I cannot succeed. With that assistance I cannot fail… To His care commending you, as I hope in your prayers you will commend me, I bid you an affectionate farewell."

The grey smoke of the locomotive swirled about Maggie's skirts as the soldiers hurried them to the awaiting car. She rested back on the plush red upholstered seats of the two-car train. The noise of the whistle, the slight swaying of the cabin, and the vibration of the rumbling wheels greeting steel reverberated through her body. She wasn't as worried about her and Father's destination as she was President Lincoln. He had said he didn't know if he would be able to return to his beloved Springfield.

Evidently, General Scott was worried about Lincoln, too. He had provided four soldiers to escort Lincoln safely to Washington. Her father, careful not to tax President Lincoln with his southern agenda too soon, looked from her to the president, began to speak, then hesitated. Did Father want her to say something first?

She did not envy her father. The hooded vigilantes, the crackers demanding to fight along with their southern neighbors, how would Father explain to a northerner the problems dear to every southerner's heart?

A waiter came through the cabin door carrying a tray laden with cups of hot coffee, cream, and sugar. "Would you care for refreshments?"

She nodded. Setting down the tray, the man began to serve her, then her father, then suddenly his hand went into his coat and pulled out a pistol.

The soldier snapped into action, grabbing the man's arm. The soldier wrestled to grab the pistol. The gun went off, blowing gunpowder across the small compartment. Smoke filled the compartment like fog on the mountainside. The man lay on the floor. The soldier heaving and winded, glanced at the president. "Sorry, Mr. President, to disturb your refreshments. I'll get more as soon as I remove the body."

Another soldier rushed in. By the looks of the brass on his shoulders, perhaps a captain? Papers rolled up like a telescope in his big fist, he plopped his bulk down in the nearest seat. "President Lincoln, we have just interceded a plot to assassinate you while escorting you into the White House. We have devised a plan, and if it meets your approval, sir, we will proceed accordingly."

He handed the papers to Lincoln, who quickly read them. Then he handed them to her father. "They want me to enter from the back, dressed as a servant. It is appropriate. After all, I am only a humble servant of God... and the people of these United States."

# Chapter 22

The crowds congregating on the White House lawns tossed Ben to and fro.

"This is going to a momentous occasion, Big Jim. One you will want to tell your grandchildren about."

"Indeed. We helped elect this fine gentleman. Abe Lincoln got his start in a log house in Kentucky. 'Tis a fine upstanding beginning, we being Kentuckians, too."

A burly red-faced man shoved Jacob, their slave, nearly knocking him to the ground. Ben grabbed Jacob and steered him behind him.

"I think you need to take your bad temper to the tavern. This is not a place to be disruptive," Ben said to the man.

"Keep your nose out of my business, or it could get bloodied."

Big Jim chuckled. "Would not be the first time. But I can wager you'll come off the worst."

"And I'm feelin' in the need to use my fists… cooped up like I've been on the train," Ben said.

A line of soldiers marched out and stood along the front of the platform, pushing the crowd aside. The soldiers' bayonets rose above the heads of the people. The man slinked away.

A tall man dressed all in black from head to toe, sporting a distinguished black beard and a large top hat, made his way onto the platform and took a seat.

"President Lincoln," someone said. "Hush. Or we'll miss his speech."

Ben searched the group of people that had followed President Lincoln out onto the wood platform.

A stately woman with a waist small enough to wrap his hand around sat down. She wore a little blue hat with a white satin ribbon that flapped in the wind. Though she be slopping through swampy waters or standing like a queen on the platform with the next president of the United States, he'd recognize that elegant class anywhere. 'Twas his Maggie.

The crowd cheered and clapped as President Lincoln rose and walked toward the lectern. "In compliance with a custom as old as the government itself, I appear before you."

"Isn't that Maggie and her father sitting like statues to the right of President Lincoln?" Big Jim asked.

"That it be and not a more beautiful looking lass than any to be seen here. But I'm thinkin' she might be sittin' a little too close to Lincoln."

"When are you going to get it in your head she's not for you?"

Ben looked away. Truly she could do better than he. And her father had more than told him so the night of the McCullen's ball. "But the Lord has made me a new man, a man of conscience and consequence…"

"Sh… listen to the president," the woman next to him whispered.

Lincoln's lanky build loomed over the lectern, his deep voice vibrated with emotion. "I have no purpose, directly or indirectly, to interfere with the institution of slavery in the States where it exists. I believe I have no lawful right to do so, and I have no inclination to do so."

"There goes my freedom," muttered Jacob. He hit his hat with his fist.

"What are you fretting over? You're free to leave," Ben whispered.

"Yeah, you eat more than the two of us," Big Jim said.

Ben smiled down at Jacob, understanding how he felt. "Get on with ya. I give you your freedom from being by my side. But it will be another type of slavery that will soon be hounding your heels—"

"Yes, be gone with ya," Big Jim chimed in.

"Fine." Jacob's bottom lip puckered out. "I accept my freedom, and 'cause I like where I am, I'll be staying." He placed his hat on his head and crossed his arms. "Besides, you two need caring for."

"You're missing the best part of the president's speech," a woman behind them hissed.

Lincoln leaned over, his large hands grabbing the wooden lectern, his face scanning the crowd. "But if destruction of the Union, by one, or by a part only, of the States, be lawfully possible, the Union is less perfect than before the Constitution, having lost the vital element of perpetuity." Lincoln paused, taking a deep breath, then hurled forward like a sprinter on a death defying run. "It follows from these views that no State, upon its own mere motion, can lawfully get out of the Union."

A sound like hornets rose stronger and stronger, blocking out Lincoln's next words. Angry fists shot up toward the sky.

Lincoln's strong, resolute voice rose above the murmurs. "That there are persons in one section, or another who seek to destroy the Union at all events, and are glad of any pretext to do it, I will neither affirm nor deny; but if there be such, I need address no word to them. To those, however, who really love the Union, may I not speak?"

"Hush, let him speak." A woman in a brown hat put her hands out as if to hold back the tide of angry voices.

"Yeah, over here, Mr. President," one southern man yelled. As he pushed his coat back, Ben was on him like a fly on honey, grabbing the man's derringer. Another man appeared, poking a gun in the would-be assassin's ribs. Ben winked and handed him the assassin's gun. A plain-clothed man suddenly did the same to another man, pocketed the pistol, then ordered him out of the crowd at gun point. The President, unaware of the turmoil, continued. Ben strained his ears to hear, but his eyes were on Maggie. She had scooted to the edge of her chair, her white-gloved hands clasped together, unaware of the danger she was in sitting so close to Lincoln.

"Come on, Big Jim, we need to get closer."

Big Jim didn't hesitate. Jacob followed. They inched their way forward.

The president's voice raised an octave higher. His feelings edged the words like a father talking to a disobedient child. A hush followed among the crowd shoulder to shoulder, leaning forward as not to miss a word.

'Why should there not be a patient confidence in the ultimate justice of the people? Is there any better, or equal hope, in the world? In our present differences, is either party without faith of being in the right? If the Almighty Ruler of nations, with his eternal truth and justice, be on your side of the North, or on yours of the South, that truth, and that justice, will surely prevail, by the judgment of this great tribunal, the American people."

"Now he's making some sense," a sturdy man said.

Ben was close enough to Maggie to jump on stage if needed. One of the soldier's stopped him. His eyes locked on Ben's.

"Best get your gun ready. The crowd is a bit argumentative," Ben whispered. The soldier nodded, returning his gaze to the crowd.

President Lincoln looked huge from where Ben stood. He crossed his arms and smiled into Maggie's startled eyes. Then he pointed to the president and to his ear.

"In your hands, my dissatisfied fellow countrymen, and not in mine, is the momentous issue of civil war." Lincoln lifted high his big palms. "The government will not assail you. You can have no conflict, without being yourselves the aggressors. You have no oath registered in Heaven to destroy the government, while I shall have the most solemn one to 'preserve, protect and defend it.'" Lincoln clutched his hands together, bowing his head.

Is he praying? Ben looked around at some of the bowed heads.

"I am loath to close." Lincoln's eyes glistened. "We are not enemies, but friends. We must not be enemies. Though passion may have strained, it must not break our bonds of affection. The mystic chords of memory, stretching from every battle-field, and patriot grave, to every living heart and hearthstone, all over this broad land, will yet swell the chorus of the Union, when again touched, as surely they will be, by the better angels of our nature."

# Chapter 23

The stagnate air of the small Maryville courtroom was laced with the heated tension of angry voices. Maggie's father had called a special meeting. Maggie wondered if the Secessionists had succeeded in swaying the citizens of Maryville to secede from the Union. Ben had ridden in early this morning with news that President Lincoln had issued a proclamation calling for militia after the attack on Fort Sumter on April 12. Father had countered Ben's news with his own that the East Tennesseans were to send delegates to Knoxville on May 30 with their vote.

Ben hadn't glanced her way, his thoughts too absorbed over the impending war. His curly head bent low over the map he and Father were looking at. However, Ben's cordial greeting earlier had told of his disinterest in her. Well, there was certainly enough to keep her mind occupied here.

Behind her, Matron Burns' shrill voice rose with excitement, retelling the attack on Fort Sumter.

"General Beauregard carried the Confederacy's new flag, a red and blue creation comprised of bars and stripes. It is really quite a striking thing and, well, Beauregard took the Union forces by surprise and bombarded Fort Sumter, nearly washing it into the Charleston Harbor."

The deep frown that creased her father's solemn face told her he had heard Matron Burns. Voices rose and fell like high tide, excited and exhilarated about the course of southern events.

"Did you hear?" Miss Peabody's fingers wrapped around her parasol in a death grip. "Richmond was made the new Capitol of the Confederacy and Robert E. Lee has just accepted command of Virginia's military and naval forces." She nodded and her hat, a flat little creation, fell across her forehead. She pushed it up, noticing Maggie.

"Dear, I am so sorry the jury did not convict Mr. Reynolds. I know it was he who flogged and killed your dear mother."

A cold draft of wind blew in. Miss Peabody glanced toward the gaping door "Oh, speak of the devil… There he is now."

"The coward." Matron Burns snorted. "He hid his personage behind a mask, and he dares to strut in here pretending to be a gentleman, rubbing elbows with decent folk."

Reynolds' bold steps came closer. Would he have the audacity to park himself next to her? Reverend Brown stepped in front of Reynolds and bowed, his kind eyes consoling; Reynolds turned away. The Reverend smiled at her. "May I sit down?"

"Please."

The meeting room was packed to capacity, riding boots beating the wood floorboards, resonating excitement. Every chair had been taken and men lined the walls like colored wallpaper, mumbling about the war and what legion they planned to join.

The gavel struck the desk and the murmurs ceased. Her father's voice bellowed over them. "The Confederacy has asked Jefferson Davis to be their president and hopes that Davis will accept the appointment."

A cheer followed.

Her father banged his gavel on the desk again. "Ordinance of Secession for the United States of America, a yes vote in favor of seceding from the Union—"

"Yeah, we'll whip those Yanks in a month!"

"We could lick them with one hand tied behind our backs!"

"Why, look how easy it was at Fort Sumter. It'll be thatta way throughout this here war. Besides, those Yanks' hearts ain't in it like ours. They'll let us go."

Her father cleared his throat. "A no vote will be to remain in these United States of America." Her father laid down his paper. "Now, before you vote, hear me out. I've known most of you all my life. Some of you are too young to remember the War of 1812. I was like you young men, and I've learned a lot through the years. I've been up north. I've seen the factories, the immigrants; Mr. McConnell can attest to them. Ben come up here."

Ben approached the front of the courtroom with confidence. His tall riding boots, tan breeches, and black coat complete with cravat, made him look like the country gentleman he had become. The crowd hushed.

"Don't let my fine duds fool you. I came off the *Dunbrody* without a shilling to my name, weighin' but a hundred pounds and my shoes having holes in the bottom of them big enough for a jack rabbit to burrow in. There's thousands like me, too, in the north, lookin' for any money they can get their hands on to feed their families instead of watchin' them starve. They'll jump for the chance of fightin' against ya, though the thought of the slaves being free is not to their fancy."

He glanced about the packed room, his head held high, his back as straight as the large oak tree standing outside the courthouse. "No, we want you to be keeping your slaves. Irishmen often are hired to do the work your slaves are too good to be doin'. Now you ask me what's my part in this here war now that I've made my fortune and become a proper gentleman."

A mumble went up like a rumble of thunder.

"It be because of me pride. Pride in my new country, it is. I had to leave my Ireland because you see… freedom is rare in Ireland. Here, you have your land and your freedom, and you have your beautiful homes. You'll be outnumbered, and your little factories and textiles will be lookin' poorly alongside the likes of the large factories in the north. Give President Lincoln a chance and you'll win not only your lives, but your dignity." Ben stepped down.

"Mayor Gatlan, may I speak?" Reverend Brown said.

"Yes, please do."

The Reverend motioned for Ben to take his seat.

Maggie closed her eyes feeling a tingle running up and down her spine. Ben kept his hands in his lap and his eyes looking straight ahead. *He thinks I don't care a shilling for him. What should I do?* If she didn't speak to him now, she'd surely loose him.

"Men, what Mayor Gatlan and Ben McConnell have said is true. The fighting will be near your homes, your families. I reiterate what President Lincoln has said repeatedly. It is found in Mark 3:25 and if I may, I would also like to read verses 26 and 27."

"Go ahead, Reverend," her father said.

"'And if a house is divided against itself, that house cannot stand. And if Satan rise up against himself, and be divided, he cannot stand, but hath an end. No one can enter into a strong man's house, and spoil his goods, except he will first bind the strong man; and then he will spoil his house.'

"The United States is strong when united, but without the South, America will be half a house, and ready for plunder to outside nations. Think about that for the sake of our children and grandchildren."

"Hand me one of those papers." Matron Burns stood up and held out her arm.

"You can't vote; you're a woman," someone in the back yelled.

"I'd like to see someone stop me. This war is going to affect all of us. Now hand me that paper."

Her father stood. The crowd silenced as his voice boomed out. "Matron Burns has put a question before us tonight. Are we to allow the women here a chance to vote on the fate of Tennessee? All in favor say yea."

"Yea!"

"All opposed say nay."

For the first time the room was silent.

"The vote carries. Hand out the papers, Clerk Jordon."

Dr. Jordon smiled as he handed one to Matron Burns and then to Maggie. "It's about time we asked our ladies' opinions."

Nothing had gone well for Ben with Maggie. He'd hoped she would ask him to the house or at least squeeze his hand. He'd given her a chance to.

He led Caedmon out of Spirit Wind's warm stable, giving him a hasty pat on his glossy white neck. "I do not understand the lass, nor do I understand her father." He laid the saddle on his horse's dappled back, his thoughts on Maggie. She'd plenty of time to tell him her feelings. He strapped his breech-loading gun onto his saddle and mounted, pulling his hat down across his forehead. "Well, there's plenty of lasses beggin' for my services." Caedmon nickered, as if in agreement.

He started down the tree-lined lane, the moon glistening through the budding apple and cherry trees. The birth of spring after a brutal winter always made a farmer's heart glad, only this spring of 1861 was different. Only twenty-four percent voted in Blount County to secede. But when the carrier brought news of the other votes, Mayor Gatlan said it was no use. Reynolds reiterated this, stating that East Tennessee would soon be surrounded by the Confederacy and forced into submission. "'Tis confusing, this democracy, to be sure." Ben reined up Caedmon. "But, I'll not leave with my tail between my legs like a whipped dog. I'll give Maggie a piece of my mind she'll not forget."

He spun Caedmon around and galloped back toward Spirit Wind. The night breezes had a hint of apple blossoms in them, but he could not enjoy their pleasures. The day's worries brushed his face with death's fingertips. Men would meet their Maker sooner than needed, and he was powerless to halt that consequence.

He reined up Caedmon under Maggie's bedroom window. The house was dark, and the hounds had welcomed him, having enjoyed the tidbits of his supper he'd brought. He surveyed his options. The rose lattice might be the tool he needed to climb to her window. He dropped Caedmon's reins, then stood on his saddle and put his boot into one lattice rectangular, testing the strength of it. It cracked beneath his weight. Instantly, he grabbed the limb of the large elm, swung his leg up, and surveyed the chances of him climbing the tree and jumping into her partially open window. Giving a shove, he was soon climbing into the massive limbs. He pushed open the window pane with his foot and jumped.

The breezes swept the shears in gentle strokes. He crept to a featherbed with a canopy made of lace. Maggie lay there, her long silk-like curls strewn on her pillow in wild abandonment. Ben's fingers ached to stroke one. She always kept it tamed within her net and hats.

This was his Maggie. Her full red lips slightly parted and her thick sooty lashes lay like hummingbird wings across her ruddy-pink cheeks.

He knelt, aching to crush this beautiful goddess of his dreams into his embrace. Who knew if he'd ever get the chance again? He bent over her and a wisp of roses, honeysuckle, and cinnamon wafted past his nose. His lips hovered over hers, and gently he lowered them to her cheek.

"Ah!" Her torrential punches, boxed his ears like his wee mother. It was all he could do not to fall on the floor and whimper like a pup. He put a restraining hand across her arms, then covered her mouth with his other.

"I did not mean to alarm ya, Maggie, merely to say farewell."

"You, you, pirate." she hissed. "What do you mean coming like this to my bedroom at midnight?"

"'Twas just a good-bye kiss I was seekin'."

Her eyes widened.

"Will be the last I'll be sharing with ya. I am on my way to New York to join the Irish Brigade."

Maggie rose to a sitting position. Her beautiful brown hair glimmered with golden highlights in the moonlight and cascaded over her white, lace-edged nightgown.

"But why must you go? The war has just started and you're not even an—"

"American? I beg your pardon, lass, but I am." He stood up. She'd gotten his dander up, to be sure, with that remark.

"Oh, you stubborn Irishman, turn around. Wait, hand me my wrapper. …Now turn around."

Ben did as he was told, careful not to alert Maggie as to the moonlight that made plain her image in the mirror. She possessed a body that could make any man weak with want.

"Alright, I'm decent now."

Decent? She was covered from head to toe with linen, silk, and lace. But for the light of the moon, he would not have seen the brief image of her he'd carry to the battlefield. He smiled. She hadn't ordered him out of her bedroom, nor had she yelled for help. She must care a little for him.

"Now what about this Irish Brigade? And for which side are you fighting?" Her sweet mouth was drawn up in a worried frown.

It was hard, he knew, for her to understand, just as it had been for his dad. "The Union side. I cannot fight to divide this country that has become my home."

Her lips pouted as he took her hands in his, her long silky fingers as graceful as a dove's wing. He kissed them. Her gleaming teardrops spilling their way down her rosy cheeks surprised him. He coaxed her toward him. She didn't need a second invitation but folded into his arms as if she had always been a part of them. They stood there gazing out into the moonlight, the soft melody of the wind playing with her hair and the whispering trees swaying their budding leaves to the promptings of the invisible caresses of the wind.

"Where in New York is this Irish Brigade?"

"Staten Island. Would you be knowing the name Thomas Meagher?"

Her eyes appeared larger in the soft light. She's so beautiful. He bent his head lower, hovering over her mouth. No, steady yourself, man. "He was born in Ireland, and very active in the Young Ireland movement. That's how many of us got to know him. He says this Irish Brigade will show the Americans we're not afraid to fight. We even have our regiment's flag, emerald, sportin' a gold shamrock." His mouth came closer to hers. She wasn't backing away, but tilted her face up.

"And… so," she whispered, slightly out of breath. "Ah… that is why—"

"Maggie." His eyes could not get enough of her loveliness. "Whatever I've done, consider this my apology." His lips touched hers, caressing her like the wind on the leaves, then grew in intensity. She wrapped her arms around his neck, drawing him to her. He swept her into his arms and glanced at the bed, its sheets inviting. He paused, smiled into her innocence, her head nuzzling his neck, and carried her to the window seat. The breezes stirred her wrapper and gown, lace and satin swirling about his arms and legs, as her hair tickled his nose. Silence cloaked their forms, fused as one, in a cocoon of blissful youth, love's sweet moments too few.

"'Tis not that I don't understand your southern cause. It reminds me of our fight to free ourselves from the British. And most of our Irish comrades are not in favor of giving the slaves their freedom. Jobs are hard to come by as it is. But the Union has promised us bonuses, extra rations, and subsidies for our families."

Maggie laid her hand on his chest. "Father might have accepted you if you fought on the Confederate side." Her eyes pleaded.

"My dad is fighting with Michael Corcoran. He has started the 69th Regiment Irish Brigade and fighting with the Confederates. Dad says Lincoln plans to free the slaves. Says he needs his slaves and don't need to be fighting after the war against them for jobs. He's threatened to disown me if I go Union. But a man has to do what he has to."

"My Ben, always the rebel." Maggie traced a finger from his forehead down to his lips. He kissed her finger. "Ah… you're my wild Irish rose, to be sure, Maggie my darlin'. I'll be off before I change my mind and sweep you on my horse and take you with me to this bonny war."

"War!" Maggie got up, laying her hand on her hips. "Why do men find war so exciting? Fighting, fighting, and more fighting. Do you get pleasure in having your face knocked in? Feeling a bullet whizzing past your ears?"

Ben smiled into her stormy face that only a moment ago was as tranquil as any lake in June. She reached up and ran her fingers through his hair. "Do you know how many times I've tried not to feel anything for you?"

He laughed. She quickly covered his mouth with her hand and listened. "You best be careful before you awaken Father and Will. Neither of whom will mind shooting you now that you have joined the Union."

Ben picked her up and whirled her about the room. "It's not them I care to kiss, my bonny lass." With that he bent low, lifted her clear off the shiny wood floor and kissed her smartly. He released her and headed for the window, blowing her a kiss before descending into the branches of the elm and then jumping onto his horse.

"Ben!"

He reined up Caedmon sharply and he reared in protest, the horse's strong legs raking the night with his hooves. Maggie's hair streamed behind her; her gown and wrapper floated like angel wings in the night breezes.

"When will I see you again?"

"When you least expect me."

Caedmon's hooves pounded in his ears as his heart skipped a beat— would he see his love again?

# Chapter 24

*A* Christmas had come and gone as the war grabbed up every man who could walk and straddle a horse. Because of their knowledge of fighting during the Indian uprising, Father and Uncle Blake were immediately commandeered into officer ranks. The war had demanded their fathers, brothers, and sweethearts. Had caused a tightening of waists and pocketbooks and an influx of fundraisers. There was one tonight at the meetinghouse in Maryville.

Standing on a stool while Hattie finished up the hem of her ball gown, Maggie fluffed the puffy sleeves done in red velvet. The gentle folds of ivory satin finished off the rest of the dress. A red satin ribbon at her shoulder angled to her corseted waist and flowed to the lace edging her ball gown. All from remnants of mother's old dresses.

She glanced out the french windows, hoping to see her father and his dappled gray stallion turning onto the lane to the house. The Battle of Fredericksburg on December 13 had sent Maryville exclaiming praises of their valiant men in gray who had won a stupendous victory over the Union armies.

The Ladies Society scheduled a fundraiser for December 15 months ago. The Fredericksburg victory encouraged heightened celebration as did the valiant solders returning home for a welcomed reprieve. Would Father be one of them? She'd not seen him since April of 1861. Only an occasional letter telling of his recent battle told her he was still alive. Now December of 1862, surely Father would be home for Christmas.

She heard the pitter-patter of shoes on the stairway and Aunt Louise entered the room slightly out of breath. "Oh, Maggie, you look beautiful! I can hardly wait to see you dancing off into the moonlight with that handsome Will. Oh, I do hope we make a sizeable amount for the Cause. Our brave men deserve our support."

The hound dogs barked, Old Reb baying a welcome to his master. "It's Father and Will—"

"And my Blake!"

The two women hurried down the winding staircase of Spirit Wind. The door burst open allowing the chilly December breezes to sweep across the room, then Father swept her into his arms.

She buried her head in his gray coat, which smelled of smoke, gunpowder, dried leaves, and tobacco, and wept for joy.

"Oh, Blake, Blake!" Aunt Louise ran with arms stretched wide and was instantly swept up into Blake's strong embrace, their bodies forming one as they kissed.

Dear Father, how he must miss Mother at a time like this. "I missed you!" She kissed him on the cheek, then poked at his coat. "Father, your coat is stiff… and wet. Frozen in spots?"

His face, a pasty shade of gray, was set with deep concaves. His only color was his twinkling blue eyes embedded in black circles, like a sparkling sapphire in charcoal.

"I suspect these twenty months sleeping on the cold ground hasn't helped your rheumatism. When are you going to admit you are too old to be fighting a young man's war?"

"Ah, daughter, what man wouldn't be proud to do so? I feel twenty years younger." His beard, more a dirty white than gray, swept his chest; his body was lean and his skin brown like a walnut and leathery as an old buck's. He rolled back his head and allowed his laughter to roar like a waterfall in his deep chest.

Will Jr. and Little Irene came clambering down the stairway, their screams drowning out any further conversation. Little Irene ran up to Maggie's father, jumping up and down, screaming, "Santa Claus came early!" She looked curiously up at him. "What happened to your red suit and belly! Did the war take them, too?"

Will laughed, gathering her into his strong embrace. "No, daughter, it's Papa Gatlan." Picking her up in one arm and his son in the other, the two children's little arms encircled his neck as they kissed him on his reddened cheek. It was clear that living in the outdoors agreed with Will. His ash-colored hair swept the back of his lieutenant's uniform and met his sloping sideburns. His beard was shorter than her father's, of a reddish-yellow color, which complemented the gold braiding sweeping his broad shoulders and the gold sash about his slender waist.

His sapphire-blue eyes swept her form with a covering glance. "My, you're a vision, Maggie. I believe you've grown prettier, though how that is possible, I can't believe. You're already heads above any southern women I've ever met, except Irene. ...Well, don't I get a kiss for that compliment?"

Maggie laughed. "If I can find room between your children." Will handed Little Irene to Ida and Will Jr. to Hattie. He stepped closer, his arms open and inviting.

Ben's dark face flashed before her mind's eye. She felt the touch of his lips burning hers as though it were yesterday. Her feet felt glued to the floor. "Aren't you glad to see me?" Will's face turned scarlet red.

"Of course, she is. Why she has prayed nonstop for you, Will," said Aunt Louise.

Maggie stepped forward and kissed Will on the cheek, her heart pounding like a war drum at Aunt Louise's remark. "It is true, Will. Little Irene, Will Jr., Miss Peabody, and I have prayed for Father's and your safe return daily." She sent a silent prayer heavenward that hers and Hattie's efforts at making over Miss Peabody would work its charms into Will's heart.

"Miss Peabody?" Will's eyebrows furrowed.

"She is a great admirer of yours."

Her father laughed. "Evidently your prayers were heard, daughter. Say, what's all the going on at the courthouse?"

"Oh, Maryville is having a fundraiser for the Southern Cause. But we won't go, you must be tired and—"

"Nonsense, that's just what we need to renew our spirits." Her father looked from Will to her uncle. "Tell Cook to start warming up the water, looks like we'll need a soaking to get off a year and a half of dirt. And get my clothes cleaned up, daughter."

Will chuckled. "It's about time we kicked up our heels instead of fighting."

Maggie and Aunt Louise entered the carriage in a flurry of hoops and petticoats and made themselves comfortable between Father, Will, and Blake. Father was in a cheerful mood and fingered his beard often as though it had given him his appointment as major general.

"Blake, tell the ladies how you managed to get through that squabble in Fredericksburg?" Her father bellowed like he was talking to a division of soldiers. Eyeing her aunt, Maggie tugged at his arm and motioned for him to be careful.

"Squabble?" Aunt Louise grabbed her husband's arm, hugging it to her chest as if fearing Blake might be a dream. "Why the papers said that over 5,000 Confederates lost their lives. I was praying you weren't one of them."

"Darling." Blake kissed her on the top of her draping long curls. "Gatlan likes to make sport of it because the North lost 12,000. Of course, I didn't see any newspaper men out on the battlefield counting the dead, either."

"You should have seen them. The Union army put this Irish regiment up first, playing their drums and waving this flag the color of grass. They were like sitting ducks." Will pantomimed holding a rifle in his hand. "Pow, pow, pow, then we got the cannons loaded and—"

"That will be enough of that, Will," her father said. "Didn't Ben McConnell join that regiment, Maggie?"

She kept her face as impersonal as she could. "Yes."

"I never saw such bravery." Blake leaned back on the carriage seat and sighed. "You could hear their voices drifting across the hill side, singing 'The Color of the Green.' You know what they call their leader?" He looked around at their faces. "Fighting Dick, right, Gatlan?"

"Yeah. And heard tell Fighting Dick's regiment is called 'the rowdy fighters of the Irish Brigade.'" Her father chuckled. "Fighting Dick didn't give them that title; the Confederates did. Remember what happened at Shiloh?"

"Oh, right, yeah." Blake leaned forward, his eyes bright and shining. "Grant was their commander then. I heard they came storming over the bunkers. They might have won, but Grant decided to retreat. We've got us the best commander in Lee. He proved that in Fredericksburg. The North is whimpering now, licking their wounds like a whipped dog."

"Isn't there a Confederate Irish Brigade in Tennessee?" Maggie asked.

"How do you know that, daughter? Have you been keeping up with the reporters following the armies?"

"No," Aunt Louise said. "We keep our ears open to all the gossip."

"Well, they have a Georgia regiment, too. Colonel Patrick Moore commands the 10th Tennessee Irish Regiment." Her father looked down at his hands. "These Irish have adopted this land with their whole heart. The Union army puts them up front to take the first onslaught of bullets. It's hard to watch at times. They fight father against son, just like a lot of our families do."

Blake rubbed his chin. "I couldn't believe that one Irishman. I think it must have been his son. ..."

"What?" Maggie was instantly alert. Ben said his father had joined the Confederacy.

"The fighting had just commenced and we were waiting our orders. There the Irish Brigade cavalry was, right out in front, the bugle sounding charge and... they were being knocked down like turkeys at a shooting match. A tall captain bringing up Fighting Dick's rear got hit... then this old Irish Reb from Colonel Moore's regiment galloped forward and knocked this other Reb off his horse before he could shoot again, and sped across the field to help the Irish blue coat."

Will's eyes gleamed into hers. "I don't see how either one could have lived through that battle." He punched his fist into his open hand. "What a waste of brave men. Well, the war can't last much longer. These Yanks know we're serious. They'll soon be scooting it back up north."

Every potted plant in town had been commissioned for the dance, turning the drab brown building into a garden of color and grace. Hydrangea, oleanders, and elephant ears had made the trip over snow dusted roads and icy temperatures.

All types of instruments from bull fiddles to accordions, banjos and knuck-bones were available. Combined with an assortment of musicians ranging from the very young to the very old, the oldest being Old George who just turned ninety. The men's voices raised in argument as to which songs to play first. Old George, due to his age and experience, won and picked a waltz.

Maggie, her father, Louise and Blake, Matron Burns, and Miss Peabody had purposely arrived early. Maggie set out the punch and glasses, arranged the cookies and refreshments, and surveyed the booths. Eli lit the candle wall sconces and her father and Blake lit the huge chandelier in the center of the room.

Days before, gracious settees and Queen Anne upholstered chairs had been brought and set in groups for the elderly ladies and gentlemen to watch the festivities of the evening in comfort.

The neighs of horses and the tinkling of bells on the harness and breastplates, coupled with the sound of carriage wheels, told Maggie the guests were arriving.

Like the roar of the great wind, the hall burst into life. Ladies, whose robin red and apple-green water silk hoop skirts gave the impression of floating in air, laughed and coquetted, their arms hugging a recovering soldier home for recuperation. The soldiers wore soft gray, with gold braids on their cuffs and collars. Red, yellow, or blue stripes on the trousers displayed the different branches of the service.

"My, too bad I have only two sides." Will winked at Miss Peabody, who was arrayed in lavender. Her golden hair crowned her kind face and aqua blue eyes. "Save the next dance for me, Miss Peabody." His gold sash swung in tempo to his quick steps. He offered Maggie his arm.

Maggie and Will joined the couples waltzing around the room.

Glimmering lace petticoats peeped shyly from beneath the ladies' rustling dresses as lace flounces gently caressed ivory bosoms and shoulders. Swans down feather fans dangled from their gloved wrists.

Will hadn't taken his eyes off of her. She glanced at Miss Peabody.

Yes, Miss Peabody noticed. She was a welcomed visitor to Spirit Wind, babysitting Will's children every chance she got between working at the hospital darning socks and gloves for the soldiers. Maggie made a note to tell Will.

Will looked dashing in his uniform. The shiny buttons captured the candlelight and the chandelier cast a glow on his blond hair, making him appear like a golden Caesar. His sweeping sideburns met his beard, which wrapped around his chin like a wooly scarf. His saber clanged with every stride of his long legs as if to remind his dancing partner that she was dancing with a gallant soldier armed to defend her honor.

"Will you keep your beard?"

"I will through winter. It helps to keep one's face from freezing, sleeping out in the elements like we do. Do you like me better with or without it?"

Will was handsome; there was no getting around it. And if he decided to shave his face or even his sideburns, he'd still be handsome what with his large blue eyes framed with the longest lashes she'd ever seen on a man. "Whatever way you want to wear it is fine with me."

The music stopped and the couples dispersed to the punch bowl, a few ladies opening their fans. She had forgotten hers.

"You are the most beautiful lady here, Maggie, so no use trying to compare yourself with the others, because, to me, there is no comparison."

Maggie dabbed her handkerchief across her forehead. No wonder she was feeling warm, with Will burning a hole through her face. How could she tell him she could never consider him as a beau? To her, he would always be Irene's husband.

Her father was suddenly by her side. "Will, Lincoln plans to sign a law freeing our Confederate slaves."

"He can't do that. Besides, we're winning this war, with less men and less equipment than the Union."

"Daughter, did you know about this?"

As if she or anyone could have stopped it. However, she could halt one catastrophe in its tracks. She needed to keep her father in good humor, at least through the evening's festivities. The Ladies Society had gone to too much trouble for this ball, and she didn't need Father getting the men up in arms.

Father gulped his whisky down. "To think I trusted that man."

"Father, I don't think you should blame President Lincoln. Congress has been busy enacting laws against the South since the war began. President Lincoln has called for both South and North to pray."

"Daughter." His eyes glared down at her like two steel swords. "He is not a gentleman of his word."

"But… didn't we give our word? And didn't we start this war by firing on Fort Sumter?"

"Might as well accept the fact," Lawyer Peabody said. "If we don't win, forget about having the South we had before the war."

"I think that you might be exaggerating the urgency. We shall still be Americans." Maggie hardly recognized the reserved Peabody in his Confederate gray. His hair appeared darker and his black beard poked out like a teacher's pointer in front of his chin. Could what Peabody say be true?

Peabody rolled back on his shiny boot heels. His eyes, as alert as a sentry, gleamed into hers. He appeared to enjoy her spirited comebacks. "Yes, we shall, but Lincoln has already signed a preliminary Emancipation Proclamation. It is only a matter of time when all slaves will be given their freedom under that proclamation, and," he leaned closer, "given the vote."

She frowned. "Women don't have that privilege."

"How can that be, most of them can't read or write," Will said.

"Which means our slaves will be voting the way their Union emancipators wish them to. We live in changing times and the South needs to quit holding onto the middle ages and change, too." Peabody turned to Maggie. "You and your mother had the right idea. We also need to give women the vote. Southern women have a lot to offer the South."

Her father looked down at his empty glass, twirling it in his hand. "We need to get France and Britain to join our side. How is that coming along?"

"What? With the Union blockading our ports?"

"Looks like the blockade runners are getting across." Maggie nodded toward the bright finery and the scarlet and gold tassels of the men who milled around the room.

"Right, but they couldn't get our ambassador through, and I don't know that France or Britain is going to join unless we can assure them a victory."

The scents of sachet and hair pomade and burning cranberry and evergreen candles floated past her nose. The hubbub of voices and occasional laughter mingling with the banjo and strings of Old George's fiddle was only a backdrop to the entertainment, and the money freely flowed. Knoxville's hospital should make a famous amount tonight.

"Well, the war should soon be over. Not even the arrogant Union can stand to lose all that many soldiers." Peabody bowed. "Miss Maggie, may I have this dance?"

Miss Peabody was instantly by Will's side, batting her silky lashes at him. Her lavender silk, with the wide insets of white lace, set off to perfection the golden highlights in her hair.

The laughter rose and the room vibrated with the firm steps of the soldiers and the dainty ones of the ladies. The pulsating spirit of the Confederacy echoed the chant that the war would soon be over. Stonewall Jackson's victories in the Shenandoah Valley and the defeat of the Yankees at Manassas on the creek called Bull Run clearly showed the bravery and excellence of their gallant men in gray. The South had the best leaders in Lee and Jackson. Neither McClellan nor Grant could hold a candle to them.

Old George struck out the first notes of "Bonnie Blue Flag" and the room echoed with the sweet sopranos of the ladies and the deep basses of the gentlemen. But it was those arrayed in their gallant gray uniforms, like a solid, immovable wall that drew the admiring glances of the ladies and onlookers. Why there wasn't a dry eye amongst them, so handsome, so reckless, so determined.

The bugler climbed up onto the platform with the musicians and standing at attention, the soldiers lifted their voices and sang. "Hurrah! Hurrah! For the Southern Rights, hurrah! Hurrah! For the Bonnie Blue

Flag that bears a single star."

It was a beautiful flag. But, oh, how Maggie's heart ached for the Stars and Stripes. She wished the South didn't need to secede. The Confederacy was so determined to erase any semblance to their northern neighbors that they had changed their currency and bonds. Only gold remained as it always was.

As Maggie scanned the crowd, she spotted Reynolds. He shoved his way toward her, his eyes staring, not relinquishing his hold on her. She shuddered. Even murderers were accepted into the South's social elite, if they would carry a gun for the cause. Lawyer Peabody glanced at her and promptly steered Reynolds toward the punch bowl.

"Hurrah! Hurrah! For the Bonnie Blue Flag that bears a single star …"

Ben loved the South, but didn't want a divided nation. Her heart was split between loving her southern neighbors and the United States. Between believing in the cause and believing in Christ. Conscience and consequence as Ben often said. With tears in her eyes, Maggie prayed. Lord, help southerners and northerners find a common ground, a common love between race and creed, and a unity of brotherly love that will forever unite this land of ours.

"Don't worry, Maggie." Will patted her shoulder comfortingly. "I swear, we'll lick those Yankees. You just watch us."

He didn't understand. Ben would. How she needed Ben, needed his common sense more than ever now. Was he lying in some forlorn ditch somewhere, his handsome face buried in the mud and blood of a tattered cornfield turned battle ground?

# Chapter 25

Ben hung onto Caedmon's reins, his legs feeling like pudding. Caedmon neighed, pulling Ben along as if he understood the urgency. Ben blinked, trying to see the shadows and deep ditches. He'd lost a day from the blow to his head that had knocked him out proper. Another day had gone by before he'd made it back to the battleground to find his dad. The date was December 15, and like a patchwork quilt, gray and blue coats blanketed the Fredericksburg's cornfield. The spiraling mountains loomed on one side of him and a forest on his other. Where could his dad be?

"When are you planning to stop?" Big Jim had been shot clean threw his shoulder.

"Soon. How's your arm?" Ben stepped gingerly around the corpses strewn across the cornfield. "Then we'll be having our supper."

"You said that two hours ago." Big Jim bent down. "Ben, we cannot find your dad."

Ben looked up. Jacob was picking his way through the battlefield. Burial squads were dragging the dead men and dumping them like so many logs in endless rows of shallow ditches. He'd never find his dad if he was piled there.

"Ben!" Big Jim slid off his saddle. Taking Ben by the shoulder with his good arm, he gave him a hearty shake. "Your dad's in heaven. He don't care where his bones lie. He's in his celestial home."

"I care." Ben stuck a thumb to his chest. "I want him buried on his land like a true Irishman. But you're right. I've forgotten to do my praying. What can a man accomplish without it, and it being so close to our Savior's birth? Bow your head. I'll be making my peace."

Ben waved his arm to get Jacob's attention, but Jacob was a black speck amidst the shadowy bodies lying about the darkened field. Slate-gray clouds danced before the moon in ghostly shapes.

"Lord." Ben fell to the ground, the dew wetting his pants, or was it blood? "Lord, look humbly upon your servant tonight and grant me my wish to find my dad so I can give him a proper burial on his land. And, Lord, send these brave souls home to be with Ye and heal our land. Amen."

Jacob yelled, waving his arm.

"Do you suppose he's found him?"

Big Jim smiled. "Well, didn't you pray? Come on, looks like we just might make it home for Christmas after all."

To what kind of home, Ben didn't know. Tangled underbrush bogged down his feet. He stepped higher and led Caedmon and Big Jim through a maze. In the thick wood, the bodies lay two deep. Jacob pointed to a half concealed emerald green flag. Ben knelt. Dad, is that you?

He turned the corpse over. The eyes stared up at him like two shiny green marbles, the flag clutched in his fists. Ben could not remember anything of the battle, how he knew his dad was here, or that he was dead. The surgeon said his memory would come back in time. He had to pry his dad's fingers open to remove the emerald flag. His dad's body and face were caked with dry blood; bullets had entered his skull and leg.

Ben's tears wet his dirty cheeks and sooty-black beard. He didn't care. He'd say his eulogy here for his friends and the dead to hear:

"Dad… bigger than life he was. Even now, I remember when he sat me upon his knee, his sharp green eyes poking into my face, and he gathering up my wee fingers in his large ones… 'Son, I'll teach ya to hunt, live off the land, ride, and shoot. But I can't teach ya how to be a man. That you'll be learning on ya own. A man is bigger than what he does. Like the Bible that is bigger than any religion… you lean on God, and He'll be showin' ya how to be that kind of man.'" He turned his eyes upward. "Dad was that kind of man to the end."

Ben scrunched his hat, twisting it about in his shaking hands. "Jesus, take good care of my dad, he being a good man, but as You know, he had a bit of the blarney in him. I thank You for allowing me to find him. Now I'll be reciting John 5:24… 'He that heareth my word, and believeth on him that sent me, hath everlasting life, and shall not come into condemnation; but is passed from death unto life.'"

"That Jesus saying that?" Jacob asked.

Ben nodded. Jacob's eyes, larger than two silver dollars in the church offering, stared from him to his dad. His dad's face was so disfigured only his eyes, his solid hands, and the mark on his wrist confirmed his identity.

A man with a stretcher said, "You taking this one with you?"

"Yes. We'll be taking him home to bury him."

"Hmm… looks a little too old to be fighting in this young man's army."

Ben hoisted his dad up on his horse. Laying him on top of the saddle, he tied him down. Indeed, young at heart his dad was, and a good soldier right to the end.

"Dad's laughing at us from the doorway of his mansion, yeah, laughing and bragging to St. Michael that he died an old man fightin' a young man's war."

"How do I gets to a be Christian?" Jacob muttered.

Death clung to the vines, the trees, like rotten meat left out in the sun. Gun smoke hovered above their heads like goblins, mingling with the dew and blood-soaked ground. Ben swallowed down a deep breath. It was a fitting place.

"Bow your head, Jacob and repeat after me. 'God, due to my hard heart, killin' my fellow man, and the altogether sinfulness of my life, I don't deserve heaven; please forgive this sinner. You sent Your Son, Jesus Christ, to die and shed His blood for me… because you loved me. I ask Your forgiveness and I ask You to come into my heart, guide and direct me and give me strength to faithfully follow the road You have chosen for me to travel until You bring me home to be with You. Amen."

"Well, I don't feel no different after saying those words." Jacob said.

"Keep believing in Jesus." Ben tapped his chest. "You'll be feeling His Holy Spirit soon enough." He laid his hand on Jacob's shoulder. "Jacob, may the road rise up to meet you. May the wind be always at your back. May the sun shine warm upon your face; the rains fall soft upon your fields and until we meet again, may God hold you in the palm of His hand."

Jacob coughed. "Well, we needs ourselves another horse."

"Or you could be giving Ben yours, seeing how he bought him," Big Jim said quietly, "that being a Christian thing to do."

Ben held up his hand. "No, it's yours, Jacob. You and the horse have a bond, and I don't mind walking my dad home. You two go up ahead, I'll be there shortly."

The smell, the gaping mouths, and staring eyes were so atrocious it was hard for Ben to breathe and step around the corpses without feeling nauseous. "Yea, though I walk through the valley of the shadow of death, I will fear no evil; for thou art with me..."

Big Jim and Jacob, their bandana's swabbing their noses and mouths, reined their horses around the corpses and were soon out of site. Ben hunched his shoulders against the northern wind. It was well he was alone with his dad. Dad didn't smell too well to be having company.

They made camp in a little grove of trees near a clear running brook. It had been the first clear brook they had come to.

Big Jim had a small fire going when Ben walked up. He slid is dad down and laid him out downwind of them. Caedmon seemed to appreciate that. Ben looked around. "Where's Jacob?"

"He lit out as soon as I told him I'd make camp here."

The warm beans tasted good to Ben, as did the coffee. The ground never felt so soft. He rubbed his swollen leg and rested it on a rock. This had been the first meal of the day for them both. A noise to the left of them had both reaching for their rifles. Jacob rode up.

"Here!" His face was expressionless in the twilight. Jacob held out the reins to him. "It's the best I could do, but I don't think your dad would mind going home on this here mule."

"Thank you kindly."

Jacob squatted down in the dirt and helped himself to the coffee. He was a curious man. Stuck to himself mostly. What destiny awaited Jacob now that he had given his heart to Jesus? It would be interesting to see.

Big Jim stirred the fire. "Thought you left us for sure this time."

Jacob gulped down his brew and said, "You've got no claim on me."

"Nor do we want any. Have you heard from your wife or children?"

"Just this here letter I got three months ago. They's in Canada waiting for me. I wrote them about your farm."

"Fine mule, Jacob. At least I can be resting my sore leg, and riding my horse will make traveling faster. Hopefully, we'll make it to my cabin by Christmas Eve." Ben looked over at Big Jim. "So, Jacob, why don't you head for the Canadian border? We can always write you when the war is over and— "

"I told ya I like where I is."

The next four days were a continuation of the last, drenching rains that often turned into big puffy snowflakes. Every pass in the Appalachians along Kentucky was guarded by the Confederacy. Unbeknownst, they had slipped past. Bone weary, they stumbled on, feeling cold, wet, and hungry. Hunching into his collar, the winter wind gnawed at Ben's exposed nose like the beak of a vulture. He squinted out from beneath his cavalry hat, trying to see if his house and barns were still standing. The picket fence welcomed them as he rounded the corner.

The stars, just appearing in the night, twinkled a greeting to him. He felt as though he was envisioning the night the Christ child was born. Only, he couldn't enjoy it. His big toe throbbed, and his stomach growled because they hadn't eaten all day. But it wasn't food they needed; it was water. He shook his canteen. Only a drop left and Big Jim might need it; he had a fever. Through the trees, a light shone in his cabin. "What's that?"

Who could it be? The snow changed to freezing drizzle. Ben burrowed into the collar of his blue wool coat.

Big Jim rode up. "Hold up, we'd best see who's in there. Could be a Confederate cavalry group getting out of the weather, and I don't care to be spending my Christmas in one of their prisoner of war camps."

"Well, I ain't standin' in this here rain any longer. I'm going to walk up and knock on that cabin door. If'n they be Union blue, I'll motion for you to come." Jacob handed the reins of his horse to Ben. "If'n they be Confederates all they can do to me is to take me back south with them. But don't you worry none; I'll get free and find ya."

Big Jim leaned over on his saddle horn, his eyes gleaming respect; however, his words held a threat. "You ain't got a dog's chance in Hades stayin' alive if you ride with us. Go to Canada and find your family. Why you want to ride with us anyway?"

"You two need tendin' to. Besides, you'd sit here all night and you with a hurt arm and a fever and Ben with a powerful smellin' dad needin' put in the ground."

Ben covered his mouth so Jacob couldn't see his grin. Clearly, Jacob felt he was a vital part of his and Big Jim's survival.

"You mean you'd come back here to find us and probably get your fool head shot off for your trouble?" Big Jim whispered.

"That's what friends are for." Jacob walked toward the cabin. His horse nickered softly, as if to a fellow friend. He turned. Put his finger to his lips and hissed. Then he was gone, swallowed in the night with his dark hair and clothes.

"Did you see that? What I wouldn't do to be that camouflaged when I'm facing Johnny Reb."

The wind blew about Ben's body. He shivered. "Goes right to my bones like I'm not wearin' a thing." He pulled his wool cap over his ears.

"Minutes move like hours when you're cold and wet."

The door opened, and out ran Jacob waving his hand, jumping up and down. Two other figures joined him, waving their hands.

"Well, maybe we'll have a joyous Christmas after all," Ben said as he and Big Jim approached the cabin.

"Meet my family, gentlemen. My wife, Prudence, and my little girl, Flora, and my son Jacob Jr. I wrote them in a letter where I be livin' and here's they are."

Ben could see why Jacob was so proud of his wife. She was nearly as tall as Jacob, with light skin and high cheekbones. Her large eyes peeked out of high arched brows and lashes thick and long enough to make any southern lady jealous. He bowed. "'Tis a pleasure to be meeting you, ma'am, only, you left a place with no war to be in the middle of a place that is."

"I couldn't be where I was doing no good. Besides, Lincoln is freeing us, and I don't see no need to hide and not do my part in this here war."

Ben noticed that the girl had acquired her mother's slenderness and eyes; the boy, being at the most five or six, would give him a bit more time to decide. He chuckled, looking about his cabin, swept clean, a fire burning brightly in the hearth, and a wild turkey turning on the spit. "My, it looks like someone knows how to trap a turkey."

Big Jim rubbed his hands together. He sat down and pulled his boots off, displaying two large holes on both big toes. He limped over to the fire and first rubbed his hands together and then turned, rubbing his backside. "I declare, I believe I might be rubbed raw, being in that saddle all those months."

In the corner of the room stood a tree about the size of Jacob Jr.

"I see you've got a Christmas tree."

Prudence continued hugging Jacob. Her long, slender arms wrapped around his waist. Jacob crushed her to his side, kissing her forehead. "Yes," came the sweet sound of her voice, as soft as a turtle dove's, but as determined as a donkey's. "Little Jacob wouldn't let up till we cut one. I think he's got his father's stubbornness."

"Mama, I cut it myself, rembers?" Jacob Jr.'s bare feet pitter-patted across the wood floor and picked up a hatchet almost as large as himself. His father was right after him like a bug on a hound. "Don't you be picking that up. Why, you could drop that hatchet and cut off your toe."

Ben sat down on a chair next to the fire and extended his legs. Some day he hoped Maggie would be here, and they would have a passel of young'uns, lusty stout lads like him and soft-eyed beautiful lasses like Maggie. His children would know the value of working hard and playing just as hard. He'd teach them how to defend themselves, how to shoot a rifle, and know the Good Book. They'd have a spirit about them that would never quit, and a love for his Savior that could withstand the devil's deceit.

He watched the boy sit down next to Big Jim, handing him a corn pone he warmed in the fire.

Ben would build another house, a big white frame house with glass windows and… well, with fluttering curtains on the windows and rugs on their shiny wood floor. Women took great store in those things. They'd have an upstairs for sleeping and a kitchen and a parlor and it would resemble Spirit Wind and be something he'd be proud to bring his Maggie to. It was so clear, yet so surreal.

"I didn't notice; is the barn still up?" Big Jim looked up grabbing his boots he'd laid before the fire to dry.

"Don't you be disturbing yourself." Ben stopped Big Jim from getting up, careful not to touch his wounded shoulder. "I'll be tending to the livestock. I need to check out the buildings, anyways."

"Master, you want me to put vittles on the table when you get back?" Prudence asked.

"No, none of that. 'Tis a bother saying master this and that and isn't true. I'm not your master. You only have one Master, and He being in heaven."

Ben motioned for Big Jim to remain by the pallet near the fire. "I'll take care of your horse better than you."

"Humpf!" Big Jim's low baritone bounced about the cabin walls with a fervor Ben hadn't heard for some time. Big Jim accepted the mug of coffee Jacob's wife handed him. "I could do more work than you with one hand tied behind my back…. Mrs. Prudence, don't you be listening to that Irishman's blarney."

"Isn't blarney something like fibbing?" she asked.

"That's tellin' it lightly." Jacob had donned his coat and now covered his thick coarse hair with his Union cap.

"You need not come, Jacob, I can manage. Take the time you need getting reacquainted with your missus."

"I'll do that tonight." He smiled sheepishly at his wife and reached for the door knob a split second before him. "I'm going to help you whether you wants my help or not."

Ben's shoulders ached almost as bad as his back. The icy rain now covered hitching posts and fences. It was going to be hard walking to the barn without falling. He started to slip. Jacob grabbed him just in time. Ben glanced at his dad. "He's faring better than I." They slowly made their way to the barn, found a kerosene lamp, and lit it. Then they unsaddled the horses, and rubbed them down with straw.

Jacob found some hard corn on the cobs and the horses crunched down on them with relish. Ben went up in the hayloft and tossed down some flakes of hay. Checking out the hayloft, an idea came to mind.

"Big Jim and I could sleep right well up in the hayloft tonight and give your wife and you some privacy." No answer. Ben climbed down, looking for Jacob.

Jacob was outside, leaning against the barn.

"What are you doing out here in the ice?"

Jacob wiped at his face. "I don't understand women. Or should I say my woman? She had a nice place, least that's what she told me. I just can't believe her comin' here alone, and I can't understand why she didn't stay put. What if we didn't make it back?"

"Maybe she and the children could go to Spirit Wind. I could write and see if Maggie could take them in. Or else, you'll have to stay here."

"I can't. Did you hear her? Lincoln's going to free us… but what she don't understand is only if'n Lincoln and this Union wins the war."

"Here, give me a hand with my dad." Together they wrapped an old tarp around Ben's dad. Ben held his nose. "Dad, you sure got an odor about you that not even the rain can wash away."

"Best we bury him tomorrow, rain, snow, or whatever."

"So, you staying here?"

"No. I can'ts. We haven't won one battle. I don't think the northern heart is in this war like the southern heart is. That's why those Rebs fights to win like they do. It's just a paycheck for you Irish." Jacob scrunched up his face, turning it heavenwards. "I'm not sure the North has what it takes to whip that kind of spirit."

"Spirit, ya say. Well, you're forgetting one thing. Many of those southern families came over on the *Mayflower*. Do they want to go against what their ancestors fought for, independence from Britain and making the likes of us a great nation?"

Ben knew he could be joining his dad soon. Yet, it was all worth the rough boat ride, going to sleep with your stomach crying, worth it all to be at these shores feeling that breath of hope, that spirit of liberty welcoming him. 'Twas not what he'd first expected. No, it was hard work, to be sure. More aches in his belly and groans in his muscles, yet, he'd not trade a moment of it. He'd found the love of his life here and had his land to boot.

"I'm not fighting for the money. I'm fighting for a dream of these United States to remain as grand to all the immigrants who want come here to be a part of America, for a better life." He lifted his arm pointing to the moon peeking through an obstinate cloud. "To the rainbow just over the rise ..."

"So, you're looking to join your dad, are you?"

# Chapter 26

*M*iss Maggie, what are we goin' to do?"

Maggie looked up from her letter to Aunt Louise. Before she could ask Cook what she was referring to—the empty flour barrel or the depleted sugar supply—her father interrupted Cook and slapped his newspaper.

"Well, look here, the Union suffered a defeat in the Battle of Chancellorsville in Virginia. But Stonewall Jackson was mortally wounded." Father looked down at his paper. Home from the war with an injured leg and shrapnel cuts, his right hand was in a sling and his head bandaged tightly around his forehead. His left hand shook the pages as if trying to read more about the battle.

Maggie jumped up in alarm. The paper was over a month old, it was nearly July… his shaking was not due to his excitement, but due to his nerves; he'd forgotten he fought in that battle.

"What year is this, daughter?"

"Father, it's 1863, you remember. You've been home now for nearly two months—from the battle at Chancellorsville."

"Well, I know that," he said, slightly embarrassed. "Look at this. Union losses are 11,000 killed, wounded, and missing. Confederate losses 10,000. We'll show Lincoln freeing our slaves with his highfalutin Emancipation Proclamation. We'll show Lincoln thinking this Grant fellow could capture Vicksburg. I don't understand why people have such long faces—"

"Maybe 'cause their starvin'," Cook interrupted. "Miss Maggie, I only got a little bacon and some cornbread and hominy to feed these folks with. What with our brave Confederacy leavin' us what theys didn't want. We all sick of hominy and done picked everything we could. Now there's nothin' in the garden ready for pickin'. Whats you want me to do?"

The cardinals and blue jays flew to the little birdhouse Mother had always supplied with ample seed. Only no seed was there. They flew away into the crystal blue sky. Maggie wished she could fly away… away from all these troubles biting at her heels like hounds on a hunt. The hay was ripe in the field, ready to be cut… only, there was no one left to cut it but her and Eli.

She wanted to fly away from the question that haunted her and kept her sleepless though her body ached for rest. Ben, will I ever see your swarthy face and jesting eyes again? Listen to your practical commonality making sense of this senseless killing?

The noise of a wagon winding its way up the drive caused her and Father pause.

"Humpf, most likely someone looking to be fed." Cook pulled at Maggie's worn apron sleeve. "We ain't got any to gives them, Miss Maggie." Her large lower lip protruded and she crossed her arms on her ample bosom.

A large black man striding a horse and a light-skinned woman driving a mule pulling a rickety wagon approached the manor. Two small children sat in the back of the wagon.

Cook narrowed her eyes at the strangers. "I don't like it. I don't likes it. These people are trouble. I can sniff it on their heels."

"Mr. Gatlan and Miss Maggie?"

Maggie shielded her eyes from the sun. "Yes."

The man jumped down as sprightly as Little Irene, whose four-year-old little legs could out run and out jump them all. "May I introduce, Mrs. Prudence… Walker of… Kentucky, here for a visit."

"Humpf! Ain't no time to be calling… what with a war goin' on," Cook grumbled.

"Now, where's your southern hospitality?" Maggie motioned Cook into the house, then turned back to the visitors. She chopped down on her lips like she was dicing up onions.

Onions always made Maggie laugh and cry at the same time; that's what she felt like doing now. The old South had floated away on the heels of want and need. Her father walked around the wagon, sniffing it like a bloodhound. So unlike Father, the war had changed him. "This wagon smells like death. In fact there are blood stains on the wood."

Of course, there are blood stains, Father. She closed her eyes, blocking out the sights and sounds of their hospital in Maryville. The men's lice, maggots in open wounds, and the groans of the soldiers who had come to them from the battles of Ft. Henry and Ft. Donelson. She would never forget the sickish sweet smell of gangrene that clung to her garments as the flies and gnats hovered above the groaning men with their severed limbs and wounds. She had nursed Father back to health. Blake McCullen was not so fortunate. He'd gotten gangrene in his leg, so Doctor Jordon had to amputate. He died anyway.

The man handed her a letter. How coincidental, she'd been writing Aunt Louise about Blake. What did this letter hold? She looked up. His face was drawn, his eyes sad, but he carried a smile on his lips.

Flipping the seal with her thumb, she read. *"Maggie, 'tis I your Ben praying daily for your safety in your war-torn Tennessee."*

Ben's alive! Maggie caressed the letter written on the back of a piece of wallpaper. She blinked away her tears, not wanting them to fall onto the parchment.

*"Please take in Prudence and her children. She is very resourceful and well able to be a proper helpmate to you. I shall write you more when time permits. Taps and lights out will soon follow and I must get this letter finished. Send Jacob back with the necessary papers to get him safely to Virginia. He's made a good soldier and a good friend to yours truly. Your humble servant, Ben McConnell.*

Maggie slipped the letter into her apron pocket. Jacob's face swam through her tears of thanksgiving.

Jacob, embarrassed, shoved a pebble aside with his toe.

"Ida, ready the guest rooms."

"How long will you be staying?" her father asked.

"She's come to help us in the hospital, Father, and comes highly recommended by… Aunt Louise." Prudence alighted from the wagon. Maggie hugged her as if she was a long-lost friend.

Jacob lifted the children out of the back, patting them on the head and silencing their questions with a look.

"Hattie, bring me my writing tablet, please."

Hattie rushed upstairs and came down with the tablet. There was no paper left. Maggie looked around; the newspaper lay at the far end of the table. She grabbed for it, skimming down the page. Then seeing the list of deaths, she tore the piece out of the paper and wrote a note asking for Jacob's safe passage to Mrs. Louise McCullen's estate. She handed it to Jacob. "Here, this is all I can do. It'll be up to you to get yourself to Virginia, but… if I were you, I'd stay to the woods. No telling if the Confederates or Yankees won't want to confiscate you and your horse for the Cause."

"Thank you, ma'am." He tilted the brim of his worn hat, staring down at her from his horse. She handed him a cloth bag of corn pone, bacon, and an apple, then his canteen freshly filled with spring water. "I wish there was more I could give you."

His eyes filled with tears. "Just take care of my family."

"Our good Lord willing, we shall all come out of this war better than worse."

"Amen." He turned to leave.

"Oh, wait." Maggie handed him her letter to Aunt Louise. "Drop this off where there's a chance it could get to Kentucky." She put a hand to her mouth. Dare she ask the question? "What part of Virginia are you heading for?"

"Ben told me to head north, to Virginia, then to a place in Pennsylvania. For me to asks people where a place called Gettysburg is." With that he spurred his horse into a canter, the dust swirling about his horse's hooves. She coughed, her mouth puckered in a round *O*. She'd never heard of that place before.

The sun beat on them like a scorching cannonball. Ben's saber clanged against his saddle, and his spurs jingled to the sounds of the horses' neighs. As the Irish Brigade galloped to their destination, they sang "Garryowen." Ben smiled; the Irish sang that song on their way to fight because it matched their horses' strides.

Pausing for a walk, Big Jim pulled up next to him. "I don't care what you say, Ben McConnell, this Union army 'tis taking advantage of our fighting spirit to be sure. Why else would they be putting us up front, but to be used as cannon fodder?"

"Well, at least we're not eating another man's dust."

Big Jim wasn't going to be put off that quickly. "They think we are too dumb to see through their shenanigans. 'No Irish need apply,' that is unless they want someone to get their head knocked off first, then it is 'Right this way, Irishman.'"

Big Jim wasn't talking blarney today. But there wasn't an Irishman alive that Ben knew could back down from a fight, even if it was an unfair one. And there was many an Irishman infuriated with that new act.

"What is that act called?"

"You means the National Conscription Act?" Jacob piped up.

Ben didn't have a clue to why they named it that.

"They just want to make sure the unmarried men fight whether they wants to or not," Big Jim said. "But if you got enough money jingling in your pants, you can pay someone to be takin' your place."

"Us Irish are just a bunch of poor men fighting in a rich man's war," another man chimed. The man looked at Jacob. "What's the likes of him doing riding with the likes of us in this brigade?"

Ben smiled. "He's a leprechaun here to bring us good luck."

"Humpf. Leprechauns are green, not black as the ace of spades."

"We'll all be black with gunpowder before this day is through." Big Jim pointed toward the fork in the road. "Is this the way to Gettysburg?"

Fighting Dick pointed up the hill of a dust-strewn pathway that the wagons, heavy with cannons, had taken. To their left was another commander ornately dressed with gold buttons traveling the length of his cavalry coat and gold braiding intricately scrolled on his lapel and sleeves.

"Who might he be? A French general?" Ben had heard that the Confederates hoped France and Britain would join their fight. He unfastened the clasp on his revolver.

"Na, that's General George Armstrong Custer and his Michigan Wolverines," replied a man with bright red hair.

As Custer and his regiment rode closer, a familiar tune tickled Ben's ears and the words of Garryowen floated about the green hillside: "Our hearts so stout have got us fame, For soon 'tis known from whence we came, Where'er we go they dread the name, Of Garryowen in glory."

"That's our song," grumbled Big Jim. "They steal our songs and then—"

"Come on, men," Ben cried, leading off singing "I'm lonesome since I crossed the hill, And over the moorland sedgy, Such heavy thoughts my heart do fill, Since parting from my Sally. I seek no more the fine and gay, For each just does remind me How sweet the hours I passed away, With the girl I left behind me."

Then looking to his right, another cavalry group appeared, the commander less ornately dressed. However, the enthusiasm of the men singing at the top of their lungs caused no one to worry about their determination and patriotism. Raising their voices, they sang. "I left my love, my love I left asleepin' in her bed. I turned my back on my true love when fightin' Johnny Reb."

Custer's Wolverines were not to be out done. "Instead of spa we'll drink brown ale And pay the reckoning on the nail …"

Fighting Dick's strong baritone led the Irish Brigade in the second stanza. "O ne'er shall I forget that night, The stars were bright above me, And gently lent their silvery light When first she vowed to love me. But now I'm bound to Brighton camp - Kind heaven then pray guide me, And send me safely back again, To the girl I left behind me."

The third cavalry group now took up the chant. "I told her she would find me in the U. S. Cavalry. Hi-Yo! Down they go, there's no such word as 'can't'. We'll ride clean down to Hell and Back for Ulysses Simpson Grant."

General Custer threw up his hand and smiled back into the soldier's faces. "Ok, men, now we need to be quiet; we're coming to Gettysburg, and may God be with each and every one of you!" Distant thunder rumbled. Over the treetops, a blaze of fire erupted in the clear blue sky.

Ben and Big Jim looked at each other realizing that it wasn't thunder they were hearing, but cannon fire.

Custer drew out his sword. "Remember, men, ride to the guns!" He pointed where he wanted each cavalry group to be. "Irish Brigade, you will join Winfield Hancock's regiment, ride to Cemetery Ridge to the hill known as Little Round Top and wait for your orders."

Fighting Dick Richardson turned and led his regiment forward. Big Jim leaned over. "Cemetery Ridge, don't believe I care for the name much."

After a meeting with the Union cavalry divisions, Fighting Dick Richardson galloped up and down the rows of the brigade. "Irish, are you ready for some brawling?"

Five hundred voices rose like the roar of the sea in high tide. A pang of homesickness grabbed Ben's chest. 'Twas like the roar outside his bedroom window just before a storm in Cork. Dad would have liked to have been here.

"Charge!" Fighting Dick yelled. The bugle boy's trumpet split through the air like a thunderbolt. The cavalry drew their sabers and yelled, "Charge!"

The ground shook with 1,000 hooves hitting the ground at once. The wind whistled in Ben's ears. The smell of horses, gunpowder, and sweat blanketed the air. The neck of Caedmon stretched taut like a bow with an arrow about to fly; his muscular legs boldly lapped up the dirt. Caedmon was living up to his name as a wise warrior. Ben drew his saber. Would he?

The cannons hadn't fired, but it was just a matter of time. Ben's eyes narrowed, looking forward, always forward, anticipating the next move of the Confederates, a solid gray wall of resistance now in sight. The light of a cannon wick glimmered in the dust. He swerved Caedmon to the right, missing the cannon ball meant for him, and spurred his stallion forward. Caedmon jumped over the barricade and landed on a man.

Ump. Deep went Ben's saber as three more men tried to pull him down. Caedmon kicked out. Ben slashed his way through, turned, and fired his pistol. Big Jim joined him and side by side they fought.

The flies buzzed around Ben's head, his mouth so dry he couldn't swallow. His eyes burned from the gun and cannon smoke. Gray coats turned red as blood oozed over the lifeless forms of the men, their glassy eyes staring—seeing nothing.

Ben was panting as hard as Caedmon. A commotion to his rear caught his attention. A rebel cry, a blood curdling scream that raised the hair on Ben's neck. More Rebs joined in, as if rising from the blood-soaked ground.

Darkness cloaked the battlefield. A hundred campfires lit the velvet blackness as the groans of the dying mingled with the popping wood of the fires. Ben, Big Jim, and Jacob made their way along the rutted and bloody battlefield, helping the medics find the half-alive bodies of their comrades. Reb or Yank, it didn't matter the color of their coat now. They worked by the light of the stars and moon above.

"Listen?" A Reb with hair so white it glistened in the moonlight held his hand up.

"It's coming from that clump of trees." As they made their way to the trees, hauling an empty stretcher between them, a hand from out of the dark earth grabbed Ben's trouser. He liked to jump out of his own skin.

"Water."

Ben knelt, giving the man a sip from his canteen, then looked up at his Rebel counterpart. "You got *him*?"

The Rebel nodded, hoisting another man up on his shoulders and walked toward Ben. "How are we goin' to carry them both?"

Reb had a Union man and Ben had a Confederate. Ben bent down low. "If you're not squeamish about sharing a bed with a Yank, we could be getting you to the surgeons right soon. But if you be—"

"Hold on there, Irish. I figure, I've shared enough dirt today to call that Yank kin. Hoist me up and be quick about it."

They passed a burial detail.

"They're hauling them on their stretchers before the bodies are cold," said the Reb toting the head end of the stretcher. "Stacking them like cords of wood on the borders of the battlefield."

The man who called Ben Irish wiped his dirty hand across his forehead. "That could have been me."

Flies riddled dead horses and gnats buzzed in the sodden air. Ben swiped his face, glancing upwards. Vultures hovered in the treetops, looking down at them, eyeing the men on the cots.

Those horses would take a great deal of effort and time to remove. So they'd likely remain for tomorrow's battle.

The next day dawned bright, with clear blue skies. Breezes came off Culp's Hill to Cemetery Ridge, whipping up the stench of yesterday's dead.

Caedmon pulled at the reins. "Easy, boy. So, you want what must come of the day's battles to be ended, too? 'Tis true. Waiting is more terrible than the battle."

Bloody charges raged back and forth along Sickles' line. Ben's long legged Thoroughbred lapped up the miles to the nest of boulders known as Devil's Den, then galloped into a peach orchard, the branches heavy with succulent fruit. When death nipped at your heels, food was an unattainable luxury.

"Charge!" Fighting Dick valiantly led the charge. Again and again the men of the Irish Brigade responded. Ben was glad he wasn't a foot soldier. The cannon shots oftentimes blasted ten men at a time.

Jacob was riding to his left when suddenly that whizzing noise that heralded another cannon ball came toward them. "Duck, Jacob!" Ben sped to the left. The earth shook beneath Caedmon's feet. Jacob's bay whinnied. Caedmon neighed back. "Jacob?" No answer. Ben jumped down.

Through the smoke and dirt flying like vultures without wings, Ben blinked and coughed, trying to see through the haze of dust and gunpowder that singed his nose as well as his eyes. He blinked again.

Jacob clawed his way to his horse, holding his stomach. Laying his head on his mare's rich blood red coat, he sobbed. "She's hurting, Ben, hurting bad, ain't she?"

Ben closed his eyes. The mare's eyes had drawn themselves upwards so all he could see were the whites. Yet, the little mare seemed to know that it would hurt her master to no end if she groaned. She nuzzled Jacob's head, as if to say good-bye and neighed softly in his ear. Ben drew his revolver.

Jacob held up his gun-powdered hand. "No, she'll take it better if I does it."

"You're gut shot, Jacob, you can't…"

Jacob pushed himself up on his horse's neck, his stomach and entrails oozing blood. Ben unfastened his belt, and then his coat. He wrapped his coat around Jacob's middle and then secured it with his belt. "That should at least keep—"

"Thanks… Ben."

Why? Why did it always have to end this way?

Jacob lifted the revolver, too heavy for his weak hands to hold, and rested it on his horse's neck, then fired, hitting her just behind the ear. He crumbled to the ground.

The cannon fire lit the smoke-clogged field strewn with men and horses. A rebel yell split the air. A man on a large chestnut lowered his sword, his hateful eyes gleaming their way into Ben's. "Thought I killed you at Fredericksburg—"

"You!" Ben lunged, pulling Reynolds down. Ben landed on his back, the wind knocked from his lungs. His gasp was fodder for Reynolds, whose eyes gleamed down at him like a demon's brimming with malice.

Jesus, give me strength.

Big Jim's bellow rose above the clamor of guns, the neighs of horses, and screams of the men. Like an outraged bull charging down the field, he hurtled his bulk on Reynolds, lifting him up and throwing him across the bloodied ground. Ben gasped, crawling toward Jacob, feeling for a pulse. Faint, but alive. A bullet whizzed past his ear. He glanced up. Reynolds was stepping over Big Jim, blood oozing from Big Jim's chest. Big Jim groaned, rolling onto his side, holding his chest.

Reynolds aimed his revolver at Ben's head.

With his last ounce of strength, Ben lunged, grabbing Reynolds' legs. Throwing him to the ground, his dad's face shone before his eyes. Reynolds. He'd killed Ben's dad and… "Jesus forgive me." He sank his sword deep, deep, into Reynolds' chest.

Reynolds gasped. His hands dug into the dirt as if something—someone—was dragging him down. His eyes bulged out, an ear-piercing scream bellowed from his gaping mouth.

"So ya saw the fiery inferno of hell." Ben shook his head. "And you thought the devil was your friend."

The morning of the third day, sunlight gleamed through the haze of gun and cannon smoke resting across the valleys like the ghosts of the dearly departed.

Ben stroked his horse's dapple-gray coat, dark with soot. Caedmon's proud head drooped to the ground, as if he, too, dreaded the call of the bugle.

The 500 men of the Irish Brigade had been whittled down to 150. Ben's heart ached for his wounded friends. He closed his eyes and silently prayed Big Jim wouldn't lose his arm beneath the surgeon's knife. For Jacob, that he'd find the strength to fight against the gunpowder infection in his stomach and God would miraculously heal him. Both the Confederate and the Union doctors had shaken their heads, saying it didn't look good. Jesus could bring the dead to life. If it were His will, Jacob would live to be with his wife and children again.

"What be the date?" the red headed Irishman to Ben's left asked.

"July 3," Ben replied.

"Tomorrow is America's Independence Day."

Fighting Dick whipped his saber in his hand and shouted. "Come on, you rowdy Irishmen, let's win this war for our land. Let's show these Americans how the Irish can fight."

From the medic cots to the rhythm of the tinkling cavalry swords to the bayonets of the foot soldiers, a wail rose and voices sang. "Yes, we'll rally around the flag boys, we'll rally once again…"

Ben's tired bones felt renewed strength, a will beyond flesh, strength beyond mortal. The Irish Brigade raised their voices in unison. "The Union forever, hooray, boys, hooray!" The Irish green, with the Stars and Stripes. "Shouting the battle cry of freedom…"

Fighting Dick was beside him, raising his sword high in the air. "Ok, you fighting Irish… charge!"

Behind stone walls and rocks and trees, the Union infantry opened fire on the Confederate guns. The Irish Brigade hit the enemy on one flank while Custer's Wolverines hit the other. Caught from all sides, Ben doubted that even a third of the Confederates had survived.

Ben lowered his sword. His arm ached from the three days of fighting. Caedmon stumbled. Discarded guns and sabers littered the ground. The Union had won a sweeping victory.

# Chapter 27

*M*iss Maggie."

Maggie looked up, shielding her eyes with her hand from the bright sunlight. She cradled freshly picked tomatoes, green beans, and turnips in her apron.

Prudence walked along the rows careful not to step on any of the delicate plants, shuffling her feet in shoes too large for her small feet. Maggie and her household made do with whatever they could obtain—even cutting up their hassocks for the fabric to use to stuff worn out shoes and making their clothes from their curtains and drapes. They had learned resourcefulness. Not wasting a yard of fabric or the thread to darn with.

Prudence clutched a letter to her bosom, then held it out to Maggie to read. It was difficult. Paper was scarce, so letters were used and reused. Between the lines of the first letter Prudence had written her husband, was a woman's handwriting.

*July 11, 1863*

*Dear Prudence:*

*Your husband has been gravely shot at the Battle of Gettysburg. Recovery shall be lengthy, if he does recover. He is at New York DeCamp General.*

"Miss Maggie, I needs to go to him."

Ben had written about that horrific three-day battle, about Jacob and Big Jim getting injured, and that he'd killed Reynolds. He asked if she could come up. A small voice whispered in her ear to go. But what about Father and the duties at Spirit Wind?

Her father lapsed from past to present, his spiraling emotions kept the household in a constant uprising. Still, a trip north might benefit him. Give him less time to ponder about the Old South and help direct his thoughts to a new beginning. Hattie and Ida were capable of handling Little Irene and the household duties. Besides, she didn't care to have Prudence travel alone.

Eli refused to stay behind, stating it wasn't right for two women to be traveling alone. Besides Mr. Gatlan needed attending to. The trip by train, with Eli warning them as to how to avoid the gentlemen's eyes, had Prudence and her covering their mouths. They had been in the Maryville hospital where Confederate and Union men alike cussed and swore about their crawling lice and cramping bowels. Not to mention the amputations and sicknesses they had to nurse.

Father seemed like his old self and the officers had been polite and respectful to him. However, when Maggie told the soldiers they were traveling to New York to visit their husband and sweetheart, Father had been taken aback when she referred to Ben as her sweetheart. Well, it was about time he knew it.

The train stopped with less than a block to go to the hospital. Maggie hesitated before descending the steps. Would Ben be waiting for them? It had seemed ages ago when last she saw him. Had he changed? She didn't have to wait long.

Captain Ben McConnell, with enough medals on his coat to start his own silver factory, swung her off the high steps amidst the whistles of a dozen soldiers. His red lips smiled broadly beneath a close-clipped black mustache, as did his black eyes, alert, and attentive, remembering as she, that breathless night he had come to her bedroom.

"Mr. Gatlan, sir," Ben tapped his heals together and saluted him. "So good to see you well and enjoying the sights. If you have time, I would love to show you New York." Ben's eyes appraised her.

"Well, that would be nice…" Her father stuttered. "I have never had the opportunity to see New York—"

"Then, I'll be your guide, sir. I know the ins and outs of the place." Ben's crown of victory, his captain's bars, glistened in the setting sunlight. "But first, let us visit the hospital."

Big Jim's grin spread from ear to ear, a cute nurse on either side of his arms. Proudly he displayed the scars of his right arm, showing where the saber had entered his upper right chest. "They thought they'd be takin' it off. But my Ben's a scrapper when it comes to prayin' and fightin', to be sure. And this being the day of my release."

Jacob rested his head on three pillows and his cheeks gleamed wet, seeing his wife. "Did you bring the children, too?"

"No, I didn't, 'cause you need to rest." Prudence fluffed his pillows, fussing that he looked pale. "Have you been eating regularly?"

"They feed me all kinds of things, to make sure everything is working proper." Jacob looked from her to Ben. "They worked on me for hours, trying to sort out my innards. They did a powerful good job, 'cause I'm feeling much better." He lifted Prudence's hand and kissed it. "When I heard you were comin', right then and there I knew I had to get better soon or you'd have the willow stick after me."

"Willow stick?" her father retorted.

Prudence looked up. "He's just remembering the first time we met. When he told me he was sick and dying and that I better be nice to him instead of tellin' him to get and quit bothering me… I was thirteen at the time."

"Well, it's good to see what ten days' worth of recuperation has done for you both," Father said. "I'll go and see the doctor, perhaps they'll allow you to recuperate at Spirit Wind beneath the gentle hands of Doctor Jordan."

"If Ben here hadn't carried me to the surgeons with all those cannon balls cutting holes in the dirt and the bullets whizzing past our ears, I would have been knocking on St. Peter's pearly gates." Jacob said.

"It takes a brave man to do that." Father patted Ben on the shoulder.

"And I am pleased that you have these friends who think highly of you."

Ben blushed. "Thank you, sir, I think highly of your praises."

Big Jim joined them on their sightseeing excursion. They headed toward the Bronx. Prudence and Eli stayed with Jacob.

Maggie couldn't believe the finely clothed women or the suit clad gentlemen all rushing to their jobs as if a war wasn't even going on. Getting off the streetcar, Ben directed their eyes to where his family first lived and to the town that had sprawled up consisting of a combination of Black and Irish communities. The streetcar pulled to a screeching stop. Ben stepped down first, offering Maggie his hand, his eyes sparkling up at her merrily. Walking down the sidewalk, a line of men as thick as ants storming a picnic basket came walking over the hill, with clubs and sticks.

"Looks like a mob has formed, but what for?" Big Jim muttered.

"Haven't they done enough fighting in this war?" Ben replied.

As the crowd drew closer, they watched. Her father remained silent.

Three men stopped in front of Ben and Big Jim. "You'd best get your lady out of here if you know what is good for you. Me and my men are tired of working for nothin', seeing our comrades dying by the hundreds in this rich man's war."

Ben placed his hand on the man's shoulder. "Give these Americans a little time. You'll see those 'no Irish need apply' signs will soon be taken off the shop windows and the new ones will say, 'Irish needed.' Give our Lord time to be changing their hearts and minds."

The man knocked Ben's hand off his shoulder. "I'm tired of seeing the want in the faces of our women and children crying for their husbands and fathers. They've treated us unfairly and this last law proves it. These people of color sit back, grabbing all the jobs and growing in numbers while we fight and die in their war." He banged his club in the palm of his hand, eyeing two men who had just come out of a building.

"Don't, friend. You'll be killin' all the good us Irish have accomplished. Don't allow Satan to get the best of ya."

"I'm not your friend if you can't see the truth. Those that takes, takes, and those that gives, gives, and that goes on for generations. I'm tired of giving to the takers and only have the grave be my resting spot."

They pushed their way past Ben and Big Jim, storming the houses.

Ben swiped his hand across his face and groaned. "'Twasn't meant to be. Irish, a respected and honored nationality. To be proper American citizens, wealthy in spirit and prosperity. Oh, why can't God be given us a little help?"

Maggie's hopes had been crushed with Ben's, seeing her father's aghast expression. She knew that look well. Father would tell her Ben, being Irish, was undesirable and not worthy of her attention. Evidently, Ben saw the same horror in her father's eyes.

He took her hand, the deep crevices of his face ashen in color. "Maggie my lass, I'll always be a dirty Irishman unfit for the likes of you. Go home." He hailed a streetcar and ushered them aboard. Then he kissed her hand. She had never seen him so sad, the look of defeat clouding his vision. "Take Jacob with ya. Big Jim and I have our work cut out for us here, mending the mess these rioting Irish have caused." He jumped off the train and ran toward the rioting men.

"All aboard," the conductor yelled. The clang of the bell echoed a shrill good-bye; her eyes were glued on the site outside the trolley car. Two colored men exited their house. The mob grabbed them. Another man lifted his torch to the building. Ben yelled and grabbed the man's arm. Big Jim followed. The men swarmed them like angry hornets. Maggie clutched her throat and gasped. What could Ben and Big Jim do against an angry mob?

"Ben!" That was the last Maggie could see. She reached for the cord that would stop the street car… her father pulled her arm down. "This is not your fight, daughter. It's Ben's and his Irish ruffians." Father clicked his tongue against his teeth. "I should have known something like this would happen. I'm just glad you're not married to that barbarian."

The fighting, ransacking, and burning continued for five days. Ben and Big Jim landed back in the hospital, with more knife wounds, cuts, and bruises than fighting in Gettysburg had given them. The federal troops had been called in and 120 people had died. The Irish Brigade was disbanded. Once their wounds were healed, Ben and Big Jim were reassigned to Grant's cavalry.

"It'll be alright, Ben, my boy. We've chewed enough leather with them to be knowing them."

The months galloped by and Grant's men accepted them. It helped when four more cavalrymen from the former Irish Brigade joined them. Grant respected them all.

"You men have made a reputation for yourselves, and I'd like to continue calling you the fighting Irish." Grant shook their hands with exuberance. And that exuberance rubbed off on them.

They ate together, shared the same dirt together, and sang the same songs. Ben and the boys taught them their Irish songs and they taught them theirs.

At last a sunny November 19 offered the soldiers a chance to sit back and rest and listen to the ceremony dedicating the battlefield at Gettysburg as a national cemetery. Ben couldn't help remembering the last time he heard Lincoln speak during his Inaugural ceremonies and Maggie's beautiful face peeked into his mind.

She'd written him. But he hadn't opened her letters. Instead, he'd see that look of utter disgust spread across Mr. Gatlan's face. How could Ben erase such complete revulsion?

"Finally, they're going to let Lincoln speak." Big Jim elbowed him in the ribs. "The old wind bag before him most likely gave everyone itchy ears."

Ben looked around. The murmurings of the large crowd had drowned out most of the speaker's words. Would they do the same to Lincoln? He hoped not; he'd waited over an hour just to hear him.

A hush fell like a downy coverlet on a tired child. Ben could have heard an acorn drop from a nearby oak, it was that quiet.

Abraham Lincoln rose, looking more like a Kentucky woodsman than a president. His tall, long-legged form dressed in black from the tip of his tall stately hat to the bottom of his leather boots. His eyes surveyed the mass huddled beneath him like a father his offspring, his brows worried, yet proud. His powerful voice spoke with the sing-song accent of a backwoodsman sitting on the hearth of his cabin and voicing his innermost thoughts.

"Four score and seven years ago our fathers brought forth on this continent, a new nation, conceived in Liberty, and dedicated to the proposition that all men are created equal.

"Now we are engaged in a great civil war, testing whether that nation, or any nation so conceived and so dedicated, can long endure. We are met on a great battle-field of that war. We have come to dedicate a portion of that field, as a final resting place for those who here gave their lives that that nation might live. It is altogether fitting and proper that we should do this.

"But in a larger sense, we cannot dedicate—we cannot consecrate—we cannot hallow—this ground. The brave men, living and dead, who struggled here, have consecrated it, far above our poor power to add or detract. The world will little note, nor long remember what we say here, but it can never forget what they did here. It is for us the living, rather, to be dedicated here to the unfinished work which they who fought here have thus far so nobly advanced. It is rather for us to be here dedicated to the great task remaining before us—that from these honored dead we take increased devotion to that cause for which they gave the last full measure of devotion—that we here highly resolve that these dead shall not have died in vain—that this nation, under God, shall have a new birth of freedom—and that government of the people, by the people, for the people, shall not perish from the earth."

Silence greeted his closing. Lincoln had managed in a few paragraphs to summarize the pain, suffering, and death of thousands of soldiers. No, the Irish Brigade didn't matter; color, creed, race, or origin did not matter. What mattered was this nation under God should continue on until Jesus returned.

As quietly as Lincoln had stood, humbly, he resumed his seat, as if he didn't expect any more from the audience but to hear him.

After the lengthy train ride to Cincinnati, Ben checked Caedmon over for any cuts and bruises. The stallion nuzzled his pockets, neighing softly. Ben stroked the wide forehead, then gave him the carrot he sought. "Well, Caedmon, my warrior, it's time to get back to business."

Big Jim had collected his saddle and saddle bags. "I know our horses liked riding better than walking and they sure earned the rest."

Now they were in the saddle again, riding thirty-five miles a day. Across the back roads and streams without let up. Grant had a powerful need to get to Chattanooga. His short, but powerful build loping along with them, he'd often drop to the back to check on his troops, his uniform as worn as his smile. He never stopped encouraging or consoling, and his grin was like a tonic for the men. It helped erase the want, hunger, and loss of their comrades.

"Looks like we could be spending Thanksgiving and Christmas at Chattanooga," Grant said. "Say, does anyone know if the southerner likes turkey for their Thanksgiving meal?"

"Na," a large man with a shock of black hair replied. "They likely prefers possum and rabbit." A chuckle went up among the ranks.

"Irish would know," someone yelled from behind. "Ask Ben."

He didn't care, nor had he paid any attention to the man who had yelled out his name. They would be marching past Spirit Wind on their way to Chattanooga. The unopened letters in his pockets crinkled noisily. Why hadn't he burned them in last night's campfire? Why? Because for all his declaration, he couldn't stop his heart from beating, nor he could he stop loving Maggie.

Grant cantered up next to him and tilted his head like the old hoot owl Ben watched last night looking down at him before he drifted off into troubled dreams. "Irish, you know anything about southern hospitality?"

"I know they have the best food, the best beds, and the best lookin' ladies in these United States."

"I expect I'll be asking for your knowledge about southern ways, seeing how you used to live here. We'll see how Chattanooga goes, might have you keep a division down here, sort of hold down the fort so to speak while I take the rest of the troop back to Virginia. I'm not planning to turn up the same dirt again and I don't trust Schofield or Thomas to not lose the ground we've taken. I'll write you the necessary orders." Grant leaned forward. "Keep this under your hat, Ben, but Lincoln has mentioned making me general-in-chief of the federal armies.

"Only, I'm not sure I should appoint Sherman to succeed me as Commander in the West. He's a bit of a hot head and doesn't understand the southerners like you or me. Can you handle the Tennessee campaign and smooth the ruffled feathers of my generals? I know that might make Schofield and Thomas angry, but I need to win this war."

Memories as painful as reopened gun-shot wounds caused Ben's vision to blur, recalling the Union soldiers looting the farms along their path. He stopped many from their needless pilfering—the blank stares of the southerners, not understanding why he, a Union officer, would care. He could read their thoughts, so like his own. They were wondering what they were going to eat with winter coming.

One little cracker boy came to mind. "Please, Mr. Soldier," his tiny voice pleaded, "don't take my little red-topped boots. They're all I got."

Ben had thrown that soldier out on his ear. He'd rolled down the steps and drawn his revolver. Ben, quick as a bob cat casing its next meal, stepped on the man's hand and grabbed his gun. "You can pick up your pistol from Grant. Now move!"

Grant upheld Ben's every action. Boldly he spurted out the words that volleyed through his mind with every bend in the road displaying the burned barns, stripped garden patches, women and children huddled on porches throwing stones at them as they rode by. "What will be left of the southerner's pride when we get through stripping them of their livelihood?"

"We didn't start this war, Ben, but I'm planning to finish it. I'm raising your rank to major. Take whatever men you'd like with you. I'll not leave a trail of hatred in my wake. You have a way with these people. I need you down here to watch that my commanders don't take any more than they need to."

Ben's new rank already felt like twenty-pound weights on his shoulders. He didn't mind taking chances with his own life, but when it came to the others, it gave him pause. Weighing lives he might lose like Cook weighed out the meat for each family in the slave quarters. The Rebs hated him and now the Union officers would distrust him.

Humpf! would be Cook's response. He concurred. Only, he knew better than to voice his opinion. Grant's face was as dirt smeared as Ben's. Grant's stogie dipped at an angle in the corner of his mouth. His eyes, though, were as alert as the troop's youngest recruit, a tow-haired boy of eighteen. Grant demanded respect and loyalty. Ben chuckled in spite of his loathing for his new orders.

"Yes, sir. But I guess I'll cross that bridge when the time comes, sir. That is if our good Lord decides to get me through this battle at Chattanooga."

Remembering the wagon ride to that tent revival and how Maggie prayed for his speedy recovery, Ben began singing. "I left my love, my love I left a sleeping in her bed…" He doubted she was praying for him or any Union officer now.

# Chapter 28

## May 1864

The dogs bayed like a hound on a fox, announcing the approach of what sounded like more than fifty horses trotting down the muddy red road toward the long winding lane to Spirit Wind. Maggie ran up the steps to the ballroom balcony. Blue or gray, she couldn't tell, the men were too far away to see the color of their coats. What did it matter? The same want would litter their eyes, the same hungry mouths, the same dirty, bearded faces.

Blades of grass heralding spring peeked out of the hoof-scarred lawn, a remnant of the Yanks trekking back from their victory in Chattanooga in late November, looting Spirit Wind on their way to Virginia.

Ben's face came uninvited into her thoughts. His eyes had been as cold as the frost that lay on their plants. He'd commandeered her horse, his stallion having been shot dead beneath him in Chattanooga. Then Grant and his men took some of their livestock, killed their turkeys, and made Cook prepare them the proper Thanksgiving Day meal. Father was so furious he struck Ben across the face. As immovable as the Smokies, Ben stood there, his eyes staring forward. He saluted her father and mounted her horse.

They left singing at the top of their lungs something about a yellow ribbon. Well, there was no getting away from the gloating faces and smirks that swept their soot-covered faces.

Afterwards, Maggie built coops and hid what was left of their chickens, turkeys, pigs, and milk and beef cows down in the low land, what once had been the swamp. She paused, remembering Ben back in those days with his tattered breeches and ragged shirt that had clung to his frame like a scarecrow. Now her people had become the ragged remnants of past wealth and plenty, their children barefoot, and their clothes threadbare. Christmas had come and gone, but the memories would haunt her for years to come.

Ben and Jacob had ridden up around Christmastime, Ben looking tall and lean as a willow, his head bandaged, his arm in a sling. Her horse nickered when she saw her. Maggie ran and gave her an apple, not offering one to Ben. She glared up at him, as if daring him to complain as the juice spurted from her mare's mouth.

Ben chuckled deep in his throat. "Jacob needs your services. I'll be leaving him."

Prudence helped her husband off his horse. He was thin like a bean pole, and he'd been shot in the leg. Tears rolled from Prudence's brimming eye lids and dripped down her lean cheeks. "Thank ya for your kindness."

"Merry Christmas, Maggie. The troops and I will be filling our canteens at your brook over there and be moving on."

Maggie sawed on her bottom lip, refusing to glance up into Ben's questioning eyes. If she did, that would be her undoing. She longed to re-dress his sodden bloodstained bandage. Instead, she kept her hands busy stroking her mare's velvet coat.

"You're hurt, too. Looks like you need a new cloth. Yours is blood soaked," she said.

"Don't you be worrying your head about me, Maggie." He saluted her and galloped off. That was the last she had seen of him. But she had heard through the gossipers, there had been heavy words spoken between General Thomas and Ben that day.

Now, hearing the clang of sabers and spurs, Maggie came back to reality with a jolt. Dirty gray wools complemented the budding apple and cherry trees dotting their lane. Out of breath from her hastened decent down the stairs, she yelled to her staff.

"What is it, daughter?"

"Father, Confederates coming."

Jacob had been sitting on the veranda. Quickly he got up, staring in the direction of the road and with the help of his crutches, made it into the house and into the hiding place they had prepared for just such an event.

"I declare," Hattie muttered. "We've got our troubles with both Yanks and Rebs."

Maggie put a hand to her mouth, stifling her cry, seeing the soldiers' dirty, worn clothes, the sleeves tied up at the corners due to lost limbs, the bare feet of the soldiers slapping the dust and rocks as they marched behind the cavalry.

"Why they're just a remnant of the army that passed here in December." They look half-starved. What are we going to feed them? Will they demand what's left of our meager supplies of clothes and food?"

Cook ran out, clutching her rabbit's foot, rubbing the worn out white fur and praying. "Mother rabbit work your charm, keep us all away from harm, ain't got me any time to kneel and pray." Cook's voice quivered with emotion. "Don't you let us down today."

The lean, impeccably dressed man swept his hat from his head in one fluid motion. "Colonel Hood at your service, ma'am. By chance, can my men rest here for a spell beneath your magnolia trees? We're travel worn and our surgeon needs time to doctor a few of our men." Hood looked around, allowing the sun to bath his face with its rays. "My, what a beautiful May morning it is."

"I can offer you some tea on the veranda, or else we could go inside…"

Father joined them on the veranda, his paper in hand. "Is it true? Or is this just propaganda? It says here that the Northern victories have just about ended the Southern resistance in the West. Is this true?"

Hood rested back, undisturbed. "If Lee is worried—"

"Sir!" Hood's aide ran up the walkway, his spurs clanging like a cymbal on the bricks, with a courier running right behind him. They immediately stood at attention. "Enemy soldiers advancing toward Maryville, sir."

"What? Preposterous!" her father bellowed.

Hood jumped to his feet, tipped his hat, then ran to his horse and sped off. A cloud of dust was the only remnant he had been there at all.

The surgeon came trotting up the walkway. "May I set up a hospital in your home?"

"Why, of course," her father replied.

Maggie grabbed all the blankets they had and cleaned off the dining room table to serve as the surgeon's operating table. Doctor Jordon arrived with the first casualties. Gray coats or blue, it didn't matter, they were all treated equally.

Matron Burns, Miss Peabody, old men, and women with children were mass exiting from Maryville and came to the first house welcoming them.

The children hovered in the corners of the parlor. Maggie had Ida take them upstairs, making a nursery and day care, while their mothers worked downstairs on the wounded and dying. Cannons rumbled in the distance, the repeated gunfire making everyone as jumpy as rabbits. Doctors and nurses worked into the night as more casualties arrived.

Their India rugs took on a new design, splotched with deep red bloodstains. "No more pillows are available, and this man's head needs to be elevated." Matron Burns knelt beside one gray-whiskered man who was choking on his chewing tobacco. She reached her index finger inside and withdrew the mass.

Maggie looked around. Seeing the books lining the study walls, she grabbed an armful and walked back into the parlor, handing Matron Burns a couple. The man with the gray whiskers smiled. "Softer than a rock and maybe some of that book stuff will rub off on me."

The door leading to the front of the house never stopped rocking from the litters of soldiers. Jacob stepped in, dressed in a pair of Eli's worn breeches and shirt. Maggie smiled. No way was Jacob going to hide like a scared mouse in a closet when there was work to be done.

"Jacob, have Eli help you move Father's desk and ready the study for more patients."

Every bowl was filled with either water or blood. Every available cloth was used. Maggie ordered her petticoats to be torn up for bandages. There was hardly any room to step, what with the men strewn on couches, tables, desks, and floors. So they turned the covered veranda outside to be used for the less wounded soldiers.

"Miss Maggie?" Hattie pulled on her sleeve as if just saying her name wouldn't be enough to get her attention. "Come quick. Mr. Will, he's bad hurt."

Maggie looked around at the groaning men lying on every available floor space of Spirit Wind. "Where is he?"

Hattie led her into the dining room to where the surgeon and Doctor Jordon were.

"Maggie, how's your stomach?" Doctor Jordon asked.

"You know that answer, Doc." She looked down at Will groaning with pain, his left leg and arm a glob of blood that oozed down his side and onto the table.

"We need a steady hand for our instruments, and to mop up some of this blood. We are going to amputate his arm, maybe his leg. But we are going try and save the leg, if we can. Can you do it?"

Doctor Jordon's face resembled one of her father's crossword puzzles—a patchwork of pain and concern. She nodded.

As they worked, only Will's arm had to be removed. She thanked God. The other surgeries did not go as well. Because there was nothing to give the patients, many older soldiers' hearts couldn't take the shock of the amputations. They died on the operating table.

No chloroform, only corn whisky was available. The screams of the men carried through the house, louder than the gun fire.

Now awake, Will called for her. She rushed to his side, kneeling next to his thin, weak body. Only his eyes were the same—soft and blue, the color of a summer sky. The memory of 1861 and the Christmas Ball came floating into her thoughts. Those had been good days filled with hope and promise of a quick victory.

"Maggie? Can you give me my left hand, it's asleep and I want to hold it, it's keeping me awake with its constant jerking."

Maggie bowed her head and kissed him on his forehead. She had nursed many a patient at Knoxville who suffered the same symptoms after an amputation. Rubbing her hand gently along his left shoulder, she held up the end of his empty sleeve. "Doctor Jordan had to amputate your arm. But he managed to save your leg."

Will took the empty sleeve from her and smiled. "I'll just hold onto it so as to remind me that it's just my imagination."

Maggie's lip quivered. Big tears rolled down her cheeks. "Oh, Will, I'm so sorry." He stroked her hair gently. Maggie felt every shudder of his body, his frazzled nerves complaining, and there was nothing left to give him for his discomfort. She buried her head into his chest and wept.

"Dear Maggie, don't you worry. We're riding on the last stretch of dirt now. The war can't go on much longer."

Maggie blinked. "What? You mean the war will soon be over?"

"We've got nothin' more to fight with. No ammunition, no horses." He chuckled. "There aren't even enough rocks anymore to hurtle on the Yankees' heads." He wiped away her tears with his good hand, giving her comfort, when she should be comforting him. "Most of my men are barefoot.... All we care about now is making a valiant finish and end with a little dignity." He grimaced. "Though to be honest, some of us are still wishing for a miracle. It's hard to say 'uncle' when it isn't part of a southerner's vocabulary."

Shortly after midnight, the rains came. Sheets of it. Deep crevices of red mud wove their way down the lane, blending with blood and discarded pieces of gray and blue cloth. Soon the wagons bearing the wounded were stuck. Eli, Father, and Jacob worked doggedly to dig them out.

The big pots boiled on throughout the night, no one getting any sleep. As quickly as a soldier died, Eli and Jacob hobbling on one crutch and holding the stretcher in the other, carried the dead away to stack next to the woodpile.

Then Father and Prudence brought in another wounded soldier and the process began again.

At noon of the second day, the rains subsided and the cannons fell silent. People who could stand rushed outside.

"I can't see the color of their coats." Maggie shielded her eyes with her hands, stepping up on her tiptoes. The victors trotted down the road and turned the corner. Was Ben alive or dead? She watched as a rainbow crested above, across the silky blue sky. Then Ben's tall form, riding just behind General Schofield, came up to the entranceway.

General Schofield was off his horse in a single bound. Ben remained in the saddle. One hand held behind his back, as if concealing something.

"Who might be the owner of this plantation?" General Schofield asked.

"I am." Her father stepped forward, dressed in his full military suit of gray, gold buttons, and braiding. "Major Gatlan."

What was Father trying to do? Irritate the general?

"Yes, I see. Sir, can you relate to me the casualties, how many Union and Confederate soldiers?"

Father, who in his meticulous handwriting had listed all the soldiers, their names, ranks, and army, handed the list to Schofield.

Schofield glanced down at it. "Major McConnell will stay. His headquarters will be here until the courthouse is properly repaired for occupancy." He tipped his hat. "Good day, ladies and gentlemen." With that the general turned and galloped back down the lane, a hundred or so soldiers following him.

A gathering of no more than thirty Union soldiers remained. Ben glanced over his shoulder at the ragged line of Confederate prisoners with bloodied bandages swathing their heads and arms. He turned his eyes on her father.

"I am sorry to impose on your hospitality." His voice low, rumbled like an impending storm in his throat. There was careful restrained savagery in his dark eyes, a ruthless abandonment of caring about anything or anyone.

"Oh …" Maggie fell back as if he'd struck her. She had seen that look once before. Where? Her mind revolved like the spokes of a wagon spinning out of control down a cliff. Then she remembered. The cracker Mr. Barns up in the Smokies. He'd been bitten by a rabid wolf. The neighbors tied him to a tree; he had looked at her like that.

"These conditions force my hand, 'tis my only choice." Leaning forward, he jerked with pain. Deep crevices of exhaustion slapped his face like a dirty rag. He lifted his left foot out of his stirrup slowly, then slid off his horse and crumbled in a heap on the ground, unconscious.

"Let go!" Ben struggled. He fought the faceless man that bound his arms. "Ben. Ben, wake up; it's Jacob. You're having a nightmare." He slapped him across the cheek. "Wake up! I say."

Ben blinked the hazy room into focus beneath his half-shut eyelids. Insolent flies buzzed about his form in the shallow light. The curtains were drawn and only a few pinpoints of sunlight penetrated the shades drawn against the noonday heat.

Jacob patted his arm. "Good, you're goin' to be alright. Doctor Jordan managed to save your leg, and once you get over this here fever, you'll be back to your ornery self again."

Ben swallowed. His mouth felt like someone had stuffed cotton in it. "Can I get a drink of water?"

"Maggie's fetching some spring water for you now." Jacob bent over. "I's didn't want her to see you at your worst… though she nursed you through most of it as it was." Jacob's worried eyes swept him. "You back to bein' your joyful self?"

Ben's bottom lip quivered. He clamped down on it. His ears rang with the earth-splitting sounds and horror of the cannons and gunfire. A bitterly ruthless noise erupted from his lips. "That man is gone, Jacob. I'll live, then I'll die like Big Jim."

"Hmmm, you sure about that?" Jacob chuckled and patted him on his stomach. About the only place that didn't hurt. "I thinks Miss Maggie will have somethin' to say about that."

As if on cue, Maggie entered the room carrying a bucket of water, with Will leaning on a cane near her side. Will had evidently said something funny, for she was laughing. Her eyes danced, her red lips smiled, showing her even white teeth as her swishing skirts raised tiny dust particles in the semi-darkened room. Her lemon verbena sachet and soap smell wafted past Ben's nostrils.

"Well, I'm glad to see you're awake."

That smell, yes, she had been the one swabbing his face. What were they saying when they walked in, something funny about him?

Jealously, like a red-hot demon, lit on Ben's shoulder, whispering in his ear. Ben had worked his way up that impossible ladder of respect in the Union army and he wasn't going to let that Reb throw it back in his face. Let alone in front of Maggie. "Ben?" Maggie looked at him aghast. "What's wrong with you?"

Ben struggled to rise. Maggie placed some pillows behind his back. He didn't take his gaze off Will. Perspiration trickled down his forehead. He felt hot and cold all at once, his rage overtaking his emotions. He was not only a dirty Yank, but a filthy Irishman to these Rebs. Ben set his face into a solid mass of determination to complete his job.

He knew it wasn't hate for Will or Johnny Reb for they were only doing what they had to, as he was doing what he had to. It was the long-standing determination he felt when first he disembarked the *Dunbrody* famine ship that had worked its way into his bones and now lodged there like a Reb's bullet. "This is war, Maggie. I'll have to send Will to the Union prison up in Pennsylvania." Ben chuckled deep in his throat. "Least he'll get three square meals and a roof over his head, not like the sorry conditions in Anderson Prison. In that hole, it's only wormy bread and sleeping on the hard ground..."

"What do you expect?" Will stepped forward, his hand drawn into a fist. "What with Sherman making an eight-mile swath through the South, burning everything in his path."

Little Irene ran into the room, her pitter patting feet making a lively tune on the wood floor. "Papa! Irene wants to go for a walk."

Will knelt and patted her on the shoulder with his good arm. "Sure, sweetheart. But Pa might have to go away for a while. Now promise me you'll mind Miss Maggie until I return."

Little Irene buried her head into her father's chest. "No, Papa, no." Her little hands went around his neck as her blonde curly head mingled with her daddy's beard.

"Ben, if there ever was anything between us..." Maggie rushed to his side, knelt and buried her head in his sheets. "Please. Little Irene has already lost her mother." Raising her head, her bottom lip quivered; her eyes, moist with tears, beseeched him.

So she cares that much for Will to kneel here and beg like this.

Ben set his jaw. He remembered the sword that had been meant for him sinking deep into Big Jim's back instead. "Jacob, you're still in the Union army. Arrest Will and throw him in the guard house."

Jacob's bottom lip puckered forward. "But there ain't no guard house."

"Well, then." Ben threw his legs over the edge of the bed, swaying as his head swam with the sudden change from lying down to rising. Maggie's arm went out to steady him. He pushed her away. "Then commission the smoke house, whatever, lock up these Johnny Rebs before someone rides out and alerts the Confederacy that we're just a remnant here holding down Maryville."

## Chapter 29

*B*en's fist pounded the glossy varnished table where he had lain only three months ago. The irritating flies and gnats buzzed around his perspiring face. The sheers swathing the tall french windows lay limp. The servants had drawn them against the blistering August sun and no breeze rustled the trees.

It was only a matter of time before the Confederate army returned to Maryville. Rolling out his maps, he prayed his plan would work. If it did not, his regiment would land in Anderson prison.

"Ben, does it help saying I'm sorry?" Maggie placed a bowl of hominy and a corn pone on the table next to him. Breakfast, lunch, and dinner consisted of the same menu. That is, unless Jacob or Eli could trap a rabbit or two. Deer had been depleted years before, as were livestock.

He sneered. Yes, she was sorry. For what? For being part of her father's little scheme, or for letting Will go? It was as clear as the hot August sky that she was feeling guilty. Well, she'd be sorrier before the day was up.

Good thing he'd learned not to trust anyone. After all, he had his men to think about. And thank God, he and his men had fortified the old courthouse in case the Rebs returned. That was the only place where he could fight and win.

"I can't believe Will would go and tell the Confederacy... I just..." She leaned forward and a whiff of her womanliness passed his nostrils. Her soft voice tickled his ears. He closed his eyes to savor the moment.

"Daughter," her father said, eyeing Ben.

Mr. Gatlan's hatred for him was obvious. Most likely, he'd orchestrated the whole affair of having Little Irene get lost in the berry patch. It had played on Ben's conscious so badly, he'd let Will loose from the guard house to help find her. It was hard for him to believe Maggie didn't know about it. Well, no matter. What was done, was done.

A volley of boots echoed down the hallway. "Sir!"

Ben saluted back. "Yes, sergeant?"

"The courthouse is ready."

Ben turned. "Maggie, get your things, you may bring Hattie with you. You are now my prisoner."

"Oh!" Her hand went to her throat.

"No!" her father cried.

Ben turned his eyes to Maggie's father looking every bit the tall, dignified southerner in his tailored coattails and impeccably groomed even in his threadbare clothing. You wouldn't think to look at him that the South had gone through nearly four years of grueling battle and was now on the brink of defeat.

Ben felt consumed with hate for this senseless Civil War that had killed his father and Big Jim and so many young men chopped down in the prime of life. "One more word from you and I'll hang you as a spy. Do I make myself clear?"

"Major, found me another deserter." The sergeant pushed him forward. Dust particles from the courtroom floor drifted behind their boots.

"Sir, I was coming on my own free will." The man turned his hat brim around between his dirty fingers. "I didn't mean… I mean I want a second chance."

This one would make fifty. The parable about the two sons came to Ben's mind. The one son had change of heart and did his father's bidding. Where was that? Oh, yes, he remembered now. "Matthew 21:30. Do you know that verse, soldier?"

The soldier bowed his head. "Yes, sir, I know the parable of the two sons well. 'Cause I'm always running when I should be staying put. When I have a change of mind and heart."

This wasn't a coincidence. He needed everyone he could get and he didn't care a hoot what the army said. If it was all right for Jesus, it was okay for him. "You fight alongside us and give us your best, well, I'll see to it the charges are dropped against you."

The man bowed his head. "Thank you, major. Only, we're powerfully outnumbered, sir. I saw a platoon of some 1,000 Confederate cavalry riding this way. That's why I came back. It's like the Alamo, only our people are going to be slaughtered. I'll do my best to fight off these Rebs."

Ben's voice softened. "I know you will, soldier." Ben had sent Jacob to ride to the nearest Union cavalry. General Schofield was the closest; they had to hold onto this courthouse until Schofield made it to them.

Seeing a cloud of dust in the distance, he rested his arms on the windowsill and looked through his binoculars. Confederates riding fast. He heard a rustle of skirts. He turned.

Maggie had stopped wearing her hoops long ago. It complemented her figure not to have them on. My, what a vision she is, standing there with the light of the setting sun behind her, her hair bouncing about her shoulders in loose curls like a wee lass in Ireland. A vision of loveliness, she is.

Get behind me Satan. Him the reason Ben was listening to his dark side. God, I should not have brought her here to the courthouse. Help me, Jesus, protect her. It was best she thought the worst of him. Best she was with her own kind. Will would be a good husband for her. He set his jaw into determined lines and in his most angry voice, said, "Didn't I tell you to stay in the basement?"

Maggie hesitated. "Why do you hate me so? I don't believe you ever cared for me." She stepped forward. He willed his hands at his sides though he yearned to take her into his arms and kiss those sweet lips.

A knock on the courthouse door pulled his attention away from Maggie. A private ran forward. "Sir, its Big Jim…"

Ben pushed Maggie behind him. What devilment was this? Ben

gaped at the large man running toward him with an ear-to-ear grin planted on his swarthy face. Big Jim grabbed Ben and shook him.

"So you left me for dead, did ya? Well be feelin' me; I'm not a ghost come back… This is Big Jim in the flesh to be sure."

Matron Burns, her handkerchief in her hands, wiped her nose. Her black mourning bonnet nodded over her forehead, and she shoved it up with her thumb. "Polly found him in the woods two days ago, wandering about." She pointed to Polly Toole who stood next to her. "He wore only a pair of dirty trousers—"

"All we could make of it was he must have got amnesia," Polly said. "We gave him a bath and got him some clothes and nursed him back to health.

"Anyway," Matron Burns continued, "when you came back to the courthouse and we were driving him up the road, I mentioned your name, Major Ben McConnell, and suddenly his face lit up and he remembered everything. Well, nothing would do but for me to drop him off here."

"You sorry Irishman, what you doing back now?" Ben slapped him on the shoulder. "You're too solid to be a ghost! You've come to your memory too soon to my likin'. We're goin' to be fightin' a battle with no good end in sight. Now get back on that buckboard. Take Maggie and Hattie with ya. Be gone with ya, I say!" Ben turned, blinking away his tears of joy. Well, at least he could save a few lives. He was destined to join his dad soon.

"Matron Burns, you heard the major," the private said.

"Oh, but Major McConnell, Polly and I have come to get the court minutes, estate records, marriage licenses, and such from the courthouse… in case of a fire."

Ben turned. "You're welcome to them and I'll supply the labor. Soldier, give her as many men as she needs. Where do you plan to take them?"

"Across the street to Elizabeth Toole's store. Her son fled southward."

"Well, take Maggie and Hattie. Big Jim can help you and guard the store—"

"I'll be stayin' I am," Big Jim said. "You ain't goin' to get rid of me that easily, Ben McConnell."

Maggie noted Ben's cold black eyes staring at her, as if amused.

"It'll be a fine fight, Maggie my—well never you mind. Your Will shall be back at Spirit Wind directly." He lifted her chin, his eyes looking jestingly into hers. "You'll be happy to see him.... He being one of your kind and all."

"Why, of course, why wouldn't I be?" What a silly question; Will's children needed their father. "Will did what he had to do as you must do what you have to do." She shrugged. Ben's broad shoulders proudly bore the major's insignia, but Maggie knew it was the responsibility of his men's lives that burdened his thoughts.

"It's war," she whispered, wishing she could feel his arms around her. She longed to feel the strength of them, weep openly, and declare her love for him. But did he love her? "My… my place is by… " she paused. His lips parted in a sneer, as if she was the most amusing female ever to swoon at his feet.

There was a suave brutality in his eyes she hadn't noticed before. His white teeth gleamed in the shadows of the setting sunlight. "That first day I met you—"

"I recollect you called me a filthy pirate."

"But I didn't know you—"

"But I knew about the likes of you." He grabbed her arm, then dropped it like it had burned his hand. "Like belongs with like." He turned his back as if she was of no more consequence to him than a fly buzzing about his head. "Big Jim, take Maggie and Hattie to Matron Burns' buggy."

"Ben, no. I want to stay here with you."

Ben ignored her cry. His deep baritone voice hurtled orders like a bugler sounding off a charge to his men.

Maggie blinked back her tears as Matron Burns' carriage paused to unload Polly and the court records, and then lumbered down the dusty road toward Spirit Wind.

Once there, Maggie retreated to her bedroom. Outside her window, the musket fire sounded on throughout the night. She had given orders for the rooms to be cleared for the wounded to come, and Dr. Jordon was already asleep in one of the guest rooms. But as she listened to the snores of her family, she remained kneeling beside the open window, praying for Ben's and Will's safety.

The shadowy forms of two men made their way toward the house. Maggie hurried down to the front door. Hattie joined her.

The Confederate politely removed his hat. "Ma'am, we are commandeering your wagon. An old one will do."

"What you want with our wagon?" Hattie said. Her hands on her hips and her bottom lip protruded, making her look as if she had just sprouted another chin.

The soldier, taken back by her brazen reply, shuddered. "General Wheeler plans to burn the buildings around the courthouse so we can use our cannon and demolish that courthouse down around those Yanks' heads!"

Maggie clutched her throat. "Buildings?"

"Got to make a clear path for the cannons, ma'am."

Elizabeth Toole's and Matron Burns' homes were just a few that stood to become a pile of ashes. "We're waitin' for our cannon, ma'am. Should be here soon. Then we'll be moving out. Do you have a horse you can spare?"

"Hattie show this gentleman where that old wagon is behind the barn. It's not much use to us."

Hattie showed him and then returned to the front porch. Maggie had changed into her riding clothes. "Where's you fixin' to go, Miss Maggie?"

"To warn our neighbors and Ben."

"Not without me, you're not!"

Maggie ran to Father's study, opened his desk drawer, and pocketed his pistol. She hurried out the front door and to the stable to saddle up two horses. Hattie's arm cradled a lantern, and in her hand, she held some candles. Maggie scooped them up and pocketed them in her saddle bags, and they took off at a gallop across the hills.

Once near town, they tied their horses in a clump of woods and lit the lantern, then ran toward town, pounding on doors, warning of the Confederates plans. Hattie went to Polly's. Bending over, Maggie gulped air into her starving lungs from running up and down the town streets. Then she ran to the storm shelter's stone tunnel and basement beneath the courthouse. She lit the lantern that hung near the entrance. Cobwebs swept across her hair. She flung her hand over her face and shuddered. Moisture from the rains had left puddles on the dirt foot.

What if Ben takes her for a Reb coming through the tunnel? He might shoot her. She would have to take that chance. As she stood in the basement, light from the upper boards gleamed down in the darkness. Smoke filtered down through them. Had the Confederates set the courthouse on fire? I'll be trapped! Burn to death down here and no one, not even Father, knows where I've gone. Why hadn't she thought to write a note? She pounded on the trap door of the courthouse basement. "Help, someone, help."

The door creaked open on rusty hinges. Ben's head popped into sight. "What in blue blazes—"

"Colonel Wheeler is going to—" She coughed from more smoke billowing through the open windows.

"You're about five minutes too late." He pulled her up, shoving her to his chest in a crushing hug. Maggie circled his neck with her hands and wept. He does love me. He must.

His lips came down on hers in an all-consuming hunger that disappeared as quickly as it had appeared. He looked down at her and scowled. "You shouldn't have come… you're in danger here."

"I, I had to warn you."

"Show me the tunnel."

Maggie led the blue clad soldiers the way out. With guns cocked, they pored through the tunnel and out the other side.

Maggie coughed, aghast, her eyes tearing from the smoke. Burning buildings lined both sides of the street. Her face felt hot with the heat of the orange and red flames licking the velvet of the night. Where's Ben? Where's Hattie?

Maggie ran toward the tunnel. A soldier stopped her as more soldiers came running out. "Major said for me to escort you to safety," a soldier said.

The cannon sent out a volley of warnings.

The soldier smiled, his chest bloated with pride. "The major's busy right now, said he has a surprise for those Confederate soldiers, but he said to assure you, he shall meet you in the by and by—"

She heard curses, then cannon fire.

"Better we skedaddle, ma'am, right quick or else we'll miss the fireworks the major has planned for your enjoyment!"

# Chapter 30

Ben couldn't believe it. General Grant had summoned him into to his tent. Whatever for?

"Sir! Major McConnell reporting."

General Grant looked up from his glass. "Everyone please leave. John, get me some black coffee."

Ben tilted his head, puzzled. What was Grant up to this time? Grant glanced up and Ben snapped to attention.

Grant pulled a chair out next to him at the oblong table. "Have a seat. I never talk to a man that looks down at me. I need some advice."

"General Grant, from me?" Ben sat down with misgivings.

"Call me Sam, all my friends do, and I'm talking to and asking your advice as I would a friend." He twirled his empty glass around in his hand, his black hair falling across his forehead like a schoolboy's. His bearded face and the deep crevices woven permanently around his deep-set eyes told differently of his forty-some years.

"Pour me a drink from that bottle, will you, Ben?"

Ben reached across the table and poured the drink, the liquid making slurping sounds in the quiet tent.

"This helps ward off a migraine. And I feel one coming on. ...You know you missed some of that siege at Petersburg with handling that Confederate cavalry raid at Maryville."

"Sorry, sir, I mean Sam. The men and I came as soon as we knew the town was contained. We left behind us an awful mess."

"Yeah." Grant moved his long arms from the table, stretching his shoulders. "But nothing to the conditions in which we left those people in Petersburg after that ten-month siege. I tell you, Ben, because you understand it better than anyone else. You being an Irishman straight off that famine ship and me a son of a leather tanner. I don't know how I even made it through West Point with my grades. I think I had the worst record for disobedience of orders than any other cadet."

Ben chuckled. "General Custer told me he broke your record."

"He did, huh? Well, it takes a rebel to know a rebel. You know, I met Robert E. Lee while serving as a regimental quartermaster during the Mexican War. He was Lincoln's right hand man up until 1861. That's when he handed in his resignation papers. Lincoln told me Lee hated to do it, but he had to remain loyal to his Virginia. So he up and joined the Confederacy with the new Southern Republic."

Grant swallowed down the remaining liquor. "I didn't mind fighting the Mexicans, but I hate fighting against Americans. I wanted to run in and save them all… even the children show gumption." Grant looked at him, his eyes bloodshot with pain. "I kept seeing the faces of my own children. But what could I do? …They've given me the title of Butcher, you know.

"Well, it's war and I can't stand the thought of these United States being sliced up into little pieces. We're family and family has got to keep the same name, even if you do quarrel. So I bombarded and bombarded again. I even thought up a new strategy, did you know that? I've nicknamed it *trench warfare*." He slapped his palms on the table, then swept them back in his lap and sighed. "Lee's surrendering." Grant rubbed his hand through his hair. "I'm glad it's over."

Ben couldn't believe it. Had he heard correctly? Maybe there was something Grant wasn't telling him about the surrender. "Where is this surrender taking place?"

"At Appomattox, Virginia. Ever heard of such a name?"

"No, but this is cause for jubilation. Mind if I have a glass? We'll toast together."

"Right. But before we have that toast, how do I deal with a southern gentleman? I mean, rumor has it that you fancy a southern gal in Tennessee? I respect Lee and hold too much admiration for the southerner. Why, he could have stayed in the hills and drawn this war out indefinitely. But he cares about his men. He cares about this country."

Ben poured himself a drink, remembering Maggie's father. A gentleman, whether victorious or vanquished, he and his southern cause were still the winners because of their invincible valor. Ben could sympathize with Grant. "They're like the gallant cavalier of old England and we're like the swashbucklers of yore." Yes, Maggie had labeled him correctly on their first meeting.

"I couldn't put my finger on it. But you have. We're a pair of swashbucklers." Grant laughed and slapped Ben on the shoulder. "Why do you think I fought so hard? Without our southern brothers smoothing our Yankee pine needles, we wouldn't have a prayer getting anywhere in the world of politics. Northerners are brash. We haven't got enough manners to impress a southern cracker, let alone a Chinese dignitary."

Ben lifted his glass allowing it to catch and reflect the sunlight peeking into their flimsy canvas walls. "With respect, General, give Lee what's humanly possible for a general like yourself to give, 'cause there's no use arguing with a gentleman. He'll find a way to outfox you in the end."

Ben allowed the drink to burn his mouth before swallowing. "Ah, 'tis a grand day to be sure, when two generals such as you and Lee meet in harmony. It has a pleasing ring about it, would you not agree, Sam?"

Ben watched General Lee dismount, his silver hair catching the sunlight. What with his grand coat without a spot on it and his gleaming gold buttons and sash he was a cavalier, indeed.

"His black boots are so shiny," Ben whispered to Big Jim. "I believe I can see my face in them if I had the notion to try."

"Look at that saber, will ya. My, grand lookin' indeed, to be losing to the likes of us."

Grant waited for Lee to enter the room. He motioned for Ben to enter. Ben could hardly believe his good fortune.

He noticed General Grant had not done the proper preparation for the event. What had Grant's aide John Rollins been doin'? Sipping the general's ale? Ben clicked his tongue against his teeth. Grant's boots were dusty, his field uniform muddied and sooty from the ride. Ben pushed down on his coat, making it as straight as possible amidst these great generals and stood sharply at attention.

"Of course, General Lee, please have a seat. Would you care for some refreshments?"

"Perhaps, after we have reached a reasonable agreement."

"How are your men?"

"Tired and hungry. No telling what they'll encounter when they get home. There's spring planting, rebuilding…" Lee hesitated. "Much mending to do."

Grant glanced down at his muddy boots and then glanced at Lee's. "For four years your army… well, gave us… " Grant slammed his fist down on the table. "Time and again, Lee, your army has beaten the strongest forces the North could send against you! We've chewed a lot of dirt together, and for some reason the Lord has managed to make you southerners come out as shiny as those boots of yours. I've no doubt the South will flourish again because North and South are united again." Grant locked his fingers together. "That undying valor and tenacity our gallant soldiers displayed, what a heritage for all generations we have accomplished here. What Satan meant for evil, God has turned to good. …'to those who love God'… God heard the prayers of both North and South— "

"Yes." Lee chuckled deep in his chest. "I see you haven't changed through the years. Always the visionary."

"I had to be to get through West Point."

"True. May I remind you why we are here, Sam. What are your terms?"

Grant nodded for his aide to get him a pen and paper. Ben prayed for God to give Grant wisdom. Once done writing, Grant looked up, cleared his throat, and read. "This Confederate army is pardoned. Rifles will be turned in; however, officers may keep their sidearms. Personal property shall be respected."

"Sounds reasonable." Lee cleared his throat and accepted the drink of water Rollins offered him, and continued. "Don't forget about the horses and mules, Sam. The men shall need them for a late spring planting."

"Quite so. And I'll include rations for your men."

"Your terms are generous. May God be with you—"

"And with this United States of America again!"

Exiting the building, brass instruments and drums split the cheers of the men. Grant raised his arm, halting the music. "No bands."

"But General Grant, we're celebrating the end of the Civil War," the band master said.

Grant's eyes swept the soldiers. He grabbed Lee's hand and gave it a hearty shake, and in his booming voice retorted, "The war is over. The Rebels are our countrymen again."

Ben and Big Jim watched General Lee mount his dapple-grey horse, and they prepared to follow him. Lee's men stood as he rode by, their hats in their hands, then unable to restrain their voices any longer, they cheered him. General Lee stopped his horse, gaining silence. "I have done all in my power for you men, and I urge you to pick up your rations and go quickly and quietly to your homes." His sharp eyes swept his soldiers directly. "Most importantly be good citizens as you have been soldiers!"

"We've just witnessed two great generals uniting a torn country," Ben said. "Now it's up to President Lincoln to complete their handshake."

"There's sure to be a big celebration in Washington. What say we go up there and see?" Big Jim clearly wanted an Irish frolic of some sort after four years in Hades.

"Well, I'll humor you this time, 'cause I'm so glad to be seeing your ugly face that I thought would be feeding the daisies right about now. But after that I'll be heading to my home and fixin' it proper for my wife-to-be."

"Humpf. You think Maggie'll talk to you after the way you treated her?"

They rode hard and in two days joined the throng of people gathered outside the White House calling for President Lincoln. Ben looked around at the torches burning in the night. Faces lit in the blackness looked strangely unreal. Then Lincoln appeared. Tall, gaunt, looking as if a strong breeze could blow him away. He stood before the open window over the building's main north door, the customary place where presidents gave speeches.

"Looks like Lincoln been in the war right along with us," Big Jim muttered, then stepped closer. Ben hadn't been prepared for that.

A man held a light over President Lincoln's papers. His young son, his head barely above the large window frame, looked up at his father. The president smiled at his son and patted his head, then took up his papers.

"We meet this evening, not in sorrow, but in gladness of heart. The evacuation of Petersburg and Richmond, and the surrender of the principal insurgent army, give hope of a righteous and speedy peace whose joyous expression cannot be restrained. In the midst of this, however, He from whom all blessings flow, must not be forgotten. A call for a national thanksgiving is being prepared, and will be duly promulgated. Nor must those whose harder part gives us the cause of rejoicing, be overlooked. Their honors must not be parceled out with others. I myself was near the front, and had the high pleasure of transmitting much of the good news to you; but no part of the honor, for plan or execution, is mine. To General Grant, his skilful officers, and brave men …"

Big Jim jabbed Ben in the ribs. "The president is speaking about us, you sorry Irishmen."

"Hush, listen, you might be learnin' a thing or two."

"We all agree that the seceded States, so called, are out of their proper relation with the Union; and that the sole object of the government, civil and military, in regard to those States is to again get them into that proper practical relation."

A man moved forward, his tall black hat blocking Ben's sight of the president. "I'm sorry, sir, can you be removing your hat?"

The man turned, his bushy eyebrows, thick downturned mustache, and curry hair gave Ben an impression of the villain in Shakespeare's

*Macbeth*. His walking cane and distinguished dinner jacket completed his appearance.

"You can't stand there and believe this president's lies," the man hissed.

Ben ignored him as best he could. He did not wish to start a brawl. He turned his attention back to President Lincoln.

"Some twelve thousand voters in the heretofore slave-state of Louisiana have sworn allegiance to the Union, assumed to be the rightful political power of the State, held elections, organized a State government, adopted a free-state constitution, giving the benefit of public schools equally to black and white, and empowering the Legislature to confer the elective franchise upon the colored man…"

"Does that mean that the black will be given the right to vote?" Big Jim whispered.

The man slapped his hat onto his head and turned. "That will be the last speech he will make."

Ben watched the man weave his way through the crowd. "I wonder why he would be saying that?"

Big Jim scratched his whiskered chin. "Sounds like a threat to me. But with the looks of these policemen, I don't think President Lincoln has anything to worry about."

# Chapter 31

he war is over; the war is over!" the courier yelled to Maggie. "Lee surrendered to Grant in Virginia April 9! And President Lincoln is dead! Shot just yesterday."

"Yesterday?"

The rider put his hand to his hat. "Yes, ma'am, the way I heard it, President Lincoln and his wife was seeing *Our American Cousin* at the Ford's Theatre right there in Washington D.C. and this fellow named Booth—"

"John Wilkes Booth?" Maggie laid her hand to her heart. She had watched his performance in Knoxville.

Maggie's father grabbed the courier, nearly pulling him off his horse. "Are you sure Lincoln's dead?"

"Yes, sir." Fright filled the young boy's eyes.

She tugged on her father's sleeve and whispered, "He's only a child."

Her father looked down at her from the tips of his spectacles. "Child? Why I had a dozen of them, fifteen- and sixteen-year-old boys in my league. There are no children in the south, just young adults."

The boy handed her father a paper, his hand shaking. "Here, this tells all about Lee's surrender." He placed his foot in his iron stirrup.

"Wait, please."

"Yes, ma'am?"

"Are there any letters for me?"

The boy fumbled in his knapsack. "No ma'am." He looked apologetically at her from the seat of his saddle. "Don't worry, ma'am, the mail has slowed down some." He sped down the road, dust flying like a thundercloud behind his horse's feet.

She should have known the war was over, or nearly so, when Noah and some of their other slaves came back saying the soldiers didn't need them to dig the ditches for them anymore.

Noah walked up with a few of their field hands. Rakes and shovels lay over their shoulders, ready to work. "Master Gatlan, what does this all mean?"

Maggie turned, joining her father and smiled. "It means you are free to leave Spirit Wind."

The men muttered with one another, then Noah shuffled his big feet toward her. "We know that, but what if we don't want to? My family 'n me, we got no place to go." His big eyes pleadingly looked into hers.

Her father rocked on his heels, his hands in his pockets. "Would you like to continue working on the work gangs with the other plantation owners? Planting the cotton field?"

Noah took this back to the growing group of men. Noah's muscular shoulders slumped forward, his tattered shirt only coming to his elbows. "No sir, we don't like those other blacks, theys lazy."

Her father smiled. "Indeed. Well you should know. We'll figure something out. But I got to tell you, I don't have much to feed you. The Yanks took it all." Father sighed. "All we've got left is land. Hopefully, my daughter's teaching will come in handy for you, if it comes to selling the farm…."

"No'um, you can't be doin' that, Master Gatlan." Noah looked at Maggie and a big smile lit up his worried face. "Yes'um, Miss Maggie's teachin' sure helped us. Will Miss Maggie be starting up the school again in the Glenn?"

Her father hadn't heard a word. He was wiping the dust from his face, staring down at the paper. "And the war's been over for a week and we're just getting the news. Should we go tell our neighbors Lincoln has been assassinated?" Her father began to pace.

Maggie turned to Noah. "Go to the back field near the swamp and dig up that burlap bag of seeds we hid. Then start on that back field. Plant the sweet potatoes, corn, and beans. We'll be needing food first."

"Yes'um, Miss Maggie. We'll head right out."

"My bonds, my Confederate money… we're ruined, daughter." He threw down the paper. "There was some hope I could talk with Lincoln, but now…" Her father punched his fist in his hand. "Lincoln. I curse the day I met him. He was going to help the South get on its feet again. Just how is he planning to help now that he's dead?"

"It's not his fault, Father."

"What about his promises? Let me see if there's anything in here about him saying what his plans were for reconstructing the South."

"Andrew Johnson's the president now, Father. He's a southerner from our state of Tennessee. Surely he'll be lenient and help restore the South back to a prosperous establishment."

"Johnson's a Jacksonian scalawag. Not fit to be bearing the title of Southern Gentleman." Father glanced down at his paper. "Says here Sherman issued orders back in January of this year to confiscate the land in Georgia and South Carolina to be redistributed to freed slaves. According to this, about 400,000 acres of farmland have been divided amongst 10,000 freed slaves. Looks like they got forty acres, and many of the slaves received mules." Her father slapped the newspaper. "Well, when our slaves find out, they'll most likely go." Father sat down heavily on the wrought iron chair beneath the veranda.

"We're bankrupt, daughter, bankrupt in every way except our land. All I can do is maybe lease some land to each family. I'll draw up a contract, that's what I'll do and plot out forty acres to each, I could buy the seed, they can work it like it was their own and give me a piece of what they harvest. Only, they'd have to be their overseer, have to be frugal with their money and time."

Maggie plopped down in the adjoining chair. "Sort of like what Ben and his family did in Ireland."

Her father looked at her. "I know what you're thinking. But it won't be that difficult for them to get ahead. They won't pay rent, nor buy the seed. I'm just asking for a fair share of their crops. I'll pay the property taxes. I'm taking more of a gamble than they are. Hopefully, I'll get enough produce to pay for next year's seed and this year's taxes."

Cook came forward, setting down the hominy for her father and Maggie. Her father pushed the bowl aside and grabbed up his paper.

"Don't you go and turn up your nose to my food. Now you eat. It's nourishing and we's got a powerful amount of work to do."

"Yes, ma'am." Father smiled. When Cook's heavy steps receded into the house, Father turned. "We don't even have a bank anymore in the whole south, Maggie. If Lincoln had lived, I know he wouldn't have allowed this to happen to us. He loved everything connected with these United States." Her father slapped his hand down on the table. "I know what I'll do, I'll go and visit with President Johnson, find out his intentions."

Maggie looked at her porridge and muttered, "I just wish you could find out a certain Irishman's intentions."

Her father's face softened. "I shall, daughter. I will go to Washington by train and stop in Kentucky to see this young gentleman of yours, this, this Mr. McConnell. Though I do not care for his manners, not one bit; we southerners should marry within our society—"

"Like marrying like."

"Yes. Will would make you a fine husband." Her father bent forward, kissing her on the cheek. He had done that to mother, oh so many years ago. She liked pleasing Father. Life was so peaceful when she did.

His footsteps on the brick walkway receded as he strolled into the house, and she was left with her memories. Ben had said that very same thing the last time he had kissed her. "Like should marry like."

After breakfast, Maggie went to her desk and drew out the copy of Lincoln's second Inaugural address. Caressing the newspaper with her fingers, she smoothed out the folds. It had been a source of strength to her father, knowing the South was on its last brave battle. A moonbeam of hope had rested upon them from Lincoln's words that their lovely world would survive after the war. She skimmed down the page for a specific passage.

"Both read the same Bible, and pray to the same God; and each invokes His aid against the other. It may seem strange that any men should dare to ask a just God's assistance in wringing their bread from the sweat of other men's faces; but let us judge not that we be not judged....

"Fondly do we hope, fervently do we pray, that this mighty scourge of war may speedily pass away. ...With malice toward none; with charity for all; with firmness in the right, as God gives us to see the right, let us strive on to finish the work we are in; to bind up the nation's wounds; to care for him who shall have borne the battle, and for his widow, and his orphan, to do all which may achieve and cherish a just and lasting peace, among ourselves, and with all nations."

Maggie blinked back her tears. She would cling to the mercy of their benevolent Savior that God would make these southern states into a mighty fortress for Jesus. For only God and His Son, Jesus Christ, could save them from hating their northern brother.

# Chapter 32

The rain hadn't let up for three days. Ben had planted his corn, vegetables, and tobacco. Still, he'd planned to plant more. But the month of May had been nothing but storms. He couldn't stay in that lonely cabin any longer. Mr. Gatlan's words plagued the very walls. "Like should marry like."

Mr. Gatlan and Big Jim had sat him down and made him see the sense in it. What was there to live for? He had only his land.

Well, he would plant in the rain. He would try a crop of cotton, though his other neighbors were planting more tobacco. Cotton had skyrocketed after the war. His land was fertile enough to grow anything under the sun. He blinked. However, the sun was concealing itself this day.

"Giddy up!" Nellie refused to take another step. "Giddy up or I'll beat your worthless hide and sell your shredded carcass to the tanners!" Nellie heehawed and sat down in the muddied puddle of churned up dirt. "Why, Lord, did you allow Caedmon to die and let this stubborn mule live?"

A lightning bolt streaked across gray clouds and slapped into a nearby tree, cutting it in two with a ghastly sound that made Ben's ears ring and frightened Nellie so that she took off at a gallop.

"Whooooaa." Ben held onto the plow reins, jumping and springing across the clumps of earth like a dancing leprechaun, then fell face down into the mud for his troubles. Spewing mud and water from his mouth, he wiped the slimy mixture from his eyes. The mule, with the new plow turned on its side like a tiny sleigh, slid down the hill toward the cabin.

Someone laughed.

Where could that voice be coming from? Getting to his knees, he looked around. The sheets of rain washed down his body, clearing away some of the mud, but it did little help in seeing… a man and mule black as the dirt he'd wallowed in only a moment ago, climbed the hill toward him. The man's lopsided grin offered Ben a welcome he could not refuse.

"Jacob! 'Tis a fine day for you to be out on a ride."

"You stubborn Irishman! Trying to plow a furrow in the rain. Why your mule has more sense than you."

Ben plopped his hat on his head. Water streamed down his face from his sodden brim. "Humpf! I'll be doing what I will with my land."

"I came all the way from Tennessee to visit you. Do you have a few minutes to be neighborly?"

"That I do." His boots sloshed with every step sliding down his hill. His army breeches felt ten pounds heavier with the mud and water he'd accumulated during his ordeal. "You go on into the cabin. I'll be there shortly. I'll tend to your mule and be taking care of mine."

"You haven't changed, Ben McConnell, not in the five years I've known ya." He leaped down from his mule and helped Ben unharness his mule and then pointed to the cabin. "I'll tend to the livestock. You need to get out of those wet things and into something warm."

Ben huffed and eyed Jacob. His confidence had improved, as had his diction. "'Tis a change in positions, I be feelin'. Being at Spirit Wind has improved ya, though I don't know that I care for your uppity ways."

Jacob grew serious. "Uppity? When a friend wants to help a friend? Besides, I believe I should be helping a ghost."

"Ghost?" Ben knew something was wrong with Jacob. Now his words confirmed this. He slapped himself in the chest. "I'm flesh and blood with a little of the blarney still in me. Though wet it may be."

"Well Maggie thinks you're died and Will is fixin' to marry her. But the marriage is postponed until after the sheriff's sale of Spirit Wind."

The rain pounded on the barn's metal roof like a man's hammering. Ben sat down on a bale of hay, wiping his face with his cavalry issued red bandana. "Saints preserve us. I pray I didn't hear what I thought I heard." Grabbing Jacob's arm, he pushed him forward. "Come, we'll go inside and do our talkin."

"Do you love Maggie or not?" Jacob's features grew grotesquely sharp in the glow of the hearth.

Ben felt their clothes drying by the fire. Still damp. He picked up a large spoon and stirred his pot of Irish stew, his face feeling hotter from Jacob's words than the heat of the fire. "You've never had Irish stew, have you?"

"Have you heard anything I said, you stubborn Irishman?"

"I'm through with Maggie." He didn't lift his head from over his pot of brew. Her father had been right. He could never give Maggie what she was used to. Oh, he'd had hopes that someday he would. He looked about his small cabin. Firm and strong, the weather could not penetrate its walls. Still, it wasn't the fine place like Spirit Wind. He did not care to be feeling inadequate, didn't like losing his hopes, but the Irish in him needed to be practical. No, Maggie would be happier with her own kind. "Like should be marrying like."

Jacob paced back and forth. His bare feet slapping the wooden floor like a Cherokee war drum. "Now, tell me what do you want?"

Ben spooned out the stew into wooden bowls, blowing on his spoonful before sampling his cooking. It went down well, warming the inside of him. He hoped to chase away the chill he felt in his bones by foolishly venturing out on a day like this.

Maggie's tearstained face came before him amidst the dark steaming brew. That night the Confederates raided the courthouse when he couldn't help but feel her lips on his once more.

Jacob stopped his pacing. He turned Ben around, peering into his face. "Tell me the truth. Did Maggie's father come here?"

Ben nodded.

"I thought so. Now it all makes sense." Jacob began to pace again. "Did you tell her father to tell Maggie you died in Virginia?"

Ben spun around. "Now why would I being doin' a fool thing like that?" He hung his head. "'Tis providence come to visit me. Perhaps I'm more valuable dead than alive."

"But why didn't you go after her? Why didn't you, Ben?"

"Her father said that she'd be contacting me if she had a change of mind. Said that 'like should marry like' and Big Jim wholeheartedly agreed with him. They both agreed against me that I would be doing a grave sin asking Maggie to make a choice, which might be more out of pity than love…" Ben turned, his broken nails diggin' into the fleshy part of his palms. "I'll not have any wife of mine pity herself for want of a better life."

"Big Jim McWilliams. I haven't seen him in quite a while." Jacob stirred the stew in his bowl, taking a hesitant bite. "Better than the food at Spirit Wind. …Maggie's father is sick and Spirit Wind is being auctioned next week for taxes. He might not even have a bed to die in and all because of his southern pride."

Was Jacob telling the truth? One conscionable act leads to a consequence. Ben walked to the painting of Jesus hanging on the far wall. He was standing in the midst of the sheep, resting on His shepherd's cane, looking right at Ben. "It takes one wee step down the wrong path to make ya lost." Yes, we are but sheep that have gone astray. Pray, bring me back upon that narrow path, Jesus.

Standing on the porch of Spirit Wind, Maggie handed out the knapsacks she had prepared for her faithful servants, each filled with corn pone, an apple, yams, a book, and a page from the Bible each individual had chosen.

The cupboards were cleared and the library shelves empty. It was all she had left to give them. "I am proud of you. And I know God has something especially good planned for each and every one of you."

"Yes'm, Miss Maggie. Thank you, Miss Maggie."

She watched them as they walked down the road. Some had placed their knapsacks on a twig they cut from a nearby tree and had rested it upon their shoulders. A ragged bunch of men, women, and children traveling down the winding road to a destiny unknown, much like Ben and his feisty Irishmen had some eight years before.

Her heart leaped within her chest, recalling Ben and his merry eyes, always alert like one of their coon dogs on a new scent. Always ready to kick up his heels to do a jig. What had he told her that first day? Something about the spirit of liberty? Her eyes filled with tears. It was so hard to believe he was dead.

Maggie leaned back against one of the pillars. The auction was just a week away. She had asked Lawyer Peabody for his aid in transferring the large estate into a park. That would please Father, knowing that Spirit Wind would remain intact. She had also proposed the Glenn, the small plot of land separate from Spirit Wind that Father and Mother had first settled on, remain to them. They had the tax money for those forty acres.

If that didn't work, they could always go to Father's home place. But Father's kin hadn't fared too well either. She looked out at the barren fields, rutted from wagon wheels, soldiers' horses, and boots. The tattered remains of their cotton and tobacco sheds had been stripped of their livelihood by one night's celebration when the Yanks rode through on their way to Georgia.

It was so quiet without the slaves, without their singing and merrymaking at all hours. So still without the horses filling their stables with their neighs and the clomping of their hooves on the brick paving stones. She even missed the old rooster waking her up in the mornings.

Will's boots clumped their way down the hallway, void now of its fine furnishings and echoing like an empty wooden tunnel. They had sold everything for tax money. In his good arm, Little Irene, not so little anymore, clung to his whiskered face. Her blonde curls floated about his face and he blew one dangling curl aside and laughed.

"Aunt Maggie, tell Papa not to cut his whiskers. I'm afraid I'll not recognize him."

Will laughed and set her down. "My, you're getting to be a big girl." He wagged his finger in her face. "I think we should stop calling you 'Little' and just Irene, would you like that?"

"Yes." Irene jumped up and down on her bare feet. "Then I'll be more like Flora and Jacob Jr. Can I go play now?"

Flora and Jacob Jr. came skipping in from one of the buildings Jacob and Prudence had made up for their house. Maggie watched Irene dash down the steps toward her friends. "Flora?" Maggie waved her hand. Flora looked up and skipped toward them. "Have you heard anything from your father?"

"No, ma'am."

"Then, perhaps, you'll stay on longer, at least until after the auction."

"Mama says that's her plans."

"Sweet Maggie, always worrying about everyone else and never thinking about her own happiness." Will's voice was low and soothing. He sighed deeply, leaning closer to her, his breath stirring her hair and tickling her ear. "I know this isn't the time or place to be asking you this. But we need to set the wedding date. These cursed northerners coming down here to rape our country won't steal our joy at having us a beautiful wedding. I'd like to see them try."

She clutched the nearby pillar as if to draw strength from its solidness. Will couldn't relinquish his hate. Oh, if only she could love Will, then Father would be content. Will would be happy because Irene would have a mother, and she should be happy because she would have a loving husband.

God, I have nothing in common with Will but our southern heritage. She, like the citizens of Maryville, was glad the South was reunited with the North. Suddenly she knew the truth.

Lord, I can't marry Will. I just can't; it would be wrong. Maggie turned. That was her undoing. She flattened her back against the pillar as Will reached for her. His eyes staring deeply into hers, his lips dangerously close. She turned her face away. He kissed her hair. "Will, I don't love you. I wish I did. You deserve a loving woman. Someone to love you back."

"Look at me, Maggie." He touched her chin and gently turned it.

Maggie raised her downcast eyes. "Miss Peabody loves you and she adores your children. Please give her a chance?"

He took his thumb and gently wiped away a tear. "I am very fond of her, and you're right, both Irene and Will Jr. adore her. Now, let's be honest. Tell me that you are not still in love with Ben McConnell."

His eyes seemed to swallow her face whole.

"I'm not going to allow you to become an old maid, Maggie, you've got too much loving in you for that." His mouth fell onto hers hungrily. She didn't fight it. Her lips felt bruised by his advances. He raised his sandy head. She met his gaze.

"That was like kissing my sister. ...I had hoped..." He put his hat on his head and walked down the stairs. Not looking back, he said, "Well, it takes longer for some, but love will come... I'll be up in the woods, chopping down trees."

Hattie walked toward her and wrapped an arm around her waist. "Go for a walk, Miss Maggie. A walk will do you powerful good."

"I think I shall." Maggie grabbed her bonnet and down the cement steps she went. Walking up the lane, she turned toward her hill, the place where she first heard the cry for help that brought Ben to her side.

There lay their cotton plants, a few puffs of cotton clinging to the vines like stubborn children to their mother. A noise came from the distant road. A wagon and six white horses galloped toward her.

Horses were scarce and to have hitched six to a team, seemed wasteful in these times of need. The man stood and waved at her. Who could he be? In this new world of theirs it wasn't a good thing for a woman to be out alone. Colored men and carpetbaggers had pilfered and raped white woman. She lifted her skirts and ran to Spirit Wind.

"Maggie Gatlan, I came for ya."

She stopped, shielding her eyes with the upturned palm of her hand. Of all the absurdity, who could this stranger be? Will was in the forest on the north side somewhere. He couldn't possibly save her if this... Oh my, the wagon had a white cover over it. It was like the covered wagon father had brought from Virginia to this new land. It was rocking back and forth like a boat on a wave-tossed sea of grass and hills. The man must be unstable; what else would be his reason for racing his horses like that?

The horses were loping in a canter, and the dust from the wheels billowed up behind the wagon. The man held the reins in one hand and a whip in the other. He cracked it and it set off a volley of noise echoing about the hillside. Hair as black as the ace of spades, his dark beard flowing in the breezes. Fear clutched her throat. She picked up her skirts and ran. Had John Brown come up from the grave after her?

The screech of brakes, the horses neighing, and she heard a man's labored breathing behind her. She zigzagged, hoping to lose him, just a few more steps toward the slave quarters, just a few.

"Wait I say, you obstinate lass!" he grabbed her and she fought him, her arms flying.

"Let me go, let me go you—"

"Pirate? Aye, my bonny lass 'tis your Irishman in the flesh, he is."

Maggie peeked out from her dark curls that had fallen across her face. She blew a strand away. "Ben McConnell?"

"Yes, 'tis me."

She gasped, gulping in a deep breath. He's alive? "I, I thought you were John Brown's ghost. Why, you arrogant Irishman, you nearly frightened me to death." She struggled to be free of his grasp. "You were alive all this time and didn't come for me?"

His black as coal eyes danced into hers in merriment. "You'll not be running away from me until you hear me out, now will you? I want to tell you about my place."

How could she ever have thought she loved such a... flirt? He's so conceited, he must have thought she'd run into his arms. The audacity. Why he's nothing but a, a happy-go-lucky Irishman who didn't have a thought in his head but for his foolish land.

She struggled. His arms were firm about her and unrelenting. Struggling wasn't doing her any good, and only made her want him the more... oh, foolish woman, she was. "Oh, alright, I'll listen to your ...your... blarney."

His eyes cloudy, a puzzled expression swept his handsome face. "I won't be taking much of your time. I understand you are to be wed."

Wed? Slightly confused, how had he known? She just nodded.

Ben looked around and seeing the cabin he'd spent so many months in convalescing, he started toward it. "Come, Maggie, we can talk in here and renew our acquaintance. Remember? The summer when I wasn't able to walk?"

"How can I forget it?"

He guided her up the steps, then politely opened the door allowing her entry first.

The room was as she had left. Maggie bit down on her lip. Would he notice there wasn't any dust on the cupboard or sideboard? She had just been there the other day. This was her prayer room. Where she came to be alone. Where she found solace to face another day without—

"Maggie." His voice was low and gentle. He walked around the room, his steps competing with the robins outside striking up a tune in the nearby blossoming apple tree.

He hadn't changed. Tall, square of shoulder, and his strong legs pounding the boards as he paced. His black beard gave him a frightening appearance. She frowned. "Why did you keep your beard? You look like the—"

"Pirate scoundrel that I am?" Ben laughed. "I've been working on my land… then I saw no point, for you see…" He grabbed her Bible from off the vanity. "Look. 'Tis here what's inspired my visit. 'Tis this that told me to come. All through the roads littered with wagon wheels and broken harnesses and dead animals too numerous to count, I wondered if anything good could come of this war. And this verse hummed in my mind, singing a new tune to my wayward feet." He flipped through the pages. "'Now the Lord is that Spirit: and where the Spirit of the Lord is, there is liberty.'

"See, Maggie, where there is no vision, no faith, there is no hope and we shall perish without a vision, perish for not believing the Almighty can do anything He so chooses… God united these States for a reason, Maggie, and where His Spirit presides nothing is impossible for us, or for America. We'll carve our fortune out of the refuge of this war the way your father and mother did out of the wilderness."

Maggie turned toward the window, listening to a singing cardinal.

He was such an idealist. Had Ben not seen the frowns on people's faces, their eyes full of hate? Maggie burrowed her eyes into his. Angry, resentful. After all, his side had won. "You speak of faith? Hope? In what? The wind blows where it wishes and so does the wrathful nature of man. Just look what your Union has done to the South. How—"

"We will overcome, Maggie, my lass, just believe. Our good Lord never intended God-fearing people to fight among themselves."

"My father curses the flag that flies at the Capitol. There is so much hate here for the northerner you can cut the very air with it." She turned away and buried her face in her hands and sobbed. "Go away. Leave me alone." She heard his steps behind her.

"It'll take more than a day." His voice was but a whisper, so soft, so gentle. "It'll take years to remove the stench of this war from the nostrils of the southerner. But have faith, it will happen." He took her into his arms. She had no strength left.

She laid her head on his chest. She could hear his heart beating, feel his strong fingers covering her arms, his arms hugging her to him. There was peace and strength and an undying faith in Jesus here. Ben's bright hope and love for his fellow man. She felt the security she longed for. New hope coursed through her veins. God had heard her pleas; only God knew the yearnings of her heart. This wasn't the end of the South or the end of her and Ben's lives, but the beginning.

"I've renamed my farm to Shushan, Maggie. For during the bloodiest battles, when I did not see how I would come out alive… I prayed for God to choose the victor, and Esther 8:6 came to my mind 'For how can I endure to see the evil that shall come unto my people? or how can I endure to see the destruction of my kindred?' The United States is established beneath God's commandments. I now claim Esther 9:2 for America: 'and no man could withstand them; for the fear of them fell upon all people.'

"Maggie, it was then I knew the commonality we had between Yankee and Johnny Reb."

"What similarity could there possibly be?"

"We were both battling Satan himself." His eyes burned into hers, infusing her with his truth and the wisdom of a man who had gone through the fiery furnace. "It was Satan who wanted to kill the idea of the *United* States, for America to lose faith in God and our Savior, Jesus. Satan wanted to stop the traveling evangelists from spreading God's Word. He wanted the immigrants to give up and leave this bonny land, but we didn't stop loving our God—we couldn't.

"We didn't stop believing in the Stars and Stripes we carried with us into battle. Only if there is no vision can a man or a country perish. I realized that watching Grant and Lee shake hands. A bloody four-year war ended with a solid hand shake and a determination to reunite and rise again! We are stronger, Maggie, because of the bloodshed. Stronger now than ever before." He took her in his arms and hugged her. "Like Lincoln said, 'there shall be a new birth of freedom.... With malice toward none; with charity for all; with firmness in the right.'"

Maggie's heart quickened. "As God gives us to see the right, let us strive on to finish the work we are in; to bind up the nation's wounds."

His eyes had not left her face. "A husband and a wife must have the same goals, same dreams, same God." Ben knelt before her, took her hands in his, and kissed them. "Marry me, Maggie, my lass."

"Oh, Ben. Yes, with all my heart." Maggie laughed. "Father will be happy now."

Ben stood. "How so?"

"Because like is marrying like. We are new beings in Christ Jesus striving for one commonality, to make this nation the best Christian nation it can be until Jesus returns to claim His own."

Ben's dark head lowered to hers, his lips gently caressing hers, then he swept her up into his embrace. "For here destiny awaits, a whirlwind of destiny our children shall decide, and they will need the shield of faith we believe in to get through the terrible battles. And faith as small as a wee mustard seed that my dad bequeathed me to believe it!"

# *Chapter 1*

*S*omething was amiss. She could sense it.

Collina May McConnell shrugged the feeling off as tiredness. Joseph McWilliams and she had loaded hay and a thousand pounds of feed on her wagon not more than an hour ago.

Joseph sat astride his sorrel gelding next to her wagon, scowling at Emerald's townsfolk. His fiery-red hair and thick beard added to his frightful appearance. *What's got into Joseph? This isn't like him.*

Store clerks sweeping the wooden porch leading to their doorways paused in midstride. Children stopped their snow ball fights. Three young men outside of Jim's Mercantile halted their chatter.

A woman ran out of the mercantile like a passel of hornets was attacking her, hauled a boy up by the inside scrap of his collar, and glared at Collina.

"If looks could kill—"

"Smallpox carrier Collina May, smallpox carrier go away, we don't want you or any McConnell to stay!" the young men yelled.

A chill went through her, the townspeople stares crushing her morale. She pulled her team to a halt and jumped down from the wagon. The thwack of her boots echoed in the silence as she slammed up the wooden steps to Doctor Baker's office. She grabbed the medicine left on the porch, then took the steps down two at a time.

Joseph jumped off his horse and barred her escape, his large hand like an iron anvil weighing her shoulder, his red head as alert as a bird dog's on a sudden shift in wind. "What you fixin' on doing, drivin' your team home in a snowstorm just 'cause some mama boys called you a name who ain't got nothin' better do with their day than pick on a lone woman?"

"Let go, Joseph." She figured the reason he'd ridden into town with her was to put a halt to her plans. She yanked away from his grip. "I can handle myself and my team as good as any—"

"Man?" Joseph interrupted. "When are you going to realize God made you a woman for a reason? You just say the word and those men won't feel like singing anymore."

Her puckered eyebrows met his scowl with one to match.

"Seems like yesterday you were just a freckle-nosed kid kicking that big Macintosh boy in the behind 'cause he'd muddied up your stockings."

"Wasn't just the Macintosh boy that got my boot, I'm recalling. And it looks like I…" She looked away. Joseph knew some of the story. She would spare him the details. Now she knew what a leper must have felt like back in Jesus' time. Well, she needed to get this medicine to Father.

Joseph's six-foot build had a width of shoulder that won him easily every arm wrestling fight from Kentucky to the Tennessee border … but he let go of her without a struggle. His arms fell to his sides as he hunched his muscular shoulders against the north wind. "These are truly bitter days in more ways than a thermometer can record."

"I'll be all right," she whispered. She swallowed down the lump that followed, seeing the pity in Joseph's eyes.

"Take Haggerman Road, not that lane you came in on. I'd go with ya, only Pa's come down with a bad case of the gout." Just the two of them were left. Joseph's ma and sister died of typhoid last summer.

Joseph's pa, Big Jim, and her pa went back a long way. Both were Irish immigrants and had fought side by side during the Civil War. She wished she could help. But her pa wasn't faring any better than Joseph's.

"Too long that way." The wagon seat felt cold and wet. She grabbed her lap blanket. Thick white flakes of snow flew gracefully downward, as if they'd sprouted wings. Wet and pearly white, they rested on her red-plaid blanket like tiny flies—little snowflies. Just a passel of fly-flakes. She could make it through the pass. Pa always says a person can make good of any situation.

Joseph stared up at her. Thick waves of hair tussled about his generous forehead that sloped to a firm jaw. It was a face unchangeable by circumstance. "Someday someone will come along and make those stubborn feet of yours want to follow. But I sure pity that gent's toes before you learn the step."

"You're not bad lookin' from up here. You might even be powerful handsome if you ever took a razor to those whiskers you call a beard." She laughed as deep crimson spread across his face like a sign post telling of his adoration for her.

He bent forward, resting on his strong forearms. "Most girls tell me I'm handsomely appealing!"

She knew that to be true. She couldn't figure why he even looked her way. "Joseph, thanks for... well, you know." She never held much store in the prating tongues of the townsfolk. So, she'd not lost anything losing their friendship. She had the friend that mattered. "I'm long overdue at Shushan." She slapped the reins. "Giddup!"

If the townsfolk want something to gawk at, she'd give it to them. "Yah!"

Her horses picked up the pace to a trot. She gave the clicking sound and with heads arched, her horses went into a high-stepping gait. The ground beneath the wagon pounded their beat.

"Yeehaw, Collina, you show them!" Joseph hooted.

She grinned. Every storeowner's nose was pressed to the window pane.

The harness and breast plate buckles jingled in unison... the ice and snow wasn't so bad, the ground was soft, and taking the lane meant she wouldn't have to endure the townspeople's gawking. Like Joseph, Pa had warned her not to, said you never know what's lurking around a bend in the road, but Pa hadn't heard the townsfolks' new song about them, either.

She burrowed into her wool collar. The snow blanketing western Kentucky had put everyone in a bad spirit. January of 1898 had started out cold and stayed that way. It being the first day of March, surely the worst was behind them. What more could happen? As Collina made her way home, the wind picked up and so did the snow. Flakes blew about her team like dandelion seeds. She wished it was dandelion seeds and not a storm she had driven her six white horses into.

The horses strained against their harness, heads bent low to the ground, their strong hindquarters digging into the hill as they pulled the heavily laden wagon through the rutted and snow covered lane and up the steep hillside.

She couldn't see for the blowing flakes. Then just as suddenly as the storm had begun, the wind seemed to sweep the snowflakes away. She could see now that the stars were just appearing in the new night, and through the scurrying clouds that swept the sky like grey ghosts, the soft, mellow rays of the full moon suddenly lit the snow-covered pathway with a luminous glow. The words of Matthew 17:20 came to mind. "If ye have faith as a grain of mustard seed, ye shall say unto this mountain, Remove hence to yonder place; and it shall remove; and nothing shall be impossible unto you." Lord, please get me and my team home safely is all I'm asking. But if You feel like moving something, please take this smallpox plague off the McConnells' shoulders.

The old vagrant Mother and Father had fed and clothed during the winter months gave the McConnells the smallpox. That old vagrant who lost his home and family after the Civil War always wintered in the McConnell's sharecroppers' cabin. Mother nursed him and Father buried him. Mother said she'd do no different even if she had known the outcome. Nine of the McConnells had contracted the pox. Only she and Mother had proved immune.

She hunched her shoulders to ward off another blow from the chilling wind. What is the matter with me? Mother always said never to look back at trouble, or else it was sure to follow you around like a long tail to a hound dog!

The left front wheel of the wagon rolled into a rut with a jolt. "Whoa, Daisy. Easy Jude." Collina braced her boots against the bumper panel, her lap blanket falling to the floor. Daisy fell to her knees, then Jude. She could feel the hay on the wagon shift. Daisy neighed, whipping her head from side to side, fighting to free her front leg from the crevice.

Collina jumped down and worked her way to the lead mare.

Daisy's nostrils glowed red in the pitch darkness. Collina blew on her hands, willing her cold fingers to become nimble and tried to loosen the taut leather straps. "Jesus, help me!"

Her horses neighed. She heard an answering neigh, then a man rode up.

"What—"

"You hurt?" A pair of strong hardened hands wrapped themselves around hers. "Are you hurt?"

The wind whipped away her words of gratitude, as snow peppered her eye lashes. The man, dressed in a large sweeping grey cape, breeches, and a wide brimmed cavalry hat, scowled at her.

"Who are you and why are you riding Pa's stallion?"

"Guess that means you're not hurt. Can you hold the harness taut?"

The soldier grabbed the slippery strap, then motioned for her to take his place. Daisy, feeling the slackened pressure, struggled to rise, thrashing out wildly with her foreleg. Collina clung on, digging her fingernails into the wet leather.

"You've got as much strength in those arms of yours as a fly does to lift an elephant."

The wagon moaned, swaying and twisting like a ship lost on a billowing wave. Flakes of timothy hay flew about their heads. She coughed, spewing fragments of the hay from her mouth. Jupiter reared and the front wheels bounced from the force, causing pressure on the shafts of the last four horses.

"Get out of here!" the soldier yelled.

"No!"

The man's large hand gripped her shoulder like an iron vice and shoved her nearly two yards across the mud and snow.

A groan escaped her. She'd landed hard. Her tongue tasted fresh blood from the gash in her lip. She stumbled to her feet, wincing with pain.

The man threw his hat off his head. His straight dark hair shone blue black in the moon's rays. Placing his broad shoulder underneath the cross bars, the glint of his steel knife shone in the moon's light.

"A knife? Don't cut that harness. It's from London, England!"

The soldier glanced up.

She gasped at the boldness in his eyes. The blade of his knife gleamed in the moonlight at her to beware. She glanced toward her wagon, recalling the shotgun on the floorboards and inched toward it. Daisy jumped to her feet. "Shove that rock behind the front wheel. Good, now you take the mare and bring me back that gelding. …Good."

He hooked up Jude, kicking the rock away from the front wheels. "Ya! Ya!" He guided horses and wagon safely onto the high side of the lane. "Only right thing you did was hitch up enough horses to pull this overburdened wagon."

He hitched Daisy to the one remaining strap, and retrieved his hat. The inside lead rein dangled like a disjointed rudder on a ship.

"I declare, I've never seen such an outfit like the one you're wearing."

"Franklin Long of the 1st Volunteer Cavalry, ma'am. Roosevelt calls us the Rough Riders." His cavalier pride was as evident as the cape that swept his broad shoulders.

She couldn't help but admire the man. Charles Dana Gibson could have acquired his inspiration for his Gibson Man from Franklin Long.

She reached down into her buckboard and produced Pa's gun and cradled it in her arms. "Just where were you heading with my pa's horse?"

Franklin smiled, sweeping his big brimmed cavalry hat from his head. "Looking for you, ma'am. Your father gave me permission to ride him when Doc Baker told me to fetch you."

"What? Now how do you know the Doc?"

"I was heading for Florida and decided to stop in to see my good friend. He, Roosevelt, and I were on the same polo team back in Long Island. Only, seems I've got enlisted by Doc Baker as a medical dispatcher for the McConnells."

Could be he's telling the truth. She placed the rifle back onto the wagon seat. After all, if he wanted to do her harm, he'd have done it by now.

"Your lip is bleeding a little, right there."

"If you recall, I encountered a nasty fall." Her hands felt gritty. She wiped them on her riding skirt. She felt the knot of her scarf playing with her earlobe. She fumbled with the crude tie. There, she had it undone. Her thick hair, once braided neatly down her back, now bounced about her shoulders in wild curls. "Oh no, it's come undone."

A half-smile teased the corners of his mouth.

"Here," he said, extending his handkerchief. The wind played through her curls like notes on a piano. His eyes followed the movement. "A young girl like you shouldn't be out alone."

"I'm old enough."

"It's a good thing there was a full moon. It helped me get your team unstuck — I apologize for that tumble I gave you." His fingers wrapped around her hand as if seeking solace for his actions. "Your hand is cold. Here take my gloves."

He was much too forward to suit her. She yanked her hand away. "I'm fine."

"It couldn't be helped... you did a foolish thing taking this lane."

"I cut two hours off going this way."

"Oh? Good thing Doc warned me not to expect the expected from you."

It was on the tip of her tongue to call him a liar. Doc Baker would never say such a thing about her — would he? Oh, the gall of this man. "Well, I almost made it. This was the last big hill. After this one I'd have been home in half the time it would take going down Haggerman Road."

Franklin's thick brows arched in deep angles above his troubled eyes. "I'd just hate to see that pretty head of yours crushed beneath your wagon bed." He raked his fingers through his hair. "Girl, you need to quit trying to fill a man's boots. But I've got to say, you've got more gumption than most men I know. Let's get you home. Take the stallion; I'll bring the wagon."

"Quit referring to me as a girl. I'll have you know I'm full grown."

He chuckled. "Sure, kid. Doc Baker wrote me how hard it's been. How you and your mother have been doing all the work on your farm. I'll stay on until I get my orders. You're going to need help now that your father—"

"Do you even know what you're volunteering for? Lincoln freed the slaves some time ago. It's not the glamorous Old South of yesteryear and hardly as adventurous as riding off to some exotic country in a shiny uniform."

His mouth contorted into a grimace. Collina met his scowl. "Then there's the smallpox. Some believe I'm a carrier, like that Typhoid Mary person. Even after Doc explained to everyone in town about smallpox, but people still part like the Red Sea whenever I walk down Main Street. I can't blame them. Smallpox leaves terrible pits on your face. No, you go back to your make-believe war and allow the rest of us to live in the real one."

Her hand gripped his handkerchief. She had the very thing that would crumble that proud and arrogant face. "Here's your handkerchief, Mr. Long. But are you sure you want it back? Some of my blood's on it."

His eyes turned an icy steel-blue color.

She shivered. She'd hate to meet that gaze when he was toting a gun. Then his fingers wrapped around her hand and she felt the strength of them.

"Yes, some of your blood is on it." Lifting the soiled cloth to his lips, his eyes never left her face. He wiped his mouth and said, "Girl, you've got a lot to learn. Now, get on this horse. I'll follow you with the wagon."

Her rifle was in that wagon. She didn't know this stranger well enough to leave him with her team and a loaded gun. She turned to climb onto the seat. Then his arms wrapped around her waist like an iron corset.

"Let go of me!" She could hardly breath, and all she could sniff was his aftershave, which reminded her what she must smell like, thanks to her horse. Next thing she knew, she was airborne and swung over his should like a bag of oats.

She beat him on his back and tried to kick herself free. Her legs felt like they were caught in a vice. What has he got for arms, lead? "I demand you let me down this instant!"

"Get on that horse," he dropped her to the ground. "Or I'll place you on him myself — you can ride, can't you?"

She swung at him. He ducked, holding her at arm's length. "I see I've got my hands full of one spitfire tonight."

"You're a bully. Picking a defenseless—" She kicked him in the leg.

"Ow …defenseless …you …why—"

She took the remaining steps to Raymar at a run and jumped into the saddle. A smirk swept his lips. Did he have to look so handsome in that uniform?

"Just as I suspected, you straddle a horse like a full-fledged Injun." Bending over he rubbed his leg. "And you have a wallop like a boxer.

Now go! I just hope you're not too late."

"Late?" She'd totally forgotten. "The medicine!" She galloped Raymar toward the wagon, grabbed the package and tucked it into her coat, then turned Raymar sharply toward the lane. He did a half-rear.

The clamor of her horse's hooves matched beat for beat the pounding of her heart. Was Franklin just being overly alarmed? Still, there had to be something seriously wrong for Doc to ask a perfect stranger to fetch her back.

The large oak doors rested partly open. Collina's older sister, Myra, gave them a thrust, then stepped back. In the kerosene lamplight, Mother's big mahogany furniture etched jagged shadows across the Indian rug, the fire on the stone hearth casting crimson hues of light. Collina walked past the small parlor into the bedroom quarters. Like silent sentries, the McConnells stood around the big four-poster bed.

Her mother's walnut colored hair tinged with silver was swept into a coiffure. A smile creased her lips. She walked toward Collina with a regal poise that always flowed invisibly about her countenance, that impeccable grace that always claimed recognition.

"Collina," her mother whispered. "Your father's been asking for you."

Doc Baker looked up. His greying hair appeared more silver in the lamplight, and the shadows etched deep lines around his forehead and beneath his eyes, making him appear older than his sixty years. Taking the stethoscope off her father's chest and clicking the earpiece out of his ears, he rested them around his neck. "Did Franklin find you?"

Collina nodded. Pa looked so pale, so tired.

"Good. Your father's sleeping now. Let him. There's nothing more I can do." He slapped his bag shut and started toward the open door, then stopped, glancing toward her mother.

"His heart's worn out, Maggie, too much for it to handle, what with the sickness. Told him before to stop harboring every tramp from here to the Tennessee line." His voice quivered, then grew gruff. "I told Ben,

I warned him, he needed a rest. Told him the work would always be there but he might not."

Her mother gently touched Doc Baker's arm. "He's a hard one, my Ben, could never stay still for long."

"Well, I'll be downstairs if you need me." Doc turned, swiping his eyes with his big hand.

"Children go on with Doc Baker. I'd like to talk to Collina alone, Maggie said.

Collina felt like someone had punched her in the gut. They couldn't live without Pa. She blinked away her tears, hurried to the large brick fireplace, and laid a birch log on the hot ashes. A popping noise, then a meowing wail followed as dying embers encircled its prey with hungry fingers, consuming the white parchment with an unquenchable appetite.

"What… what happened? Father appeared in good spirits when I left."

"A massive stroke, a blood clot somewhere caused it…"

Her father stirred.

"Come, child." Maggie rose tiredly from the large Bentwood. "Death never waits on convenience."

"Pa?" Collina bent low toward the still form.

Her father's eyes opened, fluttering for a moment. He lifted his blue-tinged hand in recognition. His lips worked their way into a crooked grin. "You got that hay and grain from the McWilliams okay?"

She nodded. "With the usual measure of trouble thrown in for flavor."

His eyes creased into a smile. "It's the pepper sprinkled on our table meat that gives it flavor, right daughter? What's the date? Are we still in February or—"

"No, Father, it's March and would you believe, I just rode our whites through what felt like a blizzard."

"It'll not last. Hard times never do… Hardened people… nursed on God's Word… endure. Collina, above all, ye must take up the armor… the shield of faith… to quench the fiery darts of the wicked one…"

"Oh, Father, you're going to lick this. Just don't give up."

"My journey's done." His lips struggled to form the words. "But yours is yet to be. Your mother, she'll have a lot to do… with tending to your younger brothers and sisters." He forced his eyes to stay open. "You can manage, Collina, without me. You being just a day past sixteen worries me, but I knew when I first laid eyes on your wee face you'd be my Joan of Arc, my Esther of Shushan.

"Like my dear departed father fulfilled his vision and I be the product. I knew when I looked into your green-blue eyes. I named you Collina, 'cause I saw you were marked to climb beyond the stars...."

She swallowed. Painful tears blurred her vision. She blinked, willing them to retreat. They fell, unheeding her wishes. As she brushed them away, her fingers, numbed from the cold, felt like a soothing poultice to her hot moist cheeks.

His forefinger touched one tear as it lay on her chin, then stroked one long dark curl. "I'm sorry, lassie. I'm putting a lot on such thin shoulders." Her pa gasped for air, his mouth making a hissing noise. "You're in charge. We'll keep our land, the good Lord willing." He coughed. Mother brought him up to a sitting position. Clutching her mother's arm, Pa said, "We've come through worse. Never forget what Shushan represents. You understand, daughter, you will oversee the fields and the breeding... and not let ... the legacy of Shushan end." His eyes closed.

Was Pa dead?

His eyelids quivered like a window shade blown by a breeze. His dark eyes penetrated hers, seeing into her soul. "Our Lord will walk with ye, directing you...."

"But why not Chester or Jessie?"

"Chester's married and his place is with his family," her mother interceded. "Jessie's just fifteen and Robert's thirteen, both are too young and headstrong for the job."

"Daughter, I always told you, you should have been a boy, what with all that ambition, you could have been someone, someday."

"Pa, I—"

"Maggie." Her pa panted, gasping. He placed a hand on his heaving chest. "Who blew the lamp out? Everything's so dim." His hand waved the air and her mother grasped it gently, guiding it to her lips.

"My darling, Maggie, what... would I have... ever done... without you? I'll love ya always."

"Yes, my darling, and I'll always love you." Maggie's tears fell on Ben's hand unnoticed. "Yes, my love, you go home now. We'll be together soon."

Collina stumbled out of the bedroom, feeling more than seeing her way down the stairs. Doc was saying something. She felt his hand on her shoulder.

"Collina, did you notice? I had Robert take down that yellow flag. If the McConnells can lick the smallpox, they can lick anything."

"Pa's dead."

"I… know. There wasn't much hope," Doc said.

She blinked back her tears. Franklin's face was a mass of pain. He glanced away but not before she saw the pity in his eyes. "Why didn't you tell me?" She glanced down at her hands. "I guess it was best this way… Pa's—"

"Collina," Doc gently shook her. "Franklin is offering his services until he receives his orders. He's willing to work for a bed and his meals. That is, until Roosevelt sends for him. But that could be six months down the road."

She felt the knot in her throat growing. She dared not speak. She nodded and fished in the large pockets of her riding shirt for that hankie, but all she could find were a few bits of grain. She stared down at them. They're all dried up… no use to anyone.

"Here," Franklin held out his linen. Her fingers again felt the warmth of his.

"I'll tell you, Franklin," Doc said. "You won't find a better family to stay with, never a harder working, long suffering…" Doc paused, clearing his throat. "Here, let me have that dang hankie."

*Coming early 2018 from CrossRiver Media*

# Author's Note

*N*o *Irish need apply."*
Ireland's great potato famine caused a massive wave of Irish emigration to America during 1845 into the 1850s. They were seeking freedom from British tyranny. Most refugees arrived destitute, almost 650,000 in New York alone. They took whatever unskilled jobs they could find. Their lives were so harsh in America that their mortality rates remained high. Sixty per cent of children born to Irish immigrants in Boston died before the age of six, and adults died in an average of six years after entry into the States.

The Irish immigrants served bravely in the Civil War and in both armies. Still, they were repeatedly targets for public and military discrimination. However, they refused to give up. Persevering through unimaginable barriers due to their nationality and poverty, they doggedly pursued their belief in America and faith in Jesus Christ and overcame.

Their heroic Civil War exploits could not be ignored. On July 2, 1888, a monument standing 19'6" was dedicated to the Irish Brigade and gently graces a hill at Gettysburg. It is a Celtic cross supported by a granite base. On the front of the cross are the numbers of the three New York regiments and a harp flanked by eagles. At the foot of the cross is an Irish wolfhound, a symbol of honor and fidelity. It is a fitting symbol of the Irish people's love for their new country and honors well the words of the "Battle Hymn of the Republic."

Young Irishman Ben McConnell's fight to rise above his "unwelcome" status provides immigrants as well as fellow Americans with a "living hope" (1 Peter 1:3). In *Swept into Destiny*, Ben's and Maggie's journeys delve into the truth about faith and devotion, our individual plight, and America's greater cause, that of "the coming of the Lord" and fighting for indivisible freedom.

*"Now the Lord is the Spirit; and where*
*the Spirit of the Lord is, there is liberty." — 2 Corinthians 3:17*

# Book Club Discussion Questions

1. Maggie and Ben come from different social classes, which meant they shouldn't associate with each other. But Ben's determination to rise above his circumstance causes Maggie to recall Matthew 17:20. How does she apply it to their situation? What verse would you give to someone struggling against poverty? *See 1 Samuel 16:7, 2 Corinthians 8:9 for further discussion.*

2. When Ben McConnell sings "Wearin' o' the Green" to Maggie, the stanza "For they're hanging men and women there for Wearing of the Green" causes Maggie to clutch the cross she wears around her neck. Why do you think she did that? Could it be possible today for Christian beliefs to be prohibited and believers put to death? *See Revelations 13:15; 14:12,13 for further discussion.*

3. The Second Great Awakening ushered in an American revival, with tent meetings and spiritual and physical healings. Why did the preacher quote 2 Corinthians 3:17 to a Southern crowd? Do healings take place today? *See 1 Corinthians 12:9; Mark 16:17,18; Galatians 5:1 for further discussion.*

4. At the Christmas Ball, Maggie schemes to have Ben risk his life so her parents' lives would be spared. This causes her to think that one conscionable act had led to this consequence. Would you sacrifice everything for your beliefs? *See Ephesians 1:11, Luke 9:62, Proverbs 3:5,6 for further discussion.*

5. The Abolitionists were breaking the law, punishable by death. Reynolds'

slaves were his property. According to the law, Maggie and her mother were wrong to interfere. Who do you think was right in their actions? If you ever had to choose between God's law and man's law which would you choose? *See Acts 5:29, James 1:22 for further discussion.*

6. Lincoln's disgust over the Dred Scott decision not only brought the nation closer to Civil War, it made him determined to fight for the presidency. What else did the decision alert Lincoln to regarding the judicial system? What line does Ben repeat from Lincoln's Gettysburg Address that inspires him to believe in America's future? Could this be applied to today? *See Judges 2:16,18; Mark 3:25,26, Psalms 91:1 for further discussion.*

7. The Irish immigrant saw a record number of deaths upon their arrival in America. "Irish need not apply" was a sign commonly seen throughout the country. How did the Irish respond? During the Civil War, the Irish Brigade became an honored fighting unit. What other ways did the Irish change the tide of hate and prejudice toward them? *See Jeremiah 17:9,10; John 15:7-10.*

8. During the Confederate surrender, Grant and Lee display their respect for each other. What terms were arranged and what biblical truth did the generals show? What Scripture applies? *See John 15:12-14, John 14:13.*

9. Southern money, bonds, and slaves are swept away. With their property auctioned off, all most southerners have left are the clothes on their backs. Some thought it John Brown's curse, others believed it was punishment from God. Why do you think the South became known as the Bible belt? *See Matthew 5:39,40; Luke 6:27-31 for further discussion.*

10. "…with firmness in the right, as God gives us to see the right…" What else did Maggie quote from Lincoln's Second Inaugural Address? Ben, inspired by Lincoln's words, uses Esther 9:2 as the foundation for life and the reason to change his estate name. How could you apply that verse to your life today? How could our nation apply that verse? *See Mark 3:24-26, Esther 8:6, 9:2, and 2 Corinthians 3:17.*

# CATHERINE ULRICH BRAKEFIELD

Catherine is an ardent receiver of Christ's rejuvenating love, as well as a hopeless romantic and patriot. She skillfully intertwines these elements into her writing as the author of *The Wind of Destiny*, an inspirational historical romance, and *Images of America, The Lapeer Area*. Her most recent history book is *Images of America, Eastern Lapeer County*. Catherine, former staff writer for *Michigan Traveler Magazine*, has freelanced for numerous publications. Her short stories have been published in Guidepost Books *Extraordinary Answers to Prayers, Unexpected Answers* and *Desires of Your Heart*; Baker Books, Revell, *The Dog Next Door*; CrossRiver Publishing, *The Benefit Package*. She recently spent three weeks driving across the western part of the United States, meeting her extended family of Americans. This trip inspired her inspirational historical romance, *Wilted Dandelions*.

Catherine enjoys horseback riding, swimming, camping, and traveling the byroads across America. She lives in Michigan with her husband, Edward, of forty years and her Arabian horses. Her children grown and married, she and Edward are the blessed recipients of two grandsons and one granddaughter.

www.CatherineUlrichBrakefield.com
www.Facebook.com/CatherineUlrichBrakefield
www.Twitter.com/CUBrakefield

Hostile indians,
raging rivers,
and treacherous trails
are nothing
compared to
marrying a man
she does not know.

*Wilted Dandelions*

# MORE GREAT BOOKS FROM CROSSRIVERMEDIA.COM

## SEEKING SOPHIE
### Melody Balthaser

Indentured servant Sophie Stalz stabs her master to protect herself from rape. Escaping through the Underground Railroad, she now finds herself stranded on an island in the hands of a stranger. Surrounded by the sea, Jackson Scott just wants to be left alone with his memories. His fortress crumbles when Sophie shows up on his doorstep. As her master is *Seeking Sophie*, can Sophie and Jackson build a life together free from their past?

## LOTTIE'S GIFT
### Jane M. Tucker

She's a little girl with a big gift. Lottie Braun has enjoyed a happy childhood in rural Iowa with her father and older sister. But the quiet, nearly idyllic life she enjoyed as a child ended with tragedy and a secret that tore the two sisters apart. Forty years later, Lottie is a world-class pianist with a celebrated career and an empty personal life. One sleepless night, she allows herself to remember and she discovers that memories, once allowed, are difficult to suppress. Will she ever find her way home?

## ROAD TO DEER RUN
### Elaine Marie Cooper

The year is 1777 and the war has already broken the heart of nineteen-year-old Mary Thomsen. Her brother was killed by the King's army, so when she stumbles across a wounded British soldier, she isn't sure if she should she help him or let him die, cold and alone. Severely wounded, Daniel Lowe wonders if the young woman looking down at him is an angel or the enemy. Need and compassion bring them together, but will the bitterness of war keep them apart?

## GENERATIONS
### Sharon Garlock Spiegel

When Edward Garlock was sober, he was a kind, generous, hard-working farmer, providing for his wife and growing family. But when he drank, he transformed into a unpredictable bully, capable of absolute cruelty. When he stepped into a revival tent in the early 1900s the Holy Spirit got ahold of him, changing not only his life, but the future of thousands of others through Edward.

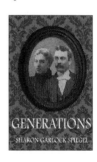

Made in the USA
Columbia, SC
30 October 2017